# DEAD RINGER

Jacob met Kendall's gaze head-on. "What I'm about to say has to stay off the record for now."

"There's no such thing as off the record." Kendall could see Jacob had something important to tell her. And if she didn't give him her word, he would walk out of her office right now. There was no way around it. "You have my word," she promised.

"Did Phil White ever mention that you look like his wife?"

That took her aback. "I do not look like Jackie White."

"He did, didn't he?" He boldly studied her high cheekbones and vivid green eyes. "She wasn't as pretty as you are, but the similarities are there. I saw it even when she was lying by the river, pale and lifeless. You had to have noticed."

"Is that supposed to spook me?"

Jacob's eyes narrowed. "The second victim looks like you as well."

"Brown hair and green eyes are common traits. Whatever similarities you see are strictly coincidence. Now if you don't have anything else to add, it's late and I want to work."

Jacob pulled two Polaroid pictures out of his coat pocket and laid them on her desk. They were of the two murdered women.

Kendall swallowed. "The women look similar, but nothing like me."

"You don't believe that, do you?"

Books by Mary Burton

*I'm Watching You*

*Dead Ringer*

Published by Kensington Publishing Corporation

# DEAD RINGER

## MARY BURTON

## ZEBRA BOOKS
### Kensington Publishing Corporation
www.kensingtonbooks.com

ZEBRA BOOKS are published by

Kensington Publishing Corp.
850 Third Avenue
New York, NY 10022

All Kensington titles, imprints, and distributed lines are available at special quantity discounts for bulk purchases for sales promotion, premiums, fund-raising, educational, or institutional use.

Special book excerpts or customized printings can also be created to fit specific needs. For details, write or phone the office of the Kensington Special Sales Manager: Attn.: Special Sales Department. Kensington Publishing Corp., 850 Third Avenue, New York, NY 10022. Phone: 1-800-221-2647.

Zebra and the Z logo Reg. U.S. Pat. & TM Off.

ISBN-13: 978-1-4201-0027-3
ISBN-10: 1-4201-0027-0

First printing: November 2008
10 9 8 7 6 5 4 3 2 1

Printed in the United States of America

# Prologue

"It's time, Ruth."

A cheerless finality hardened the man's softly spoken words. His heart truly felt heavy as he stared out the frost-streaked window. Outside, pine trees bowed under the ice's extra weight as arctic gusts rushed over the fields, swirling around, creating minitwisters in the snow.

"I don't want you to go," he said, turning toward Ruth.

The woman sat in a wooden chair, her head bent forward. Dark hair cascaded over her tear-streaked face. "Please," she said.

The room was decorated with rose wallpaper, white iolite curtains, and a large braided rug with interwoven strands of yellow, pink, and blue. A white four-poster canopy bed covered with a cherry comforter and dozens of stuffed animals dominated the space. He'd built this room for her and the others.

"Shh. I have to let you go. We both knew this time would come." Sadness tightened his throat.

Ruth raised her head a fraction. She glanced down at

her wrists, lashed tightly to chair arms. "No. No. I don't want to go. I want to stay with you."

The hoarse whisper was a lie. Instinctively, she understood what leaving truly meant. Dying.

He crossed the room, hoping to reassure her. "You don't need to be afraid." He knelt beside her and laid his hand on the ropes lashed to her pale wrists, now raw and bleeding after days of struggling. "It's okay, Ruth. It's all for the best. You'll see," he said tenderly.

Tears rolled down her face. "No. Let me stay." Desperation sparked in her eyes. "We can still be a family."

"You have to trust me, Ruth. I know what's best." He touched her cheek.

She flinched and then offered a faltering smile as she raised her pale green eyes to meet his. "Allen, please."

He liked it when she said his name. "I can't. You know that."

Lovingly he touched her chin and tipped her face back so he could look into her eyes. Fresh tears fell and dampened his calloused hand. For a moment, his resolve wavered. He really didn't want to send her away. He wanted to keep her here forever.

But he couldn't.

Wouldn't.

He rose and moved behind her. Gently he stroked her hair, which no longer smelled of coconuts and summer, but of fear and sweat. "I've really enjoyed our time as well. I've been alone for so long. But you must join the Family now."

She shook her head but was unable to lift it. She whimpered, "Please. Don't."

Allen pushed her hair away from her slender neck. "You will be grateful in the end."

He'd been searching for her for years, knowing that one day he'd find her and they'd be together again. And then he'd found her and he'd nearly cried out in joy. For weeks, he watched her attend church, drive to her secretarial job at the engineering firm, and go to the grocery store. He stood in the shadows as she'd wept at her parents' graveside. He'd scrutinized. Admired. Waited for the perfect opportunity to bring her to this special place that he'd created.

He slipped his hands under Ruth's thick mane of hair and brushed the soft skin of her neck. It felt cold. Her faint heartbeat drummed under his fingers. The drugs that had made her sleepy, almost nonresponsive, were wearing off. Soon she'd be struggling again, screaming until her voice grew hoarse.

He'd not wanted to use the drugs, but she'd been so defiant and unwilling to talk to him. She'd fought, called him names, and rejected him. The drugs had calmed her, made her see the good in him.

"I wish we had more time," he said.

She craned her head to the side and looked up at him. Desperation made her eyes spark. "We can still be a family."

A smile twitched at the edge of his lips. "Not in the way that it matters. There is too much that can come between us."

"It could be different this time. You'll see. I promise I will love you."

*Love.* For a moment he closed his eyes and let the word roll through his mind. No one had loved him in so long. "You can't really love me until you join the Family."

"I can."

He didn't blame her for the lie. He knew she was afraid of the transition. Crossing over always triggered fear in his girls. She'd say anything at this point. He understood and wasn't mad.

"Shh. It's going to be okay, Ruth."

A sob rose in her throat. "I'm not Ruth. I'm not Ruth."

He drew circles on her neck with his thumbs and then slid long fingers around her neck. Her pulse throbbed faster now. "Don't fight it. It's so much easier when you don't fight what is best for you."

"No." She jerked against her bindings and started to thrash her head. "I don't want to go!"

He tightened his hold and began to squeeze.

Initially, she thrashed harder. A muffled cry escaped her lips. But the pressure on her neck quickly robbed her of air, sound, and energy. Soon, she choked and gasped for air. She pulled against the bindings and balled her slender fingers into fists.

"Ruth, you were always the strong, brave one."

He tightened his hold, savoring the rush of power and excitement rushing through his body. His body warmed, despite the chill in the room. In this moment he felt connected, *alive.*

For so long he'd been alone, lost and wondering. Now, Ruth was about to join his Family. She would be with him forever.

"Family. It is everything. Without family life isn't worth much. People today don't get that. They are so busy rushing around they don't take the time to spend with each other."

She strained her neck and twisted her head, gagging, trying to break free.

His arms and hands ached but his grip remained tight. Her pulse drummed frantically, proof her lungs struggled for air. And then the *thump, thump, thump* skipped several beats. His heart raced faster. A few more erratic pulses followed and then stillness.

Life ebbed from Ruth's body, like water down a drain. She slumped forward. A tranquility only death could create washed over her.

Lovingly, he rested his palm on the top of her head. "It's better now, isn't it? You are finally at peace. You are free of all your worries and pain."

She didn't move. There were no more uneven protests. No pleas for freedom.

"Praise be," he whispered.

From his pocket he pulled a gold chain with an oval charm. Inscribed on the charm was the name *Ruth*. He slipped the chain around her neck. The clasp was small, delicate, and his large hands fumbled with the fastener until finally he hooked it.

He moved around the chair and knelt in front of her. The charm lay in the hollow of her neck just above her breasts. The pendant was a fine piece of jewelry that had taken him weeks to make. But it was worth it. He touched the shiny gold.

Ruth deserved the best.

He untied her wrists and took her hands in his. He kissed her cold fingers and then pressed them to his cheek. "I love you so much."

He put his hand under her chin and tipped her face back. Under partially open lids, green eyes stared sightlessly at him. He imagined he saw laughter in their glassy depths.

"You won't be alone much longer, Ruth." He laid her hands in her lap, crossing them demurely over each other. "Soon, I will find the Others and I will send them to you."

Allen smiled at the thought of the Others. Joy burned inside him. "Soon, we all will be together as the Family was meant to be."

# Chapter One

Homicide detective Jacob Warwick flexed his right hand, working the stiffness from his joints as he strode over the frozen land toward the flashing police car lights. The five patrol cars were parked on the rural patch of land near the James River's banks. Friday's snowstorm had whitewashed the landscape, robbing it of color and life. A morning haze obscured the southern bank of the river and most of the river's smooth waters.

The temperature hovered around thirty degrees, but the breeze made it feel like twenty below zero and cut through his jacket as if it were thin cotton.

The cold irritated his bruised knuckles and he regretted leaving his gloves at his apartment. He turned up the collar of his worn leather jacket and shoved his fists into the pockets. A skullcap covered his military short hair and a black scarf warmed his neck.

An hour ago, Jacob had been at the gym, enjoying his day off by giving what he had to a punching bag. Breaking a sweat sent endorphins rushing through his brain and for a little while eased the tension that stalked him.

His cell had rung midswing. He'd steadied the swaying punching bag, muttered a foul oath before wiping the sweat from his eyes, and dug his cell out of his gym bag.

His partner, Detective Zack Kier, had recited the bare facts. Female murdered. Midthirties. Caucasian. The body had been dumped on the banks of the James River at the Alderson construction site, located in the east end of the county a dozen miles past the airport. Jacob had showered, burying his face under the hot spray and regretting that he couldn't linger.

Another gusty breeze off the river sent Jacob deeper into his coat. This parcel of land was all raw fields and spindly cedar trees, but if the sales sign he'd passed on the way in was correct, Alderson Development Company would transform all this into a lush golf course surrounded by brick houses with perfectly placed trees and flower beds. The proposed clubhouse would offer tennis courts and a heated swimming pool.

*Starting in the $900,000s.* The slick marketing signs implied that the riverfront houses, with their top-of-the-line amenities, also supplied the right brand of status and a *Father Knows Best* kind of happiness. Life had taught him there were no guarantees. And thirteen years on the force had shown him misery could be found in high-dollar homes as well as low-income ones.

Jacob spotted a group of ragged-looking men standing by a muddy black Suburban. They wore jumpsuits and camouflage jackets. They were the Alderson Development's survey crew. This was their job site. They'd arrived just after sunrise to survey the north bank of the James River. They'd been the ones who'd found the body.

"Hey, when are you gonna let us get back to work or let us go home?" The shouted complaint came from one of the surveyors. Steam rose from the coffee cup in his hand.

"Can't say," Jacob said. "But stay put."

Jacob moved toward an older officer with a buzz cut and a perpetual frown. The other officer stamped his feet and rubbed his gloved hands together. "Cold enough for you? My bones can't take too much more of this frosty shit."

Jacob's body still ached from a boxing match last week. "I hear ya."

"What are you complaining about? I've been here for an hour already."

Jacob smiled. "You're tougher than I am."

"My ass." Watson's gaze narrowed as he glanced at Jacob's face. "That the remnants of a shiner?"

"Yeah. The other guy had a mean right hook." But that hadn't stopped Jacob from winning the charity boxing match.

Watson's gaze narrowed. "How old are you now? Thirty-four, thirty-five?"

"Give or take."

Watson shook his head. "You're getting too old for those kind of antics. You're not eighteen. You should stop now while you still have all your parts."

Thirty-six wasn't old in the big scheme but for a boxer it was ancient. In the army he'd been Golden Gloves. Since he'd left, he'd remained a strictly amateur boxer. Boxing gave him a thrill, reminded him he still had it. Whatever the hell *it* was.

But the sport was taking a toll. He didn't rebound like he used to. He'd taken on so many bouts these last few months there was rarely a day when his body didn't ache. Watson was right. He didn't recover as he had in his twenties. "I'll keep that in mind."

Watson eyed him. "Bullshit. You ain't gonna stop."

That coaxed a guilty grin.

Most outsiders—noncops—didn't understand how they could chat about everyday things or be so casual in the face of death. But this kind of banter, even humor, was a way of blowing off steam and cutting the tension so they didn't go insane.

Jacob pulled rubber gloves from his jacket pocket. "Forensics isn't here yet?"

"Tied up at another scene. Will be here any minute."

"Good." He ducked under the yellow tape and strode toward his partner, Detective Zack Kier.

Zack Kier faced the icy river. Tall, broad shouldered, he possessed a lean build suited so well for the triathlons he enjoyed. His unseasonably tanned skin was a souvenir from a Caribbean second honeymoon with his wife, Lindsay. A black overcoat brushed his knees and plastic gloves covered his dark winter gloves.

"So what do we have?" Jacob asked. He yanked on his gloves.

Zack turned at the sound of his voice and nodded toward the river's edge. "See for yourself."

Jacob followed Zack down the embankment toward the frozen riverbank. Where water met land, lay a woman on her stomach. She wore a camel overcoat, gloves, scarf, navy pants, and flat shoes, all soaked with water. Her gloved hands were outstretched in a T fashion. One hand lay in the water and the other on land. Her face was turned toward the river and her long dark brown hair streamed over her cheek in a gloomy curtain. Small waves lapped against her body.

Jacob moved toward the body but stopped ten feet short. He didn't want to contaminate the scene any more than he had to before forensics got there. His heavy sigh froze on contact with the air. "Do we know who she is?"

Zack shook his head. "Not yet. There was no ID in any of her pockets. And no purse to be found."

Jacob squatted. He stared at her face, mostly hidden by her thick brown hair. How did a neatly dressed middle-income woman end up here? "There are a few bridges downstream and dozens of docks. Suicide?"

Zack's expression was grim. "That's what the responding uniform thought at first."

Jacob frowned. "And?"

"He felt for a pulse on her neck when he arrived. He had to push back her hair to make contact with her skin." Zack tightened and released his jaw. "He found black-and-blue finger marks around her neck.

"Strangled."

"He also spotted marks on her wrists. Looked like rope burns."

Jacob shifted his gaze to the edge of her coat sleeve. He wanted to push up the wet fabric and see the marks for himself but he would wait for forensics. "Did the responding officer touch the body anywhere else?"

"No. Only on the neck and wrist to check for a pulse."

Forensics needed a complete record of everyone who touched the body. "Good."

Jacob's gaze settled on the victim's wrist. "Whoever did this held her captive before he killed her."

"That's what I'm thinking."

The victim was fully dressed, down to scarf and gloves. But that didn't mean she hadn't been stripped and sexually assaulted. Some killers, especially novices, often suffered remorse for their victims. In the killer's mind, redressing her would have been a way of safeguarding her dignity. "We need to make sure the coroner checks for signs of rape."

"Already noted."

Jacob flexed his right hand, trying to work the stiffness from it. He studied the partially exposed side of the victim's face. Determining time of death would be tricky. The freezing temps would have slowed down the decomposition process. "Any missing persons reports?"

A cold gust of air made Zack drop his head. "I put a call in about fifteen minutes ago. No one fitting her description has been reported missing, but that could change."

There could be a hundred reasons no one had called in a report. The victim had been traveling. She'd had a fight with her spouse. She lived alone and had few friends. Sooner or later, though, most people were missed by someone.

A glance upriver revealed no signs of a dock, boat, or landing where she might have been dumped. "She's soaked but her skin isn't discolored like it would be if she'd been in the water. And there'd be weeds or grass over her if she'd been in the river."

"The freezing rain yesterday would have drenched anyone to the skin."

Jacob could think of a dozen reasons how a middle-income woman could end up like this. Secret life of drug addiction. Domestic abuse. At this point all would be guesses.

Jacob stared at her body. "Why leave her here?"

Zack scribbled in his notebook. "Whoever did this might have thought she wouldn't be found for a while."

"Or he figured she'd be found quickly. Construction crews have been all over this place for weeks."

"That brings up a whole new set of problems."

Most killers didn't want anyone to know they'd murdered. If this killer dumped the woman intentionally, Zack was right. It opened the door to a darker scenario.

The rumble of a vehicle engine had them both glancing back up the hill. The forensics van had arrived. White with blue lettering, the side read *Henrico County Forensics.*

A young dark-haired woman slid out from behind the driver's seat of the van. Tess Kier, Zack's sister. Tess had been with forensics three years. She was meticulous and one of the best in the country.

Tall for a woman, she had sharp features and a lean body. Jacob had thought more than once about hooking up with her, but he had never made a move. Not only was she his partner's baby sister, but they interfaced on crime scenes often. *Keep your dick out of the company payroll.* It had been a favorite phrase of his army sergeant's. Sage words he was careful to live by.

Zack's grim features softened a fraction and he headed up the hill toward Tess.

Jacob remained by the river's edge, close to the victim. He turned and stared out over the river, not sure what he was looking for. This was a sad, desolate place. "No one deserves this."

Tess came down the hill in her jumpsuit, booties, and gloves. A digital camera hung from a strap around her neck and she held a clipboard in her hand. A pencil stuck out from the ponytail holding up her ebony hair. As Tess approached she glanced down at Jacob's hands.

Jacob read her mind as if it were a book. He wiggled his fingers. "I've got my gloves on like a good boy."

"Good." Tess's pale, smooth skin accentuated sharp, blue eyes. "I don't need anyone contaminating my crime scene." She cast a pointed gaze at her brother. "I know I don't have to tell you about the right gear."

Zack looked bored, as if he'd heard this speech a thousand times. "Anybody ever tell you that you're mean in the morning?"

"My ex-boyfriend." Tess tucked the clipboard under her arm and started to snap pictures with the digital camera.

In the dim morning light the camera's flash illuminated the victim with a brutal clarity. All chatter ceased and a grave silence settled on the scene.

Tess documented the body from every conceivable

angle. She stood on the bank and then moved into the shallow, frigid waters and snapped more pictures. She drew sketches and took notes.

Jacob studied the victim as the camera flash exploded. He tried to put himself in her head. To think as she had.

Her shoes and clothes were sensible. Almost prudish. Her hair was loose now, but he guessed that she normally wore it tied back in a tight ponytail. That practical style would have matched her short, neat, unpolished nails. The scarf around her neck was tied in a square knot.

She looked like a librarian. A churchgoer. Someone who walked on the correct side of the road. She was the type of person who would be noticed if she went missing.

The cold seeped into Jacob's bones and he grew restless. He shifted his weight from one foot to the other, trying to get the circulation moving. Blazing heat and humidity didn't bother him, but the cold pissed him off.

Jacob swung his gaze to the huddle of surveyors. "I'm going to talk to the crew."

Zack nodded. "Right."

The frozen ground crunched under his feet as he made his way up the embankment. He stopped in front of the men who stood in front of the black Suburban.

A tall man standing in the center of the group nodded. He weighed at least two hundred pounds, sported a thick black beard, and had a tattoo of a fallen angel on his neck. The other crewmen looked younger, maybe midtwenties, and their bloodshot eyes suggested they'd done some heavy drinking last night.

"Which one of you found the body?" Jacob asked.

The tall one answered. "I did. I'm the party chief."

"Your name?"

"Frank Burrows." A deep southern drawl drew out the last name and suggested he was a transplant from the southwestern part of the state.

"Walk me through what you saw," Jacob said.

Tension deepened the furrows on the man's brow. His gaze darted toward the river before settling on Jacob. "I was setting up the survey equipment along the river. Rob here," he said, jabbing his thumb toward the man to his right, "was a few paces behind."

Rob shifted his stance. "I had to take a leak."

Burrows rolled his eyes. "I'd just placed the tripod when I spotted the woman's coat. I thought it was debris from the storm. We're always finding stuff in the water. Tires, shoes, clothes, furniture. I walked over to get a closer look. When I realized it was a woman, I called nine-one-one."

"Did you touch her?"

Burrows folded his arms over his large chest. "Hell no. She didn't look like she was breathing and I didn't want to get too close."

"You didn't check for a pulse?"

He sniffed, his air now defensive. "No."

"Any of your men touch her?"

"No."

Jacob glanced at the crew. "See anyone around here who didn't belong?"

They all shook their heads no.

Burrows spoke up. "This isn't the kind of place people come to for fun in the winter. There's an old deer stand in one of the trees, so hunters have been through here at one point. But that was before Alderson bought the place. We've got a few illegal trash-dump sights but most of those are a few months old."

"No one lurking around?"

"The road you drove in on is the only way in by car. It ends about a hundred yards past the turnoff."

"How about tire tracks on the road? See anything different, suspicious?"

"Hard to tell what tracks are ours or someone else's. And the snow last night would have covered up anything new."

"What about river access to the site?"

"A flat-bottomed boat could navigate the area but we haven't seen one." Burrows nervously tugged at a string dangling from the edge of his coat.

"Something wrong?" Jacob asked.

A half laugh, half curse burst out of Burrows. "What do you think? I found a dead woman at my job site. All I want right now is to sit in a warm bar and drink a cold beer."

"Warwick," Zack called up from the river's edge. "Tess has found something."

Jacob turned from the surveyors. "Be right there."

Burrows shoved out a breath. "Can I let my men go now? They didn't see nothing and we have another survey job that we can jump on so this entire day isn't a waste."

Jacob shook his head. "Hang around just a little longer."

The party chief swore. "If I'd known this was going to tie us up so long I'd have called the cops after we'd finished our work. A few hours don't matter to her either way."

Jacob glared at him until the man had the sense to drop eye contact. Irritated, Jacob made his way back down to the riverbank and discovered Tess had turned the victim on her back.

The woman's cheek was turned to the side but he could see she had a wide face; high cheekbones; and pale, white skin. Her eyes were closed. The bruising on Jane Doe's neck was very visible now, as were the marks on her wrists. In the gray morning light, her frozen features made her look more like a mannequin than a human. Yet, there was something familiar about her.

Jacob swallowed. Personalizing the body could rob him of objectivity. He'd do a better job in the end if he thought of the body as just a piece of evidence and nothing more.

"Look at her necklace," Tess said.

Jacob leaned closer. A gold charm hung from a chain around her neck. The scripted engraving read *Ruth*. "Her name is Ruth?"

Zack jotted a note in his spiral notebook. "The necklace looks nice."

Tess nodded as she snapped pictures of the body and got close-ups of the neck and charm. "It's very nice. I'd say it cost good money."

"She doesn't look like one to wear expensive jewelry," Jacob noted. "She's all about practicality."

"Maybe it was a gift," Tess offered.

"Maybe." Sometimes the odd detail in a case could bother him for days or weeks. He'd had an apparent suicide last year. The man appeared to have shot himself. The house was clean, everything in its place. Only the man's tie and suit jacket were dumped in a sloppy heap on the floor. No big deal. But the detail just hadn't fit the picture. Jacob had sat at that crime scene a long time before he reasoned the man had dumped the clothes in a final act of rebellion.

And now he had an expensive charm around the neck of a woman who looked like she shopped at discount stores. It could be nothing, like the discarded clothes. But it still bothered him.

"I'll check on the charm," Zack said.

Jacob nodded as he stared at the woman. Despite the ravages of death and the elements, he still felt as if he'd seen Jane Doe before. "She looks familiar to me."

Tess nodded. "I thought the same thing. Been trying to place her since I first got a look at her face."

How did he know her?

Tess gently placed her fingertips under the woman's chin and turned her face toward them.

The full-on view of her face startled him. Recognition dawned.

Jane Doe . . . Ruth.

She looked like the news anchorwoman on Channel 10 News. Kendall Shaw.

# Chapter Two

*A woman's screams echoed in the child's ears as she huddled in a corner of a closet, her legs curled so tightly under her skirt that they cramped. She clutched her hands over her ears and panted. Sweat clung to her skin.*

*"Make the screaming stop," she whispered to herself. "Make it stop."*

*And then, in an instant, the terrified screams did stop. An eerie silence descended. The child raised her head. Light seeped in under the door frame, and in the silence she heard the steady sound of footsteps approach the door. The door handle turned.*

*"Come out, come out wherever you are." The voice was soothing, soft, yet terrifying.*

The dream had awoken Kendall Shaw last night at two o'clock and had left her so shaken she'd not been able to get back to sleep. A dull headache now pounded behind her eyes.

The reoccurring dream had plagued her on and off for months now. She'd thought the dream had been a by-product of last summer's shoulder surgery and the heavy-duty pain meds her trauma surgeon had prescribed. But she'd nearly completed physical therapy and had weaned herself off the drugs within weeks of the surgery.

And still the frequency and violence of the dreams had increased. Always they left her panicked and wide awake. Each time she got up out of bed and went downstairs and checked all the doors and windows. Always they were locked, but she never felt reassured.

Even now, the memory made her heart race and her hands sweat.

"Enough," Kendall muttered as she rubbed her shoulder. "Get hold of yourself." She reached for the aspirin bottle in the cabinet by her kitchen sink, flipped open the lid, and popped two into her mouth. She gulped down the water and set the glass down on the counter. "Stupid, absurd dream."

For the last five months, she'd been the evening news anchor at Channel 10 News. Ratings had soared since she'd started anchoring and there was talk about giving her a local talk show.

Kendall checked her slim wristwatch. Ten-fifteen. Most days she didn't arrive at the television station until three. Once there she briefly met with producers, the assignment editor, sometimes the news director, and any available reporters to discuss the day's news. They discussed what stories each reporter was covering and which would be included in the newscast. After that she touched up hair and makeup and then taped promos for the news that night.

It was still way too early to leave for work, but she was restless and in need of work's distraction. "Nicole, I'm leaving!" she shouted.

Last summer Kendall had been chasing the story of a

serial killer. Nicole had been running from an abusive husband. Both had nearly lost their lives at the hands of these two evil men.

The women had met in the hospital and had struck up a friendship. In November, when Kendall had purchased a historic townhome on Grove Avenue, she'd invited Nicole to move in with her. Neither figured the arrangement would be permanent, but in the interim each liked the idea of living with someone else. The nights were less creepy when you knew someone else was right down the hallway.

Footsteps sounded. Nicole appeared in the doorway. Dark hair hovered above her small shoulders and accentuated deep-blue eyes. She had pale skin and full lips that spread into a wide grin when she laughed. A peasant top, jeans, dangling silver hoop earrings, and worn boots hinted to her artistic nature. However, Nicole's most notable feature now was her large pregnant belly, which strained the fabric of her top. She was weeks away from giving birth to her late husband's child.

The pregnancy had been a frightening shock. But Nicole had been determined to bring the baby into the world. She was pro-choice yet couldn't imagine terminating this pregnancy. She rarely spoke about the baby and had met with an adoption agency a few times, but so far she hadn't committed to an adoption plan.

Smiling, Nicole lifted her gaze from the camera in her hands. Nicole had established herself as a talented photographer out West but had had to abandon all that when she'd fled her marriage. Now, she was rebuilding her business with remarkable success. "Leaving early today?"

"I've got a mountain of work to tackle." Kendall tossed a smile in with the words. No sense worrying Nicole over a few disturbing dreams.

"You drive yourself too hard. When are you ever gonna kick back and enjoy?"

"No rest for the wicked. And frankly I'm not the only one who's been pushing it hard. You've done your share of working lately."

Nicole's hand slid to her belly. "I've got a deadline."

"You need your rest."

"I'm resting."

Kendall rolled her eyes. "Please. I see the hours you keep. It's not good for you or the baby."

Nicole dropped her gaze to her camera and checked the battery. "I thought the carpenter was arriving today."

Abrupt subject changes were common when Kendall brought up the baby. "He called around eight. He had a problem on another job that needed his attention. He'll be here Friday."

"Kinda last minute to cancel."

Kendall agreed. She'd have chewed the guy out if she'd felt more like herself this morning. "Contractors. They flake out." She was trying to see the humor. "I lost three days of work on the bathroom renovations last November because it was Black Powder season, whatever the hell that is."

Nicole laughed. "Deer-hunting season."

"Save me."

Kendall had purchased the nineteenth-century home using the inheritance from her mother. The house, located in the city's Fan district, had great bones, including twelve-foot ceilings, hardwood floors, a staircase with a bull-nose railing, plaster walls, and working fireplaces. However, old-world charm had also come with an outdated kitchen and bathrooms from hell. She'd had the bathrooms revamped before she'd even moved in, but the kitchen wasn't as simple. Not only was the renovation expensive but she also didn't want to rush it. She

planned to entertain in this house and to do that right
required a kitchen. Unlike her mother, who'd been a
great cook, Kendall was adept only at making coffee and
hiring a caterer. But despite her lack of culinary skills
she understood the kitchen was the heart of the house.

She'd spent most of November working with the designer. And then it had taken weeks to find a carpenter.
But according to her sources, she'd landed one of the
best craftsmen in the region. Supposedly, he was worth
the trouble. So far, though, he wasn't winning any points
with her.

Nicole moved into the kitchen. She kept her shoulders
back but her gait lumbered under the weight of the baby.
"So what kitchen remodeling design did you settle on?
French country, Italian, or ultramodern? I've lost track."

Kendall reached for her black double-breasted overcoat, which hung in a small closet in the hallway off the
kitchen. She slid it on over her winter-white knit dress.
"French country."

Nicole set her camera on the counter and pulled a tea
bag from a plastic container. She dunked the bag in a
cup, filled it with water, and put it in the microwave. She
hit the two-minute button. "You have taste and style."

Kendall grinned. "I know."

Nicole laughed. "And you're humble, too."

She lifted a neatly plucked brow. "I don't have a humble,
down-to-earth bone in my entire body and you know it."
She wasn't ashamed to admit she liked nice things.

"That's one of the things I like about you, Kendall.
You know what you want and aren't afraid to go after it.
When I grow up, I hope to be just like you."

Kendall grabbed a large black Coach bag from the
counter. The bag held everything from makeup, snacks,
and notebooks to a laptop, a digital tape recorder, and

a spare Fendi scarf. It was her survival bag. "Life's too short for indecision."

Nicole's mood suddenly shifted to pensive as if her thoughts had turned back to the baby. "Right."

Kendall felt as if she'd kicked a puppy. Her straightforward manner made her a great reporter but a difficult friend. "So what are you doing today?" She injected as much enthusiasm as she could.

"I'm developing pictures." Nicole smiled, trying to shake off her mood. "I did a huge photo shoot of a family who lives on River Road. Five grown kids and the parents. They all have busy schedules. Logistical nightmare. But in the end I got some good stuff. They'll be pleased."

"Are you using those pictures in a show?"

"This work is strictly for the money. I've had so many paying gigs I've had to put the artistic stuff on the back burner."

"That's a good thing?"

Nicole shrugged. "Yes and no."

"So what's your next assignment?"

She looked pleased with herself. "A portrait for an office lobby and publicity shots for Dana Miller next Thursday. She won the contract to sell Adam Alderson's River Bend Estates."

Kendall knew the woman by reputation. "Charge her top dollar. She's high profile and she's got deep pockets."

"It's going to be a generous paycheck." Nicole pressed her hand to her stomach.

Kendall frowned. "Everything all right?"

"Fine. She's just moving a lot lately. Must be the Mexican food I had a few days ago."

A rush of panic niggled her. "You *will* tell me if you go into labor? I don't want to be delivering a baby on my kitchen floor."

"That would be bad especially if the Italian marble has been laid."

Kendall frowned. "I'm not kidding. I want that baby born in a hospital, where you both will be properly taken care of."

The microwave dinged and Nicole pulled out her brewed cup of tea. "Don't worry, I'm not that close to delivery. The doctor said at least three weeks, maybe even a month before she makes her appearance."

Kendall had promised herself not to push Nicole one way or the other when it came to the adoption. But try as she might, she could no longer dance around the subject of the baby. "So have you followed up with the adoption agency again?"

Nicole sipped her tea. "No."

That worried Kendall. "Nicole, you can't keep putting this off. That baby is coming no matter what. Three weeks isn't that far off."

"I know."

Kendall softened her voice. "You owe it to yourself and the kid to figure out what you are going to do."

Nicole dropped her gaze, her cheeks flushed with emotion. "I know."

Kendall sighed. "Hey, I know I can be overly direct. Even a bitch. But I like you. And I just don't want to see you get hurt. And I think the more you plan the easier it will be for you."

Nicole lifted her eyes. Tears glistened. "God, I wish I had cut-and-dry answers. The baby deserves to be happy and to have the best. I just don't know if I'm the person to do it for her. And still I can't discuss making an adoption plan."

Kendall thought about her own complicated relationship with her late mother, who had adopted Kendall when she was three. There'd been lots of love in the house. But Kendall had learned early on that her mother didn't like to discuss the adoption. Even to this day, loyalty to her mother mingled with fear of the unknown and kept her silent about her adoption. "Few things in life are. We just do the best we can."

Nicole tipped her head back so the tears wouldn't spill. "I know. You're right."

"So you'll at least talk to the agency and make sure you've covered all your options."

"Yes. I'll follow up." This time tears spilled down her cheeks. "*I will.*"

Kendall laid a manicured hand on Nicole's shoulder. "Don't cry, Nicole. I don't want to start my day knowing I made a pregnant woman cry. It's got to be really, really bad Karma."

Shaky laughter rumbled from Nicole as she swiped the tears from her cheeks. "No more tears."

"Good. Don't worry, we'll take this one step at a time."

"Thanks." Nicole swallowed, sniffed. "So what were you doing up late last night?"

Kendall tensed. She'd not spoken to anyone about the dreams and she didn't want to. Verbalizing validated them somehow. "You heard me?"

"I pee on the hour, remember?"

"Right." She dug her fingers through her long dark brown hair. "It was nothing. I just couldn't sleep."

Nicole sipped her tea. "Normally you sleep like the dead."

When she was a kid, her mother said she could run nonstop all day. But at night when her head hit the pillow, she collapsed and slept like the dead. That pattern hadn't changed until last summer. "I know."

"What kept you up?"

"Problems at work. The negotiations for the new talk

show have me a little stressed. It's just a fluke, I'm sure. I just need to cut back on the caffeine."

"Everything else is going really well at the station?"

"Great. I love the job." That was the truth, pretty much. But it did lack the excitement of live reporting.

"No more dangerous stories?"

Kendall had taken terrible chances last summer chasing the Guardian serial killer story. Then she'd craved the attention of the big networks, wanted to land a new job and leave Richmond. However, after the Guardian shot her, the urge to flee the past vanished. In fact, the opposite became true. She started thinking about her past more and more, and when the anchor slot became available she jumped at it.

"I did do a remote from the women's show last week," she teased. "Got a little hairy in the waxing booth."

Nicole wasn't thrown off by the humor this time. "You're sure?"

"Yes. No hard news reporting these days." She checked her watch, refusing to fret anymore. The *dream* was just a dream. "I need to get to the station and start prepping for the evening broadcast."

Nicole seemed to sense she'd hit a touchy subject but let it go. "Sure. Have a great day."

"Call me if you need me."

"Absolutely."

Kendall tossed a wave at Nicole and headed out the back door. Her high heels crunched against the road salt that she'd spread on the back porch after the snowstorm. She tiptoed down the steps, over the slick walkway to the garage door, and slid behind the wheel of her black BMW, parked next to Nicole's beat-up Toyota. She fired up the engine, noting the thermostat barely had tipped twenty.

She pressed OPEN and the garage door swung open

and she shoved the car's gearshift into reverse. She backed into the gravel one-lane alley that separated the row houses on her street from the ones on the street parallel to hers.

Absently, she glanced at the vacant house that stood directly behind hers and the FOR SALE sign that hung on the fence. She shifted to first gear, then accelerated down the narrow alley and toward the side street.

Within ten minutes she was at the station and pushing through the front doors of the Channel 10 station. She waved to the receptionist. "Hey, Sally. How goes it on the front lines?"

The young blond girl, a recent journalism grad, grinned. "Never better."

"Good." She moved down the hallway past the huge head shots of her and the other anchors at the station to her office.

Kendall dropped her purse onto her neatly organized desk. She'd hired a painter after she'd gotten the job and had had them paint the walls a soft mauve. She'd brought in artwork, a few plants, and an Oriental rug. Instead of using the fluorescent light above, she relied on the two floor lamps and a desk lamp. The office had gone from sterile to cozy.

Her news director, Brett Newington, appeared in her doorway. "What brings you in so early?"

Chiseled features, thick blond hair, and a toned body gave him a boyish charm, which had been what had caught her eye a couple of years ago. They'd started dating and they'd been incredible at first. They seemed to fit so well together. Then her mother had gotten sick with cancer. Kendall had given up her apartment and moved into her mother's house to care for her. Brett had resented the time she'd devoted to her mother and Kendall had suddenly discovered chiseled features and nicely tailored shirts weren't enough.

She'd broken it off with him. At first, he'd seemed relieved and had even gone on to date other women. Lately, however, he'd been making noises about getting back together. She'd been doing her best to ignore them.

"Tying up loose ends."

He looked suspicious. "Then you didn't hear."

"About?" She took off her coat.

"There's a report of a murder in the east end. Body found at Alderson Development's River Bend Estates' site."

"Who was killed?"

"So you really haven't heard?"

Brett thought she'd gotten wind of the story and had arrived early so she could cover it. Smart man. If she had heard, she'd have done just that. "Who was murdered?"

"I don't know. Some woman."

*Some woman.* Some woman who had a name and a life that was now over.

Nearly dying last summer had changed the way she approached stories. They were more personal now. She felt for the people involved more. "She must have a name."

Brett shuffled through the papers in his hands as if searching for an answer. "Not yet. Unidentified at this hour."

She could have been *some woman* last summer. "I want to cover this," she said.

"No. I need you here behind the desk. I'm going to send Ted."

Hearing *no* made her want this story more. "I've not been in the field for weeks and even you said research shows viewers like it when I go on location. Besides, I can do a better job on this than Ted."

Brett scratched his head. "Viewers like seeing you at

powder puff events like the tree-lighting downtown. They don't want to see you slogging it out at a murder scene."

"Let's face it, they'll all tune in when they know I'm covering the story." She hated to admit what she said next. "I've not covered anything hard since last summer and they'll all want to know how I'll react. Think of the ratings."

Ratings. It was the magic word. "Why this story?"

She couldn't explain what she didn't understand herself. "I'm really good at this, Brett. You and I both know this."

He studied her. "It's hard to say no to you."

"Oh, please. We both know you would if you thought it wasn't a good idea. And it's a great idea."

He grinned. "Okay. Take the story."

Kendall ignored the flutter of nerves in her stomach. She moved to a small closet and removed a pair of worn hiking boots she kept on hand for rough terrain. The land around River Bend was raw and covered with snow. "Call Mike and have him warm up the van. I'll be out front in five minutes."

Allen watched her move through the cold, her head tucked low against the wind. She shoved slim hands in the pockets of her large dark overcoat. Her snow boots were damp and muddy and the scarf wrapped around her neck was soiled at its edges.

It saddened him to think she had to work so hard to get through life. She struggled so much.

So bravely.

He also knew she was lonely and afraid. He'd seen her crying by her bedroom window the other night. His heart ached for her. She was adrift in the world. She needed her family.

She deserved *more*, just as Ruth had deserved more. And he intended to give her all that was owed to her.

Soon she would not be alone. She would be a part of his *Family*. Soon she would be with those who loved her so very much.

His fingers tingled with excitement. He was anxious for her to join Ruth. So anxious in fact that it was a struggle to keep his distance.

The house was so quiet since he'd sent Ruth away. So lonely. He found himself wandering from room to room, hating the silence and the way the wind made the shutters creak.

The house just wasn't the same without Ruth. She'd brought life to the house.

God but he hated the loneliness.

He swallowed a lump in his throat.

The loneliness would end soon.

# Chapter Three

*Tuesday, January 8, 12:10 P.M.*

The overcast sky added an extra bite to the ice-cold
wind that cut through Jacob's leather jacket. He stamped
his feet, hoping the extra blood circulation would warm
his body and restore some feeling to his toes.

The survey crew seemed to accept the cold as a matter
of course. They'd remained idle all morning, standing
on the sidelines watching the police work as if it were a
location set for a television crime drama. Fifteen minutes
ago they'd broken out their lunches. It was a regular
party.

As much as he wanted to leave, neither he nor Zack
considered it. They wanted to wait until Tess had finished taking her photographs, sketching out the scene,
and had released the body to the state medical examiner's office.

Tess had searched the victim's pockets, finding
wadded tissue and a grocery store receipt, but nothing
that would identify her. She also searched the entire area
around the body for evidence but so far had found nothing out of the ordinary. The wind wasn't helping matters

either and could easily have blown evidence farther afield. Jacob had expanded the search perimeter. He had ordered the uniformed officers to fan out and search the area.

Tess hoped to preserve as much evidence that still might remain on the body. She had ordered the woman's body moved away from the water and wrapped in a clean white sheet. Once it was transported to the medical examiner's office, she would go over it again and search for hair and fiber samples on the body.

Tess trudged up the hill, her expression grim. Her cheeks were pink and her lips chapped. Wisps of dark hair peeked out from the skullcap on her head.

Jacob raised the yellow tape for her.

Tess ducked under the tape and arched her back, trying to work the knots formed after hours of stooping. "Thanks."

"Sure."

Zack moved away from the uniforms toward her. "You need a strong cup of coffee."

"I intend to have one as soon as I arrive at the medical examiner's office. When I've warmed up, I'll go over the body again."

Zack looked like he wanted to argue with his kid sister, but he knew she didn't like babying. "Sure."

"I've called the body removal team," she added. "They'll be here in a few minutes."

"Did you find anything?" Jacob asked.

She shook her head. "Not yet. And it's so damn cold our killer likely didn't break a sweat when he dumped our victim."

Sweat mixed with the body's oils to create fingerprints. Without sweat, fingerprints weren't always produced. "Do the best you can."

"Will do."

Zack braced against the wind. "What can you tell us, Tess?"

She shoved out a breath. "The medical examiner will have to confirm all this but I think whoever held her also injected her with something."

"What makes you think the killer did it?" Jacob asked. "People from all walks of life have hidden addictions."

Tess sniffed. "The needle marks on her arms are fresh. And there are no signs of older marks that would suggest she was a habitual user."

"They could be behind her knee," Jacob said. That had been a favorite spot of his mother's.

Tess shrugged. "We'll see. But I don't think she's an addict. Doesn't have the look."

Many didn't have the look if it was a new habit. "Why do you think the killer injected her? Maybe she did it herself. Went on a binge."

Tess's face tightened with annoyance. "Like I said, I don't think so. Her teeth are healthy and her fingernails don't appear splintered—both would be signs of chronic drug use. I think whoever took her, tied her up, likely to a chair, kept her for several days and shot her full of drugs. And then strangled her."

The image of the woman's face flashed in his mind and again he thought about Kendall Shaw. He savagely pushed the thought away, refusing to think of the body as anything more than evidence. "Any signs of sexual assault?"

"Couldn't hazard a guess at that one. Her clothes are per-fectly intact, but you know that doesn't mean anything."

The hearse arrived and made its way down the rough construction road. It stopped a hundred yards from them. The driver kept the motor running as he and an-other man emerged. Both men were tall with broad, muscled shoulders.

They removed the gurney from the back of the hearse casually and headed toward Tess. She led them to the body, which she had bagged in a black body bag. The bag had been sealed with a lock that wouldn't be removed until it reached the medical examiner's office. The attendants hoisted the body on the gurney, carried it up the embankment, and loaded it in the hearse without conversation.

Zack and Jacob followed Tess to the forensics van. They waited as she fired up the engine and turned the heat on full blast. She closed the door but cracked the window.

Tess held out her hands toward the heater. "I'm never going to be warm again."

"When does your shift end?" Zack ducked his head so he could make eye contact.

"Four. Hopefully, I'll be done with our Jane Doe. I promised Mom I'd help pack up the Christmas decorations."

Zack nodded. "Thanks for doing that."

"Next year it's your turn."

Zack grinned. "No, it's Malcolm's. He owes me." Malcolm, their brother, worked SWAT.

"What did you do for him?" she asked, smiling.

Zack grinned. "Let's just say we had a bet and he lost."

Tess's laughter rumbled in her chest. "Should I ask?"

"No," Zack said.

Jacob envied the easy camaraderie the brother and sister shared. He'd never known anything like that. His father had split before he was born and he had no siblings. His mother had been a drunk and an addict who had found child rearing a drag. When he was twelve he'd been taken in by a good guy, Pete Myers, who had given him a stable home. Last summer, Pete had turned out to be deeply troubled.

Shit. Jacob couldn't have had a more fucked-up personal life if he'd set out to plan one.

Zack and Tess exchanged a few more words before she rolled up her window. The hearse drove off, and Tess followed in her van.

Zack rubbed his hands together, trying to stimulate circulation. "I'm headed back to the office."

"Right behind you. I just want to walk the scene one more time." Jacob was anxious to get back in his car and turn the heater on, but he just couldn't let go of this place. Not yet.

Zack had driven off and Jacob had started back toward the river when he heard, "Who's in charge here?"

The voice was deep, angry, and full of attitude.

Jacob turned, pulling fisted hands from the warmth of his pockets. Standing at the perimeter was a guy dressed in a dark business suit and a crisp overcoat. It didn't take a Harvard education to know the suit and coat cost more than Jacob earned in a month. The guy wasn't tall, maybe five seven or eight, and he had a full head of brown hair slicked back off his face. A gold ring winked on his left pinky.

The guy had "slick" written all over him.

Jacob moved toward Slick, his strides long and deliberate. He was itching for a fight, anything to burn off the unease that plagued him. "Can I help you?"

Slick raised an eyebrow. "Are you in charge?"

Again, attitude seasoned the words. The hair on the back of Jacob's neck rose. He didn't mind questions but attitude pissed him off. "I'm Detective Jacob Warwick. I'm running this murder investigation."

Slick's features softened a fraction and he thrust out his hand. "My name is Adam Alderson." His breath puffed, freezing when it hit the cold air. "I own this land development project."

Jacob had already guessed the answer to his question: Alderson's survey crew chief had called him to complain about the delay. "What can I do for you?"

Alderson's smile was impatient. "I saw the hearse leave. That means the body is gone."

"Correct."

"Great. When are the rest of you going to clear off my property? Right now I'm paying my crews to stand around and drink coffee."

"I was just about to talk to them one last time and then send them home. Forensics won't release the scene today, so your men can't work the area."

Alderson twisted his pinky ring. "But the body is gone."

"There could be evidence in the area, so it needs to be contained until we can thoroughly search it." He kept emotion out of his voice.

Alderson's eyes reflected his frustration. He didn't like hearing no. "Tomorrow then?"

"I can't say. I've ordered the patrolmen to thoroughly comb the area. And then the autopsy might reveal something that would send us back. It could be days, or weeks, depending on what they find."

Alderson shook his head. "Weeks! That is not acceptable, Detective. The surveying has to be complete by the end of January so the site plans can be finished. I need to break ground this summer if occupancy is going to happen next spring."

Jacob didn't flinch. "We'll be done when we're done. At this time I won't commit to a date."

A muscle in Alderson's jaw tensed. "Do you have any idea how much revenue this development is going to bring into the county?"

Ah, money, it made the world go round. "A great deal, I'll bet."

"A great deal doesn't begin to cover it. I can assure

you my development is worth a hell of a lot more than solving the murder of some woman."

The casual dismissal pissed off Jacob. If he had his way, Alderson's people would never set foot on this land until spring.

Alderson checked his watch and had the stones to look bored. "I need a release date, Detective."

A woman was dead. She'd been held captive, could have been tortured, and this guy looked bored.

Jacob had the urge to toss this guy off the property. "Where were you last night?"

The question caught Alderson off guard. "Me? Why the hell should that matter?"

Jacob mentally dug in his heels. No one dictated policy to him at his crime scene. "It's a simple question."

Alderson rolled his eyes. "Oh, please."

He'd stand there all day if that's what it took. "She was found on your property."

"I had nothing to do with the woman's death."

Jacob stood a good six inches taller than the guy and he wasn't above using his height to intimidate. "Then answer the question."

Alderson's lips flattened. "I was having dinner last night with my attorney, as a matter of fact." He looked smug. "We were going over contracts for another property I'm looking to buy." Alderson dug into the pocket of his coat and pulled out a business card. "Here's his name and number. Feel free to call him."

Jacob studied the name but didn't recognize it. "I will. Your men report any strange people on the land in the last couple of days?"

He shoved out a breath. "You spoke to them. What did they tell you?"

"Just tell me what they told *you*." People lied to the

cops all the time. He was hoping Alderson's men might have given him a different story.

"No one has been on-site for days. The snow and ice storm has kept the job site closed since Friday. Today was our first day back on the job. Which is why we can't afford any more delays."

"I passed a gate when I came in. Is it always locked?"

"Yes. But you can see for yourself the fence doesn't extend around the entire property. Anyone could have driven down the road and cut through the woods and walked around."

A gust of wind blew off the river, slicing through Jacob's leather jacket. He wondered if Alderson's high-end coat was any match for the cold.

"What about water access?" Jacob ventured. "How navigable is the river in this area?"

"Good, if you've got a flat-bottomed boat. The water is five or six feet deep."

Jacob kept his gaze leveled on Alderson's face. "Who's Ruth?"

The guy didn't flinch. "Ruth? I don't know a Ruth. Is she the woman who was killed?"

"Just a question."

"Then why ask?"

"I'm going to be asking a lot of questions."

"What do you know at this point?"

Again with the attitude. What was it about rich guys who thought they could take charge of any situation? "Can't say."

"You're not being very helpful, Detective."

"No."

Alderson narrowed his eyes. "Who's your boss?"

He didn't hesitate to answer. "Sergeant David Ayden. Would you like his number?" Ayden wasn't afraid to go to the mat for his detectives.

Alderson nodded. "Yes, I would."

Jacob pulled out a piece of paper from a notebook he carried in his back pocket and scratched out Ayden's name and number. He held it out. As Alderson reached for the paper, Jacob glanced at the man's hands. Smooth, pristine, long fingers; buffed nails; and, most importantly, no sign of trauma. A woman being strangled might fight back and scratch her attacker's hands. But there was nothing on Alderson's hands.

"I'm going to have more questions for you," Jacob said as Alderson tucked the slip of paper in a pocket.

"Frankly, Detective, I don't like you. I'm only interested in dealing with your boss now."

"Suit yourself." He dropped his voice a notch. "But I can promise you, Sergeant Ayden won't release this site until I give the all clear. And the more you slow me down, the longer it's going to take."

Alderson heard the underlying message behind Jacob's words: *I can be a badass too.* The developer was still annoyed but he nodded curtly. "All right, I'll play it your way now."

"I want to talk to Burrows one more time." He'd hoped the forced wait in the cold might have jogged a few details loose from the party chief's mind.

Alderson raised his hand and called out, "Burrows!"

The surveyor lumbered over to them. "Yeah, boss?"

"This is the lead detective on this case."

Burrows nodded. "We already talked."

"Talk to him again."

"But you said . . ."

"Forget what I said. Tell him what you know. And don't hold back. I want this job site reopened as soon as possible."

Burrows glanced at Jacob. "Sure."

Jacob flipped open his notebook. "Tell me again what

happened from the moment you found the victim to the moment you called nine-one-one."

Burrows sniffed, glanced toward the yellow tape. He recapped what he'd already told Jacob.

"Have you seen her around here before?" Jacob asked.

"What, that woman? Hell no. No women on the survey crew. And no one in their right mind would come out here in January unless it was for money." He glanced at his boss after realizing what he'd said.

"Did you see anyone else lurking around the property?"

"No one. It was a typical morning."

"No hunters? No cars? Tire tracks?"

Burrows shifted his stance and hesitated. "Well, there was one guy. We caught him trespassing about a week ago. He seemed harmless enough."

Most likely he was, but the detail couldn't be ignored. "What happened?"

"It was before the storm. He was out here last Monday or Tuesday. Buzz, one of the surveyors, spotted him by the river. We told him it was private property. He said he used to hunt here with his dad when he was a kid. The place had special meaning to him. Anyway, we told him to hit the road and he did."

"That's it?"

"Yep. I forgot all about him until today."

"Can you describe him?"

"Honestly, I didn't give the guy much thought. Medium height. Wearing a thick parka, and a hat and gloves."

Jacob shifted his gaze to Alderson. "Who owned the property before you?"

"The entire tract is two hundred acres and was owned by about a dozen different families. I can get you a list."

"Good. The sooner the better."

"Sure."

\* \* \*

Kendall and her cameraman arrived at Alderson's River Bend site just as the body removal team's hearse and the county's forensics van lumbered toward the main road. The rugged, pockmarked side street forced the van and hearse to move at a slow crawl. Seeing the hearse gave her pause. This was her first murder story since last summer. If the police had been half hour later last July, she'd have been removed from the scene in a hearse.

Mike, her cameraman, stopped the van on the side of the road. He stood just under six feet and his weight hovered under two hundred. He looked fierce but he was one of the most even-tempered people she'd ever met. "I doubt I'll be able to get the van down the road."

"Yeah."

"You okay?" When Mike had visited her in the hospital last summer, the sight of her had brought tears to his eyes. She had been surprised he'd care so much. They'd barely known each other, having worked together for only a year.

During that visit and any other visit from friends, she'd been the upbeat one. She'd cracked jokes about bedpans and male nurses until she'd eliminated the unease and coaxed smiles. On some level she'd understood that if she made people feel good around her, they'd not abandon her. So, she'd become adept at telling everyone that she was fine.

Kendall cleared her throat. "*Please*. And I want lots of footage of the hearse."

Mike tossed her a glance. Relief flashed in his eyes. "Will do."

She realized he was worried about her doing her job, just as Brett was worried. This story was going to be make-or-break for her. She had to prove she was really back on the job.

Mike shoved the van in park and rolled out the driver's door in one fluid movement. He opened the side door to a neatly organized mobile studio. He hefted his camera on his shoulder. The green light on the camera clicked on, signaling he was taping.

Kendall slipped off her heels and put on her hiking boots before grabbing her pad. She glanced out her window, saw the mud, and scooted toward the driver's-side door. Her coat snagged on a torn piece of vinyl on the seat, forcing her to pause and tug it free. "Mike, when are you going to get this seat fixed?"

"Talk to 'the king.'" Annoyance dripped from his words every time he referenced Brett. "He's Mr. Budget Cut."

Brett did whatever it took to get the story at the cheapest rate possible. He'd step over anyone or knife anyone in the back to get the scoop for Channel 10 or save a buck. Few liked Brett, but as long as ratings were high and the budget was in the black he was tolerated.

Mike stood in front of the van and raised the camera.

She scooted out the door and moved behind Mike, who was now shooting. The cold air whipped off the river and cut through her coat. "All go?"

"Like clockwork."

"You're sure? We're the only TV crew here and I don't want to mess this up."

He waggled his eyebrows. "Chill. I always get the goods."

That made her smile. "Mike, when have you ever known me to chill? I'm good because I'm such a domineering diva."

He kept his gaze straight ahead. "I ain't commenting."

Mike rolled tape as the hearse reached the main road and pulled onto the hard-surface road. It quickly picked up speed and soon rounded the bend a half mile away and vanished from site. The forensics van followed. The driver, a woman, shot Kendall a stinging glance.

Mike clucked. "What's with the look?"

"Disdain is part of the job." She glanced at the police car blocking the entrance to the side road. "I'd love to get down to the river and see what the cops are up to."

"It won't be by that road," Mike said. "The cops aren't going to let us in."

"You think you could find another way down?" she asked.

"Maybe. Might mean some hiking."

"No problem."

"Hop in."

They drove past the officer positioned by the development's entrance. Mike signaled to the officer that they were going to turn around.

"We're going to have to hustle," Kendall said. "He's going to expect to see us returning soon."

"Right."

He drove down the rutted road another half mile. Kendall pressed her hand to the dash and planted her feet on the floor to keep from falling forward. When they reached the dead end, Mike turned the van around and shut off the engine.

"There's a path," Kendall said. "Looks like it leads to the river."

"Let's go."

Kendall peered ahead into the icy woods. She didn't relish the thought of hoofing it through the woods, but stories rarely came to her. "Right."

Mike grimaced. "I figured you'd change your mind once you saw the terrain."

She tossed him a grin and climbed out of the van. "Faint heart never won fair maiden."

He followed. "Yeah, whatever."

Cold wind cut through her coat and she dug her gloved hands into her pockets. "Shoot as much as you can," she said as he came around the front of the van with his camera. "No telling how fast they'll run us off."

It took fifteen minutes of steady walking before they rounded a final bend. The trees opened up into a snow-capped field that ran along the river. In the center of the field were five marked and one unmarked police cars, a survey truck, and a black SUV. Beyond the vehicles, yellow crime scene tape billowed in the wind near the icy James River.

Kendall scanned the crowd. She was good at summing up a setting quickly, picking shots and getting to the root of a story. Her blood pumped with a mixture of fear and excitement. She'd forgotten how much she really enjoyed covering hard news. These last few months she'd done her reporting from the news studio, and when she did get out, the stories were soft serve.

Now as she struggled to keep from sinking into the mud, she realized she'd grown lazy covering the soft stories. Not good. Comfort was the beginning of a slow decline.

"The other news stations aren't here yet." There was no hiding the excitement in her voice. "With luck, we can snag an interview before they do. Follow me."

She knew all the homicide detectives in the department as well as a dozen others from other departments. It was safe to say none really liked her when she showed up at their crime scene, but there was a mutual respect. She hoped.

Kendall's gaze settled on the broad shoulders of a very tall man. His back was to her but she recognized the scarred black leather jacket, faded jeans, and lean body. Jacob Warwick.

He stood next to the river's edge staring into the distance. He flexed the fingers of his right hand as if they were stiff. She'd heard somewhere that he'd competed in a charity boxing match last weekend. He'd taken a beating but in the end had won the bout in points. He was a fierce fighter who never conceded.

Tenacity was something she would never fault this man for. It had saved her life last summer. . . .

The Guardian serial killer had taken her to his basement slaughterhouse. He had shot her in the shoulder and she'd stumbled back and fallen to the hard cement ground. The pain had robbed the breath from her.

The Guardian had stood over her, his ax raised high as he'd readied himself to sever her hand from her body. Tears had welled in her eyes and she'd only been able to say, "Please, don't."

Without warning, the killer had spared her hand and left her to bleed to death, alone, locked in the tiny basement room.

Even now, she remembered the cold cement floor pressing into her back. She'd tried to stand but every move intensified the agony. She'd screamed until her throat burned. But no one had come.

Blood had seeped from her wound and she quickly didn't have the energy to stand. Her limbs had grown cold as life seeped from her.

In the darkness, there'd only been the drip, drip of a pipe and the scurry of rats. Time had lost meaning and she passed out.

And then the door had opened and light shone on her face. She'd thought for a moment the Guardian had returned and she'd balled up her good hand, praying she had the strength to fight.

Warwick's face had loomed over her, his shock as palatable as her own. His large hands had gently touched her face. "Jesus, it's Kendall Shaw. Kier, call for paramedics."

"He tried to kill me," she'd whispered. "To cut off my hand."

Immediately, Warwick had run his hands down the length of her arms and to her hands. "He didn't take your hand."

What little fight she'd mustered had vanished. She'd nodded and closed her eyes. The iciness had called, beckoning her to let sleep take her.

"Kendall!" Warwick's sharp voice had cut through the fog.

Her eyes had fluttered open. Fierceness had mingled with fear in his eyes. She'd moistened her lips but couldn't seem to hold on to consciousness. God, but she had been tired. Her eyes had slipped closed.

"Open your eyes," he'd commanded. "Help will be here soon. Hold on."

Hold on. It had sounded so hard. It would just have been too easy to let her grip slip.

"Listen to me. You are a better fighter than this."

"I'm not." She'd been fighting for so long—against her mother's illness and past secrets—suddenly she had become tired of struggling.

"Listen, you bitch," he'd hissed by her ear. "Open your goddamn eyes."

Bitch had been what had gotten her attention. Her eyes had opened and she'd felt a rush of fire and outrage. "Jerk," she'd muttered.

Satisfaction had gleamed in his eyes. "Good girl."

The paramedics had arrived seconds later. They'd rushed her to the hospital and the doctors had taken her into surgery almost immediately. She'd not seen Warwick since.

And now as Kendall faced him she felt a rush of embarrassment. He'd seen her well-cultivated veneer shatter in that basement. He'd seen her terror. She'd given up.

She could play the badass diva reporter for everyone else, but Warwick knew under it all she had cracked in that basement room. Shame had her straightening her shoulders until they were ramrod straight. No one, especially Warwick, would ever see her so vulnerable again.

As if sensing her, Warwick turned. Their gazes locked. The scene around them faded and she saw only his intense gray eyes. For a moment she imagined she saw regret. And then just as quickly it vanished.

Warwick's gaze shifted from her to Mike, who taped the scene. The detective strode toward the crime scene tape, ducked under it, and headed toward her. He wasn't happy. She'd snuck into his crime scene and there was going to be hell to pay for it.

Kendall preferred his anger. She could deal with that. She turned to Mike. "Aim the camera right toward Warwick. And if he kicks us out, lower your camera but keep it on. You never know what we'll pick up."

"There's the Kendall we all know and love." Mike swung his camera around as Kendall rushed toward Warwick. He stopped and let her close the gap between them.

"Detective, can you tell us who was murdered?" Kendall asked.

He tossed a brief glance at Mike and then focused on her. "How'd you get down here? The road is sealed."

"There's another path a half mile down the road. We hiked in."

He glanced toward the uniformed cops, his frown telegraphing his annoyance.

"Can you tell us who died?" she repeated.

He shifted his attention back to her. "We aren't able to release that information yet."

This close she remembered just how tall he was. "Was the victim male or female?"

"No comment."

"How old was she?" This was a guess to see if he reacted to the pronoun.

Warwick's expression gave nothing away. "We'll release a statement soon."

"Can you tell us how she died?"

"No comment."

"Was it a suicide?"

"Time to go, Ms. Shaw." He nodded toward the uniforms. "Leave or I will have you escorted out."

"What about sexual assault?" Kendall asked. She could hear footsteps behind her and knew she was about to be moved back to the main road.

Warwick's jaw tensed a fraction as he turned and strode away from her.

Kendall started after him. "What was the color of her hair? Was she tall or short?"

He kept moving, completely ignoring her. Getting information from Warwick was like getting blood from a stone.

Two uniforms stopped within inches of her. "Ma'am, you're going to have to move back to the main road."

She kept her sights trained on Warwick, who paused to talk to an older uniformed officer. She couldn't hear what Warwick was saying but he was pointing at her and frowning.

"Now, ma'am," the officer said.

"I'm going," she said, though she made no move to leave.

"*Now*," the officer ordered.

Kendall knew when it was time to retreat. "Let's go, Mike." Round one goes to Warwick.

Mike lowered the camera, but she noted the red record light remained on as they started back up the dirt road.

Grinning, Mike shook his head. "Warwick looked like he could spit nails at you."

Kendall grinned. "Nonsense. He really thinks the world of me."

Warwick had better get used to her because this story's coverage was far from over.

Nicole's belly felt heavy and her bones ached as she climbed the carpeted stairs to her second-floor photography studio, located in a one-hundred-year-old building in the heart of the historic Carytown shopping district.

The baby kicked her in the ribs. The girl was an active kid. She'd likely grow up to be a soccer player.

*Grow up to be.* Stupid to be thinking about what the girl would be when Nicole knew she couldn't raise the child.

The baby thumped inside her, as if she knew what her mother was thinking. "Enough, kid. Enough."

Each time the baby moved in her belly she thought about her late husband. He'd been insane. He'd been a monster.

And she was having his child.

What if the baby was like her father? And could she really love a child who had been created in anger and violence? What if she ended up hating the child and making its life miserable?

The questions had weighed heavily on her mind for months now. They kept her up at night, robbed her of joy and her appetite.

She continued up the stairs, her breath puffing with each step. Last summer, she'd looked at the space on a lark when she'd been shopping and spotted the FOR RENT sign. At the time, the seven-hundred-dollar-a-month rent had seemed so far beyond her means. In those days, she'd been hiding from Richard and had barely any money to her name.

It had been a humbling moment to realize she couldn't afford the rent. When she'd lived in San Francisco, she'd owned a successful business. All the Bay Area gallery owners knew her name and quirky landscapes and she'd quickly developed a following. The money had come in so easily in the early days. It was amazing how much she didn't think about money when she had it.

Then her marriage had started to deteriorate and, in an effort to save it, she'd let the business go. The money had dried up. When her husband had turned violent she'd fled, penniless, to a Richmond friend.

That had been seven months ago. Her husband was dead. No more looking over her shoulder. No more waking up in the middle of the night searching the shadows for Richard.

She'd been given a second chance. And she was trying to move on. But reclaiming the vibrant, original photography style that had been her trademark now eluded her. She couldn't seem to produce anything that was gallery worthy.

The baby kicked inside her.

The tables had so flip-flopped in the last three years. She'd started her career as an artist and she'd lived an impulsive, selfish, and reckless life. There'd been no worries about consequences or money.

Now, she was all about consequences and money. Her desire to create art had vanished and she took portraits to make ends meet. Jobs she'd have scoffed at three years ago now paid the rent. Bridezillas, screaming kids, eccentric families, and even business portraits were all welcome.

Though she'd discovered she had a real knack for

working with people, she longed for the days when life had been so easy. She wanted to be able to grab her camera and drive into the mountains and camp so that she could rise at dawn and capture the rising sun, as she once had. She wanted to stay up late drinking wine with friends and critiquing the latest art show. She wanted to be able to button her old jeans, sleep on her stomach, and not have to pee every five minutes. She wanted her body and life back.

Nicole shoved out a breath as she dug the keys out of her pocket and unlocked the door to her studio.

She'd chosen this space not for its trendy location, low price, or history. All of which were great. She'd picked this studio space because of the light. Six floor-to-ceiling windows on the north and south sides of the room let in the most delicious light. Heavy shades allowed her to control how much came into the studio during a shooting, but most days she kept them wide open. She loved natural light. It brought with it nuances that man-made light didn't quite have.

Nicole dropped her keys and mail on a battered desk she'd bought secondhand. A high stack of papers filled her in-box, and her appointment book was filled with miscellaneous papers she still needed to file. Paperwork— another hallmark of this new life she was struggling with.

She shrugged off her coat, laid it on the chair behind her desk, and opened the shades. Even on this gray day sunshine still seeped into the studio. There were a white chaise, a couple of wooden chairs, and a stool she used for portraits. On the back wall was a selection of six backdrops that hung together. Her most recent portraits covered the bare white walls of the space. In the back of the studio was a door that led to her darkroom. The room was small, not more than five by five, but it was enough space for her to work in.

Cupping her hand under her heavy belly, she crossed the room to the darkroom. She flipped on the red light and glanced at the pictures drying on the line. So many photographers used digital now, but she loved the flexibility of film. It added richness to her work that nothing could duplicate.

But she wasn't so nostalgic that she ignored the digital side of the market. She'd managed a small business loan so she could invest in computers and software and create portraits quickly. Being adept at both forms of photography translated into more revenue.

She sat behind the desk. The answering machine's green message light blinked the number three, signaling she had messages.

Nicole pressed the PLAY button. The first message was from a bride she'd met with last week to discuss her wedding. "Nicole, this is Callie. I've set the date. December twenty-fourth. I'd love for you to do my photography. Call me. My number is . . ."

The wedding was a big-budget project. Nice. December. The baby would be eleven months by then. Nicole tried to picture what the child would look like in seven months but couldn't.

She played the second message. This one was for an engagement picture of a young couple. They'd climbed Everest together and wanted a quirky portrait to reflect their adventurous life. Good.

And the third message. "Nicole, I saw you today. You looked lovely. So, so radiant. I hope all is well with the baby."

Something in the man's voice set her nerves on edge. Who was it? She replayed the message, thinking she'd missed his name. She hadn't. He'd not left one. She replayed the message again, this time trying to identify the voice. She couldn't figure out who it was.

*I saw you today.* . . .

Where had he seen her? She'd come straight from home to the studio.

*I saw you today.* . . .

She glanced at her prized large windows. Who the hell had been watching her?

# Chapter Four

Jacob dropped his keys on his desk. His office was ten by ten, furnished with county-issue furniture, and a set of bookcases filled with technical manuals. No pictures on the wall or knickknacks on his desk.

Except for the stack of files in his in-box, the office looked as it had the day he'd moved into it two years ago.

At any point he could walk out for good and know he'd not left anything special behind. That's the way he lived his life. He was always ready to pick up and leave at a moment's notice. He knew enough about psychology to guess that the quirk stemmed from his childhood. His mother had been a drunk and an addict and they moved around a lot because she always fell short on the rent. He'd landed in foster care by the time he was twelve and found stability, but the pattern had already been ingrained for life.

He opened the bottom desk drawer and pulled out a premixed protein shake. He popped the top and drank it down. Hardly satisfying but it would get him through the next couple of hours, and it was far healthier than the burger he'd been tempted to grab on the way back from the crime scene.

His cell rang and he removed it from the holster on his hip. "Warwick."

"It's Tess. I'm at the morgue. Jane Doe has been delivered and is in a drawer."

"Good."

"I've also collected Jane Doe's clothes and bagged them."

"Anything catch your eye?"

"Not yet. But I'm on my way back to the lab to process them." She sounded tired.

"Good. What about the coroner? He going to take care of Jane Doe today?"

"Not likely. He has a backlog. Two of the doctors are out sick with the flu or something. But he expects to do the autopsy in the morning."

Impatience crept into his voice. "And he's going to call me when he's done?"

"He has his marching orders."

Jacob's chair squeaked as he leaned back. "What about the fingerprints?"

"I've rolled them and will run them through AFIS when I get to my office." AFIS was the Automated Fingerprint System, a database that held literally millions of fingerprints on file. "If Jane Doe had ever been printed she'd turn up in the system."

"You're fabulous, Tess."

"I know." He could hear the smile in her voice. "I'll call you when I have something new."

"Do me a favor. No talking to the press on this one."

"I don't anyway."

"Good."

She hung up.

Jacob absently set the phone back in its holster. All the

wheels were in motion. Time and a little luck and they'd have an identity on their Jane Doe.

His mind turned to the riverbank where the victim had been found. There'd been no footprints leading up to her body. The snow had hit the city on Sunday and kept the survey crews away since last Friday. The body easily could have been out there for seventy-two hours.

He made a note to search boat landings within a twenty-mile radius of the site.

Zack appeared in his doorway. He had two cups of coffee in hand and set one on Jacob's desk before taking the seat opposite the desk. "Any word from Tess?"

Jacob's chair squeaked again as he leaned forward and picked up the cup. The heat felt good against his bruised fingers, which still ached from the cold. "Thanks." He gave Zack the rundown. "If our victim is in the system we should know about it by closing time. If she's not, it could take a while to find out who she is." He shifted the cup to his left hand and flexed it.

Zack sipped his coffee. "I heard you won the boxing bout."

"Yeah."

Zack shook his head, his expression serious. "So why do you keep pounding the crap out of people?"

Jacob smiled. "Since when did you become the department shrink?"

"Just asking, man."

"You're one to talk. You ride that damn bike like you're possessed."

That coaxed a half smile. "Point taken."

Boxing had given him so much. He was most at home in the gym. And giving up the sport meant surrendering the best things in his life.

"Your hands are going to turn to hamburger at the rate you're going."

Zack's comment struck a nerve in Jacob. His foster father had said the same thing during one of their last meetings just before he died. Jacob had done his best to hate the old man after the truth came out, but he'd never quite managed it. He'd been so pissed. Felt so betrayed. A couple of times he'd stood at the guy's grave and railed at him. But to his shame he'd never been able to extinguish the love he'd felt for the old guy.

The old guy had saved him from God knows what kind of life and deserved his loyalty. But he never talked about the guy, not even to Zack. He let his arrest record do the talking.

The phone on Jacob's desk rang. He punched the button for line one and picked up the receiver, hoping it was Tess with identification on the victim. "Warwick."

"Detective. You're a hard man to catch up with."

The soft feminine voice belonged to Dr. Erica Christopher. She was the department shrink. Crap. She handled the mandatory mental health evaluations for the department and his number had come up more than a few times since last summer. He'd played by the rules and had gone to her counseling sessions but this last month he'd slacked off. She was getting a little too close to matters he didn't want to discuss, so he'd canceled his last session. He had promised to reschedule but hadn't. She'd been after him since, but so far, he'd done a good job of dodging her. And he planned to keep ducking. He was tired of digging deep into his thoughts.

Jacob dropped his gaze. "I'm on my way out. Can we talk later?"

Zack raised a brow, noting the change in Jacob's voice. He sipped his coffee and watched, unashamed that he was eavesdropping.

"No." She'd been easygoing up until this point, but

there was no missing the steel in her voice. "You and I need to schedule another appointment."

He drummed his fingers on the desk. "I'm right in the middle of a murder investigation."

"You're always in the middle of something. But so am I." He heard the rustle of the pages of her appointment book. "I'm at the hospital on Saturday afternoon. How's three sound?"

The muscles in his back tensed like when he was boxed in against the ropes. "Not good."

"Unless you're donating an organ, Detective, I expect you to be in my office." He imagined her piercing blue eyes peering over the edge of her black half-glasses. She'd done that a lot during their sessions last fall. She was savvy and she knew how to ferret out weakness.

"No can do."

"Do I call Ayden and have you put on leave until you do?"

Jacob's temper rose. "Like hell you will."

"Get in my office and we won't have a problem. Ditch this appointment and we've got trouble."

She had him by the short hairs and there wasn't much he could do about it. "Fine. Three. Saturday."

"Good."

He slammed the phone. "That doctor is going to drive me insane."

Zack tapped his finger against the side of his Styrofoam cup. "Dr. Christopher, I presume."

"Yeah."

"She's a smart woman who knows her stuff."

"I've seen her six times. I've done my due diligence. There's no more sense in digging up the past. What's done is done. Time to move on." He said that a lot and most days believed it.

"A few more visits won't kill you. Just do your time and be done with it."

In the ring when he was against the ropes, he knew what to do: he came out swinging. But with the doctor she made him think about things he flat out did not want to consider.

The phone rang a second time. He snapped it up. "Warwick."

It was Connie Davidson with the missing persons division. Her gravelly voice grated over the lines. "I think I might have a match for that Jane Doe you found this morning."

"Great."

Paper rustled as she flipped through notes. "We got a call from a Betty Smith. She says her neighbor has been missing for a few days. The woman's name is White and she fits your Jane Doe's description."

"What's her full name?"

"Jackie Taylor White. Lives at one-oh-three Mayberry Drive, Richmond."

"Jackie?" That didn't fit. "The charm around her neck read *Ruth*."

"Can't answer that one."

Jacob frowned. "Right. Thanks." He hung up and brought Zack up to speed.

Zack nodded. "I'll get my coat. We can drive over now."

Within fifteen minutes the two were in Jacob's car, the heater blasting, headed south on Parham Road. Rush-hour traffic combined with lingering ice slowed their progress. It took almost twenty minutes before they pulled up in front of the small, one-story brick house.

White snow blanketed the front lawn and under a large picture window hung a window box filled with brown, drooping ivy coated in ice.

Jacob and Zack got out of the car and walked up the

cracked brick sidewalk to the front door. Three newspapers lay on the porch.

Jacob pressed the doorbell, which echoed inside the
house. "Looks like she hasn't been around for a few days."

Zack frowned. "Three newspapers. Three days. She
went missing on Friday."

"Maybe." No one answered the bell so Jacob rang it
again. When that didn't work, he pounded on the door.
The two walked around to the backyard and looked in
the utility room door. There was no sign of anyone. "She
must have lived alone."

"Let's talk to the neighbor," Zack said.

They crossed the yard to another house that looked
very similar. However, this house still had Christmas
lights strung along the roofline and in several of the
naked dogwood trees in the front yard. There was a
snowman in this yard; a plastic red sled; and a blue
bucket filled partly with snow, rocks, and sticks.

Jacob rang the bell. Immediately he heard the sound
of footsteps running around and young children yelling.
A woman's voice followed before steadier footsteps
crossed to the front door. The glass storm door sucked
inward as the heavy wooden one behind it opened to a
young woman with a toddler on her hip. Clinging to her
legs was a boy who looked about four.

The older boy wore a bath towel around his neck like
a Superman cape. The toddler had green Magic Marker
scribbles up and down his arms. A haphazard ponytail
held the woman's hair. She wore no makeup, a stained
Virginia Tech T-shirt, and sweatpants.

From his back pocket, Jacob pulled out his police
badge. Zack did the same. "Ms. Betty Smith?" Jacob asked.

"Yes."

"Ma'am, we're with Henrico County Police."

The four-year-old's eyes brightened as he popped his

thumb in his mouth. He clung to his mother's leg but his eyes didn't leave the cops.

The mother was more cautious. The woman frowned and made no move to open the storm door. "You've come about Jackie?"

"Yes."

"Did you find her?"

Jacob avoided the question. "Can you tell me why you filed a missing persons report?

The woman unlatched the storm door and propped it open with her foot. Immediately, warm air scented with hamburgers and fries rushed out to greet them.

"Come on in the house," she said.

They stepped into the house. The front room was a combination living room and family room. A thick gray carpet warmed the floor and an overstuffed blue couch and ottoman hugged the wall. The coffee table was covered with crayons and coloring books. A corner hutch housed a television, which now displayed a cartoon. Beyond the family room was a small kitchen. A pot boiled on the stove.

"I haven't seen Jackie in a couple of weeks. The kids have had colds and we've not gotten out much. But yesterday I had some extra cake left over from a birthday party and thought she might like some. She loves cake." She smiled as if she sensed she was rambling. "I saw all the newspapers. Jackie always lets me know when she's going out of town."

"She could have taken off on the spur of the moment," Jacob said.

"Jackie plans out everything. She's got a thing about schedules. Washes her car every Saturday. Taking off is not like her at all."

Jacob pulled out his pad and noticed the kids were staring at him with wide eyes. He nodded, not sure what someone was supposed to say or do with children that small. "How long have you lived next to Ms. White?"

"Less than a year. She moved in last summer after she separated from her husband."

"Was the separation friendly?" Zack asked.

A crease furrowed her brow. "I don't think so. Her ex came by just before Christmas. I think they had a fight, because he drove off real fast. I know that because the boys and I were in the front yard stringing Christmas lights. Honestly, that argument was playing in the back of my head when I saw the newspapers."

"Do you know her husband's name?" Jacob asked.

She thought for a moment. "Phil White, I think." The baby started to squirm so she put him down on the floor. That made him fuss louder so she picked him up again as she glanced at the boiling pot on the stove. "Is Jackie all right?"

"That's what we're trying to figure out," Jacob said. "Do you have a picture of her?"

"Yeah." She went into the kitchen, shut off the stove, and pulled the pot of pasta off the burner before moving to a refrigerator covered with dozens of snapshots, drawings, and reminder cards. The toys, the bubbling pot, and the general chaos had a homey charm Jacob feared and envied.

Betty flipped through a stack of pictures held together by a clip magnet. On the bottom she found a picture taken last fall. "This was taken at Halloween. I took a picture of the kids with Jackie. She was our first stop on our trick-or-treat route. Custom-made bags of candy for the kids."

The woman pictured with the tiny Spiderman and black ninja had shoulder-length dark hair streaked with some gray. She wore an orange sweater, a huge smile and cradled a large bowl of safety suckers.

This was Jackie White. The contrast between this picture

and the woman he'd seen by the river caught him a little short. This woman was so full of life. Radiant.

There was no charm around her neck, but the sweater could have been covering it. Again, he was reminded of Kendall Shaw. "Did she ever mention a Ruth?"

Betty thought for a moment. "No."

"It could have been a nickname," Zack prompted.

The baby reached for her nose but she shooed it away. "Maybe, but I never heard the name mentioned."

"What about a mother, a sister, an aunt?" he prompted again.

"I don't think so. She didn't have family. I mean her parents were older and they'd passed. And she'd mentioned once that she was an only child."

"What can you tell me about her?" Zack asked.

"She was always nice to me. And she loved the kids and kept her yard up." The last statement prompted an embarrassed grin. "I liked her but with the kids I don't have a lot of time to socialize. And she was always volunteering at her church."

"You know the name of her church?" Jacob asked.

She thought for a moment. "First Methodist in Glen Allen, I think."

Zack's face looked grim. "You said her husband's name was Phil White?"

"Yes."

Jackie had been strangled. Strangulation was a very intimate form of murder that required close contact. And her clothes had been intact as if someone wanted to preserve her dignity. It wasn't uncommon for an angry husband to suffer remorse after he killed his wife. "Did she have any other friends, family, visitors?" Zack asked.

"Sorry, I really don't know." On cue, the four-year-old struck a ninja pose and then kicked a kitchen chair. Betty glared at him and then smiled apologetically at

Jacob and Zack. "It's bad not to know who your neighbors are. But honestly, there are days when I don't know up from down."

"Do you have a spare key to her house?" Jacob asked. "I'm going to call for a search warrant and it would be nice if we didn't have to break in."

She smiled. "That I can help you with." She moved to a drawer by the stove and opened it. It was crammed full of miscellaneous junk that didn't belong anywhere. She dug through the mess for a good minute before she found the key attached to a Texas-shaped key chain. "Here it is."

Jacob accepted the key. "Thanks." He took Betty's full name, address, and phone number.

Her face looked pale now. She glanced at her kids, who hadn't missed a word. "Has something b-a-d happened to Jackie?"

Jacob attempted a half smile, but he doubted it was very comforting. "I really can't get into the details until I've spoken to her husband."

Worry deepened the lines around her eyes. "But you'll let me know?"

Jacob saw the earnestness in her eyes. "We'll be in touch." He handed her back the picture.

"Keep it if you think it will help."

He nodded and pocketed the picture. "Thanks."

The two detectives strode out of the warm house into the bracing cold. They returned to their car, called their sergeant with a report, and began the process of getting a search warrant.

Twenty minutes before the six o'clock newscast, Kendall leaned forward into the makeup lights that lined the vanity mirror and finished applying her lipstick. She'd always done her own makeup, having learned some of the best tricks of the trade when she'd modeled in college. She blotted her lips on a tissue and inspected them with a critical eye.

Since her visit to the crime scene today, Kendall had reviewed the tape Mike had shot and she'd written copy. The piece wasn't going to be more than thirty seconds because there just wasn't much to say. She'd spoken with the surveyor who'd found the body but he couldn't tell her much other than the body was female. Then she spent several hours calling contacts at the medical examiner's office and the police department but no one was talking. Frustrating.

Tonight's lead story would be the construction on I-64. The other pieces included post-holiday credit card debt, homes still without electricity after the Sunday storm, and hot vacation spots. Her Jane Doe would be third on the story lineup.

Kendall fluffed her hair, picked up her copy for the evening newscast, and headed toward the hallway to the studio. The station, one of the oldest in the region, was in the midst of a massive renovation. Walls were being torn out in the front of the building; carpet was being pulled; and new, brighter paint colors were being applied. The construction had made for a hectic few months, but the station manager had said the changes were necessary. The building, wiring, and broadcasting equipment were out of date. He'd promised the work would be completed by summer.

The renovation was a pain but the good to come out of it was her carpenter. He'd worked on this job briefly and had come recommended by the job's project manager.

Kendall worked her way down the winding hallway and pushed through the doors into the newsroom. The buzz of conversation greeted her. The news station was quiet most of the day, but with ten minutes to airtime, controlled chaos ruled.

Computerized editing stations divided the newsroom's large square footage. Reporters used the stations to write and edit their stories. In the far right corner was the blue screen designed to project weather maps. In another corner was the setup for AM Virginia, the station's morning show.

Most visitors were surprised when they first toured the station. They found it was always much smaller than they expected.

On her suggestion, they'd done away with the traditional anchor desk. Instead, she gave her reports from the center of the newsroom. Brett had been resistant at first but quickly discovered the new format gave the broadcast more energy. And the change had reflected in the ratings. Viewers felt Kendall was approachable when she wasn't behind the desk.

"Kendall, time to get fitted for your mike," Larry the soundman, who had worked at the station for several years, alerted her.

She moved toward him as she glanced at her copy on the murdered woman. Larry fit the miniature microphone to the lapel of her suede jacket and ran the wire to a battery at her waistband at the base of her spine.

*Today, Henrico County Police responded to a 911 call at James River near the proposed River Bend development where construction crews discovered the body of an unidentified woman. Her body had been dumped and so far police are speculating on the cause of death. . . .*

*An unidentified woman.* The phrase bothered her. The woman had a name and for some reason Kendall felt remiss not knowing it.

"All set," Larry said.

She pulled her thoughts back. "Thanks."

"One minute to air." The announcement came from the show's producer.

Her belly fluttered, as it always did seconds before air. She didn't mind the butterflies. They kept her on her toes.

"Thirty seconds to air."

She glanced at her producer and nodded.

*An unidentified woman.* The phrase lurked in the back of her mind as she stretched the muscles in her face. When the police released her name, she was going to do a profile on the woman.

Her producer did the final five count.

Kendall moistened her lips and smiled.

The unidentified woman wouldn't remain nameless and unknown. She would see to it.

Three . . . two . . . one.

"Good evening. This is Kendall Shaw reporting for Channel Ten News, Richmond. . . ."

Several hours had passed before Jacob and Zack returned to Jackie White's house.

Jacob slipped on rubber gloves before shoving the key in the lock. "I didn't see a security company sign out front."

Zack donned gloves. "We'll know for sure in a minute."

Jacob twisted the lock open and pushed in the door. No alarm chime sounded. Jacob flipped a switch by the front door. An overhead light clicked on.

The room wasn't large and could easily have been cramped but Ms. White had furnished the room modestly with an overstuffed yellow loveseat and a small paisley chair. Three pillows neatly lined the couch. A small corner hutch housed a TV. The room was perfectly neat with not a magazine out of place. There was a fine coating of dust on the coffee table, but Jacob suspected it wouldn't have been there if Jackie were alive.

"The place is as neat as a model home," Zack said.

Jacob glanced at the coffee table. Five Hollywood entertainment–style magazines were stacked in a neat pile. Nothing in the room was overly expensive but it was all kept in pristine condition. "She ran a tight ship."

They moved into the kitchen and flipped on the lights. The refrigerator was off white and neatly scrubbed, unlike the cluttered appliance in Betty Smith's kitchen. The counters were clean, the dishes washed and put away; even the stove looked as if it had just been cleaned. The cabinets were full of organic products.

"I'd say she was obsessed with cleanliness and her health," Zack sad.

"Yeah." He moved to a small nook that had a box marked "mail." "So how does she end up by the river, strangled?"

He pulled out the mail and searched through the stack. Electric, cable, credit card. All were up to date. And the name Ruth did not appear on any of the bills. So far it appeared she'd lived her life clean and simple and yet someone had brutally killed her.

"Time to pay Mr. White a visit," Zack said.

Jacob's jaw tightened and released. "Yeah."

The case had all the hallmarks of a domestic murder. A pending divorce. A recent fight. The method of murder. And yet Jacob's mind kept going back to the charm. *Ruth.* Jacob wouldn't be satisfied until he found out who Ruth was.


"*Stop!*"

It was just past two A.M. when Kendall sat up in bed. Her heart hammered in her chest and a sheen of sweat coated her body. For a moment her eyes searched the dark room and she struggled to figure out where she was. Slowly the familiar registered with her. This was her room, her bed.

She dragged a shaking hand through her hair and glanced at the digital clock by her bed. Two twenty-one. She'd been asleep just over an hour when the nightmare had woken her.

"Damn."

This dream was clearer and sharper than the others.

The terrified screams of a faceless woman echoed in her ears. The unknown woman begged for mercy and spoke of love as she wept.

The woman felt the presence of Evil pacing around her like a caged animal. Unbearable fear and sadness washed over Kendall, tightening her chest, making her barely able to breathe. She touched her fingertips to her face and realized that she had been crying in her sleep.

"This is nuts." Her voice sounded hoarse.

Kendall swung her legs over the side of the bed. She switched on the bedside light. "It's a dream. It's a damn dream."

But it had been so clear, and the feelings had been so real. She swallowed and stood. The wooden floor felt cold against her bare feet. She glanced longingly back at her bed but knew her body and mind were too keyed up to sleep.

Kendall pushed her feet into her slippers. "This is stupid. There is enough in the daily news to keep me up but I have to dream up phantoms."

She padded down the hallway past her roommate's closed door, careful to be quiet. She moved down the staircase, past the parlor and the dining room, and into the kitchen in the back of the house.

She flipped on the kitchen lights, which cast an

anemic glow over scarred linoleum floors, chipped counters, and dated appliances.

She picked up the white teakettle on the stove. At the sink, she switched on the water, waited as the aging pipes trickled out a weak stream, and then filled the kettle. "The contractor can't arrive soon enough," she muttered.

She set the kettle on the stove and switched on the front electric burner, which was the only one of the four that worked. Then she put a chamomile tea bag into a porcelain cup and drummed her fingers as she waited for the water to boil.

From the kitchen window above the sink, Kendall stared into her backyard and the alley and beyond that into the darkened house behind her. It had sat empty for the last few months. The sagging real estate market and the cold winter hadn't helped sales. It would be nice to finally have someone move in.

The teakettle whistled, snapping her out of her thoughts. She turned to the stove and poured hot water into her cup.

She sat at the kitchen table and blew on the steaming mug. The worn walnut table had belonged to her mother. It didn't fit into the design of the new kitchen but she planned to keep it anyway. Not in the kitchen, but somewhere in the house.

When she was a kid, there were nights when she didn't sleep well. She used to go into her parents' room and her mother would wake instantly. Her dad would grumble and ask her what was the matter. Her mother always told him to go back to sleep, and then Kendall and her mom would go to the kitchen and share tea. At eleven or twelve, drinking tea with Mom felt like such a grown-up thing to do.

Those were some of the best times she'd shared with her mother. During those nighttime sessions they'd talk about

the boys at school. They'd gossip about the neighbors.
Those were the moments when Kendall felt the most
secure and most tempted to broach sensitive topics.

"I hate my hair," twelve-year-old Kendall complained.

Irene set her cup of steaming tea on the table. She smiled,
her brown eyes neutral. They'd had this conversation before
and Irene understood now that no answer would be satisfactory to Kendall. "I like your hair."

Kendall groaned and glanced at her tea, heavily laced with
sugar and milk. "You *always* say that."

Irene sipped her tea. "But it's stunning. Rich dark brown,
thick, lush. I would have killed for hair like that at your age."

"I like yours. I like blond better." Kendall really didn't care
about hair color. She was trying to ask without asking: *Who do
I look like? Where do I come from? Why was I given up for
adoption at the age of three?*

"The grass is always greener." Irene smiled stiffly, realizing
instantly where this was headed. She didn't like this topic and
avoided it at all costs.

In the last year, Kendall had really zeroed in on the differences
between them. Her mother was short, pale, blond and gained
weight even when she walked by food. Kendall, even at twelve,
was taller than her mother; her skin was olive, not pale; and her
long, limber body suggested she had a lot of growing to do. Her
parents liked puzzles and books. Kendall craved continued
action.

Night-and-day differences weren't the only reminders of the
never discussed adoption. "The Gallery of Kendall," as her
father jokingly called the dozens of framed pictures of Kendall
in their house, documented all of her achievements: dance
recitals, visits to Santa, even Easter egg hunts. But all the pictures were taken after Kendall had turned three. Once when a
neighbor had asked about the lack of baby pictures, Irene Shaw

had lied and blamed the discrepancy on a house fire that had destroyed all their pictures.

"I wish I looked more like you," Kendall said, trying a different tactic.

Irene set her cup down. "Good heavens, why? Honey, you are stunning."

"Yeah, but my skin is so dark compared to yours."

Irene frowned into her cup. Then in an about-face, she smiled brightly. "You know what we should do first thing in the morning? Go shopping. I saw the cutest dress that would look perfect on you."

Her mother knew the right buttons. Her daughter, unlike her, loved pretty clothes and shoes. Shopping always distracted Kendall. However, this time the not-so-subtle evasion wasn't lost on Kendall. She understood without hearing the words that she'd get no answers. She dropped the subject.

Later, she went to her father and asked him about her adoption. "You know this kind of talk upsets your mother."

"But why don't we ever talk about it? Is something wrong with me? Was my birth mother some space alien freak?"

Tenderness in his eyes, he patted her on the shoulder. "You are perfect and don't you ever believe different. Mom and I love you and that's all you need to worry about."

Her father had been dead ten years and her mother had been gone a year now. There was no one left to hurt or disappoint.

And yet Kendall hadn't initiated a search of her birth parents and hadn't told anyone, including Nicole, she was adopted.

Questions about her birth mother had never left her. But even as an adult, voicing questions about her birth family left her feeling disloyal and afraid.

Kendall traced the rim of her porcelain cup with the tip of her index finger. She sipped her tea.

She made her living asking questions, digging into people's lives and turning the news into stories people enjoyed. But she couldn't ask the most basic questions about her own past. *Where had she come from? Where had she lived the first three years of her life?*

Kendall rubbed her itchy eyes. The weight of it all suddenly felt so heavy on her shoulders. "Sleep. I desperately need sleep."

So far she'd been able to hide the dark circles under her eyes with makeup. But soon the television cameras would betray her sleepless nights no matter how much foundation she caked on.

Rising, Kendall moved to the sink. She poured her tea down the drain, rinsed out the cup, and set it on the counter.

"This is ridiculous. It doesn't matter where I came from. I had great parents and I *have* a great life. The past simply doesn't matter."

But deep inside her, she sensed that it did.

# Chapter Five

The last forty-eight hours had been frustrating. Jacob and Zack had tracked down Phil White's town house, but there'd been no sign of him and neighbors reported they'd not seen him since Friday morning. They'd learned from his boss at the cable company that he was on vacation, but no one seemed to know where he'd gone or how to reach him.

Interviewing Jackie White's church friends and co-workers had been just as elusive. She was an intensely private woman, and though all seemed to like her no one really knew much about her. Her cell phone records, bank statements, and credit report showed nothing out of the ordinary.

Jacob had gotten a call from the medical examiner's office this morning. Jackie White's autopsy was happening today.

As Jacob and Zack strode into the medical examiner's office, Jacob felt himself tensing. Death was a part of his job but he didn't like this place. The tile floor. The chrome. The smell. The place had an eerie feeling that he'd never grown comfortable with.

"God, I hate the smell of this place," Zack muttered.

Jacob inhaled through his mouth. "I hear ya."

The detectives pushed through the double doors into the autopsy room. The tile floor had a drain in the center. Adjustable lights hung over five different chrome examining tables, all of which were empty except the one where Dr. Alex Butler stood.

Dr. Butler was young, not much older than thirty. He was tall, lean and had a thick stock of blond hair cut into a crew cut. Blue eyes reflected intelligence. He'd finished medical school at age twenty and some called him Doogie Howser. He'd spent several years working in Hawaii for the federal government helping to identify the remains of missing U.S. servicemen. He had become an expert known worldwide and could have worked anywhere.

Dr. Butler turned and glanced at his gloved hands. "Detectives Warwick and Kier. I'd shake your hand, but . . ."

"No problem, Dr. Butler," Jacob said. It felt odd calling the guy doctor. He didn't look old enough to drive. "What do you have?"

"I'm glad you arrived before I finished." Dr. Butler stepped aside and Jackie White's nude body came into view. Her chest was open via the coroner's signature Y-cut. Her vital organs had been removed. Her hair was brushed off her face.

Zack expelled a breath.

Jacob clenched his teeth, determined to view the body as nothing more than evidence.

Dr. Butler looked nonplussed over the woman lying on the metal table behind him. This was business as usual to him.

"What can you tell us?" Jacob's voice sounded rusty. Already he was anxious to get out of the room.

"Strangulation was the cause of death." He took the victim's head and turned her face away from them, exposing her pale neck, marred by finger bruises on both sides. "As you can see by the bruising he used both hands. Also, the hyoid bone was broken, as is common in the case of hanging and strangulation. When the bone breaks, asphyxiation occurs."

Jacob's impatience rose. Dr. Butler was detailing what they'd already suspected. "What's special about this case?"

"The killer had to have been a powerful person. Her larynx was nearly crushed. And it appears he strangled her from behind. See the finger marks? They point forward."

Dr. Butler moved to the body's raw wrists. He lifted her arm. "These marks were made over several days. She was trying to get loose. There are also rub marks on her ankles and at the base of her spine."

"The spine?" Jacob asked.

Dr. Butler rested his hands on his hips. "My guess is that the killer tied her to a straight-backed chair with sturdy arms. The hard chair back would have rubbed into her skin after a couple of days. Also notice the lividity—these purplish, red marks." When death occurred blood settled at the lowest portion of the body. "The markings occur in her feet, the underside of her forearms, and her backside, suggesting she was sitting after she died."

"Lividity doesn't happen for at least thirty minutes," Jacob said.

Dr. Butler nodded. "But hers is so dark I think the killer kept her tied to the chair for at least three to four hours."

The killer had kept her dead body with him. Why? "When do you think she died?" Jacob asked.

"Her liver temp was forty degrees. That's a drop of

fifty-nine degrees. Assuming she lost a degree and a half per hour, and it was a constant thirty degrees outside, I'd say she's been dead roughly forty hours."

"Death occurred roughly around six p.m. on Sunday?" Zack asked.

Dr. Butler nodded. "Give or take."

Jacob checked his notes. The timeline he'd been able to establish so far didn't fit what Dr. Butler was telling him. "We stopped by the victim's office yesterday. The office manager said White e-mailed in on Sunday morning and said she'd have to take Monday off."

Dr. Butler shook his head. "That doesn't fit what I've found. If I had to guess, I'd say she was restrained on Saturday."

"So the killer sent the e-mails?" Zack speculated.

"Maybe," Jacob said.

"Signs of sexual assault?" Zack asked.

Dr. Butler shook his head. "None. And frankly, I was expecting it. Preliminary tox screens show that she was loaded with barbiturates."

"Like a date-rape drug?"

Dr. Butler nodded. "That was my thought. The drug would have made her pliable." He turned the inside of the victim's pale arm upward. Needle marks peppered the points around her blue-green veins. "This was done over a couple of days."

"How long before we know what was injected into her?" Zack asked.

"A couple of weeks."

"And there's a possibility she did this to herself?" Jacob challenged.

"I don't think so." Dr. Butler shook his head. "That's why I opened her up. Her heart was a normal weight and size, as was her liver. Have a look."

Jacob braced and leaned forward.

Zack held up his hand. "I'll take your word for it."

Dr. Butler shrugged. "This woman took very good care of herself. Good weight, firm muscles, healthy heart, no signs of cigarette smoking in the lungs. Good teeth. She did not use drugs."

Jacob flexed his fingers. For an instant his gaze darted to the victim's pale, still face. He thought about the picture taken of her last Halloween. Smiling. Vibrant. Alive. "So how the hell does she end up tied to a chair, loaded full of drugs, strangled, and dumped like yesterday's garbage?"

"Have you talked to her husband yet?" Dr. Butler asked. "The majority of the women I see murdered are killed by someone they know."

Zack put his hands in his pockets and rattled the change. "We're still looking for him."

Tess pushed through the doors to the autopsy room. Her tight frown mimicked her brother's. Her long dark hair was tied back. She wore khakis and a dark shirt. Dark circles smudged the delicate skin under her eyes, a sign she'd been up last night working on this case. "Your office said I could find you here. I had to be down here anyway and thought I'd be able to catch you."

The doctor's gaze darted to Tess. For just an instant, he stared before looking away.

Zack nodded to his sister. "Did you find anything unusual on the body?"

She opened the file in her hands. "There wasn't much. But I did find carpet fibers on the left side of her coat."

"The left side?" Dr. Butler asked.

Tess shrugged. "As if she'd been dragged over the carpet."

The doctor nodded. "Explains the hint of rash on her left arm."

"What can you tell us about the fibers?" Jacob asked.

Tess glanced at her notes. "Standard-grade carpet. Very new. And they were pink."

"Pink?" Zack and Jacob had searched the victim's premises late into the night, along with another member of the forensics team, who had sealed the house indefinitely. "When we went through her house there was no sign of pink."

Zack nodded. "Beige, browns, and antique whites. No color at all."

"Has her car been found yet?" Tess asked.

"No," Jacob said. "But her boss reported that it was a black Jetta, beige interior, Virginia plates."

Tess flipped through her notes. "There was no skin under her nails. No chemicals on her clothes. No fingerprints on her belt buckle."

Jacob's cell phone vibrated on his hip. He glanced at the number. "Excuse me." He walked to the corner of the room and flipped open the phone. "Warwick."

He listened as the patrolman assigned to White's house reported that Phil White had returned home minutes ago. "Good. Make sure he doesn't leave." He glanced at Zack. "The husband is home."

Zack nodded. "Let's go."


"Brett, I just got an anonymous text message. The sender tells me he knows the name of the dead woman found by the river," Kendall said as she poked her head in his office.

He lifted his gaze from Wednesday night's copy. "What's her name?"

She flicked the edge of the sticky note in her hand with her index finger. She'd received tips like this before but they always left her questioning the sender's agenda. "According to my source her name is Jackie White. I did a quick check and found that she lives on Mayberry Drive and is a secretary at Trainer Engineering. Thirty-eight years old. Separated." Ferreting out facts quickly was her specialty. She handed him the note.

Brett glanced at the address of Jackie's employer and her home address. He checked his watch. "Both places are close. You could make it by both locations before deadline if you hustle. We have five hours to air."

"I want to talk to the husband."

He seemed pleased by her assertiveness. "Go for it. Where's Mike?"

She smiled, pleased with herself. "Outside warming up the van."

Brett grinned. "I should have known." He rose and moved around the desk until he stood just inches from her. "I knew it was a smart idea to hire you."

Impatience nipped at her and she feared where this conversation was going. "It was one of your best." She turned to leave and he caught her arm in his hand. The hold was gentle, yet insistent. Emotion darkened his eyes. "I miss you, Kendall."

Since she'd taken the anchor job there'd thankfully been no conversations with Brett about their past relationship. "Where's this coming from?"

He glanced down to the hand holding her arm. "It's been chewing on me for a while."

She did not want to have this conversation. They were done. Period. Gently, she pulled out of his grasp. "This isn't the time."

His features stiffened. "We need to make the time to talk about us."

"There is no us anymore, Brett. That ended last year. And as I remember, you were glad it ended."

He brushed an imaginary hair from her shoulder. "Breaking up was a mistake."

At the time she thought it might have been a mistake, but no longer. "It was the best move for us." She realized now that Brett only wanted what came easily. He wanted a relationship filled with happy moments. The hard, sloppy times sent him running.

"I don't buy that."

Anger kindled inside her. There was a time when she'd really needed his support and he'd refused her pleas of help. "You need to accept it. We're done."

"Are you seeing someone else?" Accusation peppered his words.

She didn't like his tone of voice. "That really is none of your business."

He shoved out a breath. "It's a simple yes or no answer."

"There's nothing simple about that question."

Brett looked frustrated. "Why do you have to be so stubborn?"

She lifted a brow. "I've got a story to cover and don't have time for this."

For a moment he looked as if he would block her exit, but then he moved aside.

Kendall exited the office. She hadn't realized that she'd been holding her breath or that tension had coiled around her spine until she was headed away from him. Brett's attitude was a bit unnerving and it was something she'd not seen before.

Her high heels clicked quickly as she hurried down the hallway toward the back exit. She pushed open the back double doors and found the white news van. Mike was in the front seat; the engine was running and the heater humming.

Her career was heading in the direction she wanted. Her house was coming together. And now Brett was trying to dig up the past. *The past.* Every time she turned around the past stalked her.

She climbed into the front seat and handed Mike a sticky note with an address. "Let's head here first."

Mike glanced at the address and put the car in gear. He knew the metro area like the back of his hand and rarely needed a map. "So who's there?"

"That woman found by the river on Tuesday. We have her name. This is where her husband lives."

"Cool."

For some reason the casual word irritated her. "Cool. We're covering a woman's murder."

He glanced at her as he drove through the parking lot. "What's got your panties in a twist? She's a story, Kendall. Just like all the other stories we've covered."

Indignation burned. "She was a person."

He pulled out onto Broad Street. "Why's this chick so different?"

Kendall tightened her jaw. She didn't have an answer for him. "I don't know."

"Well, figure it out. The last thing I need is for you to go all soupy on me."

He'd thrown down a glove, knowing nothing sharpened her focus more than a direct challenge. "I'm not soupy—ever."

"That so?"

Mentally, she dug in her heels. "Watch and learn.


Jacob parked the car in front of Phil White's town house. The air had turned warmer and temps were expected to top forty today. The ice from the storm had melted and almost all signs of the weekend snow were gone. Good. One step closer to spring.

Jacob tucked his keys in his pocket. He surveyed the town house trying to absorb details. Well maintained. Neat. It looked normal enough.

But Jacob's own mother had taught him early on that the walls of a house could hide a multitude of sins.

"You want to do the talking?" Zack asked.

"Yes." He'd not been able to get this victim out of his mind. She'd lived a by-the-book life. No drugs. Hard-working. No dabbling in risky behavior. And yet someone had murdered her. All the signs pointed to a domestic situation.

Jacob and Zack strode up to the simple front door. Jacob knocked.

At first there was no sound from inside the town house. Jacob then pounded the door. This time they received a gruff, "Just a minute."

"You're messing with his beauty sleep," Zack said.

Jacob flexed his right hand. "I'm going to do more than that."

Footsteps thudded. The door snapped open.

Standing in the threshold was a midsize guy wearing a gray college T-shirt, sweatpants, and a couple days' growth of beard. His thick dark hair was brushed back, emphasizing rounded cheeks and bushy eyebrows over dark eyes.

The man sniffed. "What do you want?"

Jacob pulled out his badge. "We're looking for Phil White."

"That's me." White frowned. "What do you want?"

"Can we come in?" Jacob asked.

White shook his head. "If you've got something to say you can say it out here."

Jacob didn't want to do this on a doorstep. "Can we come in?" he asked again.

"No."

So be it. Jacob lowered his voice. "The body of Jackie White was found on Sunday."

White's jaw dropped. "What? Jackie White? My wife is dead?"

Jacob nodded. "Yes."

The color drained from the guy's face and he stepped to the side. "Come in."

The place was sparse, typical bachelor. La-Z-Boy recliner, wide-screen TV, pizza boxes on the kitchen counter. Jacob would bet the freezer only saw frozen meals and the fridge beer and leftovers. There was a fireplace but it looked as if it had never been used.

White looked up at Jacob. Tears glistened in his eyes. "Are you sure?"

Jacob nodded. "Yes.

White drug a trembling hand through his hair. "How?"

Jacob ignored the question. "You two were separated?"

"Yes."

"How long?"

"Eighteen months."

"You two fought at Christmas?"

"Yes."

"Why?"

White swallowed. "That's personal."

"We need to know."

"She refused to give me a divorce."

Neither Jacob nor Zack spoke.

White filled the silence. "I tried to work it out with her. I really tried. But she hated sex. Refused to touch me. Was I supposed to live the rest of my life like a monk?" He tipped back his head to stop the flow of tears. "Why are you asking these questions? How did she die?" he asked. "Was it some kind of accident?"

"No, it wasn't an accident." Clearing his throat, Jacob said in a deliberately softer tone, "Do you know of anyone who would want to kill Jackie?"

White shook his head. "She was a saint. She donated her time to every cause out there. Everyone liked her."

"Did she have any boyfriends?" Zack asked.

White barked out a half laugh. "No."

"Are you sure?"

"Yeah. That's one of the things we fought about in December. I told her she needed a man. She said she didn't need a man. She was married to me." He dropped his head into his hands and started to weep. "God, I shouldn't have yelled at her."

Zack cleared his throat. "Is there anyone we can call to come stay with you?"

"No." He swiped tears from his cheeks. "No. I've got it under control."

Jacob glanced around the apartment looking for any signs of pink carpeting. There was nothing. But then if White had killed her it made sense that he wouldn't do it here.

White brushed another tear from his cheek. "How come I haven't seen anything on the news?"

"You are her legal husband—next of kin. We are required to tell you first before we release information to the media."

White started to weep again. The front doorbell rang and White woodenly moved toward the door and opened it.

Jacob swallowed an oath when he saw Kendall Shaw standing in the doorway.

"Mr. White, my name is Kendall Shaw. I'm with Channel Ten News."

Jacob strode toward the door. His gaze lingered on Kendall. For a split second his gut clenched with an unquenchable craving. "This is a bad time, Ms. Shaw."

Kendall's gaze told him she was as surprised to see him

as he was her. She shook it off. "Mr. White, my condolences to you concerning your wife."

White glared at Jacob. "I thought the press didn't know."

Jacob swallowed an oath. How the hell had she found out? "They're not supposed to."

"I only just found out," Kendall said. "I'd like to talk to you about your wife."

Before White could answer, Jacob reached for the door and closed it.


Forty-five minutes later, Jacob and Zack left White with bloodshot, tear-filled eyes. They'd learned he'd been hunting with buddies the last few days.

Kendall was waiting outside the apartment. The cold outside had turned her face a bright pink. She moved toward them, her stride confident. "I'd love to talk to you about this case, detectives. Do you have a few minutes to spare?"

Jacob speared her with his gaze. "Who gave you the victim's identity?"

She shrugged. "A source."

"Who?"

"I won't say."

Jacob muttered an oath and both detectives started moving.

Fast-clicking heels told them she had to hustle to keep up with them. "I've been on the phone for an hour with friends and neighbors of the victim. They all say she was a great person. Any ideas how she ended up dead by the river?"

Jacob tossed her a glance. "Leave Phil White alone, Ms. Shaw. He's upset right now." He wasn't as concerned about White as he was about Kendall mucking with his investigation. White certainly played the part of the grieving husband, but Jacob had learned long ago not to take anything at face value.

"You can't stop me from talking to him," she said.

"No, I can't. But the guy is a wreck. Show some humanity." Jacob and Zack got into Jacob's car and Jacob fired up the engine.

He looked up and noticed Kendall was crossing the parking lot to the news van. She started talking to the cameraman, who didn't seem to like what he was hearing. The two got into the van.

So she wasn't pushing the interview today? That was a surprise. Points for her. But he knew her well enough to know she'd be back.

"Damn her."

Zack shrugged. "She can be a pain, but you've got to admit she's good at what she does."

"I don't have to admit squat."

Zack studied Jacob. "It's not like you to get so pissed at reporters. They've got a job to do, like us."

Jacob tightened his hands on the wheel. "She takes it too far."

"Not today. She's backing off."

"She'll be back sooner than later."

A grin tugged the edges of Zack's mouth. "She's gotten under your skin."

"Bullshit."

Zack laughed.

"What's so funny?" he growled.

Amusement danced in his partner's eyes. "You remind me of me when I had it so bad for Lindsay and she wouldn't give me the time of day."

"That's crap. This woman just annoys me."

Zack grinned. "Oh, I *know*."

Jacob shook his head and put the car in gear. "Shut up."

Zack's phone rang at that moment and he answered

it. His smile faded and he nodded grimly as he scribbled a memo in his notebook. He hung up. "They found Jackie White's car off of West Broad Street. Vega's getting a warrant and will meet us at the scene."

Jacob pulled into traffic. He was grateful he could push Kendall from his thoughts. Twenty minutes later he pulled into the parking lot of a big-box store and he and Zack walked to the marked police car parked next to a black Jetta located in a remote corner. The sun was dipping lower and the air temps had dropped. The air cut through them like a knife.

Jacob and Zack exchanged words with the patrolman, who said, "Detective Vega and forensics will be here any minute. Vega has the warrant."

"Thanks." Jacob shoved his hands into his pockets and walked over to the Jetta, Zack following him. Inside, there was a box of tissues on the front seat, white plastic grocery bags full of groceries, and a spare pair of tennis shoes on the back floorboard.

"I don't see her purse," Zack noted.

"No."

Zack glanced around the parking lot. "What about surveillance cameras?"

"I'll ask the manager."

"She's chosen an isolated corner."

"The woman who worked in the cubical next to Jackie's said Jackie liked to park far from the store entrance so she could get a little extra exercise."

"I'd bet money he snatched her from the parking lot," Zack said.

"Yeah." Jacob rubbed his hand over the thickening stubble on his chin. He studied the trail from the car to the store entrance.

Zack shoved out a breath. "What could he have said to her so he could get close enough?"

"He could have offered to carry her groceries, asked for the time, or feigned car trouble."

"Why her?"

"Who the hell knows"?

Watching Kendall Shaw on the news each night had become a ritual. The day just didn't feel right if Allen didn't see her.

He leaned forward on his workbench and turned the volume up on the small TV mounted on the shelf above. Kendall grinned back at him. Her soft voice soothed his nerves even if what she had to say wasn't always so pleasant. If not for her he'd not have bothered with the news. Most of it was hype and made-up crap slapped together by the networks to get ratings. No one cared about the truth.

Kendall walked about the studio. Her long, lean body moved with the confidence of a queen. Her gaze turned serious when she revealed Jackie White's identity. The camera cut away to interviews she'd done with a neighbor and a coworker. Both seemed sad over the loss of Jackie—Ruth. His throat tightened. He understood that loss. He missed her too.

Allen was glad now he'd sent that text message to Kendall.

He liked helping Kendall. He wanted to see her succeed. And he also felt confident that no one would find him. He'd been very careful when he'd laid Jackie on the bank. He'd not even stepped out of the flat-bottomed boat when he'd dropped her body on the shore.

The serious glint in Kendall's eyes told him she was frustrated by the police. She wanted more and they weren't giving it to her. Pride burned inside him. He and Kendall had much in common. In so many ways they were kindred spirits.

When he'd first arrived in town, he'd written Kendall a couple of e-mails, via the station's Web site. He had told her how much he liked watching her. She'd not responded back. But he didn't really blame her.

This time when he'd sent her a text message, she'd gotten right back to him. *Who r u? How do u know this?* Satisfaction had burned as he'd stared at the words.

Allen considered sending another text but decided now wasn't the best time. Better to stay under the radar for now.

# Chapter Six

Sweat dripped into Kendall's eyes as she simultaneously pumped on the elliptical trainer and hit the rewind button on the remote. The CD in the TV mounted on the wall clicked backward. The trainer was located in her basement. The space remained unfinished, but the addition of track lighting had banished the gloom and transformed the crude space from dank to suitable. It wasn't an optimal place to work out but practical and efficient.

She was near the end of her sixty-minute workout and felt a measure of satisfaction as sweat rolled down her face. The pinch that always seemed to be in her shoulder had eased somewhat and she felt good. Her mind drifted to the day ahead. It was Saturday but she was going to work on the White story before she had to report to the hospital for physical therapy on her shoulder. She was looking at another month of PT before the docs pronounced her totally healed from last summer's shooting.

Kendall rubbed the scar on her shoulder before she replayed the broadcast from last night. She watched as she interviewed neighbors and coworkers of White and

could see that she was *softer* than she had been last
summer when she'd covered the Guardian. The old
Kendall would have gone for the interview with Phil
White, regardless of his grief. Mike certainly hadn't been
happy when she'd announced they were backing off for
the day. But she'd been adamant.

She pumped harder on the machine.

Ironically, the viewers had loved her work. E-mail response had been tremendous. Though there'd been
nothing from her tipster. Despite a wave of unease, she'd
sent him another text message asking for an interview
but doubted he'd respond.

Four minutes remained in her workout when the front
doorbell rang. "Damn." Nicole hadn't gone to work yet
and Kendall hoped she'd grab the door. An obsessive-
compulsive streak always kept her pushing as hard as she
could until she reached exactly sixty minutes.

She listened hoping to hear the door open. The bell
rang again. "She's in the shower, I bet."

Kendall started working faster, trying to will the clock
to reach sixty minutes. She wanted to finish the workout
before the visitor rang again. Three minutes and twelve
seconds to go. Two more rings sounded from the upstairs hallway.

"Damn." She hit STOP on the machine and climbed
down. She shut off the TV and grabbed a towel draped
over a nearby table. She climbed the steps to the first floor.

The doorbell rang again.

"I'm coming!" Kendall hurried down the center hallway. She glanced out the side window and saw a familiar
face. As she opened the door, cool air chilled her overheated skin and she shivered.

"Ms. Shaw?" The grinning man standing on her front
porch was medium build and looked to be in his late
thirties, early forties. He wore painter's pants, a white

sweatshirt, and a thick army jacket. Dark graying hair framed a rounded, pleasant face.

"Todd Franklin!" The carpenter she'd been waiting for.

He tipped his head forward. "Yes, ma'am."

She clapped her hands together. "Thank God. I didn't think you'd ever come. Please come inside."

Todd wiped his feet off on the front porch mat and came into the foyer. "Sorry I'm a few days late. My job on the south side just took longer than I expected. You find all kinds of problems when you're renovating."

"Please don't say that," she said. "We're thinking only positive thoughts when it comes to this renovation."

He laughed. "I'll do my best." He glanced at her sweat-stained jog top. "Did I interrupt your workout?"

"No worries." He was the one interruption she would surrender time on the machine for. She moved down the hallway. "My roommate gave you the grand tour last month. You remember, Nicole?"

"I sure do. She was a big help."

"I'm sorry I couldn't be here. New job. My first few months were pretty hectic."

"Oh, I know how it is. I see you on TV sometimes."

Kendall had learned long ago not to ask viewers what they thought about her broadcasts. Negative reviews had a tendency to chew on her. "It's always good to be working."

"True enough."

"Let me show you the kitchen."

"Great." He followed behind her. "That roommate of yours—Nicole—did she have that baby yet?"

She crossed into the kitchen and pulled bottled water from the fridge. "Not yet. Still has about three or four weeks to go. Water?"

"No, thanks." Todd glanced around the kitchen. "I reckon she'll make a good mama."

He unwittingly stumbled to the edge of an emotional

minefield that Kendall had no desire to enter. She let the comment drop. "Well, as you can see, the kitchen is still as awful as it was when you first saw it. Frankly, I believe it's a lost cause, but the designer assures me that you can do miracles."

"I'll make it just the way you like it," he said.

He possessed a confidence she liked. And he'd come with excellent references, so for now she was ready to turn the job over to him. "Bless you." She opened a cabinet drawer. The contents were neatly organized and she found a spare key easily. "Here's a key to the house. While you're working, I'll just leave the alarm off."

"Yes, ma'am." He put the key on his own ring. "First day or two it's gonna be a terrible mess in here. And the demolition will be noisy."

"It'll be worth the sacrifice." She clapped her hands together, more excited than she'd been on any Christmas morning. "So, you are going to start today?"

"I am."

"Then I'll leave you to it?"

He nodded. "Go on and do what you need to. I've got it from here. I'll be in and out of the house a lot, dragging in tools, so expect to hear the door opening and closing. Mind if I work tomorrow?"

"Not at all." Kendall went upstairs and laid out her clothes. Her selection included a pencil-thin black skirt, a Bolero jacket, sheer black stockings, and high-heeled shoes. The sooner she dressed the sooner she could get to work on her Jackie White story. Brett felt the story would play out quickly. But she wasn't so sure. She'd backed off talking to Phil White yesterday, but today she'd do her best to get hold of him.

Nicole appeared in the doorway as Kendall pulled a silk blouse from her closet. Freshly blown-dry hair brushed Nicole's shoulders and an aqua empire shirt covered her belly and grazed a pair of maternity jeans. "That the contractor I hear moving around downstairs?"

"The one and only. I hope he gets the job done quickly. I'm so over contractors."

Nicole nodded. "Big day planned?"

"No bigger than usual." Kendall took a second glance at Nicole. "You're all dressed up."

She exhaled a deep breath and smoothed her hand over her belly. "I'm headed to the adoption agency today. I have an appointment with a counselor."

Kendall directed her full attention at Nicole. "How are you doing with that?"

Nicole's eyes watered. "Honestly? I'm scared."

Kendall dropped the blouse in her hand onto the bed. She had a million things she wanted to get done today and yet she heard herself saying, "Do you want me to come with you?"

Nicole's face brightened. "Would you? God, that would help a lot."

"When's your appointment?"

"An hour."

"I'll be ready in thirty minutes."

"You're the best."

Kendall crossed the room and hugged her. "Just don't let it get around that I can be nice. I've a reputation to uphold."

Nicole laughed and swiped a tear. "I promise."

Thirty minutes later, Kendall headed down the main staircase dressed and ready to go. Drop cloths now covered the kitchen floor and partway into the hallway. Sporadic bursts of banging hammers sounded from the kitchen. She sighed. She didn't like people in her house. She valued privacy. But if she wanted a new kitchen, sacrifices were required.

She found Nicole in the living room. She had her coat

on and was tapping her foot. Seeing Nicole like this turned Kendall's mind to the woman who'd given her up. Had her own birth mother been this nervous when Kendall had kicked in her belly and she'd thought about giving her up?

A jolt of sadness rocketed through Kendall and it took an effort to shake it off. She was starting to believe that her reasons for helping Nicole weren't as pure as she'd first thought. Maybe understanding and knowing Nicole would help her understand her own birth mother.

Kendall grabbed her coat and slipped it on. Between hammer strikes, she shouted, "Todd, we're outta here!"

"Will do, Ms. Shaw!" he shouted without even looking out of the kitchen. "I'll see you tomorrow!"

Kendall and Nicole exited the front door and moved down the narrow alleyway beside the house to the garage in back. They each got in their own cars and soon Kendall was following Nicole toward Monument Avenue. Minutes later they walked together toward a nondescript stone building with a wrought-iron railing around a small grassy yard. Five steps led to a covered porch and a black lacquered door that had a tarnished brass knocker in the center. A brass sign by the front door read SERENITY FAMILY SERVICES.

Nicole swallowed as she stared up the steps toward the door. "They've come highly recommended."

"I know." Kendall smiled. "I checked."

"You did?"

"I've got lots of connections. They come in handy."

"And you heard all good things, like I did?" Hope and fear wove around the words.

Kendall met her gaze head-on. "All good. I would have told you if I'd heard anything squirrelly." She hooked her arm into Nicole's. "Let's see what they have to say."

Nicole pressed her hand to her belly. "Okay."

They climbed the steps.

* * *

The adoption counselor's office was designed for comfort, Nicole noted. Shag carpet, pale blue walls, pictures of happy kids and families, bookshelves lined with every book on child psychology and adoption ever written. There was even a basket full of stuffed animals and toys in one corner.

But she didn't feel the least bit comfortable. She felt as if she were being pricked by a thousand pins and needles. And she felt like a failure and a quitter. Logically, she understood that adoption was a good, sound decision. A loving decision. But logic and emotion didn't always agree.

The counselor, Carnie Winchester, rose and immediately came out from behind her desk to greet Nicole and Kendall. Carnie was medium height, had shoulder-length red wavy hair and a peaches-and-cream complexion. Hip-hugger jeans, a fitted T-shirt, and a collection of beaded bracelets on her left wrist gave her a Bohemian look. Everything about Carnie belied Nicole's image of an adoption counselor. For some reason, she'd expected a matronly woman, not a woman so close to her own age.

"Nicole," Carnie said as she extended her hand. Her voice was soft and soothing. "It's a pleasure to meet you."

Nicole took her hand. "Thank you. Wow. I didn't realize you were so young."

Carnie smiled. "I'm sorry I'm so casually dressed but I've got my teens' support group meeting tonight and don't have time to go home and change. We'll be playing dodgeball."

Nicole could picture Carnie with the kids and bet she was good with them. "No problem. I'd like you to meet my friend Kendall Shaw."

Kendall put out her hand. She looked positively regal and very out of place here. "It's nice to meet you."

Carnie didn't hide her surprise when she met Kendall's gaze head-on. "I watch you every night. You're great."

"Thank you," Kendall said.

"You've really added some life and glamour to the station."

"Thank you." Kendall accepted the compliment with ease. She was never arrogant, always gracious. She reminded Nicole of a queen.

Kendall lifted a brow. "May we sit?"

That was something else about Kendall that Nicole admired. She had a way of politely, but definitively, directing the people around her.

"Of course," Carnie said.

Nicole and Kendall settled on the couch and Carnie sat across from them in an overstuffed chair, tucking one of her legs under her.

Kendall, looking so smooth and sleek, crossed her legs. Nicole struggled to get comfortable. The baby had chosen this moment to sit on her bladder and her swollen feet felt as if they were overflowing her shoes. When she did finally get comfortable, she suddenly found that she was at a loss for words. What did a woman say when she was considering giving away her own flesh and blood?

Nicole glanced to Kendall trying to convey her sudden panic.

Kendall seemed to sense all this and without betraying any of Nicole's worries turned to Carnie. "This is a very stressful situation for Nicole, as you must know."

Carnie's gaze was soft. Bracelets jangled softly as she leaned forward and touched Nicole's arm. "I don't want you to worry or feel any kind of pressure. We are here today just to talk."

Nicole managed a weak smile and didn't feel so boxed into a corner. "I know."

"I haven't relinquished a child, but I was adopted, so I have a personal connection to the process."

Kendall shifted, but her expression didn't show any emotion.

Nicole swallowed. "You were? Do you ever see your mother—your birth mother?"

"I haven't found her yet. I've become something of an expert on searches, but no luck with my mother yet. My adoption wasn't exactly black market but very gray." She seemed relaxed, as if she'd told this story a thousand times before. "My murky roots are why I'm so committed to open adoption."

The tightness in Nicole's throat didn't vanish but it eased. "Do you know anything about her?"

"Only that she was young when she had me. My associate, Debra Weston, couldn't be here today because her youngest is in the winter play at his elementary school. But Debra gave up a child when she was in college. She'd be the first to tell you that it was the hardest thing she's ever done."

"Was she able to keep up with her child?"

"She lost track until he turned twenty-one. Then he came searching for her. Now they exchange pictures and his parents have even sent her a scrapbook filled with pictures of him growing up."

Kendall removed an imaginary piece of lint from her skirt. "How does someone go about searching for a birth parent? I know you support open adoption, but what if Nicole chose a closed adoption?"

"Then the petitioner—the birth child or parent— would request a court order and ask the state to unseal the adoption records. It can be a very complicated and long process."

"How long would something like this take?" Kendall asked.

"It varies, depending on the original adoption order. Adoptions done pre–nineteen eighty-nine are a little harder to open. I've one client who's been searching for three years."

"I didn't realize it was so complicated," Kendall said. "Somehow I pictured this room full of files that could be opened at will."

Carnie smiled. "I wish."

By all appearances, Kendall looked relaxed and cool. But Nicole had learned over the last couple of months that strong emotions ran under her cool exterior. Something was brewing behind her eyes.

"You'll have to excuse me," Kendall said easily. "I've a reporter's mind. It's hard not to ask questions."

Carnie didn't seem to mind. "Of course."

The interlude between Kendall and Carnie gave Nicole a chance to collect herself. She was far from comfortable but she could think a little better now. "Can you show me that book of families you were talking about?"

Carnie smiled. "I'd be glad to."

Kendall leaned forward. "Do you want some privacy?"

As much as Nicole had appreciated Kendall's help getting her this far, she knew the next steps she'd have to take alone. "Do you mind?"

Kendall's face softened. "Not at all. I'll talk to you later."

"Thanks."

Kendall rose and left the office. Carnie reached for the binder on the coffee table. It was blue with flower stickers. *Our Families* was written in black Magic Marker on the cover. "Let's have a look at some of our profiles."

\* \* \*

When Jacob knocked on Dr. Christopher's office door, he was fifteen minutes late and unapologetic. He had a murder investigation on his desk and he didn't have time to waste with a shrink.

"Come in." She sounded annoyed.

He pushed open the door. "Dr. Christopher."

She sat at her desk, her gaze on a magazine. A silver barrette held gray hair back in a tight ponytail. Black-rimmed glasses perched on the edge of her nose, and she wore a loose black sweater, jeans, and sneakers.

Dr. Christopher's office was located in the medical office building of Mercy Hospital. The office was neat, organized, small, and efficient, like the woman herself.

She didn't rise from her desk or look up from the magazine she was reading. Slowly she turned a page. "You're late."

"Yes."

He shrugged off his jacket and moved into the office, closing the door behind him. The space always felt cramped once he entered it. He took his place on the couch across from her desk and felt a little like a kid summoned to the principal's office. "Let's get started."

She finished the line she was reading and closed the magazine. "So what are you working on these days?"

He'd expected a lecture on tardiness and was grateful she skipped it. "A murder investigation. A young woman strangled, dumped by the river."

She frowned. "I read about that in the paper. That must be tough for you."

He set his jacket aside and sat back on the couch, determined to look relaxed. "No tougher for me than the other cops working the case."

Her gaze narrowed. "Why do you say that?"

"I can see their faces. The strain. Each one of them is thinking about a wife. A sister. A daughter. It's hard not to personalize a case like this when it appears the woman lived her life by the straight and narrow."

"Do you personalize it?"

His shrug was meant to look casual. "I feel bad for the victim. It's a waste to die so young, but I don't have a woman in my life whom I'm particularly close to, so I don't personalize it."

She lifted a brow. "There's no woman in your life whom you are close to?"

He crossed his leg, resting his ankle on the opposite knee. "You know this." Tension crept up his spine. "We've been through this before." He'd stopped short of confessing his real fear—that if he were tested again in the line of duty he'd freeze, as he had last summer.

"I'd like to revisit some things."

"Why? It's water under the bridge. I know a lot of women. I like to date around. But I have no desire to settle down."

"You've never been in love?"

Shit. He didn't like these questions because honestly he didn't know what to say for fear she'd peg him a nut. "Look, we've discussed my mother. She was a drunk who cared more about booze than me. It was a fucked-up family. I get that. Anyone who went through that would have trust issues. But I don't dwell on it."

"Knowing you have trust issues *and* understanding how that affects your life are two different things."

They were traveling down the same path again. "It doesn't affect me. At least not in my job."

"There's more to life than work."

He picked at the cuff of his jeans. "I'm good at my job. I stay in shape. I help a neighbor in need. What else am I supposed to do?"

She leaned forward. "When is the last time you felt joy?"

"That's easy. We arrested a guy in late December. He

was a dealer and he killed two of his teenaged mules. It felt damn good to take him down." He'd ridden that high for several days.

"That's satisfaction. What about joy? Laughter?"

He tipped back his head trying to hold on to his patience. "I'm a homicide detective. Joy isn't part of the job description."

"It is part of the description of a balanced person."

He could see where this was going. It wasn't enough he caught killers. Now he had to prove he was happy. At the rate he was going with the doc she was going to write an unfavorable evaluation. He had to come up with something. Before he thought too much, he went back to the last happy moment in his life. "The last time I felt joy. Last summer. July. Pete and I were in the gym. He was checking the laces on my boxing gloves. He kept warning me that I was going to injure my hands if I didn't ease up. It felt good to know someone had my back."

She was silent for a moment. "You miss him."

He didn't answer. He clenched his jaw until a muscle in his face pulsed.

"You miss him." This was new ground for them.

His chest tightened. And with as much attitude as he could muster he said, "Yeah, I miss him."

"And that's okay."

He leaned forward and laced his long fingers. The words caught in his tightening chest. "It doesn't feel right."

"I'm not here to defend the guy or the choices he made, but when you were young and vulnerable he never failed *you*, did he?" She spoke softly.

Jacob tightened his jaw. "No."

She sat back relaxed, as if she'd got what she was after.

"What are some of the good times you remember with Pete?"

He blew out a breath. "How did we end up on this line of conversation? I don't like it."

"I know." She smiled. "Think of it this way. Today is your last mandatory session."

He tapped his finger on his thigh. "I don't like talking about Pete."

"But you should talk about him."

Cracking the door to the memories now could easily lead to a flood.

"Tell me about a happy time for you two."

Damn. "The sooner I dish the sooner I can get back to work?"

"Yes."

"One memory?"

"I'll take it."

He flexed his fingers. He stared at the corner of the coffee table and let his mind drift. It quickly landed on a memory. "When I was fifteen, he decided we needed to go camping. I was full of mouth that summer and as usual a handful. So Pete took me camping." The corner of his mouth lifted. "It was the worst two days of our lives."

"How so?"

"You name it, it went wrong. Neither one of us knew what the hell we were doing. We were city guys. We arrived at this campground late on a Friday. It was hot and we were tired. We tried to pitch this tent that he borrowed. We got it all staked in the ground and then figured out it was upside down. It took another hour to flip it and get it up. Then it started to rain. Buckets of the stuff. After a month-long drought, it rained. The land around the tent flooded and then the tent roof started to leak. Pete grumbled and cussed all night."

Doubt darkened her eyes. "This was a happy memory?"

"We got up the next morning, dumped the soggy tent into the back of his van, and drove into some small town. We picked the first diner we spotted and ordered breakfast. We were so damn hungry at that point. Best flapjacks I ever had that morning." His throat tightened as he recalled the memory. "Pete told me that morning that no matter what, he'd never give up on me. He was the first person who ever told me that."

Dr. Christopher let the silence settle as he drew in deep breaths. He collected his emotions, which in an instant had turned raw. "It's okay to mourn that loss, Jacob. There was goodness in Pete Meyers and you have to honor that."

Jacob flexed his right hand, aware of the stiffness. "He was right about the sparring."

"I don't understand."

"I overdid it last weekend. Pete would have been so pissed if he'd seen my hands after the bout. I've got several hairline fractures in my right hand and the doc thinks I'll end up with bad arthritis if I don't stop."

"Then stop."

So like a woman. She didn't get it. "Easier said than done."

"Why do you love boxing so much?"

"The rush. The exercise. The excitement when I step into the ring."

"And you're closest to Pete when you're in the ring."

He'd never once considered that angle. But she was right. "Maybe. Yeah."

She leaned forward. "Honor Pete now by taking care of yourself. That's what he'd want."

Emotion choked Jacob's throat. "Why the hell does everyone want me to feel when *feeling* sucks so bad?"

She smiled. "Life's about the highs and lows. You need both to be balanced."

The egg timer behind her rang. She turned it off. "Looks like our time is up."

He relaxed back on the sofa. "Thank God. So I've completed my mandatory visits?"

She looked amused. "You are free and clear."

"Great." He rose but noted the tension that had normally lingered in his lower back had eased. And he could breathe without feeling a weight on his shoulders.

She picked up her appointment book and scanned the pages. "See you in two weeks?"

"You just said I was in the clear."

She stood, straightening to her five feet two inches. "You're correct. You don't have to come back. I thought maybe you'd want to."

Committing to therapy felt extreme. It was the kind of thing wimps and bleeding heart liberals did. And yet he heard himself say, "Let me think about it."

She shrugged and closed the book. "Fair enough."

Jacob left her office, shrugged on his jacket, and crossed to the elevator. He punched the DOWN button, feeling better than he had in a long time. He no longer had the urge to pound on a punching bag. A weight had lifted from his shoulders. Seconds passed and the doors dinged open.

A woman stood on the elevator. Her gaze was lowered, but judging by her body language, she looked as if she'd gone a couple of rounds in a ring. She raised her head and her gaze met his.

It was Kendall Shaw.

"What the hell happened to you? Are you all right?"

Concern for *her* in Jacob Warwick's voice had Kendall Shaw lifting her head. She'd not heard *that* in a long time.

He was just about the last person she wanted to see. She'd just finished a round of physical therapy on her shoulder and wasn't in the mood for sparring.

Still Kendall lifted her chin. She refused to show the pain she felt in her arm. "My physical therapist is a sadist."

Confusion darkened his eyes as he stepped onto the elevator and hit the button for the lobby. "How's that?"

His natural masculine scent permeated her senses. His presence added energy to the bland elevator car. Both softened the tone of her voice. "My shoulder. I was shot. Rehab."

Jacob frowned as the doors closed. "Right."

A silence settled between them as they both tried to ignore the fact that his foster father had shot and nearly killed her. He flexed his fingers.

Body language spoke volumes and she was a master at reading it. Just like a gypsy read tea leaves, she read people. It was killing Detective Warwick that his foster father had been a killer. As much as the guy could make her blood boil, she couldn't help but pity him. He'd been blindsided by the revelation.

"The doctor says I'll make a full recovery." She kept her voice upbeat. She didn't mind going toe-to-toe with the guy when he was 100 percent but she never took satisfaction kicking someone when he was down.

He met her gaze and searched her face for something. "I'm glad."

When she was around him she always felt alive and on her toes. "So what brings you here on a Friday afternoon? A case?"

He hesitated. "Yeah."

"Care to tell me about it?"

He rolled his eyes. "Are you always this nosey?"

She laughed. "It's one of the things I do best."

The doors opened. He blocked them with his hand so they wouldn't close. He faced her. "I'm sorry."

"About what?"

"Pete."

She understood that this exchange cost him emotionally. "Why? You didn't know what he was doing."

"I should have."

So like a man. "Are you a mind reader?"

"No."

"Then stop beating yourself up."

"He nearly killed you." He ground each word out.

It would have been so easy to wallow in self-pity. She'd refused. "I'm a big girl, Detective. And I goaded him on purpose. I wanted a story. Wanted a reaction. And I got one. I blame no one but Pete Myers."

Jacob knitted his brow. He was silent for a long moment. "You can let it go just like that?"

"Yes."

"I thought you'd be pissed as hell with me."

Kendall stepped forward and he dropped his arms so she could pass him into the lobby. She stood straighter and kept all traces of emotion from her voice. "Victims wallow. They fret over what they cannot control. And I'm no victim. And if I may say, Detective Warwick, neither are you."


The sun had set when Allen stood in the shadows watching her emerge from the liquor store near Mercy Hospital. Holding a brown bag close, she cut across the street and stepped around a plume of steam rising from a storm-water drain.

Judith was beautiful. Her dark brown hair was shorter than he'd have liked and the purple and red streaks didn't suit her, but he could see past all of that. She wore ragged jeans and a leather jacket. She looked more like a bum than the dignified woman he knew she could be.

Despite her faults, he wanted to touch her hair. Was it soft? Did it smell like coconuts, as Ruth's had?

Allen's muscles tingled with anticipation. It was hard to hold back when he wanted to run his hands through her hair, to touch her skin and kiss her lips. He wanted her to join the Family.

He'd hoped to wait another week before he brought her to the fold, but the loneliness ate at him day and night. He crossed the street keeping a discreet distance from her.

As she approached the alleyway she paused. She glanced down the cut-through as if weighing the merits of passing down a dark alley to save time.

Squaring her shoulders, she headed forward.

He followed and waited at the lip of the passageway until she was midway down and passed under a dim overhead light. He sprinted down the narrow alley, which smelled of garbage and urine. "Judith!"

She didn't turn around and he realized she was wearing earbuds. She was listening to music. Teetering between annoyance and relief, he hurried closer and reached out to her.

She whirled around. "Who the hell are you?"

He stammered, "I . . . thought I knew you."

Up close he could see her heavily lined eyes and streaked hair more clearly. Both made her look so cheap.

She interpreted his hesitation for weakness. "Well you don't."

Her perfume triggered a shameful hardening of his body. God, but he wanted to touch her. He lifted his gaze to Judith's eyes. The set of her jaw telegraphed her distaste. "I didn't mean to be so bold."

"Buzz off, freak!" She turned and started to walk away.

The dismissal made Allen feel like a fumbling boy and it also enraged him. He didn't deserve this disrespect. He was owed better.

Only a couple of feet separated them but the gap was growing. If he was going to stop her, it had to be now. He quickly closed the gap between them and put his hand firmly on her shoulder this time.

She recoiled and faced him. "Don't touch me."

From his pocket he pulled a gold chain. It dangled in front of her. For a split second, the quality piece of jewelry caught her eye. She wasn't used to pretty things. "This is for you."

"Nice."

"Women always like pretty things, don't they?"

Her gaze narrowed as she stared at him. "Who are you?"

His hand shot out with lightning quickness. He grabbed her hand and wrenched it around her back as he pushed his other hand over her mouth. Using his body weight, he shoved her against the wall. Before she could scream he jabbed his forearm against her throat and held her in place. "You're not going to leave me again."

Terror blazed in her eyes. She kicked him and clawed at his hands, her actions unpinning her from the wall. "Who are you, you crazy fucker?"

Her chest rose and fell quickly under him and he wanted to touch her, to do things to her that were so wrong. Angry, he slammed her back against the brick wall a second time. "Temptress."

He fumbled in his pocket for a hypodermic and stabbed it into her chest. He pressed the liquid into her system. She collapsed almost immediately.

Glancing from left to right, he made sure no one had seen; then he wrapped his arm around her shoulders, pulled her upright, and dragged her down the alley. To anyone who glanced at them it would appear he was helping her to his truck.

His truck was parked at the lip of the alley. He dragged her to the passenger door, opened it, and gently set her upright in the seat. He clicked her seat belt over her body so she wouldn't slump forward.

When Allen slid behind the wheel of the truck, his heart raced and sweat dampened his shirt. But he felt good. He had Judith. And soon she'd join the Family.

# Chapter Seven

Jacob leaned against the counter in the break room. He cradled a cup of coffee in his hands. He'd just popped two aspirin and wasn't in a good mood.

"You look like shit," Zack said as he moved into the room and poured himself a cup of coffee. "You've been here all night?"

"Yeah. The tapes from the store's parking lot arrived. I decided to review them."

Zack frowned over his coffee cup. "Why didn't you call me?"

"No sense ruining both our evenings. Besides, you and Lindsay don't get much downtime."

A hint of a smile reached Zack's eyes. "It was nice just being with her." He sipped his coffee. "So what did you find?"

"It took a while but I found the sixty-second bit of footage we needed."

Zack leaned forward. "You saw Jackie on the footage?"

He nodded. "Ten twenty-one p.m. Friday a week ago. Come into the conference room and see the tape."

They moved down the carpeted hallway and pushed through the double doors of the conference room. The walls were covered with dry-erase boards and a large map of the county. A U-shaped conference table faced the front of the room, where a TV and VCR sat on a metal stand.

Jacob sipped his coffee and picked up the TV/VCR remote.

Zack leaned against the conference table, crossed his ankles, and sipped his coffee. "Did you get a clean picture?"

"See for yourself." Jacob hit PLAY.

The grainy, color image showed Jackie White approaching her car with a cart full of groceries. She loaded the first three bags without incident but the fourth split at the bottom as she lifted it. The cans rolled away from her.

"Enter our suspect," Jacob said.

A hooded figure emerged out of the shadows and started collecting the cans. He approached Jackie with the cans cradled in his arms.

"He startles her," Jacob said. "And she tries to take the cans from him."

Zack frowned as the scene unfolded. "But Mr. Helpful refuses. He wants to put them in her car. Probably accuses her of being too proud and that she should accept help. Standard predator bullshit."

Jacob sipped his coffee. "Yeah. And it works. She lets him put the cans in the car."

Zack leaned forward. "The guy could be her husband."

"He's the right build."

They both watched the film. The man convinced Jackie to move, taking her out of the camera's view. She never returned into view but he did. He locked and closed her car door.

Jacob's jaw tensed. "He must have had a car waiting."

"Yeah."

"Let's have that chat with White now."

The drive to White's town house took twenty minutes. His paper lay on the stoop in front of the door. Jacob picked it up and knocked on the door. When no one answered he knocked again.

The door snapped open and White glared at him. He didn't look broken, as he had on Thursday. Now he looked haggard. Dark stubble covered his chin and the shirttail of his wrinkled cable TV uniform hung loose.

"What do you want?" he snapped.

"We'd like to talk to you." Jacob took a bit of satisfaction knowing he wasn't the only one who'd not gotten much sleep last night.

"About?" White prodded.

"Jackie White," Jacob said.

The two detectives stared at him. The challenge in Zack's gaze left no room for argument. White let them come inside and closed the door. "Have you found Jackie's killer?"

Zack folded his arms over his chest. "We're working on it."

White kept his hands at his sides, his fists clenched. "So what did you find?"

"Tell me again where you were this past weekend?"

"I was in Bath County hunting. I left Friday and came back late Monday."

"How far is Bath County from here?"

"Three hours."

Jacob nodded. "It can be done in two hours if you're pushing it."

"Well, there'd have been no 'pushing it' this past

weekend because of the snow on Afton Mountain." The mountain was just west of Charlottesville and in bad weather was the first stretch of the interstate to become impassible.

Jacob glanced at his notes as if reading something important. "What time did you arrive?"

"I don't know. Late."

"How about a time?"

White sighed. "I had a flat tire outside of Staunton and had to change it. I didn't get to the cabin until about one."

"Where did you fix the tire?"

"I don't remember. Like I said, a station in Staunton."

White swallowed and leaned forward. "I didn't kill my wife."

"We didn't say you did," Jacob said.

White's eyes were wild with grief and fury. "Then why all the questions?"

Zack unfolded his arms, ready to react if he had to. "Routine."

Jacob thought about the tape. Jackie had vanished at 10:21 P.M. on Friday. Which would have given White enough time to stash her and make it to Bath by one. "Can you give us the names of the men you hunted with so they can confirm when you arrived?"

White's lips flattened. "I don't see why you need the names."

Jacob's eyes narrowed. He'd been waiting for that. "I can get a warrant and have your tires examined for patches. And I'll track down and talk to your hunting buddies no matter how long it takes."

White shoved a trembling hand through his hair. He swallowed and sank into a nearby chair. "I didn't have a flat."

Jacob tensed but said nothing.

White shoved out a ragged breath. "I didn't have a flat

and my friends will tell you I didn't get there until nearly two. I was at my girlfriend's house. Her name is Kelly Green."

Jacob wrote the name down.

"She's pregnant. That's why I stopped by. She'd not been feeling well that day. I didn't leave her house until eleven."

"Why didn't you tell us about her before?"

"I didn't want to drag her into this mess."

"Is Kelly the reason you and Jackie fought at Christmas?" Zack asked.

"Yes. I begged Jackie to give me a divorce. Our marriage had been a sham since our disastrous honeymoon. Kelly wanted to be married by the time the baby was born. We were running out of time."

"Jackie didn't agree," Jacob said.

"No. She said divorce wasn't an option. She refused to be a real wife but she wouldn't let me go. Said marriage was a sacrament. For better or for worse. How the hell was I supposed to know she'd be frigid as ice?"

"Did she ever see a therapist?" Jacob asked.

"Yeah. Finally after months of expensive sessions she told me that hypnosis revealed she'd been molested as a kid."

"Do you have the doctor's name?"

"Thompson, I think."

Jacob's jaw tightened. "Who molested her?"

"She said she couldn't remember. But I knew she did. She wouldn't tell me."

He couldn't decide if White was telling the truth or spinning another lie. "I'm going to need Kelly Green's phone number. Also the full name of Jackie's therapist." Jacob handed a piece of paper and a pen to White.

White's hand trembled as he wrote. "I didn't kill Jackie."

Jacob recited the Miranda rights to White.

"Why the hell should I need to be read rights?" White bellowed. "I didn't do it.

"Get an attorney, Mr. White."

Kendall had a break in the Jackie White murder story. Phil White had called her and agreed to talk to her.

Still she was in a foul mood when she arrived at the news station just after eleven. She'd taken extra care with her appearance today. She'd chosen the dark wrap dress, black boots, and silver necklace. She'd swept her hair into a French twist and applied her makeup with extra care, ensuring there was no hint of the dark circles under her eyes.

The dream stalked her several times a night now and she was more and more convinced that it was a clue to her past.

The increased frequency of the dream had to be linked to the visit to the adoption agency. Since the meeting more and more questions about her birth mother plagued her. Had her birth mother struggled with the decision to give her up, as Nicole was now struggling? Or had she tossed her away without a second thought?

When Kendall was a teenager, she'd secretly conjured daydreams about the unknown woman who'd given her away. In one scenario her birth mother was homeless and unable to keep her. In another she was a rich movie star who'd been forced to relinquish her by manipulative managers. No matter what the scenario, the primary theme remained the same. Her birth mother had not wanted to give Kendall up.

"So why not just search, you coward?" she mumbled. "Put an end to the questions. That's what you do."

She knew the answer. Fear kept her from searching. She was afraid of what she would find.

"Get a grip, Kendall. *Today* is what counts. Jackie White's story is what counts."

"Talking to yourself is supposed to be a sign that you're insane." Mike had poked his head around the corner of her office.

She straightened, embarrassed she'd been caught mumbling to herself. "I've been called worse. Are you ready to go?"

He bowed. "Ready and willing. Where to?"

"Jackie White's husband called. He wants to talk to me."

"Excellent."

Despite her sour mood, Mike made her smile. Nothing ruffled the guy.

A half hour later Kendall and Mike were climbing the steps to Phil White's town house. Kendall knocked on the door.

Almost immediately, the door snapped open to a man dressed in a gray suit, a white shirt, and a pink striped tie. "Yes?"

"I'm Kendall Shaw with Channel Ten News. I'd like to talk to Phil White about his wife's death."

The suit frowned. "He's not talking to reporters."

She didn't back down. "And you are?"

"His attorney."

Ah, there was a detail worth noting. "Mr. White called me."

"Doesn't matter. He's not talking to the media."

He moved to close the door but she stepped forward and blocked the threshold with her foot. "If he has a story to tell, then I'm the one who should tell it."

"Go away."

"I want to talk to her." The male voice came from inside the town house. The man whom she'd only glimpsed the other day approached her. He had dark circles under his eyes and two days' growth of beard.

"Phil White," Kendall said, now ignoring the suit.

"Yeah."

"Did you kill your wife?"

Bloodshot eyes studied her. "No, I did not."

The urgency in his voice struck a cord in her, but she was careful not to be drawn in. She'd interviewed some charming killers in her time. "Then let me say how sorry I was to hear about your wife's death."

White seemed to be mollified by the comment. "Thanks."

She didn't budge from the doorjamb. She wanted this interview. "I'd like to talk to you about Jackie. I want to hear your side of the story."

The suit frowned. "Phil, it's not a good idea to talk to the press. You need to keep a low profile right now."

White shook his head. "If I don't talk to the press, then no one is going to know what *I'm* thinking and feeling."

"They don't need to know," the suit said. "As long as the judge knows."

White set his jaw and considered the advice. "No, Harvey, if the police have their way I'll be railroaded to prison."

Excitement burned in Kendall. The cops had to warn White of his rights so he wouldn't incriminate himself, but she didn't have such restrictions. "Then tell me what's going on."

The suit tried to close the door one last time and change White's mind.

Kendall kept her foot planted on the threshold. "Talk to me, Mr. White," she coaxed.

White nudged his attorney aside and opened the door wide for her. She stepped into the town house, letting her gaze absorb details.

"You kinda remind me of Jackie," White said. "Not like she is now but back when she and I met."

The comparison didn't sit well but she managed a smile nonetheless. "I'm not sure what to say about that."

White shrugged. "Nothing to say. Just an observation."

*The camera pans across the icy James River.*

*In a voice-over, Kendall Shaw begins to speak. "Last Tuesday, construction crews discovered the body of Jackie White not a hundred yards from where I'm standing. Investigators have not named a suspect in the case. And Jackie White's husband is desperate to find her killer."*

*The camera cuts to White sitting in his living room. He is holding his and Jackie's wedding picture. They are somewhere tropical. White is wearing a grin. Jackie is beaming.*

*"We honeymooned in Hawaii," says Phil White. "She'd never been on a plane and I wanted to do something special for her. So I surprised her with a trip to Hawaii."*

*Phil White turns away from the picture. Tears glisten in his eyes as he stares into the camera. "It was a magical time. She was one of the best people I ever knew. Kind, loving. I don't know who could have done this to her."*

*There is a quick shot of Jacob Warwick and Zack Kier getting into their car. "Police aren't releasing details and refused all requests for interviews. But sources close to the case say that Phil White is a person of interest."*

*"It's easy to point the finger at me," White says. "The husband is always the first to be suspected. But I didn't do it. And the longer the police focus on me, the longer the real killer will be free."*

Jacob couldn't listen to any more of the broadcast. He hit PAUSE and turned to face Sergeant David Ayden in the conference room. "She makes it sound like a damn witch hunt."

Ayden sipped his soda and then grimaced at the flat taste. "It's all about the story with her. Ratings are king in her business. What I want to know is how did she find out about the victim's identity?"

None of the photos White displayed for the interview had been visible when Jacob and Zack had spoken to him. The whole scene was staged. "I don't know," Jacob said.

"And he plays the grieving husband." Disgust dripped from Ayden's words. "With a pregnant girlfriend itching to get married on the sidelines. Wonder why Ms. Shaw didn't mention that?"

Just last night when Jacob had seen Kendall in the elevator all pretense had been dropped. It was just the two of them, and for a moment each had been able to get a glimpse of the other.

And he'd liked what he'd seen in Kendall. She had tremendous spirit and courage. He'd felt a connection with her. But in a few seconds she'd managed to irritate the shit out of him again.

"How the hell did she get that interview with White?" Ayden asked again.

"From what I understand, he called her," Jacob said.

Ayden frowned. "There'll be hell to pay when I find out who leaked the information."

"I've asked around. Everyone swears they didn't talk." Jacob would be damn sure to keep his distance from Kendall.

"What about White's story?" Ayden said.

"His girlfriend backs him up. Says she was with him until eleven P.M. on Friday. She's also got two neighbors who'll swear to the same." He recalled the facts he now knew so well. "Phil White's cell phone records haven't revealed anything unusual. Bank records were clean and showed no large cash withdrawals."

"So there's nothing to link White to the case except circumstantial evidence?"

"So far. Jackie White was seeing a therapist. Dr. Herman Thompson. He's on vacation. Won't be back until Monday. He might be able to give us some insight into his patient."

"Have you tracked down Jackie White's parents?" Ayden asked.

"They passed away fifteen years ago. They were older and she has no other relatives."

"What else do you have?"

"Tess has returned to the crime scene twice. She and a dozen uniformed officers have walked the area several more times and have gone over the terrain inch by inch. But nothing new has been found."

Ayden rested his hands on his hips. "Who the hell else would have the motive for killing Jackie White? She was a damn saint by all accounts."

"There's another angle that's been eating at me." Jacob nodded toward the image on the television screen. "Jackie White resembles Kendall Shaw."

Ayden looked skeptical. "That's one hell of a long shot."

"Maybe. Maybe not. But I'd like to poke around and see if Kendall has had any unwanted attention lately. Maybe whoever tipped her off is behind the killings. She has a knack for pissing people off."

"True. But the look-alike connection is far-fetched."

"Doesn't hurt to ask the questions."

"Fine. Tread carefully or she just might turn this angle into her next story."

* * *

It was past ten on Saturday night when Kendall climbed the back stairs of her house, more exhausted than usual. Normally, stories like this left her jazzed, but not this time. White's comment this morning still bothered her. *You kinda remind me of Jackie.*

The offhand comment had been a brutal reminder that she didn't know anything about her past. She had no idea where she came from. She could have relatives living next door and she'd never know it.

She opened the door slowly, unsure if there'd be drop cloths or debris from the renovation. She flipped on the lights. What she found was a neatly swept foyer, sawhorses butted against the walls, and a precisely arranged set of tools in a nicked red toolbox. Todd was as good as her architect had said.

Her footsteps echoed as she walked into the kitchen. The cabinets had been stripped off the walls. All the appliances had been removed except for the refrigerator, which had been angled away from the wall but was still plugged in. The microwave was set up on a makeshift table made of plywood and sawhorses. "Bless you, Todd."

Nicole's footsteps sounded on the steps as she descended from the second floor. She appeared in the kitchen doorway.

Her dark hair hung loosely around her shoulders and she wore a blue robe tied loosely over her protruded belly. Fuzzy slippers peaked out from the hem. Her face looked pale.

"I was wondering where you were," Nicole said.

Kendall shrugged off her coat and hung it in the kitchen closet. "Why aren't you asleep?"

"Just can't get comfortable. The baby's doing a dance on my bladder."

Kendall was accustomed to tossing her purse onto her

mother's old kitchen table but it was gone. She felt a jolt of panic. "What did Todd do with the table?"

"Basement."

"Good." Relieved, she put her purse in the hall closet and made a mental note to remember it was there. "So did Todd put in a full day?"

"I saw him late this afternoon. He was cleaning things up for the day. Seems like a nice guy."

Kendall placed her hands in the small of her back and stretched. The tight muscles eased and the tension was released. "Let's hope he continues to work hard. I'd hate to see him lose steam and give up on us."

Nicole absently rubbed her tummy. "You always do that?"

"What?"

"Expect people to quit on you?"

That hit a nerve. "Not people. Contractors. There's a difference."

Nicole lifted a brow. "If you say so."

Kendall didn't like the direction of the conversation. "So why are you really up?"

"I've been going through the adoptive family profiles. I just gave up about a half hour ago. I've read them so much my eyes are crossing. I think I'm driving Carnie nuts."

"How so?"

"Asking her a million questions. The woman has the patience of Job."

Kendall followed Nicole into the living room. On the coffee table was a large three-ringed binder stuffed full of pages. She felt an odd tightening in her chest. "Those the families?"

"Hmmm. There are dozens in there and they all really want a baby."

They sat on the couch. Kendall flipped through the pages. Each page came with basic stats: ages, years married, children, jobs, etc. Along with the pictures of the couples were photos of their houses, their family pets, and their children—anything that would entice an adoptive mother to choose them.

She wondered if an adoption agency had carried a similar profile on Irene and Henry Shaw. Had her birth mother filed through the pages of a book like this and chosen them?

She was careful to keep emotion out of her voice. "See anyone you like?"

"They all seem great. But it's all overwhelming." Her eyes widened and she pressed her hand to her belly. "This kid never rests. Sometimes I think she senses my stress."

Kendall turned one of the pages to the profile featuring a thirty-something couple with bright smiles. With their golden retriever, they stood in front of a gray clapboard house. The leaves were green and daffodils filled the flower beds. "I've heard babies do sense their mother's emotions."

"I hope not. She shouldn't have to worry. That's my job." She rubbed a protective hand on her belly.

"You don't have to opt for adoption right away." Kendall wasn't sure where the comment came from.

Nicole frowned. "Carnie said that as well. But I'm so afraid I won't love her. I'm scared I'll see Richard and I'll end up hating the baby. That would be the greatest tragedy of all." She glanced at the "Waiting Family" profile. "And they want a baby so much."

Kendall closed the book. Not telling Nicole about her own adoption suddenly felt selfish. "There's something you don't know about me. In fact, I don't think anyone does." Disloyalty, nerves, and a need to talk all collided in her mind. No doubt White's comment was fueling some of this. *You kinda remind me of Jackie.*

Nicole lifted a brow. "What? Are you an international arms dealer?"

A smile tugged at the edge of her lips but she felt no mirth. "I'm adopted."

Nicole's mouth dropped open and her cheeks reddened as if she'd bumped into a china display and nearly knocked it over. "Wow. You never said a word about that."

It felt good to say the words. "My mom, my adoptive mom, never wanted me to talk about it. She always treated it like a big secret."

"Why?"

"I've no idea." She relaxed back against the cushions. "I guess it was just a sign of the times. People weren't that open about it twenty-five years ago."

Nicole's gaze sharpened. "Still, not to tell anyone. You're so open about most things."

"I know, I know. But I learned from an early age not to talk about it. Like telling was somehow bad. I tried to ask Mom and Dad about it a couple of times. Mom avoided the topic and her eyes got all hurt looking and Dad said it was best to leave well enough alone." Kendall had trouble holding Nicole's gaze.

Nicole looked baffled. "I've never known you to let an unanswered question go."

"This is the only one I ever have. I guess I loved them so much I didn't want to disappoint them. So I dropped it."

"Your mom has been dead over a year? And your dad's been gone how long?"

"Ten years." She sighed. "After Mom died I was really grieving. I missed her so much. So I became hell-bent on getting out of Richmond and making the big time. Last summer changed all that. Lying in the hospital with all those tubes hooked up to me made me think about what was important. I didn't want to leave behind what little roots I have."

A frown knitted Nicole's forehead. "But don't you want to know about *her*?"

"Her" was Kendall's birth mother. "I can miss her and hate her in the blink of an eye." She smiled, hoping to soften the comment. "It's just complicated and hard to explain. I'm so curious about her. I was six inches taller than Mom. And my olive skin didn't match Mom's pale Irish skin and freckles. I don't even know who I look like."

"But you never went searching." There was sadness in Nicole's voice.

"No."

Nicole swallowed. "Do you know *anything* about her?"

"Nothing." Kendall shoved out a breath. "The point of all this isn't to lay more on your shoulders. It's to tell you that I'm adopted and I had a really great life with the people who adopted me. They adored me. I couldn't have asked for more." And still there'd been something missing. A hole in her heart. But she couldn't tell Nicole that.

"Thanks. I don't know if it makes any of this easier," she said, nodding to the full binder. "But I am glad to know you had great parents."

Kendall rose. "Do me a favor and keep this under your hat. I'm not ready to go public yet."

"Oh, sure, of course."

Kendall suddenly felt very weary. "I'm going to bed. Are you okay?"

Her too bright smile was lame at best. "I'm good."

Kendall didn't push. There wasn't more she could say to Nicole to make any of this process easier. "Okay, good night."

"Hey, you should talk to Carnie. She's good at finding lost family members."

"I don't know."

"She's kind of an adoption detective. If you want answers she's the one to go to."

Was she brave enough to seek the answers? "Thanks."

Kendall's legs felt like lead as she climbed the steps. She couldn't wait to slip under the sheets. Fifteen minutes later, she'd hung up her clothes and washed the makeup from her face. She opened her medicine cabinet and pulled out a bottle of sleeping pills prescribed to her after her surgery. She glanced at the bottle in her hand. "No. I don't need this."

She set the pills back and got into bed. She wasn't going to set her alarm clock. She'd wake up when she woke up. As she drifted off to sleep, her mind was on the family she'd lost.

*The little girl was afraid.*

*Soft arms with surprising strength lowered her to the floor and pushed her into the darkened closet. She huddled in the corner. Shag carpet scratched her legs. Above, winter coats on hangers brushed her head.*

*The woman laid a baby next to her. Immediately, the baby kicked its feet, balled tiny hands into fists, and started to wail.*

*The little girl resented the baby. It was always in the way. "I don't like the baby!"*

*"Be quiet," the woman warned. "Don't argue with me." The woman's voice was normally soft and patient. Now it was angry, afraid, and desperate. "And keep the baby quiet."*

*She didn't want to be left alone with the baby. The baby cried and smelled bad.*

*The girl held up her hands and started to stand. "No, no! Take me! Take me!"*

*The woman, already retreating, roughly pushed her back. Tears streamed down the woman's eyes. "Stay put. Don't leave this closet."*

*The door slammed shut. The key in the lock twisted, flipping the deadbolt in place.*

*The little girl was plunged into darkness. The baby cried. The little girl's lips puckered out and she put her thumb in her mouth. She hated the dark. Hated the baby. Hated being left alone.*

*Outside the closet door the woman started to scream. Angry. Hysterical. Frightened.*

*The little girl huddled in the corner, drawing herself up into a small ball. She squeezed her eyes shut and ducked her head.*

*She tried not to cry. She wanted to be brave. But it was all too much.*

*The child hugged her knees close to her body and began to cry. The infant, sensing her distress, cried even louder.*

*The child's throat constricted with fear and she burrowed her head back in the corner. The screams outside wouldn't stop. She was so afraid that she peed.*

*And then she heard footsteps moving toward the door. Suddenly, someone started shouting on the other side. The footsteps moved away. Then the room exploded with more screams and terrified yelps.*

*The little girl raised her hands to cover her ears and block out the frightful sounds. "Mommy, don't leave me."*

Kendall awoke with a start, sitting bolt upright in her bed. Her heart thundered against her chest. Her gown was soaked in sweat and she realized she'd been crying.

She shoved shaking fingers through her hair and then wiped the tears from her face.

"Damn it! This has got to stop."

# Chapter Eight

*Sunday, January 13, sunrise*

The side of Vicky Draper's head ached as if it had been slammed into a wall. Her mouth felt as dry as cotton. And every muscle in her body felt so heavy, as if lead weighted down every fiber. Time was a blur and she was so disoriented.

Crap. She'd not felt like this in a long time. She'd sworn after the last time she'd done coke not to get so fucked up when she partied.

Had it been the shots of tequila at Brian's house? Maybe the coke Ronnie T. had given her was cut with some shit like Drano.

Vicky's temper rose. That damn drug dealer was always taking a fucking shortcut to squeeze a dollar out of someone. She wasn't fooled by his easy grins. Under it all she knew he'd sell his mother for a buck.

The drugs were gonna kill her if she didn't knock this shit off. She resolved then and there never to touch the stuff again. Going forward, she would be all about clean and sober.

Her eyes were still closed as she tried to move her

hands. She quickly realized she couldn't lift her arms. Fear mingled with anger. Damn, Ronnie T.! What had his drugs done to her? Digging deep, she opened her eyes and looked down.

Her blurred vision cleared slowly, and when it did she really thought she must be tripping. Pink. The dimly lit room was filled with pink everywhere. It was like she was trapped inside a ball of cotton candy.

Shit. This wasn't right.

Squinting, she focused on the room's sole source of light: a small bedside lamp with a low-wattage bulb. Her gaze darted to the right to a canopied bed covered in a pink chiffon comforter. Stuffed animals—rabbits, puppies, ducks—crowded the bed.

The faint scent of urine rose up and assailed her nose. She realized her pants were wet and she'd soiled herself. Embarrassment washed over her.

Sitting straighter, she said, "Where the fuck am I?"

Again, she tried to lift her arms and couldn't. Her mind had cleared enough for her to realize her hands were tied to the chair.

Panic sliced through her. Oh crap, was Ronnie T. behind this?

Her head pounded. "If this is some kind of joke, I'm not laughing."

Her gaze skipped around the room again as she jerked at the bindings. She was in all-out survival mode.

She was in a little girl's room and she was tied up. This kind of setup wasn't Ronnie T.'s style. The drug dealer wouldn't have gone to this kind of trouble if he was pissed at her.

Crap, maybe she had hooked up with a kinky john. She'd turned a few tricks in her time, but it was always straightforward—no weird sex. But the kinky stuff paid really well. And she'd been short on cash. What had she gotten herself into?

Outside a frosted window, she saw an orange sun through naked trees. Sunrise. There was no snow on the branches of the trees. It had melted. How many days had passed?

Desperation rising, she tried to think where she'd last been before this room. She'd called in sick to work because Brian had invited her over for shooters. And then they'd run out of tequila so she'd headed to the corner liquor store for more.

And then that guy had approached her in the alley. He had followed her like some freak. And when she'd blown him off he'd looked hurt and then mad. And then he'd hit her.

"Hey!" Her voice sounded weak, raspy. She cleared her throat. "Whoever you are, I'm sorry I got so mad. My name is Vicky. Vicky Draper. Can we talk about this?"

A song started to play, drifting into the room on an unidentified speaker. The song was old. Pop crap from the 1980s. Duran Duran, or something like that.

She craned her neck toward the closed door. Her heart hammered in her chest. She needed to get out of there. She jerked at the ropes. "I don't know who you are, but I don't do tricks anymore."

Footsteps sounded in the hallway outside the door. Vicky sat straight, clenching her fingers into fists. She'd talked her way out of some bad stuff before. Hadn't Ronnie T. wanted to cut her hand off last year for stealing from him? She'd sworn never to cheat him again and as an extra measure said she'd pledge to work for free. He'd relented and given her another chance.

Sweat rolled down her back. *Stay calm. You can get out of this.*

The knob twisted and the door opened. A man

stepped into the room. He was dressed in jeans, a dark shirt, and work boots. Muscular build. Short hair. And wore an odd grin on his face that didn't sit well.

"You're up," he said pleasantly. "I was beginning to think you wouldn't wake up in time."

She tried not to look as terrified as she felt. "What am I doing here? Do you work for Ronnie T.?"

"I've never heard of Ronnie T. He a friend of yours?"

He softly closed the door behind him. The room was large enough, but with him in it the space shrank. She felt trapped. "He and I have worked together before."

"I see." He crossed the room and pulled a wooden chair from a desk and set it in front of her.

This guy was the guy from the alley. The guy who'd hit her. Like in the alley, he appeared so average. Like Richie Cunningham on *Happy Days.* Just an ordinary putz. If she'd passed him on the street, she'd never have given him a second glance. The straight-laced types had never done it for her. "Who are you?"

He straddled the chair and leaned toward her. "You don't recognize me?"

"From the alley."

"I'm talking about earlier."

"No."

Leaning a fraction closer, he clasped his hands together. "I thought you'd remember."

"Man, I don't. And if you've snatched me because you think I can remember something, I don't. You can let me go because I don't know nothing about anything. Ask anyone."

He looked disappointed. "I was hoping you would remember."

Vicky twisted her hands. She felt as if she were going to jump out of her skin. "Mister, I don't."

He shook his head. "That's too bad."

Too bad? Was he an old john? "If you want me to remember I'll try harder." If she could get the guy talking maybe she could come up with something to convince him to let her go.

He shrugged. "There's no point in going into it all. Once you've joined the Family, you'll understand."

"What family?"

"My family. Our family."

He rose and reached in his pocket as he moved around her.

Vicky's heart pounded against her chest. What the hell was the family? Maybe a cult. "What are you going to do?"

"I've got a present for you." He gently brushed her hair away from the nape of her neck. "You have pretty skin."

Tears welled in her eyes. She wasn't a crier, hadn't been since she was a kid. But something about this guy scared the piss out of her.

She twisted her head and tried to meet his gaze. "Mister, you've got the wrong girl. Really. I don't have a family. My name is Vicky."

He pulled a gold chain from his pocket. On the end was a small oval medallion. It caught the dim light and sparkled.

"Remember this? I showed it to you in the alley."

Her pulse thrummed. "Yeah, it's pretty."

He draped the necklace around her neck and fastened the clasp. The medallion felt cold against her skin and hung just above the vee of her sweater. Looking down, she could see it had writing on it but couldn't make out the script.

"Do you like it?" Gently, he stroked the top of her head.

Tension exploded inside her. Dear God, no matter what she said she feared it wasn't going to be the right answer. "Yeah, it's nice. You were sweet to give it to me."

"I'm glad you like it."

She clenched and unclenched her fingers. "Look, mister, how about letting me go? I don't want trouble. I just want to leave."

He came around her, squatted beside her chair, and laid his hand on her knee. "I can't let you go. It's just too dangerous out there for you."

"I can take care of myself. Really."

He frowned, clearly saddened. "You should be with your family."

"I don't have a family. I was a foster care kid. And my ex-husband and I don't really like each other."

"We should honor our father and mother."

A desperate smile lifted her trembling lips. She did her best not to think about her mother and father. She'd not seen them since she was eight and thinking about them only made life all that much harder. "I would if I knew them."

The more she talked the more distressed he seemed. "You've been alone too long. You've picked up so many bad habits."

"I'm not perfect. I get that." She had no idea what he was talking about. The guy was a nutcase. He could do anything to her. And then it hit her that she'd told him she was estranged from her parents and her ex-husband. "I have lots of friends. And they're expecting me."

He rose again and moved behind her. He laid his hands on her shoulders. Her pulse jolted wildly under his fingertips. "Friends come and go. Family is forever."

She was about to argue the point when she felt his hands move up to her neck. "What are you doing?"

"Sending you to the Family. Ruth is waiting. And I know she is so anxious to see you."

The growing pressure of his hand made it hard to swallow. She gagged. "I don't know any Ruth."

He started to squeeze. "Yes, you do."

She started to twist her head from side to side and kick her feet. God, if she could only bite him. But his hands were amazingly strong, and despite her flailing he maintained a steady pressure.

"Don't fight it." His voice was so soft and gentle. "I'm giving you what you always needed."

Getting air into her lungs became the priority. At first she could manage sips of air between gags but quickly that became impossible. She was going to die because he'd mistaken her for someone else.

Soon her vision blurred and she felt light-headed. Her body screamed for air. Her muscles cramped. Black dots formed in her eyes. Her chest burned.

Her mind skidded to a memory she rarely allowed. Her mother. Smiling at her. Calling her Peaches.

And then her heart stopped beating and everything went dark.

# Chapter Nine

*Sunday, January 13, 9:00 A.M.*

"Thank you for meeting me so early," Dana Miller said.

Nicole smiled and extended her hand to the woman dressed in mink and a sleek Armani suit. Dark hair was brushed back in a smooth chignon and one-caret diamond studs winked from her earlobes. Dana had made a fortune in real estate in the last decade.

Nicole smiled. "No problem. I often meet with clients early in the morning.

"But Sunday is above and beyond the call. My schedule is insane right now." Dana shrugged off the mink. A diamond broach clung to her lapel. "And then my marketing director called me yesterday and said she absolutely had to have the new publicity shots by Monday afternoon. We're revamping the Web site and my marketing director needs new head shots of me."

"You live a hectic life." Nicole accepted her coat and hung it on a rack by the door. The shades were open and morning light poured into her studio. Outside the winter sky was a crystal blue.

"Usually it's manageable. But I'm selling the units for the River Bend site, and with all the recent headlines I've had my hands full with damage control."

"Didn't they find a dead woman on that property?"

Dana grimaced. "Yes. Horrible. Poor woman."

"The murder must be hurting business."

"Actually, traffic by the sales office has skyrocketed. The problem is the cops won't release the scene and Adam Alderson is falling behind schedule with the surveying, which of course delays the site work. It's a mess." Dana's gaze flickered to Nicole's belly. "I guess you know firsthand about unexpected surprises."

The reference to the baby caught Nicole off guard. Dana's boldness put her on the defensive and that made her angry. As color rose in her cheeks, she reminded herself again that she had done nothing wrong.

"My comment has made you angry."

"Frankly, yes."

Dana wasn't put off. "This baby must be turning your world upside down."

Nicole lifted her chin. "Nothing I can't handle."

"Good for you. I like women with a spine." Dana grinned. "You are a doll for working me in today."

Nicole needed the interruption of work. She'd spent most of last evening looking at adoption family profiles. Again, she was left conflicted, worried, and confused over the decision. "I'm just glad you called and we could find a time to meet. Can I offer you coffee or tea?"

Dana smiled. "Tea would be lovely."

Nicole moved past the camera set up in front of the backdrop and settee. She had a small kitchen with an electric teapot and a white porcelain jar filled with a collection of teas.

"You will join me, won't you?"

Nicole shook her head. "My taste for tea has diminished somewhat since my pregnancy."

Dana chose a flavor from the jar and Nicole poured the steeping water into one of the antique porcelain cups she'd found at a flea market. The mismatched style of the cups suited her.

Dana sipped her tea. "I've heard a woman's taste buds change when she's pregnant. I've also heard her sense of smell becomes stronger."

"Very true." She could barely stand the smell of her dark-room chemicals, which she told herself was a valid reason for not working on anything for an art show. All the work she'd done of late was digital. After the baby was born, her life would get back to normal.

*After.*

"While you enjoy your tea, I'll set up the camera."

"I'm in no rush," Dana said. She sipped her tea and moved around the room, studying Nicole's prints on the walls. Outwardly calm, Dana exuded an energy that barely seemed contained. "So when is the baby due?"

Nicole pressed a hand to her belly. "About three weeks."

Dana grinned. "Wow. You must be very excited."

Scared was a better answer. But she wasn't about to share that with Dana. "Lots of changes are happening very fast."

"It must feel wonderful to feel the baby moving inside you."

More like an alien invasion. Nicole extended her arm toward the waiting settee. "If you need those pictures quickly, we'd better get started. Touch-ups will take me a few extra hours."

"Of course." She set her cup down by the hot pot and moved into the photo area.

Nicole stood behind the camera. She felt a measure of control return. "Would you like to touch up your makeup?"

"No."

That didn't surprise Nicole. The woman's makeup was perfect. "Then have a seat."

Dana sat down as Nicole started to turn on the spotlights around her. "So have you chosen a name for the baby?"

Bands of tension squeezed her chest. She adjusted the lights.

In the last few months, talk often turned to babies around her. Women of all ages reminisced about pregnancies and children. Some even touched her stomach as if it were public property. All of it made Nicole unhappy. Not knowing if she could love her child, she felt like a fraud when people asked her questions. "Not yet."

Nicole held a light meter next to Dana's face and took a reading.

Dana stared up at her. "I'm in sales, Nicole. I'm an expert at reading people."

"Really?"

"You're worried about something."

She swallowed but managed a smile. "The only thing I'm worried about is taking a great picture of you."

"Oh, I don't think that's true."

Nicole ignored the comment. "Here, turn your legs to the side and face the camera."

Dana complied. "So do you have family in the area?"

"No. My folks passed several years ago."

"Brothers and sisters?"

"Only child."

"So it's just you and the baby now."

Nicole retreated behind the camera and peered through the viewfinder. "Let's get started on your pictures."

Dana's eyes narrowed a fraction. "You dodge questions about the baby."

"I'm here to take pictures of you, not bore you with talk of the baby."

"I love to talk babies." Dana settled on her perch and smiled toward the lens. Her eyes brightened. "Not having a baby is my one regret. I was always so busy making money. I didn't want to stop to raise a child."

Nicole didn't respond. Dana's gaze grew pointed. "Are you going to keep the baby?"

"That's personal." Nicole could feel her cheeks flush.

"I know. I'm sorry." She didn't seem the least bit sorry.

Nicole had been excited about this job this morning, but now she just wanted to be done with it. She snapped several dozen pictures. Dana's practiced smile came easily. "You're very photogenic."

"I know." No conceit in her voice, just confidence in an asset.

Nicole moistened her lips. The baby kicked hard. "Would you like to see what I've shot so far? I have at least forty pictures now."

"Yes."

Nicole pulled the memory card from her camera and they walked to her desk. She popped the card in the computer and within seconds images of Dana appeared on the screen. Dana was photogenic but Nicole knew she'd also done an excellent job of capturing her. "What do you think?"

Dana leaned over Nicole's shoulder and studied the pictures. "Start flipping through them and I'll tell you what I like."

Nicole hit the NEXT button and another image appeared.

"No."

Nicole hit the button again.

Dana lifted a brow. "Maybe."

This went on for five minutes. By the end, Dana had chosen three pictures. "Excellent."

"I can take more pictures. I have other backdrops. Different lighting."

"No. What you've shot is excellent and it does the trick. Just send the disk to Brenda and she'll cut you a check."

Nicole glanced at her watch. "We've only been at this thirty minutes. Most sittings take several hours."

Dana moved across the room and retrieved her fur coat from the rack. She smiled. "Not necessary. I got exactly what I came for."

After the woman breezed out of the room, Nicole didn't feel the relief she'd been expecting. Instead, she felt as if she'd just played a round of cat and mouse. She'd dodged the cat today but wondered when it would return.

Jacob had not gotten into bed until after four A.M. He had watched and rewatched the parking lot surveillance tape hoping to see something more. There had been nothing, and finally, his eyes were so tired he had had to stop.

He had turned off his alarm clock, determined to sleep in. However, his eyes had popped open at nine-thirty. His mind was alert, jazzed even, but his body was exhausted. He had tossed and turned and going back to sleep had proven impossible.

Groaning his frustration, he swung his legs over the side of the bed. He hung his head in his hands and then pushed his fingers through his short hair. He rose and walked naked into the bathroom, took a leak, and then turned on the shower. When steam filled the bathroom, he climbed into the stall and ducked his head under the hot water stream. He leaned his head against the tile wall and let the heat flow down his back.

Jacob soaped off and rinsed. He shut off the water and stepped out of the stall. After grabbing a towel, he dried off, dressed in jeans and a black T-shirt, and slipped his feet into worn leather shoes.

His apartment was simple to the point of Spartan. La-Z-Boy couch, wide-screen TV, coffee table, and a few lamps. The beige walls had a few framed posters on them from boxing bouts he'd fought in when he was a teenager. Several bookshelves lined the walls. They were crammed full of biographies, history books, and the random bit of fiction. No plants. No knickknacks. He kept his life simple, uncomplicated.

The coffee tin was empty and what was left in the coffeepot was a couple of days old. Jacob never had time to go to the grocery store. When he did, it was always a surgical strike: eggs, cottage cheese, cooked lean chicken, and of course coffee. Only he'd not even made a fleeting pass at a store in a couple of weeks.

When he'd dated Sharon last year, the fridge had been stocked. She loved buying, cooking, and eating. And she had a killer body. She'd brought life to the apartment and he'd known he could fall for her. That had scared the hell out of him. Love equaled vulnerability. He had broken it off.

Sharon had been devastated. She'd cried. Staring at the mascara bleeding around her eyes, he'd felt like hell. He'd let her call him a coward and a bastard. And yet he didn't try to make it work.

Dr. Christopher would have a field day with that tidbit. No doubt she'd link the incident back to his mother.

He opened the refrigerator and discovered he had three boiled eggs and a juice carton. He peeled the eggs, ate them right over the sink, and then drank the remains of the juice from the carton.

Kendall Shaw's face flashed in his mind. He couldn't picture her drinking her morning juice from a carton. If she were standing here right now, she'd no doubt bust his chops for being such a slob. The image made him grin. When she was mad her eyes sparked, and he got hard.

The juice tasted all that much sweeter just knowing he could get under her skin.

The carton spent, he tossed it into the trash can under the sink and shrugged on his leather jacket. He retrieved his nine millimeter from the locked box in the hall closet and clipped it to his belt. He'd just snagged his cell from the charger by the back door when it rang. "Warwick."

"This is Zack." He sounded awake and alert. "I just got a call from dispatch. A convenience store owner found a murdered woman. Her body was dumped behind his store. She was strangled."

Jacob tensed. "Anybody see anything?"

"You know as much as I do at this point." Zack gave him the address.

"You call Ayden?"

"Not yet."

"Let him know what's going on. I'm on my way to the crime scene."

A second murdered woman meant the stakes had jumped exponentially. Jacob snapped his phone closed and headed down the stairs of his apartment complex. The cold burned his lungs as he crossed the parking lot to his car, a police issue Crown Vic.

The windshield was covered in ice. He slid behind the wheel, turned the heater on full blast, and then got out and scraped the windshield.

Two women strangled. The press would be all over this case. The press. Kendall. Damn.

# Chapter Ten

The trek across town on I-64 took Jacob twenty minutes. He took Exit 195 and continued east on Laburnum. Soon he spotted the blue lights of the squad cars flashing next to a convenience store called Ned's. He parked behind the county's white forensics van. From his trunk he grabbed rubber gloves.

Ned's was a one-story building covered in vertical siding painted a muddy red. In a large picture window hung signs for beer, cigarettes, and lottery tickets. The parking lot was crushed gravel. The officers had closed the store and driven off morning patrons.

Jacob walked up to the young officer who stood by the yellow crime scene tape, huddled in his jacket, his face pointed down away from the wind. "Officer."

The young guy stuck out his hand. "Detective Warwick."

"Where's the body?"

He stamped his feet to stimulate the circulation in them. "By the Dumpster. Hasn't been there long."

Jacob frowned. "How do you know that?"

"Ned, the owner of the store, said when he opened the

store at five she wasn't there. But when he went outside to dump stock boxes at nine-thirty she was."

"He see anything?"

"Said no. But he was rattled. Said he needed a ciga-rette."

"I'll talk to him later. Make sure he doesn't leave."

"Will do."

Jacob rounded the corner and saw Tess. She was snapping pictures of the victim. "Can I come closer?"

She didn't stop shooting. "Sure. You know the drill."

He ducked under the tape and moved toward the body as he put on rubber gloves. The dead woman lay curled on her side, her knees drawn up by her chest. She wore ragged hip-hugging jeans, black boots with heels, and a tight sweater that accentuated her breasts. Her leather jacket hugged her midsection and looked like it was designed for fashion, not warmth. Dark hair was cut short with purple and red streaks tinting the strands.

This woman was the polar opposite of Jackie White. "What about her neck and wrists?"

Tess squatted. She lifted the cuff of the victim's jacket. Red marks marred the pale skin of her wrist. Then Tess pushed back the woman's hair. Bruises indicating strangulation appeared.

"Shit," he muttered.

"Yeah," Tess said.

"We have ourselves a guy who likes to hold women and then strangle them."

She straightened. "But I can tell you she hasn't been dead long. Liver temp was ninety-one degrees."

"About five hours?"

"That's right." The first victim had died late Sunday.

"Turn her face so I can see it."

Tess gently turned the woman's head to reveal pale

skin, high cheekbones, and full lips. "She looks a lot like the first one."

Jacob expelled a breath. And Kendall Shaw. "Yeah."

He spotted a glint of gold around the victim's neck. It was a gold chain. "See the chain?"

Tess pushed back the leather jacket. Resting on the woman's chest above her breasts was a charm like the one worn by the first victim. It read *Judith.*

Jacob's gut tightened as he scribbled the name in his notebook. "Any ID on her?"

"No."

Her ID was missing. Dark hair. A charm. "Bet money her name isn't Judith."

Tess shook her head. "I'm not taking that bet."

Bells above Nicole's head jingled as she pushed through the front door of the coffee shop. A blast of warm air greeted her and she was grateful to be out of the wind.

The coffee shop was small. One look and anyone could see it wasn't part of a chain. Quirky furniture— round tables covered with shellacked postcards and chairs that didn't match—and a collection of old Virginia license plates on the wall. The front counter sported a cash register and a glistening display case filled with cookies and tarts. The tables were full of patrons.

Behind the counter stood a teenaged girl with blue hair and a nose ring. Nicole had learned on her last trip here that the girl was an art student at Virginia Commonwealth University.

"Hey, Ceylon," Nicole said. "How goes it?"

Ceylon smiled. "Excellent. The usual?"

"I'll take a biscotti today along with the tea."

"Living dangerously, I see." She put a bag of green tea

into a porcelain cup, poured hot water over it, and with a napkin in hand grabbed a biscotti.

Nicole handed her a five. "I don't know what's up. I can't seem to stop eating this week."

Ceylon gave Nicole her change. "The kid is growing."

Nicole dumped a dollar in the tip jar. "I suppose."

Ceylon nodded as if she were the authority. "My mom has had eight kids. She ate whatever wasn't nailed down."

"Did she lose all her baby weight?"

Ceylon rolled her eyes. "Oh, no."

Being saddled with extra weight didn't sit well with Nicole. She wanted her body back. Wanted her life back as soon as possible.

Still, her stomach grumbled and she knew she'd eat every bite of her cookie. The place hadn't cleared out a bit and no tables had opened up. Everyone seemed content to stay hidden from the cold. Looked like she'd be sitting in her car.

"Nicole Piper."

The deep male voice had her turning. A man with blond hair rose from his chair. He was a cop. She'd met him last summer but the name escaped her. That was another thing she wanted back—the other half of her brain that had gone into hibernation sometime during the second trimester.

She smiled, digging through her memory for a name. "Hi."

His smile was rich and warm, signaling he knew she couldn't recall his name. "David Ayden."

Color rose in her cheeks. "Sorry. My memory isn't so great these days."

"Would you like to join me?" He had a relaxed smile. "Tables are at a premium."

Her knee-jerk reaction was to say no. Her late husband's brutality had done that to her. "I don't want to intrude."

"The tables are full and I'm killing time waiting for my son." He moved around the table and pulled out the chair. "Sit. Please."

If she refused she'd look silly or ungrateful. And after all, the guy wasn't asking her to marry him. He was just offering her a seat. "Sure. Thanks."

She set her tea and cookie down on the table across from his black coffee and neatly folded newspaper. He held the back of her seat. She cupped her belly and eased into the seat. His attention made her feel oddly pampered. It had been a long time since anyone had held her chair for her.

Ayden was dressed in a dark turtleneck and faded jeans. She guessed his age to be about forty but he was fitter than most men half his age. A well-worn wedding band winked on his left ring finger. Her memory was coming back in bits and pieces. Ayden was a widower. Had a couple of kids. Boys, if she remembered.

"So what brings you down here?" he asked.

"I come in here at least once a week."

Sipping his coffee, he sat back in his chair, his body relaxed. He was comfortable in his own skin.

Nicole dunked her tea bag, amazed that she felt at a loss for words. That wasn't like her. She could carry on a conversation with anyone. Making people relax and feel comfortable was part of being a good photographer. "Do you come here often?"

"First time. My son is taking a one-day S.A.T. prep course at the university. He should be finishing up in the next twenty minutes or so."

"S.A.T. So he's looking at colleges?"

Pride shone in his eyes. "We plan to start driving around the state this spring and looking at a few colleges."

"That must be exciting."

"For him. Frankly, it makes me feel old. I remember when his mother was pregnant with him."

She shifted. There was no escaping this pregnancy. "Time flies."

He frowned, sensing her unease. "Everything all right?"

She traced the rim of her cup with her finger. "I just get a little weird when people mention my pregnancy." She glanced down at her belly. "But when your stomach is the size of a barn, it's kind of hard for people not to talk about it."

"Everything all right with the baby?"

"Oh, yes. She's fine," she rushed to say. A sudden weight bore down on her chest. And suddenly, the words tumbled out. "I'm thinking about giving her up for adoption. I'm not sure if I can be the kind of mother she deserves."

There was no judgment in Ayden's gray eyes, just a hint of sadness. "Have you chosen a family?"

"No," she said. "And I know I need to make a decision soon." Emotion threatened to overwhelm her and she sipped her tea, hoping it would calm her. "Sorry. I didn't mean for this to turn into a therapy session."

A warm smile curved the edges of his lips. "You're fine. Were you working today?"

God bless him for changing the subject. "Yes. I was taking head shots for a client. In fact, I stayed late so I could get the retouches done and get the project off the desk."

"Rush job."

"Not really. My client gives me the creeps and I just wanted the work off my desk." She voiced her fears out loud so he could tell her she was being silly.

"Who's the client?"

She broke off a piece of her cookie, not sure why

she'd even brought up the topic. "I'm probably being silly, but it's Dana Miller. I'm being silly, right?"

He shrugged. "I've crossed her path a couple of times."

This was the part where he was supposed to tell her not to worry. "And she was fine, right?"

"I wasn't impressed."

"Oh."

He leaned forward. "You're finished with her, right?"

"Right."

"Then don't sweat it. Just say no to any other jobs."

"You're right. I'm just overreacting." She needed to hear the words.

"I didn't say that. I'm just saying I wouldn't work for her again."

She sighed. "Thanks."

"For what?"

"For just letting me babble. I work alone so much, I don't get the chance to talk to people very often."

Creases formed around his eyes when he smiled. "You are doing me the favor. I've got two teenaged sons who only talk about bodily functions and cheerleaders."

She laughed out loud.

Ayden sat back, savoring the sound of Nicole's laughter. When he'd first seen her last summer she'd worn her hair shorter and she'd dyed it blond. In the last seven months the bleached strands had grown out and been cut away. Now ink-black hair framed her round face. He preferred the dark to the light. It made her blue eyes all the more expressive and alluring.

Pregnancy agreed with Nicole. The extra roundness of her face was preferable to last summer's gauntness. And despite her protruding belly she still possessed an air of grace.

"What are your boys' names?" she asked.

He sensed genuine interest. "Caleb and Zane. Sixteen and fifteen, respectively."

"They keep you busy, I'll bet."

"You've no idea." He thought about the fiasco this morning. "At six this morning, Caleb remembered he was supposed to be here for the S.A.T. session at eight. He woke me up oblivious to the fact that I've worked a lot of late hours this week on a case."

She rested her chin on her hand. "I could be a little spacey when I was a teenager. I drove my mom nuts. She was always a sport, though."

"Caleb's mom, my late wife, was the calm one. I wish she'd been there this morning to smooth the explosion."

Since his wife's passing two years ago, Ayden had never been able to talk to another woman without first thinking about Julie. Guiltily, he realized he'd not thought about her at all since Nicole sat down. "Julie was always good at getting the boys where they needed to go. I never had to worry."

Nicole's face softened. "I remember Zack saying you're a widower. How'd she die?"

"Cancer." He liked Nicole's directness. He'd grown tired of dancing around other people's discomfort over Julie's death.

The familiar lump formed in his gut, but the sharp pain of loss was finally starting to ease. "I do the best I can to keep her memory alive for the boys. But it's getting harder and harder for them to remember."

She nodded, her expression serious. "If I look at pictures of my mother I remember her. Otherwise, it's hard."

"How long has she been gone?"

"Eight years. Car accident." She straightened as if the baby kicked.

It was none of his business how she was doing, but he wanted to know. He'd worked with the Richmond and

San Francisco police who'd unraveled her late husband's murder sprees. They'd all been violent, vicious crimes.

"I gotta say," Ayden said, "you appear to be doing real well."

She nodded, understanding his meaning. "I'm just putting one foot in front of the other. I figure as long as I keep moving I can hold it together."

"That's exactly how I felt when Julie died."

She sipped her tea. "But I didn't love my husband. Not at the end anyway."

"But you did at one time."

"Sure. In the beginning."

"It's logical to mourn that loss."

"I mourned that loss a long time ago. The real struggle has just been learning to live again. To think for myself. I wanted to buy shoes the other day and for a split second wondered if Richard would approve. Moments like that make me angry."

She had a fighter's spirit. "You buy the shoes?"

A wicked grin curved the edge of her lips. "In brown and in black."

The front doors of the shop opened. A blast of cold air rolled in with a gangly boy who had the same color of eyes as Ayden. The kid's gaze scanned the shop and landed almost immediately on him. The boy grinned.

Ayden was glad to see his son but sorry his visit with Nicole would have to end. "Number one son has arrived."

Nicole twisted and looked up at the boy. She smiled.

Ayden rose. "Caleb, I'd like you to meet Nicole Piper."

Caleb shook her hand. "Hey. Nice to meet you."

"How'd the test go?" Ayden asked.

"Good."

"Any problems?"

"No."

He wondered if the boy would ever speak in complete sentences again.

Nicole grinned. "I remember my S.A.T. I think I got a two on the math."

Caleb nodded. "Math was a bear but I aced the English part."

"When I took my test, the proctor opened the windows. Outside, the university was hosting a charity carnival. The noise was a big distraction."

"Yeah, some kid in our classroom kept tapping his foot. It was a real pain."

Ayden watched the exchange, thinking he'd just witnessed a minor miracle. Caleb had completed sentences and was engaging in a conversation.

"Hey, Dad, can we head out? I've got a paper to finish for science."

Ayden glanced at Nicole's half cup of tea and uneaten cookie. "I hate to leave you like this."

Nicole's eyes twinkled with amusement. "I'm never alone when I have a cookie."

"Right." Still, it bothered him that he was leaving behind a very pregnant woman to fend for herself. He reminded himself that she was none of his concern. But the argument fell on deaf ears. He dug five dollars out of his pocket. "Caleb, grab yourself a cup of coffee for the road and then we'll head out."

Caleb took the money without question. "Cool."

Ayden sat back down. "Don't let me hold you up. Eat."

Nicole started to eat her cookie. "He's a good kid."

"Yeah. I credit his mother. I've always worked insane hours."

"Don't sell yourself short."

For the next few minutes they sat and talked while Caleb flirted with the girl behind the counter. They talked about Nicole's photography and she told him an amusing story about an uptight bride. The exchange was, well, nice.

As luck would have it, Caleb came back to the table just as Nicole was finishing off her cookie and tea.

Ayden rose. "We can walk you to your car?"

Nicole lumbered to her feet. "Oh, don't worry. I'm just a few blocks from here."

"A few blocks. We'll walk you."

Caleb glanced at him. His expression was a mixture of amusement and surprise, but thankfully the kid didn't blurt out whatever thoughts pummeled his mind.

Nicole picked up her purse off the floor. "It's twenty degrees outside. Save yourself."

"I'm parked out front. I'll drive you." The more he thought about her walking down city blocks alone, the more the idea bothered him.

She seemed grateful for the favor and allowed him to guide her out of the shop. Caleb lumbered behind.

Ayden opened the front passenger seat of an unmarked white Crown Vic and waited as she lowered herself into the seat. When she was settled, he closed the door.

"You gonna open my door?" Caleb muttered.

Ayden glared at the glint in the kid's eye. "Get in the car."

Caleb climbed in the back while Ayden slid behind the wheel. He fired up the engine and pulled into traffic.

Nicole directed him to the parking lot where she'd left her car. Her skin looked a little pale now and he guessed she was exhausted.

"Thanks for the ride," she said.

"Take care."

"Will do." She climbed out and moved to her car. Once inside, she fired up the engine and then waved an all clear to him.

Caleb got out of his seat and into the front. Ayden waited until Nicole pulled out and waved her thanks.

"Jeeze, Dad, she's like a hundred months pregnant and you're giving her 'the look.'"

Annoyed, Ayden pulled onto Cary Street. "I wasn't giving her a 'look.'"

Caleb clicked his seat belt and leaned back in his seat, pleased with himself. "Oh, it was a look all right."

Ayden shot his kid a good-natured glare. "Stow it, kid."

Then Ayden's cell phone rang. He glanced down at the number displayed.

Zack Kier.

A call on his day off couldn't be good.


Standing in her spare room, Kendall wore jeans, a faded T-shirt, and paint-spattered sneakers when the cell in her pocket rang. She glanced at the yellow paint can she'd been preparing to open and flipped open the phone. "Kendall Shaw."

"There's been another murder," Brett fired off. "How soon can you be ready to cover it?"

Kendall's heart raced. "Give me fifteen minutes."

"Good." He gave her the address. "I'll have a cameraman meet you there."

Adrenaline rushed her system. "I'll be there in a half hour."

The paint job forgotten, Kendall showered quickly, pulled her hair into a neat French twist, and donned a chocolate cashmere sweater, dark suede paints, and boots. Good to her word, she was mobile in fifteen minutes.

On the way to the crime scene, she mentally ran through the questions she wanted to ask. She prided herself on not only looking her best but also having the sharpest questions.

*A woman should be more than a pretty face.* Henry Shaw, her father had said that a lot. He had never let Kendall trade on her looks. He'd expected her to work hard in school and prove she could succeed in spite of her looks.

Her dad had provided ballast for his type-A wife, Irene, and his daughter. The women's personalities were so much alike and her dad had often said they were "two peas in a pod." Kendall had always liked it when he said that because it made it easy to pretend that Irene had given birth to her and that there wasn't another woman out there who'd given her away.

"What made me think of that?" Kendall muttered as she slowed for a red light. She forced her mind back to the story and the victim. Minutes later, she turned right on Laburnum and quickly spotted the flashing blue lights of the police cars. The Channel 10 van was waiting in a Chinese restaurant parking lot across a side street. The other television crews had arrived. This was going to be chaos.

She parked behind the van and got out. The cameraman on the scene was new and she'd only worked with him a couple of times. "Hey, Lin. Where's Mike?"

Lin was tall and lean. He couldn't be more than thirty but his shoulders stooped like those of an old man. "Don't know."

It wasn't like Mike to miss a story like this. "Follow me. Let's cross to the crime scene and see what we can see."

He nodded, reached in the van, and hoisted a camera onto his shoulder. "Will do, boss."

The wind cut into her skin as she crossed the intersection toward the crime scene. She made it as far as a sidewalk before she reached yellow tape and a patrolman stopped her.

Kendall tossed the officer her trademark smile.

But before she could ask her first question, he said, "No one's getting close to the scene. Especially you."

Her smile held, though annoyance rose in her. "Can you tell me anything about the victim?"

"No."

"Is Detective Warwick here?" This was a long shot. "He'll talk to me."

That made the man laugh. "He's busy."

Frustrated, she glanced at the store. There'd be no getting in now. She turned and started back across the street toward the van. The corner was lined with other stores and a growing number of onlookers. Someone had to have seen something.

Lin's long legs kept pace easily. "So what now?"

"There's more than one way to skin a cat."

Jacob had been waiting for Kendall since her station's news van had arrived. He'd seen to it that she didn't get close to this story.

A flutter of movement caught his attention and he watched as Tess turned the body on its side. She pushed up the victim's shirt. Pale blue speckles covered the dead woman's lower back.

Tess looked up at him. "She died sitting in a chair. But she didn't sit as long as the last one. Whoever did this didn't keep her as long."

"Almost as if he was in a rush."

"Right."

The similarity between the two victims and Kendall had to be addressed. The likeness could have been dismissed as coincidence with one victim, but not two. Jacob needed to talk to Kendall.

Over the last year, he'd managed to collect an odd assortment of facts about Kendall. He'd never gone out of his way to dig up information on her, but when she was mentioned, he paid attention.

Both her parents were dead. No siblings. Model. Loved Paris. Won several awards. He didn't want to talk to her here. A conversation between them would not go unnoticed and he didn't want to draw the attention. He'd wait. Until he could find her alone.

Kendall spent the better part of the morning talking to bystanders, store owners, and anyone who might have seen something. People were happy to talk to her, but all rambled on about details that couldn't be built into a story. At four she and the other members of the media had gotten a briefing from the police department's public information officer. But the details had been scant. Female. Caucasian. Manner of death yet to be determined.

She'd called Phil White a couple of times to get his reaction, but he'd not answered his phone.

So when she returned to the station at about five, she was frustrated, tired, and hungry. It would be a long night piecing together the bits into a story.

Kendall passed reception and headed down the hallway toward her office. She stopped short at the threshold. Detective Jacob Warwick stood in her office.

Warwick stared at the pictures on her wall, the paperweight from her desk in his hand.

He studied her space. She did the same thing when she entered someone's office. Furnishings and styles revealed a lot about a person. Neat freak. Slob. Pack rat. Hobbies. She'd been careful to choose furnishings that telegraphed cool and sophisticated. All part of the Kendall Shaw persona that she'd nurtured for the last few years. She wasn't sure why she now felt like a fraud.

"Detective." She couldn't decide if this was a stroke of luck or not.

He turned, unrushed and seemingly not caring that he'd been caught staring at her pictures. He set the paperweight down. "About time you got back."

Kendall pulled back her shoulders and smiled. She refused to betray the flutter of nerves in her belly. "This a social call, Detective, or are you going to give me an interview?"

A second glance at him and she noted the dark circles under his eyes. She'd bet he and his partner had been working around the clock since the first body had been found. "No to both."

That puzzled her. "Okay. Why are you here? I've got a story to write."

Warwick hesitated as his gaze lingered on a picture of Kendall and her parents. "You look happy in this picture."

"It was taken at my high school graduation." She wasn't sure why she felt the need to explain. "That was the last picture taken of the three of us. Dad died three months later."

A hint of regret darkened his eyes. He understood her loss. He had loved and lost a foster father who had been just as dear to him as her father had been to her. Losing a parent left a wound that would never quite heal no matter how much time had passed. Suddenly, she felt sadness for Warwick.

"You don't look like your parents."

She cleared her throat. "Mom always said I was a throwback to another generation." Her mother's lie had been told so often that it rolled off Kendall's tongue automatically. "Why are you here?" Impatience had leaked into her voice.

He met her gaze head-on. "What I'm about to say has to stay off the record for now."

Her senses perked up. "There's no such thing as off the record."

His gaze pinned her. "If you can't give me your word that none of this will leak out, then I'll go."

Reporters were nosey by nature and she was no exception. Warwick had something important to tell her and not knowing would drive her nuts. But she could see in his expression that he would walk out of her office right now if she didn't give him her word. Damn. There was no way around it. "You have my word."

"I mean it, Kendall. No leaks."

That irritated her. "When I give my word I keep it. Period."

He hesitated and she couldn't tell if he was trying to read her or gauge his own words. "Did Phil White ever mention that you look like his wife?"

That took her aback. "I do not look like Jackie White."

"He did, didn't he?" He boldly studied her high cheekbones and her vivid green eyes. "She wasn't as pretty as you are, but the similarities are there. I saw it even when she was lying by the river, pale and lifeless. You had to have noticed."

Kendall drew in a deep breath. "Is that supposed to spook me?"

His eyes narrowed. "The second victim looks like you as well."

Her stomach dropped. "Brown hair and green eyes are common traits. Whatever similarities you see are strictly coincidence. Now if you don't have anything else to add, it's late and I want to work."

He pulled two Polaroid pictures out of his coat pocket and laid them on her desk. They were of the two murdered women. Unexpected sadness washed over her as she stared at the lifeless faces.

She swallowed. "The women look similar, but nothing like me."

"You don't believe that, do you?"

"Yes, I do."

He tapped the desk with his index finger. "Have you had any odd e-mails lately? Obsessed fans? Irate ex-boyfriends?"

There had been the tipster who'd sent her the text message. "Nothing out of the ordinary. Some send me notes frequently but none have been menacing." She tried to look nonplussed. "I think you're grasping at straws."

He stared at her as if trying to read her thoughts.

Those thoughts flashed to the dreams she'd had. The unknown woman's screams echoed in her head. She pushed aside the memory and focused on logic. "I've had no threats. No creepy guys. No odd phone calls. It's been business as usual. You'd think if someone was living out some strange fantasy I'd have some sign."

"Not necessarily." He was a dog with a bone. "What about ex-boyfriends?"

"My ex-boyfriend would like to patch things up." She folded her arms over her chest, not sure why she mentioned it. "I've been very clear we are not getting back together."

Warwick raised a brow. "Did he say anything to make you concerned?"

"No. I mean he was a little frustrated with me but Brett's always frustrated with me."

"Brett Newington?"

Loyalty made her hesitate, but then she answered, "Yes."

"Why would he be frustrated with you?"

"I'm too independent, I suppose. He likes his women a bit more biddable." She frowned. "I've known Brett for years. He's stable."

"Right."

"Hey, this is the kind of thing that could really hurt his career."

"I can be subtle when I ask questions."

She arched a brow. "You're about as subtle as I am biddable."

A smile tugged the edge of his lips and for a moment it transformed his face. He didn't look so fierce. He looked attractive even.

She rubbed the back of her neck with her hand. "You went out on a limb to tell me this."

"Yes."

"Why?"

His face tightened. "I owe you."

That surprised her. "You don't owe me anything."

"That's not how I see it." He shrugged. "Just keep your eyes and ears open, Kendall. Do you have an alarm system in your house?"

"Yes."

"Good. Use it."

"All right." She held out her hand to him, trying to prove to them both that there was no snap of energy between them. "Thanks."

Strong powerful fingers wrapped around hers, and for a moment she felt a jolt zigzag through her body.

"You'll keep me posted," she said.

"When it's necessary." He released her hand, picked up the Polaroids and tucked them in his pocket, and left her office.

Kendall stood stunned and not quite sure what had just happened. If he'd come to her about anyone else, she'd have a dozen ways to crack the story without breaking her word to him. But the angle he'd brought her put her dead center in the middle of the story. She'd been

there once. And knew that was a place she never wanted
to be again.

Brett Newington sat in a chair and stared at the
woman standing before him. She had a long, lean body
and the dark wig he'd supplied draped her slender
shoulders. The woman wore black heels, a pencil-thin
skirt, and a silk blouse, all of which he'd supplied as well.
In the dim light he could almost pretend it was Kendall
standing before him.

"Unbutton your blouse," he said.

She'd been instructed not to speak except when she
was spoken to. And then she only said, "Yes, sir."

Her hands trembled as she unbuttoned the blouse.
He smiled. She was afraid of what was to come. The
others had told her. Good.

She let the blouse fall to her shoulders and then slide
to the floor. Full breasts rose up over the black lacy bra.

"Now the skirt."

She wriggled out of the skirt and kicked it toward the
blouse puddled beside her.

The woman was curvier than he liked, her belly not as
flat as it should be. But she would do.

Brett rose, walked toward her, and stopped when he
was only inches away. She stared up at him. Under the
heavy makeup he could see the pockmarks on her skin.
He could see that she wasn't Kendall. That she was a
cheap imitation.

Rage rolled inside him. He raised his hand and slapped
her hard on the face. The impact sent her to her knees.

She touched the back of her hand to her lips, now
crimson with blood. But she didn't scream or fight back.
She'd been paid well for the violence as much as the sex.

"Stand up," he ordered.

She rose up and faced him. Fear darkened her eyes. The money was good, but he suspected she was wondering now if it was worth the pain.

He grabbed her arm and yanked it back hard. "You're going to earn every dime."

"Yes, sir."

Brett smiled, pleased by her obedience. He slapped her a second time and then pushed her down on the bed.

Dana sat in her car and watched as Nicole drove off. In the dimming light, Dana smiled. She flipped open her cell phone and dialed a familiar number. "I need to buy a gun."

# Chapter Eleven

*Sunday, January 13, 8:00 P.M.*

Jacob leaned against a wall on the first floor of the medical examiner's building while Zack finished his call to his wife. Zack and Lindsay had barely seen each other in the last week, thanks to the murders. But Zack made sure he called whenever he could. Jacob admired the couple. They'd pulled a failing marriage out of divorce court and found their way back to each other.

Zack frowned as he snapped the phone closed and tucked it in his belt holster. "She sounded tired."

Jacob pushed away from the wall. "She all right?"

He frowned. "Yeah, it's just that she's trying really hard to get her new women's center together. It opens soon."

"Lindsay thrives on work. She'll be fine."

Zack shoved out a breath. "She's pregnant."

Jacob straightened. "No shit."

Zack grinned. "Yeah. She's only about six weeks along. She doesn't want me telling anyone for another month, so keep it under your hat."

Jacob clapped him on the back. "Good job, old man."

Zack looked pleased with himself. "We hadn't expected to do this so soon, but it's pretty damn cool."

They started down the hallway. "That explains why you've been calling her every five minutes."

"She'd overdo it if I didn't remind her to slow down."

Jacob shook his head. "She's smart. And she'll do whatever it takes to protect the kid."

"Yeah."

A wave of emotion burned through Jacob. He couldn't decide if it was jealousy or relief. He didn't have a family and told himself that he liked it that way. His ex-girlfriend could testify to that. But there were moments when he did wonder what it felt like to really love someone and have them love you back.

He doubted he'd ever know. Love required trust and he had none of that to give. For the first time, he was sorry.

They strode down the hallway to the medical examiner's office and found Dr. Butler behind his desk. The space was small, crammed full of books and a half dozen diplomas on the walls. Papers piled high in an in-box.

The doctor sat facing a laptop computer on the side of his desk. He was typing furiously and didn't notice Jacob and Zack in the doorway. Jacob knocked.

Dr. Butler started and his gaze swung around to the two cops. "Crap, I wish you wouldn't do that."

"Do what?" Jacob couldn't help but smile.

"Move like a damn cat. Both of you never make any noise. Do me a favor and make some noise once in a while."

Jacob smiled. "What do you want me to do, tie bells to my ass?"

Dr. Butler's face was deadpan. "That'll work fine."

Jacob found himself wondering if the guy was serious or not. Shaking his head, he followed Zack into the office. He sat in one of the two government-issue chairs in front of the desk. With all three of them in the office the place felt very small.

"So I hear you did our Jane Doe's autopsy," Zack said as he propped an ankle on the opposite knee.

"She's not a Jane Doe anymore." Dr. Butler's eyes glistened with pride.

"That was fast," Jacob said.

The second body had ramped up the pressure on all of them. "I rolled her prints an hour ago and Tess came up with a match. Your victim's name is Vicky Draper. Her ID came up so quickly because she has a record. She did five years for drug trafficking. She was released two years ago."

Zack tapped his finger on the arm of his chair. "What else can you tell me about her?"

Dr. Butler read his notes. "She was strangled from behind. And she also had a pronounced bruise on her right jaw. Someone hit her hard before she died." He raised his eyebrows. "And she had a nasty scar on her right hand. It's got to be years old. Reminds me of a defensive wound."

Jacob grabbed a rubber band off of Dr. Butler's desk. He strung it around his index fingers and started to roll it in circles. "Someone tried to stab her?"

Dr. Butler shrugged. "It was my first thought when I saw the cuts. She also had nicks on the inside of her arm. Also old."

Jacob shoved out a breath. "What about needle marks on her arms?"

"Scars of old ones. But they're a couple of years old. Nothing fresh. But there's no doubt she was a heavy user at one time. Her teeth are a mess. I'll need a few days before I'll have results of a tox screen to tell me what was in her system when she died."

Zack leaned forward, his gaze full of interest. "Vicky and Jackie look alike. Jackie could have been at the wrong place at the wrong time. The killer could have been after Vicky. Maybe she'd gotten back into drugs and had pissed someone off."

Jacob shook his head. "Vicky was wearing a charm."

Dr. Butler nodded. "*Judith.*"

"If not for the charms, I'd agree with you, Zack. But the charms change everything," Jacob said.

Zack nodded slowly.

Dr. Butler leaned forward. "A serial killer."

"I sure as hell hope not," Jacob said. But he already knew he'd return to the office and file a report with ViCap and make sure Tess had entered her DNA evidence into CODIS. ViCap was the FBI's primary database of violent offender profiles. CODIS was a national DNA database of offenders. Jacob wanted to know if this killer had struck elsewhere.

"Any other similarities between the victims?" Zack asked.

"I've run a battery of tests. But it's going to take time before I get any results back."

Jacob could feel a headache forming behind his temple. "The press is going to eat this one up." He'd told Kendall about the murder, and now he wondered if she'd be good to her word.

"Like a pack of wild dogs," Zack said.

The rubber band snapped in Jacob's hand. Would Kendall Shaw be leading the pack?

*The screams had stopped. Only the child's quick, panicked breaths broke the silence. Even the baby that lay beside her was quiet, as if it too sensed a momentary reprieve. She huddled in the back of the closet her face pressed in the corner. Coats hanging*

*above brushed the top of her head. She didn't trust that it was safe.
Her heart pounded in her chest.*

*And then footsteps.*

*Slow, unhurried footsteps creaked outside the closet. "Come
out, come out wherever you are."*

*The familiar voice was soft, kind even.*

*The little girl wanted to trust the honey-coated words. She
wanted to be held in a safe, protective embrace, but she didn't
move. Behind the sweetness she sensed evil lurked.*

*The baby started to flail and kick its legs. Kendall laid her
hand clumsily on the baby's chest, hoping to calm it. The infant's
rapid butterfly pulse thrummed under her fingers. But her touch
only agitated the baby more. The baby started to kick, to whim-
per, and then to cry.*

*Outside someone moved closer to the closet door. Fear burned
in Kendall's chest as fresh tears filled her eyes. She pressed her
back against the hard wall behind her and held the baby's arm.
The baby started to wail. The closet door snapped open.*

*A man stood in the doorway. The light behind him obscured
his face but caught the steel edge of the knife in his hand. Blood
dripped from its tip.*

"No!"

Kendall sat upright in bed. Sweat soaked her nightgown and tears streaked her face.

She raked a shaking hand through her hair and shoved
out a deep breath.

She glanced at the clock and groaned. It wasn't even
eleven o'clock. Soon she'd be a walking zombie.

She got out of bed and grabbed the robe she kept on
the bedpost, then shrugged the robe on.

Moving to her dresser mirror, she stared at her tired
expression as she rubbed her aching shoulder. All the

dreams had one thing in common: in each, she was a little girl—afraid, alone.

She had no memory of the house or the infant. The closet or the man with the knife. Yet the dream kept coming to her. Night after night.

"Damn." She prided herself on control and this dream was stealing it from her.

She drummed her fingers on the dresser and continued to stare at her face. What had happened to her before she was adopted? She thought about the pictures displayed in her parents' home. From the age of three onward the Shaws had proudly documented every moment of her life. Birthdays. Halloween costumes. Awards. Graduations. They'd savored every moment and cherished her.

But before the adoption her life was a glaring blank slate. No pictures, birth records, birth parents' names. She had nothing.

"Who are you?" she whispered as she stared at her image.

When her mother had died, Kendall had been too upset to go through her papers. She'd simply boxed them up and put them away. And when she'd moved into this house, she'd had the movers stow the untouched boxes in the attic room. They'd sat there for the last five months. Forgotten. Ignored.

Kendall moved to the closet in her room that accessed the attic. She opened the door and shivered as a cold blast rushed down from the eaves above and cut through her robe. Shaking off a quiver, she clicked on the light and climbed the unfinished stairs to the landing. The single lightbulb cast shadows in the darkened corners.

There wasn't much in the attic. The few decorations she bought for Christmas, files from old stories she'd done and her mother's papers. There were six of those boxes and they stood grouped in the far corner.

Kendall crossed the plywood floor to them. She uncapped the first box and started to thumb through the records. This box contained Irene and Henry Shaw's tax records for the last three decades. She picked up one of the files and opened it. Her dad's handwriting was neat and precise and he'd pressed down on the paper so hard with the black ballpoint pen that the letters still indented the page. She smiled and traced her fingers over the page. Her throat tightened. Ten years since his death and she still missed him.

Kendall shoved out a breath, replaced the file, and covered the box. The cold made her hands tremble and the bottom of her bare feet prick. In another box she found a dusty album filled with black-and-white pictures that documented Irene's life from early childhood up until her marriage to Henry.

They'd been married in the midseventies and Irene wore her blond hair loose, no veil, and a slim white dress that had chiffon sleeves with thick cuffs. Henry wore a blue tux, thick sideburns, and a large bow tie. Kendall smiled as she studied her father's full crop of hair. For as long as she could remember, his hair had been thinning.

Kendall closed the album and gently laid it back in the box. She set the box aside and dug through the others. More financial papers. And then finally, in the last box, tucked in a brown accordion file full of tax records she found a slim file that had *Kendall* written in her mother's neat cursive.

Kendall had never seen the file before. And she found her hands shook anew, not from cold but fear. She smoothed her hand over the dusty manila folder.

A chill snaked down her spine.

She tucked the file under her arm and headed back

down the stairs, then shut off the light and closed the attic door before climbing back into her bed.

The sheets had grown cold and it took a moment for the chill to leave her body. She rubbed her hands together and opened the file to find a picture and a single sheet of paper.

The picture stapled to the left side of the manila folder was of Kendall. Unlike the hundreds her mom and dad had taken of her, this one wasn't in color but black and white. Kendall's hair was cut short and her face was pale. She frowned as she stared off into the distance as if she were searching for something.

Kendall traced the outline of her young face. "You look so unhappy."

What had happened to her before the picture had been taken? Had her birth mother just left her? Was she mourning the loss?

Her heart heavy, Kendall flipped the picture over, but the reverse side was blank. She shifted her attention to the single sheet of paper in the file. It was a letter from an adoption agency informing the Shaws that the closed adoption of Kendall Elizabeth Shaw had been finalized. All birth records had been sealed by the courts.

The letterhead read *Virginia Adoption Services*. Her heart thumped wildly in her chest. This agency had the key to her past. Its staff could tell her where she came from.

For so many years, she'd pushed thoughts of her birth family from her mind. Now they were all she could think about. Years of denying vanished in a heartbeat. In its place rose an intense need to *know*.

Nervous energy bubbled inside Kendall. She glanced at the phone and then back at the picture of the little girl who looked so lost. Afraid she'd back out if she hesitated, she picked up the phone on the nightstand and called information. When the automated operator came on the line Kendall requested the agency's listing. Seconds clicked by as she waited. And then the operator informed her that the number was *no longer in service.*

Kendall squeezed her eyes closed and swallowed an oath. She repeated her request for the number. More seconds passed and then the operator returned with the same answer.

Kendall hung up the phone. "Damn."

Impatient, she flicked the edge of the letter with her thumb. Whatever adoption papers Irene and Henry Shaw had had appeared to be long gone. There'd been nothing in her mother's safety deposit box. The only hope Kendall had of finding out about her birth family was this agency. And it no longer had a phone listing.

She glanced again at the letter. *The infant child, now known as Kendall Elizabeth Shaw, is now the legal child of Henry and Irene Shaw. All birth records for the infant child have been sealed.*

Sealed.

Kendall remembered Carnie Winchester, whose own adoption records had been sealed. Nicole had said that connecting adoptive and birth families was one of Carnie's specialties. She could untangle this mess.

Each time questions had arisen in her, she'd run away from them. Now, she felt as if she had no choice but to dive right in.

Jacob and Zack arrived at Outer Limits tavern just after eleven on Sunday night. The pub was located in a strip mall, sandwiched between a hardware store and a wine shop, on the border of Henrico and Goochland Counties. Christmas lights outlined the big picture window and a Miller sign flashed in neon. The parking lot was filled with the tavern patrons' vehicles.

The detectives got out of the car. Jacob braced against the cold, which cut through his jacket and stung the exposed skin on his face. He ducked his head and pushed through the tavern's front door. Warm air, the buzz of conversation, and the blare of music greeted them. Zack closed the door and stood behind him.

The tavern was long and narrow. To their right a long oak bar with stools. Behind it, spotlights shone down on shelves filled with hundreds of bottles of booze. Booths filled with patrons lined the left side of the bar and in between were a half dozen full café tables.

"The place is packed," Zack said. He had to speak loud enough to be heard over the music.

Jacob glanced at a sign that read *RICHMOND'S #1 BURGER*. "The owner's name is Paul Jefferson."

At that moment a man moved behind the bar. Tall and slim and muscular like a runner, he had a thick stock of red hair bleached by the sun. In his midforties, he wore a blue T-shirt that read Kona and khaki pants. "The guy looks like he just walked off the beach," Jacob said.

Zack's eyes narrowed a fraction as recognition dawned. "I know this guy. Ten years ago he won several Ironman competitions. Busted a knee or shoulder in a cycling accident. Ended his career."

Jacob shook his head. "Lycra and spandex. Bikes that barely weigh a pound. I've never seen the attraction."

Zack shrugged, unoffended. "He's one hell of an athlete."

But could he take a pounding in the ring? "Let's see what he knows about Vicky Draper."

They moved across the room and pushed through the mob of people at the end of the bar. Jacob pulled out his badge and as Paul turned he held it up.

Paul didn't appear intimidated and turned to hand a

couple of draft beers to a waitress waiting by the bar. "My liquor license is up to date."

"We didn't come about your liquor license," Jacob said.

The guy didn't bother a glance in his direction. He filled two beers from the tap. Foam washed over the side onto his hand. "I'm very busy. We're packed, as you can see."

Irritated, Jacob tucked his badge back in his pocket. "We're here to talk about Vicky Draper."

Paul muttered a curse under his breath. "She's one of the reasons I'm busting my balls tonight. She hasn't shown up to work in a couple of days. I left messages on her cell when she didn't show last night for her shift. But she never called back. What'd she do this time?"

Someone in the crowd picked that moment to crank a jukebox with a Bruce Springsteen song. Jacob wasn't about to shout what he had to say. "Is there anywhere we can talk?"

Paul glanced down the row of patrons at the bar. One held up an empty glass in the air. "Can we do this another time? Christ, I'm slammed tonight."

"We need to do this now," Jacob said. There was some satisfaction knowing he was pissing the guy off. Did he think cops showed up this late on a Sunday to chat for no good reason?

Paul frowned. "Let me fill a couple of orders and get a waitress to cover."

Jacob nodded and watched as Paul filled two beers from the tap, made a gin and tonic and a rum and Coke. He pulled a waitress from the floor and moved to the end of the bar, where he lifted the end piece and came out from behind.

Paul motioned for Jacob and Zack to follow him through an office door at the back of the tavern. The office was small and cramped. On the walls was a picture of Tour de France cyclists riding through a field of sunflowers. Under it stood an old desk. The surface of it was covered with loose papers and a computer that looked fairly new. The chair behind the desk looked ergonomic. As if *he* needed the support.

Paul closed the door, muffling most of the loud music. Still, Jacob could feel the beat in his chest. With the three clustered in the room, there was almost no room to maneuver.

Paul stayed by the door.

Zack slid his hand into his pocket and relaxed his stance as if he had all the time in the world. "Is it true you finished second at Kona about ten years ago?" Kona was one of the world's most grueling Ironman competitions, consisting of a 2-mile ocean swim, a 112-mile bike ride over rough terrain, and a 26-mile run.

The compliment relaxed Paul a fraction. "Third."

Zack's grin was boyish but calculated. "I've done a few longer triathlons, but an Ironman, that's a big bite. How long did it take you to finish?"

"Nine hours, twenty-two minutes."

Zack nodded. "Impressive."

Paul folded his arms over his chest. "So has Vicky been arrested for drugs? Because I can tell you if she has, I had nothing to do with it."

Jacob glanced down at Paul's desk, which brushed his thigh. "Why would Ms. Draper mention your name?"

Paul shoved out a breath. "Because that's what Vicky does. She lies. She uses drugs, deals occasionally, and she can be a real pain in the ass."

Zack tore his gaze from the framed poster. "So why not fire her?"

"Because when she is here, she's a damn good waitress. Few can handle tables like she does. And the customers love her. Liquor sales always go up twenty percent when she's behind the bar. She knows how to work the men."

Zack folded his arms. "Weren't you worried when she didn't show Friday?"

"Sure, a little. But I figured it was like the last time. She had drank too much and was sleeping it off. I knew she'd call, promise to make it up, and we'd get back to business as usual. Employees not showing in this business isn't unheard of. You learn to be flexible."

"She never called to check in with you at all?" Zack asked.

"Nope." Paul shook his head. "But that's her. Once she didn't show for a week." His gaze darted between the two detectives.

"When is the last time you saw her?" Jacob asked.

"Wednesday night. She has Thursdays off. Mind telling me what this is about? Do I need to bail her out or something?"

Jacob flexed his fingers. "Vicky is dead."

The color drained from Paul's face. His stance wavered. "What?"

Jacob kept the tone of his voice steady. "Her body was found this morning."

"Shit." Paul dragged his hand through his hair. "Shit. God, I wish I could say this is totally unexpected, but it's not. She hangs with a hard crowd."

"Can you tell us who she hung out with? Friends, boyfriends, anyone we could talk to?" Jacob asked.

Paul shook his head again. The guy looked shocked but that didn't mean squat. Jacob had crossed his share of talented liars. "I don't know."

"There must be someone we can talk to about her."

Paul shrugged. "Vicky knew everybody and everybody knew her but she was like a butterfly. She flitted around a lot but rarely landed. She wasn't close to anyone. Her ex-husband moved out of state at least a year ago and her latest boyfriend is in jail, from what I hear. There could be someone new in her life but I don't know who it is."

"Meaning?" Zack asked.

Paul sighed. "She partied with everyone but, like I said, she never got close to anyone. Hell, I slept with her."

"You two were lovers?"

He grimaced at the word. "Nothing that serious. It was a little quick, free love kinda thing. That's it. No strings. Hell, I think she was doing the bartender the night after she was with me."

"And that didn't bother you?" Jacob asked. The guy was a little too easygoing for his taste.

"Like I said, it was sex." He shook his head. "I know as much about her today as I did the day I met her. She played her cards close."

"Ever wonder why?" Jacob asked.

"As long as she showed up for work, I didn't care. And I didn't ask. Vicky wasn't the kind of woman you had deep conversations with."

"But you had to wonder about her a little," Jacob said. "Where she came from, what she did when she wasn't here."

Paul shoved his hands into the front pockets of his jeans. "Maybe once or twice. The woman didn't encourage deep thought. She was strictly about fun."

"The coroner said she had an old scar on her hand. Looked like an old defensive wound." Jacob had checked with the women's prison and asked if she'd been in a fight. She hadn't. "She was sliced up pretty badly. Know anything about that?"

Paul shook his head. "Yeah, I saw that. I asked her once. She made some glib joke that told me nothing."

The small office was warm and Jacob considered removing his jacket, but the confined space made it not worth the effort. "Do you have her home address?"

"Yeah." Paul turned to his computer and punched a couple of keys. An address popped up and he wrote it down on a slip of paper. Jacob noted the guy was left-handed. Vicky had been hit on the right side of her face, suggesting her attacker was a lefty.

Jacob accepted the paper. "Don't stray too far. We may have more questions."

Paul nodded. "Sure. This all seems like overkill, don't you think?"

Jacob paused. "How so?"

"She died of an overdose, right? I mean, why does the county need two cops to figure out why a junkie died?"

"Why would you say that?" Zack asked.

"Come on, the life she lived—it was a matter of time before her liver gave out."

"She didn't die of an overdose," Jacob said. "She was murdered."

Paul's face tightened and paled. "What?"

"That's right."

"Hey, will you keep me posted?" The question seemed to come more out of a morbid curiosity than concern.

Jacob ignored the question, simply saying, "We'll be in touch if we need more."

The detectives left Paul standing in his office, his face tight with shock. They plunged back into the noise of the tavern and out the front door into the cold. Jacob felt the chill all the more after leaving Paul's overheated office. The two got into the car and Jacob fired up the engine.

"Let's see if we can get into Vicky's apartment tonight."

Zack nodded. "Let me just call Lindsay and tell her I'll be late."

"Sure."

Zack dialed the number as Jacob pulled into traffic. After a moment's pause, Zack said, "Hey, babe, I'm gonna be late."

Jacob didn't hear the response, but judging by Zack's expression she accepted the change in plans with grace.

"Please do me a favor and don't overdo it. Put your feet up." Zack frowned, an indication that he was already worried if his wife would ease up. "I love you." After a moment's hesitation, he hung up.

Jacob tightened his hands on the wheel as they came to a stoplight and did his best to convince himself that a solitary life was the only kind for him.

Zack closed his phone. "She's at the women's center unpacking boxes."

"Is she doing all right?"

"Yeah, great. I just wish she'd ease up."

"You need to ease up."

Zack tapped the phone against his leg as if he was debating whether or not to call her again. "You're right."

The light turned green and Jacob moved through the intersection. Zack punched the victim's address into the computer. Seconds later a map appeared. "It's about five miles from here. It's not an apartment but a motel."

By the time they arrived at the address, Zack had also contacted the motel's manager and told her to expect them. The building was all brick, one story, modular squares, and no character. The place looked as if it had been built in the early fifties. A collection of cars was parked in front of the motel doors.

Jacob parked in a spot in the lot and the two walked to the manager's apartment. Jacob knocked. From inside they could hear the blare of a television.

Seconds passed and the door snapped open. The woman standing in the doorway was in her sixties. A rubber band bound thinning salt-and-pepper hair into a low ponytail. She had shrugged on a parka over what looked like pajama pants and a T-shirt.

"Mrs. Mullin?" Jacob asked.

Her eyes narrowed. "You the cops, aren't you?"

"Yes, ma'am. We've come to see Vicky Draper's room."

She nodded, fished keys out of her pocket, and closed the door behind her. "Be glad to show you her place. But technically it ain't her place no more. It's mine."

The wind blew across a courtyard illuminated by security lights and the random light from the motel rooms. "How's that?" Jacob asked.

"She ain't paid her rent in two weeks. Yesterday was her drop-dead day to pay or get out. I changed the locks on her place this morning."

Jacob swallowed an oath. "Did you remove any of her belongings?"

"Was planning to do it first thing tomorrow. You lucked out, coming when you did. Another day and I'd have cleaned the place out."

"So you don't mind if we search the place?"

"Naw."

Jacob and Zack ducked their heads against the wind and followed the manager up a flight of stairs to the corner room, Number 4. The keys rattled as she searched for the right one. She tried the key once, cursed when it didn't work, and then after a second try turned the lock. She pushed open the door and flipped on the lights. "Here is Ms. Draper's apartment."

Jacob and Zack moved past her into the tiny space. An unmade bed on the left side of the room was covered with candy bar wrappers and empty take-out food cartons. The bureau across from the bed was cluttered with makeup, hairbrushes, more candy wrappers, pill bottles, and empty paper coffee cups. Ashtrays overflowed with butts and ashes. Clothes littered a filthy brown shag carpet.

The room smelled of trash, stale cigarettes, and booze.

Mrs. Mullin shook her head. "The girl is a pig. No doubt about it. White trash is what she is. I'm gonna have to have the place sprayed for roaches, and the carpet is so stained in places I just may have to replace it."

Jacob started to move around the room, careful not to disturb anything. Vicky's place had all the signs of a junkie's pad—the candy wrappers, the coffee cups, the pill bottles. "Did she have many visitors?"

"All the time. Men mostly. I didn't like the looks of most of them, but as long as she paid her rent and kept the noise down I didn't question too much."

He moved to the nightstand by the bed. A black rotary phone sat beside stacks of receipts, another full ashtray, and old magazines.

Zack moved to the bureau and studied the contents. He was careful not to touch anything.

"What about family?" Jacob asked.

"None that I knew of. I asked her once where her people came from but she just mumbled out an answer about a couple of losers.

"So what has Vicky done this time? Bad checks? Drugs?" She reached into her coat pocket, fished out a cigarette, and lit it up. Smoke curled around her head.

Jacob frowned. "Ms. Draper is dead."

Mrs. Mullin choked on the smoke in her lungs. It took her a moment to get it out. "Hey, when I said her drop-dead deadline, I didn't mean that literal like."

Jacob nodded. "I understand."

"I mean, the girl and I had words often enough. She had a mouth like a trucker." She puffed on her cigarette. "We had some knock-down, drag-out fights, but it was always over rent." Mrs. Mullin shifted her feet nervously, as if she gauged each word. "Nothing personal."

People tended to get nervous around cops. Everyone gauged his or her words when cops started asking questions.

Zack leaned over the bureau studying a mound of

pills that looked prescription. "Prozac. Was she seeing a psychiatrist?"

Mrs. Mullin's laugh sounded like a snort. "She could have used one, if you ask me. But she didn't have the money to pay her rent, let alone a shrink. She had friends who worked in doctors' offices. I'm sure they hooked her up with the pills."

Two victims. Both strangled. A prude. And a drug addict. Their only link was their physical appearance. And the charms.

Dark hair. Tall. High cheekbones.

Like Kendall.

"Warwick, have a look at this." Zack stared at an ashtray at the end of the bureau.

Mrs. Mullin leaned forward to see what he was talking about. She started to follow Jacob, but he shot her a warning glance that halted her in her tracks.

In the center of the ashtray laid remnants of a piece of yellow paper that had been burned. Most of the paper was blackened ash, but there was a tiny section in the center that hadn't burned.

Jacob frowned as he stared at the script. Damn. "Do you see it?"

"Yeah," Zack said.

"What is it?" Mrs. Mullin asked. She'd inched forward and wrinkled her nose as she tried to peer toward the nightstand.

"Don't worry about it," Jacob said. He reached in his pocket and pulled out rubber gloves.

Mrs. Mullin sniffed. "This is my property. I got a right to know."

Jacob flipped open his cell. "Ma'am, you need to consider this room sealed for the duration. It's a crime scene now." He dialed the station and requested a forensics van.

The writer's heavy hand had practically sliced through the paper with the tip of the pen. Though most of the note had been destroyed, the remaining four words were very clear.

*Judith, when I find you.*

# Chapter Twelve

The Channel 10 news station was Jacob's first stop of the day. Deliberately, he'd arrived early, knowing Kendall generally arrived around two. He wanted to talk to her boss, Brett Newington, uninterrupted.

It had continued to plague him that the two victims looked alike and both resembled Kendall.

The lobby had undergone a massive renovation. The art deco style and faded gray carpet were gone. Now there was a sleek modern look that featured lots of glass, a polished receptionist desk, and new carpeting.

On the walls were the pictures of the station's different anchors. Kendall's image was the centerpiece. Her gaze was direct, her smile bright. Behind her green eyes was an intelligence that sparked and set her apart from just about everybody. The arch in her left eyebrow suggested she knew a secret or a private joke that the rest of the world didn't know.

Jacob slipped his hand into his pocket. Since he'd first seen her on TV last year, he'd dreamed about her. There'd been other women in his life, but his thoughts kept returning to her. She'd gotten into his blood. And it annoyed the hell out of him. Nothing like wanting what you could never have.

He turned to the receptionist, pulled out his badge, and introduced himself. "I'd like to see Brett Newington."

The receptionist's eyes rounded in surprise. She picked up her phone and dialed a number. She dropped her voice an octave. "There's a Detective Warwick here to see you." She listened, then replaced the receiver. "He'll be right out."

Jacob didn't have long to wait. Brett Newington appeared within seconds. The guy wore gray creased pants, a white shirt with his initials monogrammed on the cuffs. His shoes were polished, expensive. No tie. One thousand–watt smile that didn't touch his eyes.

So Kendall and this guy had been an item? Jacob never would have put the two together. Her personality was too strong, too vibrant. She'd have eaten this guy for lunch. He could see a guy like this—the kind who thought he was hot shit—getting pissed that a woman like Kendall had dumped him.

"Detective Warwick," Brett said, extending his hand. "Is there a problem?"

The receptionist had bowed her head but Warwick knew she wasn't missing a bit of the conversation.

"I have a few questions for you. Is there somewhere we could speak in private?"

"Sure." He glanced at the receptionist, who had become very interested in a memo. "Sally, would you hold my calls?"

"Sure, Mr. Newington."

Brett nodded and without a word turned and headed down a hallway. Jacob followed. The renovation had extended down the hallway, leaving behind the faint smell of new paint and carpet.

They passed by one office and Jacob noted the name Kendall Shaw on the door. An intern stopped Brett with a question right in front of her open door. Jacob glanced into her office and, like yesterday, was surprised the space was so small. Like everything else about Kendall, it was tasteful, discreet.

"She wouldn't take a bigger office," Brett said. He answered the intern's question and it was just the two of them again. "She likes being close to the action."

Jacob would have figured she'd have wanted all the bells and whistles that went with fame. He nodded and followed Brett into his corner office. This space was three times the size of Kendall's. In the corner there was a small round conference table with three chairs around it and across the room Brett's wide desk. It was glass, sleek, and covered with files and tapes. Certificates documenting Brett's accolades covered white walls. The guy had had an impressive career.

Brett closed the door. He chose to sit behind his own massive desk instead of at the conference table. "Have a seat."

Jacob sat across from Brett's desk. If the guy thought a piece of furniture could intimidate him, he was wrong.

A collection of pictures on the credenza behind Brett stared back at him. One of the larger ones was of Kendall and Brett. Kendall stared directly at the camera, her smile brilliant. Brett was grinning but he wasn't staring at the camera, but at Kendall. There was no missing the fact that the guy had a thing for her.

"Nice picture," Jacob said. "When was it taken?"

Brett followed his gaze. "It was taken about five months ago, the night Kendall did her first broadcast as the evening anchor." Everyone around them in the photo held up champagne glasses.

Jacob remembered the broadcast. "Looks like it was a big party."

"It was. Convincing Kendall to join our anchor team was a huge coup. She cost me a small fortune, but she's been worth it."

Newington made Kendall sound like a prized mare.

"How are your ratings?"

"Never better. The public can't get enough of Kendall. She's a beautiful woman, if you hadn't noticed."

"Hard not to."

"Between you and me, she's high maintenance."

The woman Jacob had seen yesterday seemed anything but high maintenance. She was smart and hardworking. "Really?"

Brett frowned. "It's no secret that we dated once. I broke it off because she was calling me at all times of the night. It got very tiring after a while."

The guy's candor surprised Jacob. "That would have been last winter."

"Yes."

"Her mother was dying about that time."

"Yes."

"Seems natural a woman would call her boyfriend for support."

He straightened. "Look, I tried to be sympathetic. I really did. But it got to be a terrible drain. I couldn't work during the day because she'd had me up all night." He dropped his gaze and removed an imaginary piece of lint from his pants. "It might have been different if Mrs. Shaw liked me. But she made it clear she wasn't happy about me or the fact that Kendall was on television."

"Why's that?"

"Mrs. Shaw was an intensely private woman. There were times when I thought she wanted to keep Kendall

all to herself. I tried to mention this to Kendall but she wouldn't hear of it. She was very loyal to her mother."

"No other relatives?"

"None. Frankly, it was her lack of family that appealed to me. My ex-wife had a shitload of relatives who were always getting between us." Brett sat back in his high-backed chair. "So what's this about?"

"Has Ms. Shaw gotten any odd fan mail lately? E-mails or letters that didn't sit right?"

His eyes narrowed. "She's had a couple of e-mails. But that can be par for the course. The world is full of losers who think they know a TV personality. Why are you asking this?"

Jacob let the question slide. "Would you mind getting me copies? I'd like to look them over."

Brett's chair squeaked as he leaned forward. "Has Kendall reported some kind of threat? She should have come to me with a problem like that first."

"No threats."

Brett checked his watch. "What's the point of this conversation?"

"Just following a train of thought. If you'll get me those e-mails that should be it."

He picked up his phone. "Can you make a CD of Kendall's fan e-mail? Great. When? Right now." He winked at Jacob as if to say no problem.

Brett hung up the phone and leaned back in his chair. "You ever consider granting an interview to Kendall on the Guardian killings from last summer?"

Jacob stiffened. He'd had the question often enough and had always refused. "Does Kendall want an interview?"

Brett dodged the question. "It's still big news. We'd do a first-class job." The bastard's eyes gleamed with anticipation. Jacob's life had been gutted and Newington wanted to turn it into a show.

"What does Kendall say?" His voice was low, more like a growl.

"So far she's said no. She refuses to do the piece. She's being hardheaded about it. But if you said yes, maybe she would say yes."

Jacob's body radiated menace. "No interview. Ever."

Brett cleared his throat, surprised by the ferocity in Jacob's voice. "Right."

The secretary appeared in the doorway with a disk in her hand. "Mr. Newington, I have those e-mails for you."

Brett appeared relieved by her appearance. "Great." He took the disk, dismissed her, and handed it to Jacob.

Jacob pocketed the disk but didn't trust his voice to speak.

Brett swallowed. "Well, you know your way out."

"Yeah, sure."

Jacob made his way to the lobby. He paused at the receptionist's desk. It was amazing what a receptionist knew about people in the office.

What was her name? Sally. "I bet Ms. Shaw gets a lot of e-mail, Sally."

The woman's eyes perked up at the sound of her name. "She gets at least two marriage proposals a month from some fan."

"She must get a kick out of that."

"She tries to answer as many as she can."

"Any regulars sending her e-mail?"

"I hear she's got a few who e-mail her regularly."

"Is Ms. Shaw dating anyone?"

The woman's eyes took on a knowing look. "No."

"What about Newington?"

That question made her frown. She didn't like the guy. "No."

Jacob thought about the photo behind Brett's desk of

Brett and Kendall. The son of a bitch still had a thing for Kendall. "Thank you for your time."

"Sure, no problem."

Jacob strode out of the building and climbed into his car. He thought about Brett's request for a Guardian interview.

*She's being hardheaded about it.*

Clearly Brett had put the pressure on Kendall to conduct one. But she'd refused.

Ironic. He'd felt so much damn guilt over her shooting, she would have been the one person who would have gotten a *yes* had she ever asked him for an interview.

He fired up the car engine.

His sense of obligation to Kendall deepened. If there were a nut out there threatening her, he'd do whatever it'd take to protect her.

Kendall was running late. After she'd found the letter last night, she'd been wired and figured she'd not sleep anymore. But just before dawn, she'd dozed off and hadn't awakened until nine-thirty.

She clamped on a gold shackle bracelet as she hurried down the center staircase. She'd chosen a winter-white dress that accentuated her slim figure and set off her olive skin and dark hair. Along with the bracelet she wore matching gold earrings that dangled just a little.

She'd planned to leave the house by nine so she could swing by Serenity Family Services before work. It hadn't been a part of her adoption but she wanted to talk to Carnie Winchester about performing a search. When Carnie had spoken to Nicole, she'd seemed to understand the ins and outs of the adoption maze, and Kendall realized this was an area where she'd need help.

But she had to hurry. She would have loved to devote

the day to Carnie but it was just a matter of time before the cops would announce the name of the latest murder victim to the press and she wanted to be on hand to cover the announcement. She had sent another e-mail to the tipster who'd helped her with the White murder but there'd been no response.

The front doorbell rang. Her high heels clicked across the floor as she hurried to answer it. Through the oval window by the door, she saw her carpenter, Todd. A part of her was grateful he was there, so he could get closer to finishing up the job. Another part was already weary of having a stranger in her house. The sooner the job was completed, the better.

She snapped open the door. "Good morning."

The man touched the bill of his ball cap. In his other hand he held a dented toolbox. "Morning, Ms. Shaw."

She braced against a cold gust of air and stepped to the side. "Come on in. You know the way to the kitchen."

He grinned, wiped his feet, and came inside. "Yes, ma'am."

She closed the door and rubbed her hands together. "So how is it going?"

"Real well. I got the plumbing and wiring done for the new appliances and the cabinets will be here later today."

"So you're on schedule?"

"Yes, ma'am."

"You're an angel."

The comment made him blush. "Just doing my job."

She followed him as he headed toward the kitchen. "Believe me, a contractor who runs on time is a rare and wonderful thing." She stopped at the coat closet in the hallway, pulled out her white coat, and slipped it on. "So I'll have new cabinets tonight?"

"That you will."

"Great." She tied the coat's belt into a knot. "I've got

to leave early today. "My roommate is still here but she's up and awake."

"Good. I don't like waking her. She needs all the sleep she can get. When is the little one due?"

"Just a couple of weeks."

"She must be excited."

"She's ready to have this baby born." She checked her watch. "I've got to run."

"Go on ahead."

Just as she snapped up her purse her cell rang. Biting back an oath, she dug it out and pushed it open. "Kendall Shaw."

Brett was on the other end. "Warwick was just here."

Kendall smiled at Todd, turned, and moved toward the front door. "What did he want?"

"He was asking questions about you. And any e-mails you received."

That shocked her. She thought about the tipster's text message. It wouldn't be on the station's server but would show on her phone records. Warwick's tenacity could easily lead him to her cell records. "Why?"

"That's what I want to know."

The two victims looked like her. She'd promised not to tell. And she wouldn't, though it was the worst decision she could make as a reporter. "I have no idea what he was after."

Kendall heard Brett close the door to his office. "I don't like being treated like an outsider, Kendall. You aren't telling me the whole truth."

The emotion in Brett's voice caught her off guard. "Why would I hold back?"

"That's what I'm wondering."

Todd clanged open a toolbox and pulled out a wrench.

"I don't have time for this now. I'll be at the office soon," she said.

"Are you and Warwick dating?"

"What?" Her surprise was genuine. "No."

A tense silence followed. "When you get to the office we need to talk. About us. And this time I'm going to do the talking." He sounded angry, frustrated. "We have a lot to iron out."

Iron out? There was nothing left for them. She wasn't sure if there had ever been anything between them. Aware Todd was in earshot, she bit back a retort. "See you later."

"Everything all right?" Todd asked, poking his head around the side of the kitchen door.

Her heart pounded in her chest. The exchange had made her angry. "Yeah. It's nothing." She grabbed her purse and smiled. "See you tomorrow."

The cold air cooled her flushed cheeks the instant she stepped outside. She hurried to her car, started the engine, and pulled out of the garage. At this time of the morning, the heavy traffic of commuters had subsided, so the drive through the city took only minutes. She pulled up in front of the adoption agency, then drove to the parking lot behind the building and parked.

Kendall hurried up the brick front steps of the simple building and pushed through the front door. The directory in the foyer read SERENITY FAMILY SERVICES, ROOM 204. She dashed up the side stairs and down the second-floor hallway. She entered the suite.

No one was at the receptionist's desk. She glanced to the two offices behind the desk, one open and one closed.

"Hello? Kendall Shaw here."

"Come in." The voice came from the open door.

She peeked into the office. Behind the desk sat Carnie. She'd pulled her red hair into a ponytail. Soft curls framed her pale face and accentuated the freckles covering her slim nose. She wore a dark green turtleneck, black drop beaded earrings, and jeans. Smiling, she rose. There was a relaxed easiness about her that Kendall envied.

"Carnie," Kendall said with a rush of relief.

"Kendall Shaw."

"Thanks for agreeing to see me." She shrugged off her coat and draped it over her arm.

"What can I do for you?" She gestured toward a chair in front of her desk.

Kendall sat down and fearing she'd lose her nerve spoke quickly. "I wanted to talk to you about an adoption."

Carnie nodded. "I can't discuss anything about Nicole's adoption plan."

"No. No. I understand that. This isn't about Nicole. It's about me."

Patient green eyes focused on her. Waited.

Kendall moistened dry lips. "I want to talk about . . ." Even now the words stuck in her throat. She sat a little straighter. "About my adoption."

Carnie's eyebrows rose. "What can I do to help you?"

Kendall tapped her foot. In the span of seconds, she felt disloyal to her mother and angry that the same woman had so completely hidden the truth of her past. She pulled the letter from her briefcase. "I found this in my mother's paperwork." She handed the paper to Carnie.

She studied the paper. "What do you need from me?"

Her mouth felt dry. "I want to find out about my birth parents. Can you help me find them?"

Carnie sighed. "It's not that simple."

"What do you mean? I'm over twenty-one." She hesitated. "My adoptive parents are dead. Why can't you just point me in the right direction? Isn't there someplace where these records are kept?"

Carnie sat back and set the letter on the pile of papers in the middle of her desk. "Your adoption was a closed adoption and it took place before nineteen eighty-nine."

Impatience welled. "Okay."

"The search process is much more detailed in cases like yours."

"But they are *my* records. I have a right to know where I came from."

Carnie kept her voice even, but the frown lines around her mouth deepened. "Hey, I'm on your side. I'm an adult adoptee and I'm searching for my birth family too. And for the record, I've been searching for three years."

"*Three years.*" God, she couldn't go three years of more dreams.

A bitter smile tipped the edge of Carnie's full lips. "Don't get me started."

"So what are you telling me, that it's going to take years to find my family?"

"Virginia has very clear laws about closed adoption searches. But that doesn't mean all this is impossible. Who knows? You might get lucky and the search will go quickly."

Kendall was good at masking her emotions. Anger or frustration could shut down an interview in a flash. She had to keep her cool. But it was a struggle to keep calm. "What do I do?"

Carnie looked truly sorry. "The search has to be done through the agency that placed you." She glanced at the paper. "Virginia Adoption Services. I know them. They had a fire in their building last fall. They lost a lot of paperwork and were forced to close their doors. I'll have to do a little checking to see what records survived and whom they turned their records over to."

"Then what?"

"The social worker who now has charge of your file will contact the birth parents, and if they are willing to meet or have contact, they will let the social worker know."

"And if they don't want to see me?"

"Then that's the end of it." Carnie's eyes softened. "There's another wrinkle. If your birth parents have passed, then the search gets more complicated."

Kendall leaned forward. "What do you mean?"

"The social worker would have to determine if you have any siblings and if they are aware of the adoption. If they're not, then the social worker can't pass any information on to you."

Resentment and desperation collided in her. "I need to know where I came from."

Carnie pulled out a stack of forms. "I know. I know. It can be frustrating."

"My life feels like a movie. Like I've walked in the middle of the first act. Only what is happening now directly relates to the first moments of the movie."

"Look, let's get the process started. See what happens. It may go faster than you think."

Kendall pursed her lips. "Fine. Whatever."

"I'll do what I can to help you."

Kendall sighed. "Look, I know I'm being a bitch about this. And I do appreciate your help. I'm just frustrated."

"I understand."

Kendall clenched her fists. "I can't believe this is going to be so difficult."

"Did your mother have friends at the time of your adoption?"

Kendall shrugged. "I suppose. Why?"

"The adoption process can be quite emotional for the adoptive parents. Often they confide in friends or family about what is happening."

"My mother wasn't the chatty type."

"You'd be surprised how women talk when it comes to becoming a mother."

Kendall's heart raced at the possibility. She thought back to the photo album her mother had kept and remembered seeing a picture of a woman her mother had once been close friends with. "There was one woman." What was her name? Jenny somebody. Her name was in the album.

"Start with her. In the meantime, I'll track down the contact person who is now handling the agency's records."

Already her mind skipped ahead to finding this woman. She rose. "Carnie, thanks. I mean that."

"No sweat. Keep me posted, will you? I want to know how this goes for you."

"Sure." She paused. "No one knows that I'm adopted and I'd like to keep it that way for now."

"Of course."

Kendall left Carnie's office and drove straight back to her house. For so many years she'd pushed the thought of a search out of her mind and now it consumed her as if her life depended on it. As she waited for a light to change from red to green, she pushed open her cell phone and dialed Brett's number. He picked up on the second ring.

"Brett, it's Kendall."

"Kendall. Where are you?" He sounded annoyed. Typical.

"It's a long story, but I'm going to be late today. I'll be back in time for the editorial meeting at two."

He huffed into the phone. "Kendall, I need you here. The day is jam-packed."

"I edited the footage from the double murder story last night. My copy is written. If the police announce the name of the second victim call me. I'll come back." No sense telling him she was sorry. She wasn't.

"This isn't like you."

No, it wasn't. Work and deadlines had always come first for her. But she couldn't explain to Brett that she needed to find her birth family. She needed to finally fill the hole that had been inside her for as long as she could remember. "Like I said, I'll be there as soon as I can."

Brett's voice dropped. "Are you with a guy?"

"What?" She would have laughed if not for the bite in his voice.

"That cop who was here this morning. You're seeing him, aren't you?" Anger hissed.

Her spine straightened. "Who I spend my time with is none of your business."

"It is if it impacts this station."

She could picture him sitting at his desk staring out the window, his back to his office door. "The station isn't going to fall apart because I'm a couple of hours late today."

"Get back to the station now, Kendall."

"I'll be in soon."

"I hired you; I can fire you."

She couldn't believe they were having this conversation. "My ratings are too good. You'd be a fool to fire me."

"Everyone's replaceable."

She gripped the phone. "You manipulative worm. How dare you threaten me. I'm good at what I do and the ratings went up because of *me* just as much as your advertising campaign."

"Don't be so sure."

"I can leave Channel Ten and get picked up by another station." The money wouldn't be as good, but she'd manage, even if she had to sell her house and move to another market. Of course, leaving Richmond now was not what she wanted. But pride kept her from backing down.

Brett was silent for a moment before he sighed into the phone. "Kendall, just come by the station. We need to talk. You're making me nuts."

A horn behind her blared and she realized the light had turned green. "I'll see you at two and if that means you have to fire me, then so be it."

She hung up, tossed the phone onto the passenger seat, and punched the gas. Anger roiled inside her. Her cell phone rang. She didn't need to glance at the phone to know it was Brett. She turned off the phone and headed to her house. She parked in front and dashed up the front steps.

When she pushed through the front door of the house, a heavy haze of sawdust lingered in the air. A machine blared in the kitchen. Todd was sanding floors today. The cabinets were coming today. Todd was friendly and liked to chat, but she didn't have the patience for small talk so she bypassed the kitchen and dashed upstairs to the second bedroom, where she kept the photo album tucked in a box under the bed.

She flipped the pages of the album until she found the picture of her mother and Jenny. The caption read *Irene and Jenny Thornton celebrate their fortieth birthdays.*

Kendall had forgotten that Irene and Jenny shared the same birthday. She moved to her bedside and pulled out a phone book. She scanned the *T*'s until she found Mrs. Jennifer R. Thornton. Shoreham Drive.

She dialed the number. Her heart raced.

On the third ring the phone was picked up. "Hello." The woman's voice was old, fragile.

Kendall cleared her throat. "I'm looking for Jenny Thornton. She was a friend of Irene Shaw."

Silence followed. "Who is this?"

She gripped the phone. "This is Kendall. Irene's daughter."

"Kendall. I haven't seen you since you were a toddler."
Running water from a tap in the background shut off.

Her throat felt dry. "I was wondering if I could come
by and talk to you about Mom."

"Sure, honey, when?"

Emotion welled inside her. The hectic pace of these
last few months had pushed thoughts of her mother
from her mind. She'd almost thought she was immune
to the grief. Now she realized she wasn't. Her mom
would be so disappointed if she knew about this search.
She shoved the guilt aside. "Now."

"Sure. You come on by. I'd love to see you. My word,
it's been so long."

The distance of the phone annoyed Kendall. She
needed to see Mrs. Thornton, look her in the eye when
they spoke. "Thanks."

Kendall hung up the phone and hurried down the
stairs. Todd had turned off the sander, and when she
reached for the front door he poked his head out of
the kitchen. Sawdust covered his hair. "Ms. Shaw. I
thought you'd left for work."

She forced a smile. "I forgot something. I was just
heading back out."

He nodded as he dug his hand into his pocket. "I
found something I thought you might be interested in."

"Please don't tell me you found rotted floorboards or
a dead body behind the wall."

He grinned. "Nothing so serious." He pulled a small
mirror from his pocket. "Found this behind the wall."

She crossed the hallway toward him and accepted the
mirror. Trimmed in silver, it fit into her palm. The silver
had tarnished and the glass had grown dull. It wasn't an
expensive piece but it possessed a charm. She turned it
over and scrawled on the back was the initial *E*.

"Where did you say you found this?"

"It was behind the cabinets. Must have been put there when the last kitchen renovation was done."

"That would have been in the late fifties."

He shoved worn, calloused hands through his dark graying hair. "Maybe. Likely some little girl tucked it away and then lost track of it."

She turned the mirror over in her hands trying to imagine the owner. A flicker of a memory danced at the edge of her mind and then it was gone.

He took a step back. "Well, I best get back to work. And you look like you're in a rush."

She tore her gaze from the mirror. "Yeah. Thanks, Todd."

"Glad to help. And you'll be glad to know that your cabinets are on schedule. I gave the manufacturer hell when he told me he was going to be late."

The renovation had been so important to her just days ago and now it felt so unimportant. "Thanks."

She tucked the mirror in her pocket and left him standing in the hallway. The cold morning air bit her skin as she dashed toward her car. Just in the last few minutes, the heat had dissipated and the interior was cold again.

She slid behind the wheel and fired up the engine. She glanced at her phone and saw that she'd missed two calls. She checked the numbers. Brett. For the first time since she'd taken the job as news anchor, she wondered if she'd made the right decision. Money and fame hadn't satisfied her as she'd thought they would.


The muscles in Jacob's lower back bunched painfully as he pushed through the doors of the conference room. The county's four other homicide detectives were waiting when he strode in. At the head of the table was his boss,

Sergeant David Ayden. To the right sat Zack and across from him sat Detectives Nick Vega and C.C. Ricker. Vega was a New York transplant who'd lived in Virginia fifteen years. Dark hair hinted at Hispanic heritage. C.C. had red, curly hair and an athlete's short, compact body.

Jacob laid his folder on the table, opened it, and removed head shots of the two victims pre- and postmortem. He moved around the conference table to a dry-erase board, where he hung up the pictures with magnets.

Jackie and Vicky were from opposite ends of life. Jackie's straight, conservative haircut contrasted with Vicky's short, spiked hair with purple and red highlights. Vicky had painted her nails black and had six tattoos. Jackie had neatly trimmed nails, no polish, and no tats.

Still, the women shared stunning similarities. High cheekbones. The shape of their lips. And their vivid green eyes.

David sipped his coffee. "Do you think we have a serial killer?"

Leave it to him to voice the fear lurking in all their minds. "Before we go there let's look at what we have so far," Jacob said.

David nodded. "Fair enough. I want my facts crystal clear when I go to the chief."

"Jackie White is our first victim. Thirty-eight. Separated. She and her husband fought a month before she died. Several of her neighbors heard the exchange. He left before anyone thought to call the cops. He had motive and opportunity. The last sighting of Jackie White was on a surveillance tape on Friday night. A man approaches her; then she vanishes from view."

"Is Phil White linked to the second victim?" Nick asked.

"No," Zack answered. "He has an airtight alibi for that

murder. He was marrying his pregnant girlfriend in a church in Northern Virginia. There were twenty witnesses."

A rumble of disapproval echoed in the room.

Jacob shuffled through the file in front of him. "Vicky Draper, age thirty-five. Did five years for drug trafficking. She's been out of jail two years. Her motel room was chockful of prescription drugs. She was last seen on Friday morning. She and a friend of hers were drinking. She went out for more tequila and never came back."

Jacob nodded toward the pictures "Both women were strangled from behind. Both the bodies appear to have been kept in a sitting position before being moved. White's lividity discoloration is more pronounced and suggests the killer kept her body longer."

Zack took over. "Dr. Butler believes the killer had very large, powerful hands. Both women's larynxes were crushed. Both women had rope burns on their wrists and feet."

"We have victims who share similar facial features and they both were wearing identical charms," Jacob said. "Each charm was inscribed with a different name."

Zack continued. "Gold, oval shaped with a name inscribed on them. 'Ruth' on White and 'Judith' on Draper." His gaze settled on Vega and Ricker. "Anything on the necklaces?"

Nick drew circles on the legal pad in front of him. "Nothing. We've hit at least thirty jewelry stores. No one knows anything. We've got detectives in robbery scanning the Net and checking pawnshops as well."

David tapped his pencil on the edge of his legal pad. "So how is he choosing his victims?"

"We don't know yet," Jacob said.

"Ruth and Judith are women in the Bible," Nick offered.

David pressed his fist to the spot above his right eye as

if he had a headache forming. "So we have a religious freak on our hands?"

"My Bible is lacking," Jacob said. "What else can you tell us about these two women—Ruth and Judith. I mean the ones in the Bible."

Nick shrugged. "Both very virtuous. Ruth stayed with her mother-in-law during a great famine. And Judith was a bit of a warrior who helped save her people from the enemy."

C.C. folded her arms. "I'm impressed, Nick."

He shrugged. "Thank Sister Mary Margaret, my Sunday school teacher in the third grade. She made us memorize a good bit of the Bible."

"It's not only the mode of murder but the charms that link these killings," Jacob said.

"Which brings us back to the Bible theory," David said.

A headache throbbed behind Jacob's eyes. "Maybe. But I don't think so." He flipped through the pages of his file.

"Why?" David challenged.

Jacob tapped his finger on his thigh. The Bible theory looked good on paper but his gut told him it wasn't the key to this case. "I don't know."

David arched a brow. "Did these women grow up near each other?"

C.C. rechecked her notes. "No. Jackie was an only child. She went to VCU and got a degree in teaching. Her parents were older. Both passed about eight years ago. Vicky was a foster kid. She bounced around a lot but never could be placed. Trouble from day one."

Two unrelated backgrounds.

Jacob tapped his thumb on the table. The killer saw something in these women that had attracted him to them. Was it simply the brown hair and similar facial features?

David tapped his thumb on the file. "Send a report to ViCAP and CODIS. Let's see if our guy did this thing somewhere else."

"I did that last night," Jacob said.

"Good. These killers don't always just pop up out of nowhere. Often killing is the last step in a string of events."

It was early afternoon when Nicole sat in Carnie Winchester's office and flipped through the pages of the prospective parents. The couples all looked so happy. The descriptions all conveyed their palpable desire for a child.

All were quite capable of giving her child a good home.

She'd narrowed her list down to three couples. She couldn't put into words how she'd narrowed the search. She just knew.

The Latimers. The Davidsons. And the Snyders. They all lived in Richmond. All spoke of love, quality parenting, stable marriages, and nice homes. The Latimers had a son, Billy, who was eighteen months old. The Snyders owned a jewelry shop. The Davidsons had a golden retriever.

They were all perfect.

So why did she feel more frightened than she did when she first walked in here?

Nicole cupped her hand under her belly and rose. She crossed the room and moved to the picture window. Frost covered the glass. The sky was gray and it looked like the city would get more snow.

The baby kicked as if to remind Nicole that she was waiting for her to make a decision.

The door opened. Carnie stood in the doorway. She held two cups of tea. "I thought you could use a break."

Nicole's shoulders sagged with relief. "I wish that would solve all my problems."

Carnie closed the door. The two women met halfway and Nicole accepted the hot cup of tea. Decaf. Herb. Just as she'd asked for the other day. Carnie had remembered.

"So have you made any progress?" Carnie always kept her voice light and soothing.

"I've narrowed the pile to three."

"May I look?"

"Sure."

Carnie sat on the couch, sipped her tea as she stared at the profiles. She nodded. "They're all very good families. They all desperately want a child."

"I can see that." Nicole faced the window. "Then why can't I choose one?"

"It's a big decision, Nicole. Maybe the biggest you'll make in your life."

"I'm paralyzed, Carnie. I've always been able to make decisions. Now I can hardly decide which pair of shoes to wear, let alone who should raise my child."

"This situation is difficult even in the best of times. Toss in a bucket of hormones and it's that much harder. Ease up on yourself."

"Do you have kids?"

A bit of light faded from her eyes. "No." She sighed. "As I told you, I'm adopted. My past is a huge mystery. Having a baby just feels like genetic roulette to me." She offered a wan smile. "It was a big issue for my husband and I. He wanted lots of kids. We divorced over it."

Nicole's back ached and her breasts felt like melons. "I'm sorry to hear that. Do you think my baby will feel this way?"

"My adoption was closed. Yours is going to be an open adoption. Your baby will know how to find you. My guess is that you'll be good with sharing information when the time comes."

Nicole smoothed her hand over her belly. "Of course."

Carnie studied Nicole. "Can you tell me about your baby's father?"

Nicole stiffened. Even now, talking about Richard sent a bolt of fear through her. He was dead, couldn't hurt her. But an illogical part of her brain whispered that he could somehow return from the grave and harm her. "I figured you read the papers last summer."

"I did. But I want to hear it from you."

Nicole straightened, annoyed at her fear. "My husband, Richard, was the most romantic man I'd ever met when he first strolled into my photography studio. So charming. So handsome. So funny."

She dropped her gaze to her thumbnail and studied the rough cuticles. Richard would have been furious if he had seen her right now. For an instant, fear tightened her chest and she had to remind herself that he was dead. Gone.

"After we married everything slowly started to change. He started monitoring my cell phone calls and e-mails. He'd drop in at work and insist I have lunch with him. And then he began hitting me."

Carnie traced the rim of her cup. "I'm sorry."

So was she. "He started to hit me more and more. The last time was the worst. He . . ." She stopped, still not able to put the event into words. Counseling had helped enough that she could say the word. "He raped me. The baby was conceived then."

Carnie's face tightened with sadness. "I can't imagine what you've been through."

"I ran here to Richmond. I moved in with my friend

Lindsay O'Neil and she hid me. The rest was covered by the papers. Richard found us. Nearly killed Lindsay." Nicole's heart rate quickened. The baby kicked. "So here I am unable to love the child growing in my belly."

"You can't say that you don't love this baby. You're bringing it into the world. You're seeing a doctor and you want the best for the child. You're more maternal than you realize."

"So why do I just want this damn pregnancy over with? I want my career to get restarted. I want my life back!"

Carnie smiled. "That's very normal, Nicole. My partner is pregnant with her fourth, and she's ready to jump out of her skin. All she can talk about is seeing her toes again and sleeping on her stomach."

"So I'm normal?"

"You're very normal."

The tension eased from her chest and she was able to sip her tea. "Thanks, Carnie." She glanced at the profiles, still not ready to decide.

"Sleep on it. Another day or two won't matter."

That made her feel better. "Thanks." She checked her watch. "I've got to run. I have an appointment to take pictures of a couple and their dog. All three are wearing matching red sweaters."

Carnie laughed. "Sure."

Nicole grabbed her coat and purse and headed out. When she stepped out the front door, the cold hit her across the face. She turned up her collar and fished her keys out of her pocket. She hurried down the sidewalk and climbed into her car. Breath puffed from her mouth. She stuck the key in the ignition and turned on the engine. Then she turned the heat on full blast. For several minutes it blew cold air. Her toes felt numb. She glanced in her rearview mirror. Someone had written a message on her back windshield. The roughly scrawled letters were backward and hard to read. She got out and waddled around to the back of the car.

Written in the frost was *Hi*.

Most likely a kid had written it. Much like "Wash Me" or some other nonsensical statement.

But it reminded her of something Richard would do in the early days. A simple gesture that no one but her would ever see as a threat. It had been his way of letting her know he was following her. Tracking her.

A chill passed down her spine. She stared at the word until the back window defroster melted it from sight.

Allen sat at the small workbench. An overhead light shone down on the large magnifying glass. He rubbed his dry eyes and stared at the tiny gold oval pendant. With engraver's tools, he carefully started to write the first letter. He added an extra swirl to the *R*, paying close attention to the loop at the end of the letter. His engraving skills were expert.

His first charms, way back in the beginning, had been crude and sloppy. Like a child's. But he'd been a child in so many respects then. It had taken years to hone his skills. He'd started preparing for this moment in Alaska, the frozen land where he'd fled to so long ago to escape the demons. He'd thought that up there he could begin anew. But the demons had followed.

The first woman in Anchorage who had caught his attention had flowing black hair like Her. The woman had been a waitress. The first hint of winter—Termination Dust, snow on the distant mountains that encased the city around the bay—had arrived. The wind had been blowing and the air possessed a chill like nothing he'd felt before.

For one moment he'd stopped short, his breath

frozen in his chest as he'd watched her. The hair had reminded him of the woman he'd loved and despised.

The woman's skin wasn't smooth or pale. It was olive and pockmarked. And she didn't smell like fresh peaches, but of old cooking grease.

But her hair had captivated him. It had allowed him to pretend that she was someone else.

After he'd paid for his meal he'd waited across the street in the cold for her shift to end. He'd waited for nearly three hours.

When she emerged bundled in a parka and smoking a cigarette, he had watched her move down the street to a lot where her car was parked.

She was unlocking the door to her beat-up VW Bug when she'd seen him. He'd smiled, slid his trembling hands into his pants pockets.

Pale moonlight had washed over her face. "Who are you?"

"Sorry," he'd said, careful to keep his body relaxed. "I saw you in the restaurant. Waiting tables. I thought you were someone I knew."

She'd frowned her distrust. "I don't know you."

His gaze had slid to her slim neck, where he imagined he saw the throb of her pulse in the hollow. "My name is Jack." That had been a lie. He'd not given his real name in so long. "I didn't mean to scare you."

Allen had kept his posture relaxed and dropped his gaze before raising it again. He'd wanted her relaxed so he could get closer. He'd just wanted to touch the soft skin of her neck.

The woman had remained suspicious. She'd unlocked her car door and tossed her purse inside. "It's fine. Have a good night."

She'd started to lower herself into the front seat. He'd clenched his fists in his pockets. He hadn't wanted her to leave. Not yet. "Hey, can you suggest a good place to stay tonight? Someplace not too expensive."

She'd shrugged. "There's a motel at the edge of the city. It's called Trail's End. Low prices. Fairly clean."

He'd edged a few steps closer. "Thanks. Now, which way do I head out the main road to get there? I still get turned around here."

Impatience had darkened her eyes. She'd gotten in the car and closed the door. Dismissing him. Rejecting him. An old rage that had lain dormant inside him had flickered and caught fire. In seconds, it had rumbled inside him.

She'd fumbled for her ignition key.

He'd forced a smile and knocked on the glass. To keep her calm, he'd stepped back.

"Hey, I'm sorry to keep bothering you, but I still don't know how to get there from here."

She'd rolled down the window, feeling more relaxed now that she had the car to protect her. "Just follow this road. You can't miss it."

"Right, thanks." He'd watched as she turned her attention to the keys in her hand.

Bitch. How dare she? He was trying to be nice.

With her attention distracted, he'd lunged toward the car and grabbed hold of her neck, her pulse throbbing under his calloused fingers.

Her gaze had shot up to him, panic glistening. A surge of desire had shot through him and he'd squeezed harder. She'd dropped her keys and reached up to his hand trying to pry his hands from her neck and clawing at his skin.

The pain had pissed him off and he'd squeezed harder, making her cough. Tears had rolled down her face. He'd never felt more powerful than he did at that moment. Then the life had drained from her eyes.

She'd passed out. He'd opened her door and lifted her out of the car. He'd put her in the back bed of his truck and covered her with a tarp before driving back to his place in the woods.

For sixty-two days he'd kept her. Those had been good times. And then the day had come to send her home. He'd strangled her and left her body in the woods for the animals.

Allen's mind refocused on the charm in front of him. The engraver's tools shook in his unsteady hands. Even now the memory had the power to excite him.

He blinked and stared through the magnifying glass at the charm. He drew in deep breaths and tried to calm himself, but he couldn't. His hands weren't steady enough to finish the work tonight.

"It's okay. There's still time. No rush."

He studied the *R*. He smiled.

"Rachel isn't going anywhere."

# Chapter Thirteen

Kendall pulled into traffic and ten minutes later was crossing the Huguenot Bridge, which took her to the south side of town, where her parents and she had lived. Gray, overcast clouds hovered above as she turned into the neighborhood that had been built fifty years ago.

Each house was different from the one next to it, a sign that the houses had been built individually over time, rather than all at once by a single developer, like the newer neighborhoods. The yards were large and the trees tall with thick trunks.

She found the mailbox that had THORNTON on it and pulled into the gravel driveway. Her heart pounded in her chest as she stared at the tri-level. The winter sky dulled the house's white color, making it look tired and worn. Boxwoods and a pine tree offered a touch of color in garden beds that were otherwise stripped of greenery.

Kendall got out of the car and crossed the uneven slate sidewalk to a set of steps that led to the front door. She climbed the steps and rang the bell. Seconds passed and there was no sound. For a moment she thought Mrs.

Thornton hadn't heard her and she was tempted to ring the bell a second time. She smoothed damp hands over her skirt.

Then the lace curtains covering a large picture window to her left fluttered. Seconds after that the door opened.

Standing in the doorway was a tall, heavyset elderly woman who was wearing wire-rimmed glasses. A gray pageboy framed her round face. She greeted Kendall with a wide grin. "Kendall Shaw. You are a sight for sore eyes."

Kendall smiled. "Mrs. Thornton."

The screened door creaked open. "You call me Jenny. Now get yourself in here out of that cold."

Kendall stepped over the threshold and was greeted by a rush of very warm air. The house smelled of mothballs and fried eggs. "Thank you for seeing me."

Jenny closed the front door and motioned for Kendall to sit on a couch covered with an afghan. "You could have knocked me over with a feather when you called. Can I get you anything to eat or drink?"

"No. No. I'm fine." Kendall sat.

Jenny eased into a wing chair across from her. "I'm sorry I never made your mother's funeral. I was in the hospital then."

"The flowers you sent were very nice." She tried not to let her impatience show, but it was a struggle to make small talk. "I hope you're feeling better."

"I am. Thank you for asking." She grinned. "But you didn't come here to talk to an old lady about her heart."

Kendall shook her head, relieved by her directness. "No. I came to talk about my mom and my adoption."

Jenny swallowed. "Irene and I used to be such good friends. I never thought we'd ever not be friends, but when she moved across the river we just lost touch."

"Why did she move?"

"She said she and your dad liked the schools over

there better." Jenny shook her head. "There was more to it than that, but when I pressed her, Irene wouldn't say." She reached into her pocket and pulled out a stack of photos. "I dug these out right after you called."

Kendall accepted the pictures. The images were of Kendall and her mother. Kendall couldn't have been more than three. Irene was beaming, but the toddler in her arms was frowning and staring off into the distance as if lost.

"I took those."

Kendall felt as if she held a precious link to her past. She traced the outline of the child Irene held. "Why do I look so sad?"

Jenny shifted as if she wasn't sure how to answer. "I don't know. You were very clingy and fretful those first weeks with Irene. She said you cried a lot and would have terrible tantrums."

She scooted to the edge of her seat. "Can you tell me anything about my birth family? I've been to the adoption agency, but a search is going to take months, possibly years. Did Mom say anything?"

"Your mom and dad had tried for years to have children. Did your mom ever tell you about the baby she had long before you were born?"

Kendall shook her head. "No."

"Irene had a baby when she was twenty. Just a year before she married your dad. It was born out of wedlock. She said the baby died of a heart problem days after it was born. She never could get pregnant again."

Kendall glanced at the picture of a much younger Irene. There was no hint of sadness in her smiling eyes. "I never knew."

"It broke her heart, not having a child. She wanted to adopt but your dad didn't. She worked on him for years to change his mind. Finally, he gave in and they submitted their paperwork. They thought it would be years before a baby would become available, and then out of the blue they got a call in the middle of the night about a little girl who needed fostering. They went right then and there and got you." Jenny smiled. "I'd never seen your mom so happy. And your daddy, despite his misgivings, was as pleased as punch."

"Where did I come from?"

"Your mom never did say. She said it was best to leave the past buried."

Kendall's hopes dashed. "She never told you anything?"

"Well, I do know you came from someplace close."

"Why do you say that?"

"Your mom called me before she left to go get you. Said they'd gotten 'the call.' That was around midnight. They were back by the next morning. That's when I took that picture of Irene holding you."

"And Mom never said anything about my birth family. I was three. I had to have spent some time with my birth family."

Jenny pressed her hands to her lips as she seemed to force her mind to the past. "I remember you were wearing a little blue dress, white socks, and brown lace-up shoes. There was a stain on the dress. Irene threw it out."

"Do you know what it was stained with?"

"No."

"And you smelled like apples and cinnamon."

Kendall clung to the details as if they were precious gems.

"I asked Irene a few times about where you came from. She was very tight-lipped about it. And then out of the blue, Irene announced that you three were moving across the river. I remember she seemed rattled when she told me you all were leaving. Within two weeks the house was sold and you three were gone."

Irene Shaw had been one of the most levelheaded, practical people she'd ever known. Picking up and moving wouldn't have been like her.

"Do you have any idea what rattled Mom so badly?"

Jenny leaned forward. "I was sitting on the back porch. It was winter, but I was having hot flashes back then." She smiled. "You're too young to know about that yet. Anyway, your mom and dad were on their back porch. They didn't see me. I heard them talking about you. Your mom had gotten a call that day and it scared her. She was worried for your safety. Your dad was worried too."

"Did they say anything else?"

"No. But they weren't the kind of people who spooked easily."

Kendall's frustration showed on her face.

Jenny nodded. "I got the impression that the call was about your family. Your *other* family."

She eased forward on her chair. "My birth family?"

"Yes."

"Do you know who called?"

"No. Irene never mentioned the call to me. But she kept talking about *him.* Whoever that is."

Kendall glanced down at the photo taken of her as a child. *What had scared Mom so badly?*


It was nearly midnight when Kendall pulled into her garage.

Earlier, she'd made it to the station with time to spare, but her thoughts had been distracted. She'd mispronounced a name on air and fumbled as she'd struggled to get it right. Kendall had never messed up a name before.

She blamed the mistake on her own wandering

thoughts. She kept replaying her conversation with Jenny and found with each rewind she grew more frustrated.

Brett, thankfully, was cordial and there was no mention of their fight. Of course, he was too much of a professional to upset her before a broadcast. He'd lower the boom later, when it suited him.

But now, she didn't care about that. She was physically and emotionally exhausted. The air was bitter cold and thick clouds blocked the stars and moon. She shut off the car engine and grabbed her purse.

Despite the late hour, her mind was spinning, not with the eleven o'clock broadcast but with her visits to Carnie and Jenny. She was no closer to finding her birth family.

She got out and shuddered against the cold. She couldn't wait to get out of her heels and make a cup of tea. She clicked the keyless entry and the car beeped, signaling it was locked.

Kendall's heels clicked against the garage's concrete floor as she moved toward the door. A motion sensor light mounted in the garage clicked on and cast a circle of light fifteen feet around her.

Normally, she closed the alley door from the inside and left through the door that connected to her backyard, but it was recycling day and Nicole had promised to leave the bin out. Now, she needed to grab the bin. Honestly, she didn't want to fool with it but the last time she'd left one out overnight, it had gotten pinched. City living.

A cold wind sliced down the alley and she braced against the blast as she reached down and picked up the green bin.

As she turned to cut back through the garage, gravel behind her crunched. Footsteps sounded. She whirled around, annoyed that she'd not bothered to pull out her mace.

Standing in the alleyway was a tall man, well over six feet. He wore a heavy coat, faded jeans, and work boots. His hands were thrust into his pockets. Shadows covered his face.

He moved toward her.

Kendall's senses went on overload. She dropped the recycling bin and dug her cell out of her purse. Jacob's comments about her looking like the victims rattled in her head.

She dialed 911 and put her thumb on SEND. "Whoever the hell you are, sport, the cops are on their way."

The man pulled his hands out of his pockets and held them up in surrender. "Hey, lady, don't freak out."

She ignored him and hit SEND, pressing the phone to her ear as she backed up. Her heel caught a patch of ice and she slipped. Adrenaline surged as she righted herself. Her heart felt as if it would burst through her chest.

"Lady, I'm your new neighbor. I live on the other side of the alley."

Kendall swallowed and listened as the operator picked up and said, "Nine-one-one operator. State your emergency."

The guy inched forward so that she could get a good look at his face. He was a rugged-looking man, not handsome, but his face would have caught her eye in any circumstance. Dark hair brushed his collar. There was an edge about him that whispered danger, but he seemed to be doing his best not to look too frightening. He smiled, baring even, white teeth.

"I'm your neighbor. Cole Markham. I've got ID."

"This is Kendall Shaw. I live at one-oh-two Grove Avenue. I'm in the alley and there's a strange man."

Markham let out a sigh and shook his head as if he couldn't believe this. He pulled out his wallet and from that his driver's license.

The 911 operator said, "We will dispatch a car to you right now."

Kendall kept her gaze on Markham. "I'd like to stay on the line until I see the squad car."

"I'll stay on the line," the operator said.

Markham held out his hands. "Honestly, lady, I'm your neighbor."

Kendall lowered the phone away from her mouth. "Explain yourself to the cops."

He shook his head. "You're making a mistake."

She tapped her foot. "We'll see."

Seconds later the flash of blue lights appeared at the alley's entrance. A Richmond city police car screeched around the corner and down the unpaved lane toward them. It stopped just feet from Markham.

Kendall thanked the operator and hung up her phone.

Markham held up his hands as if to show he was no threat. He faced the squad car.

The cops got out, hands on their guns, and strode toward Markham.

"Officers, this is a mistake," Markham said. "I live right here." He nodded his head to the house on the other side of the alley. "I have ID in my right hand."

One of the officers nodded. "Slowly, stretch your hand with the ID out to me."

Kendall glanced at the house behind Markham. Doubt niggled her senses. That house had had a FOR RENT sign on it a few weeks ago. Still, everyone in the area knew it. It would be an easy excuse to toss out. She let the officers do their job.

Markham handed the license to the cop who approached him.

The officer, a short man with powerful arms and a full mustache, shone his light on the identification. "What were you doing outside this late, sir?"

"I was taking out the trash. You can check the bin, if you like. It's full of moving boxes."

The second officer was slim with drawn features. He moved to Markham's bin and peered inside. "It's full of boxes."

Markham looked smug.

The first officer glanced at Kendall. "It's a Virginia license and it does list his address as the property behind you. Let me just run a quick check."

Kendall shoved out a breath. Damn. She'd overreacted.

Markham lowered his hands but kept his body relaxed and nonthreatening. He looked at Kendall as if to say, "I told you so."

She lifted her chin, refusing to admit she was wrong until the officer returned.

The officer came back and handed Markham his license. "You check out. No warrants or alerts."

Markham tucked the license into his wallet and shoved it in his back pocket.

"Sorry to trouble you," the officer said.

Markham smiled. "No sweat. You're just doing your job."

The officer looked at Kendall. "Would you like us to escort you inside?"

"No, I've got it from here. Thanks."

The duo nodded, got in their car, and backed out of the alley.

Kendall glanced at Markham but didn't apologize. She had every right to look out for her own safety. "Welcome to the neighborhood."

He tossed her a half smile that looked almost boyish. "Is this how you greet all your neighbors?"

She shook her head. "Just the tall, scary ones who surprise me in the alley in the middle of the night."

Markham didn't look offended. "So what are you doing out here?"

The question surprised her. "I just got home from work."

He lifted a brow. "Which is?"

Her ego bristled. She was accustomed to being recognized. "I'm Kendall Shaw, the Channel Ten News anchor. I report the news at six and eleven o'clock during the week."

"Sorry." But he didn't sound sorry at all. "I don't watch television."

"Who doesn't watch television?"

"People who read."

"Some of us manage to do both."

"Right."

The adrenaline had eased from her body and she'd become aware again of the cold and the late hour. "Well, you should check out Channel Ten sometime. We're the best in the city."

"I've no doubt."

She picked up her recycling bin. "So are you from Richmond?"

He inched closer but still remained at arms' distance. "No. I'm from out West."

"Where? I've traveled out there quite a bit."

He shrugged. "You name it and I've lived there. But Denver was my home originally."

"And what brought you East?"

"Work."

Asking nosey questions was in her DNA. "What do you do?"

"Insurance."

That was a letdown. She figured him for something more adventurous. "Ah."

He grinned, clearly reading the tone in her voice. "Not as exciting as reporting the news."

She was being rude. "I'm sure it has its moments."

"It can."

"I would think you'd have more of a nine-to-five schedule."

"Oh, I do. I just don't need much sleep and I'm a night owl."

A silence settled between them. She needed sleep more than she needed to stand here and chat with a stranger. "It's late and I've had a long day. You have a very good evening, Mr. Markham."

"I'll do that, Ms. Shaw." He held her gaze just long enough to make her feel the tiniest bit uncomfortable before he smiled. "Sleep tight, Kendall Shaw."

She called herself Amanda now. But Allen knew her true name. Her real identity. To him she was *Rachel*. And she would soon be a part of his Family.

He stared up at her apartment window. Her lithe form passed in front of the window shade. He could make out her trim waist and full breasts as she paced back and forth. She appeared to be on the phone. His groin tightened with desire. He wanted to touch her.

His thoughts were sinful. Evil. And yet he couldn't banish them. Didn't want to banish them. With Ruth he'd kept his desires at bay and Judith had been so full of fight there'd been no room for lust. But Rachel was different. Sweet, soft Rachel pranced in front of him like a wanton goddess. He knew it would be nearly impossible to restrain his sexual desire.

Normally, he didn't like the cold. It reminded him of the days he was on the run and hiding. There'd not always been money for food or heat. But tonight he welcomed the cold and prayed it would cool his sinful thoughts. He unzipped his jacket until a fierce shiver passed through him.

And still the temptation to take her boiled his blood. Slowly, Allen started to pace up and down the sidewalk. Thoughts swirled in his head. It wasn't Sunday yet. It wasn't time to welcome Rachel into the family. But waiting four more days felt like forever.

He reached into his coat pocket and pulled out a cigarette. With a trembling hand, he raised it to his lips, lit it, and took a drag. Inhaling, he savored the burn of tobacco in his lungs. He held the smoke a moment, then exhaled slowly.

"Patience is mine," he muttered.

# Chapter Fourteen

Kendall's cameraman, Mike, turned on the light above his camera and gave her the nod to start speaking.

She flashed her trademark grin. "This is Kendall Shaw reporting from the Central Virginia Women's Center, a new vocational facility to assist women rebuilding their lives after enduring domestic abuse. The center is the brainchild of Lindsay O'Neil Kier, a noted advocate for women."

Public appearances were part of a news anchor's job. Kendall didn't like it but accepted it. However, this event was a project near and dear to her heart.

Mike panned the camera past Kendall to the facility. The building had originally been a tobacco warehouse when built over 150 years ago. It had also served as a food storage facility. The structure had been abandoned for several years until Lindsay and her board chairman, Dana Miller, had convinced the city to donate the facility to them. The two women had marshaled an army of volunteers and within six months had converted the space into meeting rooms and classrooms.

Once inside the building, Kendall casually walked toward Lindsay, who smiled radiantly into the camera. Lindsay was a tall, slim woman who wore her blond hair loose around her shoulders. Beside her stood Dana. Sleek and sophisticated, Dana wore heavy makeup and her black hair smoothed into a tight ponytail.

"Ms. O'Neil and Ms. Miller, congratulations on your grand opening," Kendall said. "This must be an exciting day for you."

Lindsay nodded. "Thanks, Kendall. We're very excited about this new place."

Dana grinned. Not to be outshined, she added, "Lindsay has done a phenomenal job pulling this all together. She is a marvel."

Kendall noted the very slight tension in Lindsay's gaze. The women's advocate understood politics and was willing to go along for her facility. "I couldn't have done it without Dana. She rallied the city and business leaders and made this grand opening happen."

The large front room was filled with local dignitaries who had been invited to the opening. Colorful balloons decorated every corner, a large table laden with food dominated the center of the room, and against an exposed brick wall stood a bar stocked with sodas and non-alcoholic drinks.

Kendall asked Lindsay about the facility and listened as she gave a recap. Dana added her two cents. They'd rehearsed what Lindsay and Dana were going to say moments ago and the interview went precisely as planned. Kendall signed off and Mike cut off the camera.

"Thanks, Mike. Why don't you get something to eat," Kendall said.

Lindsay nodded. "We've got enough food to feed an army."

"Thanks," he said. He patted his tummy. "I never say no to food."

Dana smoothed her hand along the line of her hair. "Thanks, Kendall. I think that went great."

Kendall clicked off her microphone. Her smile was quick and easy but she didn't like Dana. She would not have personally covered this event if she didn't admire Lindsay so much. "Wonderful job, Dana."

Dana spotted someone across the room and smiled. "I see Adam Alderson. Would you two excuse me?" Without waiting for an answer, she moved into the crowd.

Kendall's smile turned genuine. "You've got yourself a winner here, Lindsay."

Lindsay grinned and stared around the room proudly. "I think I do."

Kendall dropped her voice a fraction. "So how did you snag Dana Miller? I thought she was done with you after last summer." Dana had been the board chair of Lindsay's domestic abuse center. When the Guardian killings had been linked to Lindsay, Dana had fired Lindsay and completely distanced herself from her.

"Off the record?"

"Of course," she said honestly.

"She came to me. She wanted to fund a project like this one. I said no at first. Zack was the one who talked me into it. You don't always have to like the people you do business with. And this center is going to help a lot of people." Lindsay smiled and waved to someone. "So how are you doing?"

"Never better." That wasn't true. Sleep was becoming a distant memory, and the lingering questions about her adoption and her birth mother chewed at her almost constantly now. There'd been no more answers since she'd spoken to Jenny a couple of days ago. But the old woman had promised to search her attic and see if there was anything that might help.

A camera lens flashed and Kendall looked up. Nicole was snapping pictures. Lindsay frowned as she watched her very pregnant friend move across the room. "I wish she'd put her feet up and rest."

Kendall shook her head. "I have visions of delivering that baby in the back of a taxi as we race to the hospital. But she shows no sign of slowing down."

"Has she made a decision about the adoption?"

"No." Kendall sighed. "I hear her rattling around the house a lot at night. She's narrowed it down to a couple of families but can't choose."

Lindsay stared at Kendall with a critical eye. "I know what's keeping Nicole awake. What's keeping you up?"

"I sleep like the dead."

"I can see the dark circles under your makeup."

Kendall resisted the urge to check her makeup in the compact in her purse. "Don't worry about me. I've never been better."

A rush of movement by the main entrance caught Kendall's eye. Ever curious, she turned to see Lindsay's husband, Zack, appear and seconds behind him Jacob Warwick.

Lindsay's face softened when she saw her husband and a blush warmed her cheeks. Her face reflected her deep love for the man.

Kendall felt something quite different when her gaze settled on Jacob. Sharp sexual desire shot through her. Her heart beat faster.

Lindsay's gaze shifted back to Kendall and then followed her distracted friend's line of vision to Jacob. She grinned. "Down, girl."

* * *

David Ayden didn't like functions like this, even if the cause was the Women's Center. He understood their place in the world of politics but in his mind they were a waste of time. He had two unsolved murders and yet he and two of his best detectives were making small talk. All the leads on the two women had dried up. They'd learned a great deal and yet nothing that linked the women or could lead them to a killer.

Ayden downed the last of his seltzer and lime and set it down on the bar. He checked his watch. He'd been there twenty minutes. Another ten and he could excuse himself, knowing he had covered his political bases.

These were the times he missed his wife the most. Julie had loved people and she'd loved to talk. She'd never met a stranger. She'd have been in her element in an event like this. A pang of loneliness had his temper rising.

"You look like you just swallowed glass." The familiar feminine voice had him turning and, despite his foul mood, smiling.

"Nicole Piper," he said.

She was wearing a loose peasant top that hugged her round belly and covered the top of faded jeans. Her dark hair curled into soft waves and framed her delicately round face. She wore only a hint of makeup, but it was enough to accentuate her eyes and her full lips. Damn, but he was glad to see her.

"Detective Ayden."

The title reminded him that he was at least a decade older than she was. "David."

Color rose in her cheeks. "David. So are you here to celebrate the big opening?"

He was glad now that he'd come. "It's a big day for Zack and Lindsay. I wouldn't have made the time for anyone else."

Her gaze softened as if she understood. "This place is all she's talked about for weeks."

"Zack has done his share of talking about it as well." David wanted to say something clever to her—something to make her laugh. "Take any good pictures?" He groaned inwardly at the lame question.

Nicole glanced down at her camera. "I did take a great one of Zack and Lindsay." She switched the display to VIEW and flipped through several pictures before she found the one she liked. She leaned toward him and turned the screen so he could see it. This close he could smell her perfume. Soft. Delicate. And yet she was one of the strongest people he knew.

He gave himself a mental shake and stared at the picture. Immediately, he was impressed. It was a great shot. Not your typical grinning faces. Instead, Lindsay was smiling at someone off camera and Zack was staring at her as if she meant the world to him. In one shot, Nicole had captured the essence of their relationship.

"You're a very talented photographer."

Color rose in her cheeks. "Thanks."

Since Julie's death he'd not given much thought to finding someone else. Friends had arranged a few blind dates, but no one had sparked his interest like Nicole. She was an artist. Ten or twelve years his junior. And very pregnant. She'd have been the last person he or anyone else would have chosen for himself. And yet it was all he could do not to grin like a fool. His son Caleb had been right. He liked her.

Before he could come up with something else to say, Dana came up to them. He resented the intrusion and then felt foolish. Nicole wasn't his.

Dana shook his hand. Her grip was firm. Despite her smile, her gaze was cold and accessing. "Sergeant Ayden. Enjoying the party?"

He raised his glass to his lips and then remembered the glass was empty. "It's great."

"I'm glad you're having a good time." Dana turned her attention to Nicole.

He sensed a shift in Dana's energy. Accessing turned to something akin to hunger. Hadn't Nicole said the woman gave her the creeps?

"Nicole, you look wonderful," Dana said.

Nicole smiled, but he saw the tension behind her eyes. "Thank you."

David shifted his stance so that he was a fraction closer to Nicole. "You should be very proud of yourself, Ms. Miller. This is a great project."

Dana beamed. "I'm very proud of it."

Small talk was bullshit as far as he was concerned. But somewhere deep in his memory he heard Julie say, *Play nice.* Someone across the room called Dana's name. She nodded, squeezed Nicole's hand, and then said her good-byes.

Nicole's stance relaxed when she left.

"What's going on?" David said. No sense mincing words. Tension radiated between the two women.

Nicole looked up at him. He expected her to deny any trouble. Instead, she was silent for a moment. "She hasn't really *done* anything that should worry me."

"But . . ."

She dropped her voice a notch and leaned into him like Julie used to when they were at parties. "It's just that it's something about the way she looks at me. The way she always mentions the baby."

His gaze flickered to her stomach. "You *are* very pregnant."

Her hands trembled a little as she fiddled with a button on her camera. "Yeah, but it just feels like more than that."

He didn't like seeing the worry in her eyes. "She made any threats?"

"None." She smiled almost apologetically. "I think the hormones are just making me a little nuts."

David smiled but his concern didn't ease. The brain had a way of processing threats on an unconscious level. People called it intuition or a sixth sense.

Someone like Dana wouldn't make a threat outright. But that didn't mean she wasn't planning something.

He dug his card and a pen from his breast pocket. He scrawled his cell number on the card. "This is my private number. I want you to call me if you even get a whiff of trouble from her."

She accepted the card. "I didn't mean for you to take up my cause. I can handle Dana."

"Why go it alone if you don't have to? Everyone can use a wingman from time to time."

She seemed relieved as she flicked the edge of his card with her fingertip. "Thanks."

Lindsay came over to them and wrapped her arm around Nicole. "David, can I steal Nicole from you for a minute? I need a couple of shots taken."

David didn't want to see Nicole go. For the first time since he'd arrived he was actually enjoying himself. "Sure."

Nicole smiled up at him. "Thanks. I enjoyed seeing you again."

"Me too."

He watched her walk away. The weight of the baby made her lumber only slightly. She moved with a grace and confidence he found very appealing. Life had thrown her a ton of crap but she was rising above it.

He glanced across the room at Dana. The woman's gaze was locked on Nicole as Nicole raised her camera toward a group of city dignitaries. There was no denying

that the woman had something on her mind. And he'd
bet the farm it wasn't good.

He resolved then to check into Dana Miller's past and
to keep an eye on her.

He didn't question his need to protect Nicole. He
simply would.


Jacob's gut twisted into a knot the instant he saw
Kendall Shaw. As always, she looked sleek, sophisticated,
and in command of the situation. She wore a pale blue
dress that hugged her full breasts, narrow waist, and delicately curved hips. Her spiked heels conjured erotic
thoughts well worth savoring.

He spent the first ten minutes at the Women's Center
pretending to listen and care about the conversations
buzzing around him. He managed to sling good-natured
bullshit of his own, but his thoughts remained on
Kendall.

"That rose has got nasty thorns." The gruff comment,
loud enough for only Jacob to hear, had him turning.

The man standing in front of him was in his late forties. Jim Mundey was with the city of Richmond police.
They served different jurisdictions but often worked together on cases that crossed city and county lines. Jim
was medium height, wore wire-rimmed glasses, and had
thick graying hair and a paunch that strained the seams
of his dress uniform.

Jacob sipped his water, knowing Jim referred to Kendall.
"I have no doubt."

"But she is fun to look at. Damn. Those legs are to
die for."

"Be careful; this might get back to your wife."

"A man might not be able to go into the bakery but he

can still smell the bread." Jim sipped an iced soda. "So you gonna make a play for her?"

"I'd rather take a beating in the ring."

Jim laughed. "It might be worth a black eye to tap that."

They'd talked like this about women before. But knowing the woman was Kendall bothered Jacob this time. "Sure."

"She had a bit of excitement at her house the other night. The queen dropped a dime on her neighbor."

He kept his expression blank but his senses went on alert. "What happened?"

"Seems her new neighbor was taking out his trash as she arrived home around midnight. He got too close and she called nine-one-one."

Jacob frowned. "Was he trouble?"

"Naw. We checked his license. He'd just moved into the house and was tossing packing boxes."

Kendall wasn't a faint heart and it wasn't like her to get spooked so easily. She must have been paying attention to him when he'd told her the victims looked like her. Good.

"You remember his name?"

"Markham, I think."

"Do me a favor," Jacob said. "Run a thorough check on the guy. Couldn't hurt."

Jim shrugged. "Yeah, sure."

The two talked for a few more minutes about department crap and then Jim moved back toward the food table.

Jacob stayed his ground, turning his attention back to Kendall. When the group she was chatting with moved away and she was alone, he strode toward her. He came up behind her, savoring the energy that radiated from her. "Break any stories today, Kendall?"

She turned at the sound of his voice. Even in her

three-inch heels she had to look up at him. Her grin was slow and lazy. "Catch any bad guys today, Detective?"

"The day is young." This close he could see that under expertly applied makeup there were dark circles under her eyes. She hadn't been sleeping well.

"When are you gonna ID the second murder victim?"

"Got to notify next of kin first." Plus, the less information circulating now, the better.

"Any more leads?"

He sipped his ice water, unhappy with the turn of the conversation. "It's always business with you."

"What else is there?"

Jacob could think of several things as his gaze flickered very briefly to her breasts. Hell, if she gave the nod, he'd take her to bed in an instant. Just the thought was making him hard.

"My cameraman is here. Let me interview you about the murders."

"Nope." He liked sparring with her. Her eyes sparked when she was pissed.

"Why not? We can have tape rolling in thirty seconds. You can just share a few thoughts, theories."

He sipped his water. "No."

"You could challenge the killer. Try to lure him out."

"That kind of stunt could just get another woman killed. Is that what you're looking for?"

She frowned, clearly offended. "No. Why would you say that?"

He shrugged. "You're jonesing for a headline."

She faced him head-on. "I care about what happened to those women."

A smile played on his lips. "Yeah, right."

From behind the anger, genuine hurt flickered. "You don't know anything about my motives."

"I've watched you in action before. You take stupid chances."

Her face tightened. "At least I don't hesitate to do my job."

Her barb hit its mark. Last summer when he'd seen the Guardian serial killer holding a gun to Nicole's head, he'd hesitated, unable to fire. Zack hadn't and had killed the Guardian with one shot. But how had she known? Zack or Lindsay wouldn't have talked.

He didn't always like Kendall, but he respected the fact she wasn't afraid to take a swing when backed into a corner. "The jugular is your favorite spot, isn't it?"

Some of the wind left her sails. "It's what I do best."

Kendall took a step back and her gaze scanned the room. He felt her mentally disengage, as if he'd been dismissed, even before Nicole Piper approached them.

"Hey, Nicole," Kendall said. "Everything all right?"

Nicole's face looked pale. "I'm headed out. My back is killing me. See you back at the fort."

Kendall's features softened. "Will do."

When Nicole had left, Jacob couldn't resist asking, "She's your roommate?"

"For the last few months." Ice coated the words.

That's how she knew about the final confrontation. "I wouldn't have put you two together."

She shrugged a slim shoulder. "Wondering what's in it for me?"

"Frankly, yeah."

"I have a huge house and Nicole needed a place to land until the baby was born. End of story."

"You're not angling to write a tell-all book about the Guardian?" He studied the dark circles under her eyes. "Is writing the book what's keeping you up at night?"

The statement had her straightening. "There is no book."

He believed her. Had no reason to, but did. "So why the dark circles? They weren't there last week."

She touched her cheek with her fingertips and then quickly dropped them. She tossed him a killer smile and cracked, "No, Detective, it's dreams about you that are keeping me up."

He laughed, but the image sent a bolt of desire ricocheting through him. He'd like to keep her up at night. "So what *has* been keeping you up?"

Her face paled. "Suddenly, this room is too full and the sounds are too loud for me. I've got what I needed, so I'm headed out."

He'd struck a nerve so sensitive it was driving her off. Before he could say anything else, she left his side and cut through the crowds to Lindsay. She said a quick good-bye and shrugged on her coat.

Jacob set his drink down and followed Kendall. What the hell had he said? Outside, the cool air felt good on his hot skin. He caught up to her easily.

"Where's your car?"

"I can find my own car, Detective."

He fell in step beside her. "What did I say in there?"

High heels clicked on pavement. "I don't know what you're talking about."

"I said something that rattled you."

"I'm just bored."

"That why you took direct aim at me?"

She sighed. "That was uncalled for. I'm sorry."

Kendall crossed the street to a small pay-as-you-go parking lot. Her car was sleek. Black. Top of the line. Very Kendall. And a far cry from the beat-up, mud-splattered SUV he drove.

Jacob watched as she dug her keys from her purse and clicked open the lock. Her hands trembled slightly. "What's keeping you up at night, Kendall?"

"I told you, dreams of you." She laced the words with tartness.

"Cut the crap. What is it?"

She fumbled with the keys and couldn't seem to find the right one. She stopped, sighed. "Dreams, okay? Bad dreams."

"About last summer?" His voice was tense.

She turned and met his gaze. "No." Some of the fire had left her. "The dreams go back to when I was a small child."

Oddly, he felt relief. "Tell me."

Defiance sparked in her eyes. "Why? Why would you care about something like that?"

Kendall held on to her emotion and control with a white-knuckle grip. Like him. "Just tell me."

For a moment, she was silent as she searched his eyes. Trust did not come easily for her. "I'm in a closet. I hear a woman screaming and a baby crying. I have no idea who these people are or what's going on. But the damn dream wakes me up almost nightly now."

"What about family? Friends of your parents? They might help."

"I've no one."

She was alone. Like the other victims. Like him.

"What about a therapist? A hypnotist?"

Kendall shook her head. "It's not that serious. It'll work itself out."

He glanced around to make sure no one lingered close. "I know a doctor. She's not bad. Erica Christopher."

"I don't need a doctor. A solid eight hours of sleep will fix everything."

So stubborn. "Just remember the name."

"Right. Sure."

A slight breeze blew the hair back from her face. The street sounds faded. He didn't even feel the cold.

She stared up at him. Her lips looked soft. No doubt

tasted sweet. He wanted to take her right here, right now, and fulfill the fantasies he'd harbored so long for her.

He leaned toward her. She stood frozen, staring up at him. He wanted to kiss her. And he sensed she wanted him to. His body thrummed with desire.

Jacob reached out to brush her hair from her shoulder. He angled his head ready to kiss her when a passing car horn honked. The noise startled her and she pulled back as far away from him as she could manage.

"I've got to go," she said. "Do you mind?"

The sharpness in her voice annoyed him, reminded him of a queen speaking to one of her minions. He'd been dismissed. The jab inside moments ago had stung but this rejection hurt.

Jacob stepped back to give her a wide berth. He slid his hands into his pockets.

Her hands still trembled. "Good-bye, Detective."

"Sure."

Kendall got into the car, started the engine, and drove off a little too fast.

He stood in the chilly parking lot as the wind tunneled between the buildings toward him. The scent of her perfume still lingered. Jim Mundey was right. She had too many thorns.

"Shit, Jacob," he mumbled to himself. "Stop wanting what you can't have."


Nicole fumbled with her house keys, her fingers stiff from the cold. The porch light cast a ring of light down on her. She wanted nothing more than to take a hot shower and crawl into bed. It was only six in the evening but she was exhausted. The baby weighed heavily in her belly and her back ached. Thank God she had no evening appointments.

Behind her in the darkness a cat screeched and a trash can tumbled over. She whirled around and peered into the darkness. There was nothing. The houses across the alley were lighted up, including the upstairs bedroom of their newest neighbor.

Relaxing, she unlocked the back door and pushed into the house. She was greeted by the scent of sawdust. The contractor. Todd. She'd forgotten all about him. She sighed, hoping he was gone and she had the place to herself this evening.

She hung up her coat in the closet. The coats inside had been covered with plastic, and she realized Todd had taken the precaution to protect the clothes from the dust when he'd been sanding. His attention to detail was impressive.

"Hello? Is anyone here?"

No answer. She moved down the back hallway to the kitchen. The floor had been sanded and the dust wiped from the walls and swept up from the floor. The walls had been patched and primed and were ready for the new cabinets. She checked the date on her watch. They were supposed to arrive today. No doubt he'd hit a snag, an all too common occurrence with renovations.

She only hoped Todd had left for the day and she could get some much-needed quiet time. A cup of tea in the microwave and a few cookies and she'd be off to her room to finish a book on photography she'd checked out from the library.

Nicole opened the refrigerator and dug out a tea bag from a plastic bin. Since the renovations she'd taken to keeping a clean mug in the refrigerator as well. It was the one place she could count on to find one. From the sink in the hallway bathroom, she filled up her mug and then went back to the kitchen, where the microwave sat on a chair and was plugged into the outlet.

When she hit the two-minute button and the machine started to hum, she felt a sense of accomplishment. "Commando cooking."

Barely thirty seconds had ticked off when the front doorbell rang. She was half tempted not to answer it. But immediately she felt guilty. What if it was Kendall and she'd forgotten her key?

Cupping her hand under her belly, she moved down the center hallway to the front door. She clicked on the light and peered out the vertical window that ran by the door. Dana Miller.

Nicole groaned. *What the devil does* she *want?*

Dana waved to her.

There was no ignoring her. Nicole unlatched the chain lock and opened the door. She managed a smile. "Dana."

Dana hugged her fur coat under her chin. "Nicole. I was hoping I'd catch you in. You left the party before I had a chance to talk to you again."

Nicole shivered against the cold. "Was there a problem with the pictures I delivered to your office?"

"No, no. They were fine. Can I come in?"

All she wanted was her tea and a quiet evening. "Now is not really a good time."

"Oh, I won't take long. Just give me five minutes. We need to talk."

"Can't it wait?"

She inched toward the threshold. No wasn't a word she liked. "I promise to be quick. You're not going to let me stand out here and freeze?"

Nicole stepped to the side and Dana hurried past her into the foyer. Nicole closed the door. "What can I do for you?"

Dana rubbed her manicured hands together. "You look great."

Her back ached. Impatience crept into her tone. "Thanks. Dana, can you make this quick? It's been a long day."

She frowned. "You work much too hard. It can't be good for you or the baby."

Nicole's hand slid protectively to her belly. "We're fine."

Dana's gaze traveled the foyer. "Elegant. Smart. Very Kendall."

Nicole didn't want to be rude. "She's got an eye for style."

"That she does." Her gaze skimmed a gilded mirror on the wall. "I didn't realize until today that you two were roommates. How long have you been living here?"

The hairs on the back of Nicole's neck rose. The sensation warned her to tread carefully. But she dismissed the feeling. Her senses had been on overdrive since she'd run from her husband. "A while. Dana, what can I do for you?"

Dana brushed a dark curl from her pale face. "I've heard you're thinking of putting your baby up for adoption."

Nicole stiffened. "Who told you that?"

Gray eyes hardened. "It doesn't matter who told me. Is it true?"

"That's none of your business."

She leaned an inch closer, as if they were conspirators. "You can tell me, Nicole. I'm very discreet."

Nicole felt the color rise in her cheeks. "It's none of your business."

"But it can be my business."

"What?"

"I want to adopt your baby."

A shiver ricocheted down her spine. "*What?*"

Dana held up a hand. "Don't discount me before

you've heard me speak. I've put a lot of thought into what I need to say."

Nicole stared dumbfounded. What planet had this woman come from?

"I've made a fortune in real estate and I've got a wonderful home on River Road. The baby wouldn't lack for any material possession." Her smile was nervous, brittle. "I spent my twenties and thirties making money and getting ahead. I needed to prove to every man out there that no one could outsell me. And I did just that. But now that I've hit my midforties, I realize that I want more. I want a child."

"You can't have one?"

"No. I tried several rounds of in vitro last year, but none of them took. The hormone shots I took have caused premature menopause. There's no chance now I'll ever conceive."

"I'm sorry."

Dana straightened her shoulders. "Don't tell me you're sorry. Tell me I can adopt your child."

"I can't tell you that."

"Why not?"

"Because if I choose to put the baby up for adoption, I want her placed with a married couple."

Hope brightened Dana's eyes. "Her? It's a girl?"

"Yes."

"A girl. I would love her and give her everything. I've already picked out names, if you can believe it. Elise. How do you like that name?"

Nicole felt backed into a corner. Her husband had been an expert at forcing her into corners and of making decisions for her. She'd vowed last year when she'd left him with only a couple hundred dollars in her pocket that no one would ever corner her again. "I want my baby to have a mother and a father."

"That's silly. I can give the baby more than any couple ever could. My daughter would have my undivided attention." Desperation darkened her eyes.

Nicole thought about the fact that she was alone in the house with Dana, and that thought began to worry her. "Dana, you need to leave."

"But we've not decided anything. We need to figure out what's best for the baby."

Nicole's temper rose. "We don't need to do anything. This is *my* baby. *My* decision."

"I'm what's best for that baby. You should see that."

"This is not for you to decide."

Anger deepened the lines on Dana's face. Whatever kindness had been there was gone. "I haven't made it as far as I have by accepting no."

This woman would be the last person on the planet to get her baby. "You need to leave."

She didn't move. "We need to talk this through. You aren't seeing clearly right now." She drew in a deep breath. "It's the hormones, isn't it? I've heard they can make pregnant women a little unreasonable."

Nicole's patience vanished. "I've never been more certain of anything." She brushed past Dana and opened the front door. Cold hair rushed into the foyer. "You need to leave."

Dana shook her head. "You're making a mistake, Nicole."

"No, I'm not."

"The baby needs me."

She set her jaw. "You will never adopt this baby. Now leave."

Dana grabbed Nicole's wrist, her hold tight to the point of bruising. "Close the door."

Nicole glanced out the front door and down the long

concrete steps. She jerked her arm free and stepped out on the front porch.

Dana followed. "Get back inside."

Nicole thought about her cell phone, which was in her coat pocket in the closet. She glanced up and down the street. A few streetlights burned but there wasn't another person in sight. What was she going to do? "Leave me alone, Dana, or I'm calling the police."

"Don't be so dramatic." She looked smug.

Nicole edged toward the first step and glanced down the seven concrete steps. She could barely walk, but now knew she might have to run to get away from Dana.

Footsteps sounded in the hallway behind them. "There a problem here?"

Nicole glanced into the house and saw the silhouette of a man. "Todd?"

Todd moved out onto the front porch to stand within inches of Dana. He towered over her and his hands were clenched as if he was ready for a brawl. He kept his gaze on Dana. "There a problem, Nicole?"

Dana had the good sense to step back. "There's no problem. Nicole and I were just having a talk."

Todd reached around Dana and took Nicole's elbow in his hand. He gently tugged her around Dana so that she stood behind him. "You shouldn't be out in the cold. It's not good for the baby."

Nicole's breath puffed from her nostrils. "I should get back inside."

Todd glared at Dana. "You were finished talking, weren't you?"

"Yes," Nicole said.

Dana's eyes narrowed. "Maybe we can talk another time, Nicole."

"I've said all I need to say. Stay away from me."

Dana looked as if she'd argue, but when her gaze

tipped to Todd's face she held her comment. She turned and walked down the stairs, her high heels clicking. She crossed the street and slid behind the wheel of a deep blue Mercedes.

Nicole didn't release her breath until the car's taillights vanished around the corner. "Thank you, Todd."

He guided her inside and closed the front door.

"No problem."

The foyer's warmth warmed her chilled skin. Now that Dana was gone her mind sharpened. "What are you doing here?"

"I forgot my toolbox. Left it in the kitchen."

She nodded. "I saw it."

"I used the key Ms. Shaw gave me and let myself in. I figured I'd be in and out before anyone knew it. I heard that lady's voice. It sounded odd."

"More than odd."

"Anything I can do?"

"No. I'm fine now." She turned and locked the front door's dead bolt and for extra measure slipped the chain in place."

"You sure I can't do anything for you? I could call Ms. Shaw."

She smiled, grateful good guys still existed. "No, no. Please don't bother her. I'm fine. Really."

"Well, all right. I'll just get my toolbox then and head on home."

"I'm glad you came by."

He nodded knowingly. "That lady is part barracuda. You be sure to stay clear of her."

"I will."

His smile was quick and genuine. "Get yourself to bed. You look beat."

She followed him to the kitchen. "That sounds like a perfect plan."

He picked up his toolbox and opened the back door. "Sorry about the cabinets. The supplier was delayed. They'll be in tomorrow."

"Sure."

"Good night to you."

"See you tomorrow."

"You can count on it."

He left and she double locked this door as well. She shut off the hall light. The microwave in the kitchen dinged, a reminder that her tea was waiting. She opened the microwave door. The tea was lukewarm now. And she realized she no longer had a taste for it.

Nicole poured the tea down the bathroom sink and rinsed out the mug before replacing it in the refrigerator. Then she headed down the hallway and went up the stairs. The top step creaked, as it always did. But tonight it sent a chill down her spine. She glanced over her shoulder toward the long vertical windows by the front door, searching for any signs that Dana had returned.

Her heart hammered and instinct had her cupping her belly. No one was there. "Dana is gone."

But deep in her gut she had the feeling that Dana wasn't finished with her. Dana was the kind of woman who didn't stop until she had exactly what she wanted.

And what she wanted was Nicole's child.

# Chapter Fifteen

Kendall couldn't shake the feeling of dread. It had stalked her since she'd left the party at the Women's Center earlier this afternoon. Maybe talking to Jacob had spurred her fears. Detailing The Dream out loud made it all the more real and underscored the fact that she knew nothing about her past before the age of three. Maybe something terrible had happened to her.

She thought about the search forms she'd filled out for Carnie. She'd sent them by courier to the social worker and had called Carnie. The social worker hadn't made any promises.

The reality was she might not ever know the truth about her past.

Kendall slowed the car as she approached her garage. She'd enjoyed sparring with Jacob tonight. He had a way of churning up her insides, pissing her off, and making her feel alive all at once.

And then he'd leaned toward her and wanted to kiss her.

And Lord, but she'd wanted to kiss him. She didn't

care someone might see them. She'd not felt such desire in so long she'd nearly forgotten what it felt like. Jacob Warwick would no doubt make her body sing in bed.

But at the last second she'd backed away. It was what she did. When people got too close she backed away. Nicole had been right when she'd said Kendall always expected people to quit on her.

And still she couldn't resist wondering what it would be like with Jacob.

She parked the car, got out, and headed across the frozen backyard to her back door. She tried her key in the lock but the door didn't budge. It took her a second to realize that Nicole had locked the dead bolt. She slid her key into the second lock and pushed the door open. She double locked the door behind her.

Within twenty minutes, she was climbing out of the shower. Her face was freshly washed. She dried the water droplets from her skin and slid into the nightgown she kept on a hook mounted on the bathroom door.

Once in the bedroom, she slid under the covers. The sheets were cold and she burrowed deep, trying to get warm. After several minutes the heat of her body warmed the bed and she relaxed. Soon after, she was asleep.

*Kendall stood in the shower savoring the water as it beaded on her skin. She dunked her head under the spray, savoring the warmth. She heard the door to her shower open and close. She smiled, knowing it was him.*

*Strong hands encircled her narrow waist and pulled her back against a muscled chest. A jolt of desire shot through her body as those hands moved up to her breasts and cupped them.*

*"What took you so long?" Her voice sounded throaty.*

*He kissed her ear, nibbling the lobe with his teeth. "Good question."*

*Brushing the hair off her face, she turned and looked up into Jacob's gray eyes, now dark with desire. She wrapped her arms around his neck and kissed him hard. His erection pressed against her belly and she anticipated his lovemaking.*

*He lifted her and she wrapped her legs around his waist. He pressed her back against the shower wall. Desire throbbed inside her as the water washed over them.*

*Kendall didn't question if this was smart or not. There was only need and want.*

*She wanted him inside her more than she could say. She waited for him. But he made no move to enter her. The warm water stopped. Suddenly she was cold.*

*She opened her eyes. Jacob was gone. And she was no longer in the shower.*

*Kendall was in a dark closet. She reached for the door handle and discovered it was locked. Desperation grew. She knew she needed to get out.*

*The air grew thick and hot. The walls seemed to close in around her. In the distance, the cries of a baby mingled with a woman's screams.*

*"Stop! For the love of God, don't!" Fear etched the unknown woman's frantic voice.*

*Desperate, Kendall started to rattle the door handle. "Let me out! Please let me out!"*

*The infant's cries grew louder and this time when Kendall glanced down she saw the child at her feet. It kicked and squirmed its tiny hands as it wailed. The baby, like her, sensed the evil around them.*

*The woman screamed louder. And then there was silence.*

*Kendall's heart thrummed in her chest. Instinct told her to be quiet. She gathered up the infant and held it close to her chest as she pressed her back against the wall.*

*Seconds passed and the silence stretched. The baby wailed.*

*Footsteps sounded on a hardwood floor. Slow and deliberate, they moved toward the closet.*

*"Kendall." The voice was eerily calm. "Come out, come out wherever you are," it sang.*

*The lock on the door clicked open. And the doorknob started to turn.*

Kendall woke with a start. She sat up in bed. Her body was drenched in sweat. Her hand shook as she threaded it through her thick hair.

She moistened dry lips. "Enough."

She snatched up her phone and dialed information. What was the name of that doctor Jacob had suggested? Two first names. Erica. Erica Christopher. She gave the name to the automated operator, waited for the number, and scribbled it down on scratch paper. She dialed the number and waited for an answering machine. "Dr. Christopher, I need to make an appointment with you." She detailed her information and ended the call.

She climbed back under the covers and lay back down against the pillows. But she didn't fall asleep for fear the dream would return.

It was nearly one A.M. Jacob was alone in the police headquarters conference room. He'd returned to the office to read through the e-mails Kendall had received. But at this late hour his eyes itched and he'd been forced to take a break.

Now, he sat on the table, his arms folded over his chest as he stared at the dry-erase board in front of him. Mounted on the left were pictures of Jackie White—both alive and dead. On the right were similar pictures of Vicky Draper. He had also tacked up a picture of Kendall.

He'd sent Zack home an hour ago and should have gone home himself then. But he couldn't let the case go. So far all the leads hadn't produced anything.

The door to the conference room opened. He craned his neck toward the door.

Tess Kier poked her head in. "I heard you were still here."

He nodded. No secrets here.

She moved into the conference room, letting the door close behind her. She had long legs, and large breasts for a woman with such an athletic build. Dark hair framed her oval face and she had bright eyes that were so much like her brother's. "Zack still here?"

"I sent him home an hour ago. He should be home with his wife."

Tess nodded. "I'm glad. She was exhausted after today's opening."

"She's doing all right?" He didn't begrudge the time Zack's wife needed. If he were honest, he was a touch jealous. He talked a mean game about not needing family, but there were more and more moments when he was sorry he had no one.

"She's sick to her stomach every morning. But otherwise she's doing well."

"Good."

She moved beside him and sat on the table. She stared at the board in front of them. Her shoulder brushed his. "Any leads on the case?"

"Not one. Not one." He swallowed an expletive. "The killer doesn't want to be found."

Her brow knitted as she stared at the photos. "What's Kendall's picture doing up there?"

"I don't know. Just a hunch."

"Theories?"

"Lots. We first thought the case was domestic. Then

when the second victim was found and we discovered her record, we thought it was all drug related. But both wore those damn charms."

"Ruth and Judith. C.C. thinks it's a religious thing."

"The killer sees something in them that we don't."

She narrowed her gaze. "They do look alike. In fact, they look like Kendall."

He didn't like hearing his worst fear spoken out loud. "I know."

"She got any obsessed fans?"

He rubbed the back of his neck. "She's got a strong following, but there's no sign of any nuts stalking her. The station saves all her fan e-mails and copied the backlog to me. New ones are being forwarded here. I've been going through them. Lots of folks admire her. A few didn't like some of the stories she did, but none have made any threats."

"Any repeaters? Fans who e-mailed or wrote her excessively?"

He gripped the table, his frustration palpable. "Three. We're backtracking their e-mails and we plan to visit them if we can find them." His gaze bore into the eyes of the first victim. "Who the hell would do something like this?"

Tess laid her hand over his tense fingers. "Jacob, you need to take a break, if only for a few hours. You're not going to figure out anything if you don't get some sleep."

"I can't sleep."

Her lips curled into a seductive smile. "Maybe we could find something more interesting to do."

His gaze dropped to her long, warm fingers draped over his hand. Her thumb drew small circles on his wrist. He thought about Kendall and realized he wished it were her touching him now.

"We could go back to my place," Tess said.

For a moment the words hung in the air. "I'm not sure what to say about that."

"How about yes?"

His ego liked the attention. "Sleeping with you could lead to a lot of complications."

She shrugged. "I'm a big girl. My brother stopped worrying about whom I dated a long time ago."

"Don't count on it."

She rose and moved in front of him. She laid her hands on his shoulders. Her thigh rubbed his. He felt the first stirring of desire. Still, he held himself at bay.

Tess Kier was a warm, seductive woman. And he sensed making love to her would be pleasurable. Without warning, Kendall's face flashed in his mind. His erection pulsed hard. It frustrated him that the woman had invaded his thoughts. He didn't owe her anything. Hell, she'd rejected him.

Jacob needed to prove that Kendall didn't hold anything over him, so he grabbed Tess by the wrist. He pulled her between his legs and his hands settled on her narrow hips.

Smiling, she dipped her head, wrapped her arms around him, and kissed him hard on the lips. Her sweet taste intrigued him. Her firm breasts pressed against his chest. She smelled of clean soap and a hint of roses clung to her hair.

The scent wasn't right. It wasn't Kendall's.

He thrust his tongue into her mouth and savored the feel of the soft contours. A soft moan rumbled in her chest. She matched him thrust for thrust.

Jacob had tried to kiss Kendall, but she'd pulled away from him. He was a fool to think he and Kendall had any kind of chance. She moved in different circles, different worlds.

Annoyed with his thoughts, he broke the kiss. For a

long moment, he stared into Tess's eyes, wishing they were Kendall's eyes. "Thanks, but no."

His abruptness cooled the desire in her eyes. "What's wrong?"

"It's not you. Just bad timing."

"You kissed me like you wanted me."

His gaze wavered.

And in that instant she seemed to read him. "It's not me that you want."

Jacob didn't speak.

Tess released a weary smile.

"I'm sorry."

She shook her head. "Don't be. Believe it or not, I do understand."

His male ego absorbed the punch. She had another man on her mind. "Who is he?"

Unsteady laughter rumbled inside her. "I'll tell if you tell."

Jacob shook his head. "Point taken."

She moved away. "Better get back to work."

"Yeah." He shoved his hand through his hair, relieved she wasn't angry. "Thanks."

Shaking her head, she reached for the door. "Any time."

Jacob moved back to the pile of e-mails. A few minutes passed before he could really concentrate again. When his mind and libido calmed, the words came into focus. He'd read six more e-mails when he lifted his gaze to her picture on the dry-erase board. Smiling eyes stared back at him.

The woman had gotten under his skin. "Damn it."


It was late Friday night when Allen returned to Rachel's apartment building. He parked, got out, and stood in the shadows and stared up at her window. Light peeked through the edges of the curtain that covered the window. She was home, as he expected. Now all he had to do was wait until someone opened the locked apartment building door and he could slip inside.

If he took her now, they'd have the weekend together.

He had to wait another twenty minutes before a car pulled up in front of the building. He watched as a man and woman got out. They walked hand in hand up to the front door. Allen followed. The man pressed a four-digit code into the keypad. 1-9-7-1. The door buzzed open and the couple vanished into the building.

*She is yours for the taking.*

Ducking his head, he moved to the door and punched in the code. The door buzzed open. He went inside.

Smiling, he bypassed the elevator and took the stairs to the third floor. The long, carpeted hallway was quiet, and all six apartment doors were closed.

Quickly, he moved down the hallway until he reached 3-A. He knocked gently on the door.

Footsteps sounded inside the apartment. His heart raced. Rachel was within inches of him. Soon she would be his. He shoved his hands into his pockets so she wouldn't see his erection.

The door snapped open.

She stood before him and for a moment he was awestruck. Blond hair framed a pale oval face and accentuated blue eyes. She was an anomaly in his Family. A blonde with blue eyes among brunettes. But she was Family. She was his.

Rachel seemed surprised to see him. But, like Jackie, she was ever polite, wanting to please. She managed a smile. "Can I help you?"

His throat felt dry. Silly, but he was tongue-tied or nervous. "Yes, you can."

"What do you need?"

He stared at her unable to tear his gaze away. Why was he sexually attracted to her and not the others? Why was his control slipping? It didn't make sense.

Her smile faltered. And he knew his hesitation and lingering stare set off alarm bells in her. She started to close the door. "You must have the wrong person."

Allen knew if he didn't act now the element of surprise would be lost. He shoved his foot in the doorjamb. The next seconds unfolded quickly. His reflexes were quicker than those of most skilled hunters. In one fluid move, he shoved open the door, barged into the apartment, and slammed the door behind him. Before she could scream he cupped his hand over her mouth and shoved her against a wall. Her head popped back and her skull hit the wall hard. The impact left her dazed, stunned, and pliable.

He pulled a handkerchief from his back pocket and shoved it into her mouth. He dragged her across the room to a couch. She started to struggle. He slapped her hard across the face and used his full weight to press her body into the cushions.

"Don't say a word, Rachel. Not one word."

The menace in his words further ignited the fear in her pale eyes. Tears welled inside.

He pulled a needle from his pocket and shoved it into her arm. She flinched and whimpered. Power surged in his body and desire lighted up every nerve ending. With her under him, her heart beating hard and fast against him, the world felt right. She couldn't join the Family until Sunday.

They had forty-eight hours.

But there was plenty they could do together.

Plenty indeed.

# Chapter Sixteen

*Saturday, January 19, 7:10 A.M.*

Jacob awoke with a start.

Sunlight streamed into the room, and for a moment he felt disoriented. He glanced to his right and left, as if he expected Tess to be there. And then he remembered that he'd turned down a sexy, willing woman. Why? Because of Kendall.

Dumbass.

Jacob realized his phone was ringing. He snapped the cell off the nightstand and flipped it open. "Warwick."

"Did I wake you?" Zack's voice sounded bright, alert.

He cleared his throat. Big brother. "What's up?"

"We got a hit from ViCAP."

Jacob had taken several hours filling out the forms for ViCAP and submitted them to Quantico. He'd not expected a response so quickly.

His heart started to pump. "I didn't expect to hear back so quickly. What did he say?"

"The agent left a message on my phone at work. Briefly, he said there were two similar murders in Anchorage, Alaska, five years ago. The women looked like our two victims and were approximately the same age. Both women were strangled. Their bodies were dumped, and it appeared as if they'd been held several days before they were killed."

Jacob rubbed the back of his neck. "Were the victims wearing charms?"

"No."

That was a major difference, but he couldn't rule out the link yet. He checked his watch. It was too early to call Anchorage right now. "I'm going to the gym and then the office."

"I'll meet you there."

"Don't. Enjoy the day with your wife." Plus he didn't want to face Zack right now. He'd been a nanosecond away from sleeping with the guy's sister.

"Okay." Zack would need no arm-twisting to convince him to stay home. "But if you need something, call."

"Will do." Jacob closed his phone. Then stared at the other side of his bed.

He thought about Kendall and wished she was there curled up on her side with nothing on but the white cotton sheets of the bed. Opposites did attract. They also exploded like matches and gasoline.

Jacob was sexually attracted to Kendall, but long term anything between them was a long, long shot.

He thought about Tess's breasts pressing against his chest. God, but she'd tasted good. And he'd said no.

"Dumbass."


Cole Markham stamped his feet to ward off the cold that had seeped into his bones as he'd waited outside Kendall's house. He'd tried to look busy, like he was just out for a morning stroll, but he was growing tired of the cold. Sooner or later she had to come out.

And then, just after nine, she emerged from her house. She'd donned jeans and a white parka with a fur-trimmed hood, tied her hair up in a ponytail, and wore large dark sunglasses. Even dressed down, she was dressed up, and she moved with an elegant grace that set her apart from most. She was a fine woman and given a different set of circumstances he'd have tried to hook up with her.

But he wouldn't.

She was too valuable.

The other night he'd caught her by surprise and she'd freaked. Understandable. Smart even. He was glad he'd taken the time to put a few boxes in the trash. They'd been enough to convince the cops that he was legitimate.

He didn't want a scene this time. So he'd waited for daylight.

The morning air was cold, but he hardly noticed it as he crossed the street on an intercept path.

When she reached the corner she looked both ways. That's when he caught her attention with a wave of his hand. "Howdy, neighbor."

Kendall paused and then smiled. "So we meet again. But then, I guess that stands to reason."

Cole's shoulders tensed. "Why's that?"

"We're neighbors."

"Right."

"What has you out so early on a cold Saturday?"

He shrugged. "Breakfast. Care to join me?" When she hesitated, he added, "Come on."

She shook her head. "In the last few months I've been working so hard I've barely gotten out at all. It's been a while since I've done more than grab a meal to go."

"Then you must come."

Kendall shrugged. "What would it hurt? A friendly

breakfast with a good-looking man is just the distraction I need."

He flashed even, white teeth. "Great. There's a diner on the corner that's become my home away from home."

"O'Malley's? Good strong coffee and great omelets."

They walked across the street, took a right, and headed up to the corner. The O'MALLEY'S red neon sign blinked in a large glass window frosted by the morning chill. The place was open twenty-four/seven and served a steady stream of customers. This morning was no exception. Over half of the restaurant's thirty tables were filled with patrons.

Cole opened the door for Kendall. Bells on the doorjamb jingled above. He escorted her past the PLEASE SEAT YOURSELF sign to a table in the back. A few patrons recognized Kendall, a couple gawked, and one pointed. She'd grown used to being recognized and he could tell she enjoyed it.

The top of each square table was covered in pictures of Richmond and sealed with resin for quick cleanup. There was a jukebox in the corner and a bar in the back.

A redheaded waitress arrived at their table. She glanced briefly at Kendall and blasé recognition flickered in her gray eyes. That told Cole she saw Kendall here regularly.

When the waitress shifted her gaze to him, a genuine smile warmed her face. "Here again?"

Cole leaned back in his chair as if he were a veteran patron. "Can't resist your smile, Faye." It always paid to be nice to the help.

The older woman rolled her eyes at the blatant flattery in a way that showed she enjoyed it. "You want what you had for breakfast yesterday?"

Cole didn't even glance at the menu. "You've got it."

"I'll have tea, dry toast, and an egg-white omelet," Kendall said.

Faye's smile faded. "Will do."

Kendall waited until Faye left before saying, "So, it looks like you've made quite an impression."

"I like to talk to people. Faye and I struck up a conversation a few days ago."

Faye delivered Kendall's tea and a coffee for Cole. The waitress hesitated a moment as if hoping Cole would say something else. When he didn't, she moved on to another table.

Kendall swirled her tea bag around in her porcelain mug. "So how do you like Richmond so far?"

He picked up three sugar packets, opened them, and dumped the contents into his coffee. "I like it."

"Settling in at work?"

He sipped his coffee and noticed a gold watch that looked vintage hugged her left wrist. "You know how it is in a new job. There's always a period of adjustment."

"I know." Her accent was neutral and he'd not have guessed she was from the south if he'd not done some asking around.

"How long have you been at the station?"

"A few years, but I've only been the evening anchor for a couple of months."

"That a big shift?" He rested his elbows on the table and wove his fingers together. He stared at her with intensity because he wanted her to believe she was the only person in the world.

"Yes."

"I'll bet you're a huge hit."

She shrugged. "I can't say everyone was thrilled about the change."

"Why?"

"Ex-model turned anchor. Some don't think I have the chops for the job."

"Does that bother you?"

"It has spurred me to work harder than everyone else. And I'm good at what I do. I've worked hard for what I have. The doubters will come around eventually."

She was just as intense as he'd suspected she'd be. "I have no doubt you'll win them over."

Faye appeared with Cole's French toast, bacon, and eggs and Kendall's egg-white omelet and toast. "Anything else I can get for you?"

Cole picked up a slice of bacon. "We're good, Faye. Thanks." Kendall was a beauty, even more attractive than her publicity shots and the on-air interviews he'd screened. "So are you from Richmond?"

"Born and bred."

"No hankering for the big-city lights?" He popped the bacon in his mouth.

She sipped her tea. "There was a time when that was all I could think about."

"And now?"

"I like it here. I can't promise I'll be here forever, but for now it works."

There was more behind her words. More of a reason why she'd chosen to stay in town, but he didn't press the issue. "I saw that piece you did Friday on those murdered women. Tough stuff."

Kendall frowned. "It is, and very unsettling."

"Any ideas about motivation?"

"Lots of theories but no facts."

Silent, Cole cut his French toast and took a bite. Then he asked, "Did the women have any family?"

"None that I can find. One was an only child and her parents have passed. The other's identity hasn't been released yet." Thinking about the murdered women dampened her mood. "Enough with murders. Tell me about you. You'd said you were from out West?"

He was careful to keep his answers simple. Otherwise he could trip up. "Denver mostly. A little time in Alaska."

"And insurance brought you to Richmond?"

He heard the questioning note in her voice. "My own agency. I decided to strike out on my own."

"But why so far away?"

He picked up his fork. *Keep it simple.* "I just finished up with a nasty divorce," he said. "I wanted a clean start."

"Any children?"

"No, thank God. Be a shame to drag them through something like that. My folks live in Boulder. And I have a younger sister. Have you ever been out to Denver?"

"Went through the airport a couple of years ago. My flight was delayed and I spent a few hours there. But that was it."

Cole could tell Kendall was trying to sum him up. Always the reporter. But he knew he was a hard man to read. He was accustomed to hiding his thoughts.

"You don't like talking about yourself, do you?" she asked.

He grinned. "It's not that. I'm just boring. Thirty-five. Divorced. Insurance. Boring."

She shook her head. "I suspect you are far from boring."

He cut into his French toast again and stabbed a section with his fork. "I'd rather talk about you."

"University of Virginia graduate, did some modeling, and then got into reporting," she recited like a standard resume.

"I heard someone mention that you cracked a big story last year."

She shifted as if the question made her uncomfortable. "Yeah, but I'd just as soon not talk about it over breakfast."

"Oh, yeah, sure." She was friendly to a point, and then a wall thicker than a glacier dropped down.

Cole asked Kendall a few more questions. She answered them. After an hour of idle chatter he walked her home. All pleasant, all nice, just as he'd wanted it to be. He wanted her to think he was a nice guy. He didn't want her to look too close and figure out that the pieces in his own story didn't add up.

Jacob spent the better part of an hour jumping rope. He stayed away from the punching bag, instead opting for ab crunches and an upper-body workout with weights. He showered, staying under the spray until the tightness in his muscles eased. He dressed, snapped up his gym bag, and headed out.

As he crossed by the ring in the center of the facility, two young boxers sparred. He paused to watch. The shorter of the two boxers held up his gloves, signaling the other fighter to take a break. Jacob had seen the shorter boxer fight before. Had a good left jab but let his right hand drop too often. His name was Lenny something. He recalled a few scant details. Foster care kid. Hard worker. Ambitious.

Lenny spit out his mouthpiece and moved to the ropes. Sweat drenched his T-shirt and dripped from under his headgear into ice-blue eyes. "Hey, you're Jacob, right?"

"Yeah."

"You took a hell of a pounding a couple of weeks ago."

"Not too bad."

The kid sniffed. He couldn't have been more than fifteen or sixteen. "You ever thought about sparring with me? I could use the practice."

In the last couple of days Jacob had just started to feel

human after the last bout. He'd be a fool to take on another match with the healing fractures in his hand. It was a no-brainer. Still, ego and frustration over Kendall had him considering it. "You training for a fight?"

"Yeah. It's a big one."

Jacob set his bag down and walked to the ropes. "Don't you have a trainer?"

"Can't afford one. I get tips here and there. I watch other fighters. I've watched you in the ring." He crossed gloved hands over the ropes and leaned forward. "I've seen you fight, even seen some of your old fights on tape. You've got *instinct*, old man. I need to get me some of your instinct."

The kid was a big puppy and didn't mean "old man" in a bad way. Still, it stung. "Call me old man again and I'll show you some instinct."

Lenny grinned. "So you'll go a round or two with me?"

"Let's start with me showing you a few moves, and then see how it goes from there."

"Cool. When?"

The kid was hungry. Jacob respected that. "Got a case right now. I'll call when it's settled."

Lenny nodded. "I'm here every day."

"Right." Jacob picked up his bag. "In the meantime, keep your right hand up. It drops too much."

The kid grinned. "Will do."

Jacob headed to the corner bagel shop and ordered an egg sandwich and an extra large coffee. The food tasted good and he actually felt human.

He arrived at the office by noon and read the Teletype left by the FBI. As Zack had said, the report detailed the strangulation of two women who shared physical features of the women killed here.

Jacob checked his watch. Noon here meant eight there. He dialed the number supplied, hoping to reach the officer listed in the report. The phone rang three times before he heard a gruff, "Alaska State Trooper's Office."

Jacob identified himself and waited as the operator transferred him to the trooper. After introductions and a few pleasantries, he brought Trooper Mike Payne up to speed on the local murders. "What can you tell me?"

Payne's chair squeaked and Jacob imagined him leaning back in it. "I pulled the file last night when I got word there'd been a hit. Tragic cases. Hit the family hard."

"Family? Not families?"

"The women were sisters. Their names were Maria and Anita Gonzales, ages thirty and twenty-eight. Maria was the first killed. She'd just gotten in her car after her waitress shift. The killer apparently approached her seconds later. Her keys were in the ignition and partially turned as if she'd been interrupted. Her attacker must have yanked her out of the car. We found her body two months later. She'd been dead only a few days."

"He'd held her?"

"Yeah. And there'd been no sign of sexual assault."

Frowning, Jacob wrote the women's names on a legal pad. "And the sister?"

"She vanished three weeks after her sister's body was found. She'd returned to work at a local gift shop. Her killer nabbed her from the back storeroom. We found drops of her blood and tire tracks behind the store. We think he hit her, maybe knocked her out, and then put her in a waiting vehicle."

"Where was her body found?"

A shuffle of papers crackled through the phone. "She wasn't found for two weeks. And by the condition of the body, we estimated that she'd not been killed for at least ten days."

"Sexual assault?"

"None."

"And these women weren't wearing charm necklaces?"

"No."

Jacob drew circles around the word *sisters*. "Forensic evidence?"

"Pink rug fibers."

Jacob expelled a breath. "Just like my victims."

"Yeah."

His heart pounded. "Got any theories on this one?"

"We had lots in the beginning. Interviewed ex-boyfriends, coworkers, and neighbors. You name 'em, we talked to 'em. But nothing came up that led us anywhere. It was big news up here for a while."

"And no other murders in the area?"

"None like these."

"We have two victims, each with pink fibers. Each appears to have been held for several days before they were killed. Both strangled, except our victims weren't sisters and they were wearing charms."

"They weren't sisters?" the trooper challenged.

"They look alike but we checked into their family background. One's a foster kid and the other grew up in a respected family. Both had dark eyes and dark hair."

The trooper sighed. "I'd say our guy killed the first victim here on impulse. He put more thought into the second killing."

"And now his planning appears to be even more detailed."

"Can you overnight me a copy of your file?"

"Sure. You'll have it tomorrow if the snow lets up and the planes can fly. Blizzard just hit."

"Thanks, Trooper Payne."

"Call me if you catch this guy."

"I will." Jacob hung up the phone.

He stared at his notes. "What the hell was setting this guy off?"

Kendall was a bundle of nerves when she stepped into Dr. Erica Christopher's office. She'd never done therapy and didn't relish the thought. But something had to give.

The fifty-something woman rose from her desk, smiled, and extended her hand. "You must be Kendall Shaw."

Kendall pulled off her dark glasses and accepted her hand. "Yes. Dr. Christopher?"

"Yes. Won't you have a seat?"

"Thanks." She sat on the edge of the couch, ready to spring to her feet if need be.

"Why don't you tell me why you're here?"

Kendall gave her the highlights. Dreams. Adoption worries. All of it. "I want the dreams to stop."

"You never had anything like this before?"

"No."

"And the dreams started when?"

"Last summer. They were just flashes at first. Nothing too startling. It's only been in the last couple of weeks that they've gotten to be overwhelming. I have pain meds from last summer when I had my shoulder surgery. They make me sleep but I'm so groggy all day. And I don't want to cover the problem. I want to get rid of it."

Dr. Christopher pulled off her glasses and studied Kendall. "Would you be interested in trying hypnosis?"

"I'll try anything at this point."

"How about now?"

"Sure."

The doctor rose, turned on a small side lamp, and then turned off the overhead light. The room took on a cozy, more intimate feel. Kendall straightened her back and tried to look relaxed.

Dr. Christopher scooted her chair to within inches of Kendall. "What do you know about hypnosis?"

"A little. I'm going to feel relaxed. You can't make me do anything I don't want to?"

"That's right. You will be in a totally relaxed state and your mind is going to open. What we are going to try to do is get you back to that closet and see what else we can discover about it."

Kendall's stomach churned. Everything in her told her not to go back to that place. "Okay."

The doctor smiled. "Close your eyes. Relax your hands. Take a deep breath and release it." In a deep, soothing voice, she took Kendall through the process of hypnosis.

Soon the tension seeped from her body and the millions of details that always filtered through her mind faded. She lost track of time and was only aware of feeling warm and relaxed.

"Now, Kendall," Dr. Christopher said. "Let's go back to your dream. When you are in the closet. For now there is only silence, as if you've put the world on mute. Tell me what you smell and what you feel with your fingertips. Is it hot or cold?"

For a moment, Kendall's mind was blank. And then her senses kicked in. "I feel the scratchy shag carpet under my legs. My left knee sock has fallen to my ankle. The air is chilly and I smell something sweet."

"That's good."

"Have you been in the closet before?"

Eyes closed, Kendall smiled. "It's my favorite place to play. I can be alone here."

Dr. Christopher laid her hand over Kendall's. "Now, I

want you to turn the volume back up. I want you to let the sounds grow gradually louder."

Kendall imagined turning the volume up on a TV. At first there was nothing, only silence. And then in the distance, the screams began. It sounded like someone was running toward her and yelling.

Her heart racing, Kendall put down her crayon and stood up. She peeked through the keyhole but couldn't see anything. And still the screams grew louder. For several long seconds there was only the terrifying noise.

And then the door to the bedroom outside the closet burst open and she saw a woman. Her face was frantic and her eyes were crazed. In her arms she held a small bundle. The woman raced to the door and jerked it open.

Kendall darted back, certain she was in trouble. The woman pushed Kendall into the back of the closet.

"Sit down," she ordered. "Sit down and be quiet."

"But why?"

The woman laid the bundle at Kendall's feet. It was a baby. Pink and small, its arms and legs punched and kicked at the air as if to convey displeasure.

"Stay here. Keep the baby quiet. For the love of God be quiet."

And then the woman slammed the closet door and locked it. Kendall was left in the darkness with the baby, who was starting to fuss.

She jumped to her feet and pounded on the door. "Mommy, don't leave me!"

"Kendall." Dr. Christopher's voice was stern. "Kendall, I want you to wake up now. Kendall, do you hear me?"

Eyes fluttered open and focused on the doctor's face. Kendall's fists were clenched so tight her knuckles were white. Slowly, she uncurled them.

Sweat dampened her back and her heart pounded in her chest. "The woman in the dream was my birth mother."

The doctor patted her on the hand. "What do you remember about her?"

She searched her mind for details that might reveal what the woman looked like. "The image is out of focus." She concentrated harder. "Dark hair. She smelled like apples."

"Do you know why she was screaming?" The doctor's voice was calm and soothing.

Kendall drew in a ragged sigh. "I think someone was trying to kill her. I think she was trying to protect me and . . . my sister."

Amanda awoke to the sharp smell of ammonia. Her head jerked back and she coughed as her eyes popped open. Her vision was blurred, but she could see that there was a man sitting in a chair directly across from her. They were so close, their knees touched.

"Good, you are awake. I was beginning to worry." His smile was warm and welcoming.

"Where am I?"

"Don't you know?"

Amanda's head ached and her fingers felt numb as fear coiled around her chest. Her vision cleared and she looked around the room. Pink. Gaudy splashes of pink that covered the bed, the walls, and the curtains. It was a wretched shade.

She turned her gaze back to the man's face. She stared at him a long moment. She'd never seen him before and yet she *knew* him.

Her blouse was askew and her bra had been unsnapped. She also realized her panties were gone and she was sore inside. Disgust and shame knotted in her stomach. "What did you do to me?"

Color warmed his cheeks. "I'm sorry. I shouldn't have touched you like that, but I wanted you so much. Forgive me."

She never thought she could hate so much. Whatever was going on here wasn't just about rape. Ice coated her words. "What do you want?"

He met her gaze. "You know who I am, don't you?"

She stared into the man's eyes. Her memory rushed back in a blinding flash. This was the man who'd forced his way into her apartment. She moistened dry lips and glanced down at her wrists. "You broke into my apartment."

"Yes. But think back. You know me from before."

*Before.* Initially, she didn't understand. And then, as if a curtain had been lifted, she knew who he was. "Allen," she said softly.

Smiling, he nodded. "Yes."

Memories she'd long buried deep in her mind clawed their way to the front of her mind. Time had changed him. He'd filled out and grown stronger. If she'd not been looking directly into his eyes she'd never have recognized him. "You disgust me."

He winced. "Forgive me."

"No." It was the one thing he wanted from her and it would be the last thing she would give him. "You've taken so much from me."

His eyes filled with unshed tears. "I've not come to take any more. I've come to bring you home, Rachel."

"Rachel." She'd not heard the name in so long. "Don't call me that."

"It's your name."

"It *was* my name. You stole it from me." Years of anger welled inside her. She had no desire to beg or plead with the man she hated so much. "And home. How can you take me home when you destroyed my home?" She twisted her bound wrists, wishing she could pummel him with her fists.

He laid his hand on her knee. "That's my fault and I'm sorry."

"Don't touch me." Bitterness twisted her heart. Long ago, he had ripped her life apart. "I hate you."

Allen flinched as if she'd struck him. "You don't mean that. We're family."

"Family. You sick bastard, you have no idea what family means." Provoking him was foolish and dangerous. But she didn't seem to care, as if the demons that had stalked her for so long drove her actions now.

Allen rose to his feet, his fists clenched. "Rachel, you just don't understand."

She craned her neck as he walked behind her. She saw him pull something from his pocket. It sparkled in the light. When he moved close behind her she flinched. She braced for an attack. Instead, he laid a gold necklace and charm around her neck. The metal felt cold against her skin.

"Do you like it?"

Unexpected relief washed over her. She'd tried to provoke him but was now grateful he'd not attacked her. Still, she couldn't bring herself to show him any kindness. "No."

He leaned forward until his lips were close to her ear. His hot breath brushed her skin and sent terror rocketing through her body. "You haven't even looked at it, Rachel."

"My name is Amanda."

"It's Rachel."

She kept her gaze ahead, shoving back the fear that tightened her skin and made her heart race. For years she'd wished she could go back to the life she'd known as Rachel. Now, she hated the sound of the name. "Asshole."

Long fingers wrapped around her neck. "You shouldn't talk to me like that." His grip tightened.

Quickly, her breathing grew labored. She didn't want to die but knew there was no avoiding it. In some ways she'd known this day was going to come. She'd always thought she'd die young.

He squeezed hard.

Blood pounded in her temples and her body screamed for oxygen. Choking, she was aware of a clock ticking. Of life seeping from her body. The details in the room blurred into a pink haze and then nothing.

"I'm sorry," he whispered.

Then he kissed her on the cheek and began to cry.

# Chapter Seventeen

*Sunday, January 20, 9:15* A.M.

"Warwick." Jacob barked his name into the cell phone. He'd just returned from a run and his body was covered in sweat.

"It's Vega. We've got another victim. A woman. Strangled."

"Shit." He dropped his forehead to his hand and leaned against the kitchen counter. "Where?"

Vega gave the address. It was an office park near the Goochland County line. "And she's wearing a charm. This one reads *Rachel.*"

"Rachel. Another biblical name."

"The mother of Joseph. You know, the one with a coat of many colors."

"I'll take your word for it." Jacob frowned. "I'll be there in thirty minutes."

He dialed Zack's number. Zack's wife, Lindsay, picked up on the fifth ring. "Hello?"

"Lindsay. Is Zack there?"

"Hey, Jacob. He's in the shower."

"Get him out." His tone told her this wasn't a social call.

"Sure thing."

Nearly a minute later, he heard, "What's up?"

"Another body." Jacob relayed the stats and the two agreed that Jacob would pick Zack up in twenty minutes.

Jacob showered quickly, dressed, and headed down the flight of apartment stairs to the first floor. He backed out of his parking space, pulled into Sunday morning church traffic, and headed west. Within a half hour he and Zack arrived at the murder scene.

A half dozen squad cars and the large white forensics van were parked in front of the low-lying office building. Most of the buildings in this wooded office park were covered in brick and glass. Jacob parked his car and both men hung their badges around their necks on lanyards. The uniforms nodded as the two detectives ducked under yellow crime scene tape and moved around to the back of the building.

Bitter cold air whipped around the corner of the building, bringing with it the sick smell of death. Tess stood inside red tape that she'd used to mark off the crime scene area. The red tape was her signal that no one but forensics entered the area. The flash of her digital camera popped repeatedly. "Shoot your way in and out of a scene," she always said.

Jacob kept a respectful distance. She needed to do her job, and if they were lucky they could pretend Friday night had never happened and they could get back to the friendship they'd had.

His number one question right now was, What did the victim look like? Tess blocked his view of the body's face. Tension tightened the muscles in his back. He didn't want the victim to look like the other two victims. He didn't want her to look like Kendall.

Zack slid his hands into his pockets. "The shit's gonna hit the fan when this gets out."

"I know." Jacob tore his gaze from the scene. "I need to

find out who found this body." It took only a few questions to the uniformed officers to discover that a Jeff McNamara had found it. He was the CEO of JN Civil Engineering and he'd come in to catch up on work. He'd looked out his office window and seen the woman.

Immediately, he'd called 911. McNamara was a bookish guy with thinning blond hair and a lean, slightly stooped build. The discovery of the body had really rattled him, but he'd done his best to recount what he knew to the officers, which wasn't much.

Jacob and Zack did a search of the surrounding office buildings and discovered they were all closed for the weekend. If McNamara hadn't come in, the body likely wouldn't have been found until tomorrow.

Zack pulled a stick of gum from his pocket and offered it to Jacob. When Jacob declined he unwrapped it and popped it in his mouth. "Tess," he called out.

She came over to them, careful to keep her expression neutral when her gaze jumped between the two of them. "The bruising on her neck indicates that she was strangled."

Jacob steeled himself. "What does the victim look like?"

Tess stared at Jacob. "Have a look for yourself." She stepped aside.

Jacob had his first good view of the body. She was blond. Petite.

"She doesn't look like the others," Tess said. "Or like Kendall Shaw."

Kendall had been up most of the night. This time she'd stayed up intentionally. She'd been searching the Internet for any kind of old news story that would tell her about the woman in her dreams. If a violent crime had occurred, chances were the story had been covered.

She had scant details. Twenty-five or so years ago. Two small children. A woman with dark hair. Screaming. She had no location or manner of death. And not surprisingly, none of her searches had revealed anything.

Nicole's plodding footsteps sounded in the hallway and she appeared in the doorway. She wore a pink empire top, maternity jeans, and her dark hair back in clips. Her stomach looked more pronounced and low. The baby would be here soon—a week or two at the most.

"Are you working on a story?"

Kendall brushed bangs off her face with the back of her hand. "Yes. When I get a lead in my head I can't sleep."

"No bad dreams?"

"None." For the first time in a long while, she felt as if she was gaining a little control. She'd scheduled another appointment with Dr. Christopher for Monday so she could be hypnotized again. The more details she got, the faster her search would go.

"Do you ever stop moving?"

Kendall shook her head. "Not often." She'd barely gotten the words out when the doorbell rang. "Damn."

Nicole smiled. "That's probably Todd. He has tile samples."

Kendall had forgotten. "That's right. He said something about a supply problem with the tiles the designer had picked." The redesign had seemed so important last week and now she was sorry she'd jumped into the project. She didn't need the interruption right now.

"I'll get the door," Nicole said.

"Thanks." Grateful, she turned back to the screen. She heard voices downstairs but ignored them.

Seconds later Nicole reappeared, Brett following close behind. He was dressed in a sleek overcoat, a dark turtleneck sweater, and ironed jeans that topped polished Italian loafers.

He frowned when he saw her. "How soon can you be dressed and ready to leave?"

She minimized the computer screen. "Why?"

He glanced at Nicole as if he didn't want to speak in front of her.

Kendall's annoyance took root. "Go ahead, Brett. She can keep a secret."

Nicole smiled and stood her ground. Nicole had said more than once to Kendall that she didn't like Brett. She'd remain now just to irritate him.

Brett frowned. "There's been another murder."

Kendall felt sick. "*What?*"

"I don't have all the details, but I've got a friend who works in the office park where the woman's body was found. She called me about thirty minutes ago. The cops are trying to keep a lid on this one."

Nicole crossed her arms over her belly. "Go ahead. I can talk to Todd about the tile."

"You have good taste and you know what I like. Just pick what you think is best."

"Will do."

As Kendall moved toward the door, she realized her hands trembled slightly. God, another woman dead. "What can you tell me about the victim?"

"No name or background—yet."

She was headed to her room, already mentally cataloguing the details she had on the last murders. "Right. Give me twenty, and I'll be downstairs and ready to go."

Kendall jumped into the hot shower and washed the sweat from her body. She skipped leg shaving and hair washing, knowing she could hide one and work around the other. Out of the shower, she toweled off, pulled her hair into a French twist, and applied her makeup. She dressed in a white silk blouse, dark pants, and high-heeled boots. She was downstairs in seventeen minutes.

Brett sat on the sofa in the living room. Nicole stood by the fireplace.

"Let's go," Kendall said. She dug her coat out of the front closet and grabbed her purse.

Brett looked stunned by her transformation. "Now that is the Kendall I know and love. Very nice."

His compliment irritated her. "I'll follow you."

"Better ride with me. It'll save time. I want Channel Ten to have the scoop on this one."

He was right. Traveling with him was more time efficient. But she didn't like it. "Okay."

Brett opened the door to his sleek, black Audi and she slid into the seat. He got behind the wheel and fired up the engine. His eyes gleamed. "The cops are gonna be pissed when we show."

"They'd expect media."

"Yeah. But not this soon. They're only about an hour ahead of us."

"How'd you hear about the story?"

"Got a text message. A tip."

"Who?" Last time she'd received the tip. She wondered if the informant was the same person.

"Don't know. Don't care."

Thick aftershave coiled around her. "Why do you look so happy about this?"

He showed no hint of apology. "Nothing would make me happier than to rattle Detective Warwick's cage. I didn't appreciate his insinuations the other day."

"He was doing his job. Just like we are."

His grip on the steering wheel tightened. "Yeah, well some cops take the authority thing too far, if you ask me."

"Maybe some. But not him."

Brett shot her a glance. "It sounds like you like the guy."

She did. A lot. But that was the last thing Brett needed

to hear. "He saved my life last summer. I'd have bled to death if not for him."

That mollified Brett a fraction. "Just don't go soft on him. I want you to attack this story. This story will go national now that there are three victims, and I want Ten to get the credit."

She wanted to report the story because the murdered women deserved to have their stories told. *They* deserved to be heard, to be remembered, and to have justice. Fame or the need for publicity did not drive her on this case.

Fifteen minutes later they pulled onto the office development's main road. They had wound down the neatly manicured road about a half mile when they spotted the flashing blue lights of the police squad cars. Brett parked in the lot of a midrise building a hundred yards from the crime zone. The Channel 10 truck with Mike behind the wheel arrived seconds behind them and parked near Brett's car.

Kendall got out and braced herself against the cold. She was anxious to find out more about the victim. She spoke briefly to Mike and they crossed the lot and a grassy patch of land to the next parking lot, where crime scene tape held back the growing crowd, made up mostly of morning joggers and contentious professionals anxious to get to their offices.

The crime scene appeared to be extended far beyond the norm, and try as she might she couldn't see past the collection of officers or around the low brick building where she guessed the body was found.

It took only a few minutes of questioning the crowd to discover who had found the body. When she spotted the man, standing by the tape smoking a cigarette, she went directly to him.

Kendall held out her hand. "Hi, my name is Kendall Shaw. Could I ask you a few questions?"

The man looked nervous as he puffed on the nearly spent cigarette. "Yeah, sure."

"And your name is?"

His face was pale. "Oh, yeah, sorry. Jeff McNamara. I'm a little rattled."

"I would be too if I found a body. Can we get you a soda or a coffee?"

He dropped the remnants of the cigarette to the ground and crushed the glowing tip with his tennis shoe. "No. No. I'm fine."

"Jeff, what were you doing here so early on a Sunday?"

"Catching up on work." He laughed nervously. "No good deed goes unpunished, right?"

She flashed a practiced smile. "Tell me about it." She didn't want to sound too anxious but her nerves were wound tight. "Jeff, can you tell me what the victim looked like?"

"Oh, yeah. Fact, I doubt I'll ever forget her face." He reached in his breast pocket and pulled out a packet of cigarettes. He removed one, lit it, and took a deep puff before he said, "Petite. Young. Blond."

"Blond?" That was different from the profile. "Can you tell how she was murdered?"

He shuddered. "No. But I didn't see any blood."

Brett came behind Kendall and looked at the man. "Do you think she could have been strangled, like the other two women?"

The man gasped. "What?"

Kendall glowered at Brett. "We don't know the others were strangled."

Brett looked unapologetic. "My texter said they were."

Kendall grabbed Brett by the arm and pulled him away. "Why didn't you tell me this earlier?"

"I'm telling you now." He leaned toward her. "Since when did you become so spineless?"

"I'm not spineless," she said, her teeth clenched. "But if you start blurting out facts to people while I'm interviewing them you make me look like a fool. Now back off."

He held up his hands, a glint of pleasure in his eyes. "Now that's the fighter instinct I want to see. Go for the jugular."

Disgusted, she turned from him. "Jeff, I'd like to interview you on camera."

Jeff sniffed and took another drag. "Yeah, sure. Why not?"

She motioned to Mike, who headed toward them. He clicked on his light and started taping. Kendall asked Jeff a dozen questions and he answered them well. It was a good interview.

When they'd wrapped up, she and Mike moved toward the ring of police cars that stood as a barrier between her and the yellow tape. The police had seen to it that no one was going to get too close. They were careful with all their crime scenes, but this one was locked up tight like Fort Knox.

She started to work the crowd, moving among the few bystanders trying to find out what she could about the victim. After an hour, she had little more to go on than when she'd started.

And yet, as the moments passed she felt a tremendous sense of loss as she thought about the dead woman. She'd not known her but she felt as if she had. What was wrong with her?

When she spotted Jacob, who was ducking under the yellow tape, she jogged, with Mike in tow, after him. "Detective! Sources tell me that the latest victim was strangled, like the other two victims." She didn't know for certain the women had been strangled but was looking for a reaction.

At the sound of her voice, his head whipped around and he glared at her. He strode toward her, mindful that the camera was trained on him. "We have no comment, Ms. Shaw."

"Was she strangled, like the others?"

Jacob didn't speak, but the subtle shift in his expression told her that she'd hit her mark. The women *had* all been strangled. Dear God. "The county has a serial killer in its midst, doesn't it?"

His expression turned fierce. "We don't know that."

She knew he was just mad enough to lose it and give her a quote. "The other two victims were in their mid- to late thirties with dark brown hair. This victim had blond hair. Do you think the serial killer is changing his M.O.?"

Jacob ground his teeth. She sensed that controlling his temper required all his resolve right now. "No comment."

Mike kept taping, but Jacob didn't rise to the bait. He ducked back under the yellow tape.

"Why do you think he's killing them?!" she shouted after him. The need to know felt more personal than professional.

He kept walking.

"Come on, Detective! Give me a comment!"

Silent, he disappeared around the side of the building. She turned away from the tape and shoved out a breath. Mike stopped taping.

*Why was he killing them?*

The question replayed over and over in her head as she headed back toward the crowd to ask more questions.

From a distance, Allen watched the chaos at the crime scene. The text messages had certainly stirred things up today. He smiled as he stared at the worried faces of the crowd. Their worry and fear excited him. He felt more alive than he had in years.

# Chapter Eighteen

*Sunday, January 20, 1:00 P.M.*

Kendall got under Jacob's skin every time she was in shouting distance. The woman was a damn pit bull who'd push any button to get a quote. He'd have asked her how she knew the other victims had been strangled, but the damn camera was rolling and the last thing he needed was for his comments to end up on the news.

Tess approached him, her face bright red from the cold. "Jacob."

"Yeah."

He was so consumed by Kendall and the case he didn't even feel awkward about their kiss on Friday night. "What do you have?"

She was all business. "I've found a driver's license tucked deep in the victim's pants pocket." She handed him the license, now sealed in a plastic evidence bag. "The victim appears to match the picture. Her name is Amanda Sorenson."

Jacob shoved out a sigh. "Right. Thanks."

He flipped open his phone and dialed the missing persons officer on duty. He quickly learned that the parents of an Amanda Sorenson had filed a missing persons report on their daughter thirty-six hours ago when she didn't show up for work on Friday night.

He tucked the phone back in his pocket and glanced around at the growing number of cops for Zack. When he spotted him talking to Ayden, he made his way to him.

Ayden's expression was grim and he looked as if he'd aged twenty years in the last two hours.

Jacob quickly updated the two. "We need to talk to the Sorensons before the media gets to them."

"Agreed. Someone is leaking information," Ayden said. "I want hourly updates on this."

"Sure."

Jacob and Zack ducked around the back of the building and got into Jacob's car, which was parked away from the media cameras. Jacob fired up the engine and they drove out of the development onto the main thoroughfare.

Zack telephoned the contact number for the Sorensons, identified himself to Mr. Sorenson, and the two agreed to a meeting. He closed his phone. "The guy sounds like a wreck."

"Wouldn't you be?"

"Yeah."

Somberness settled between the detectives as they drove to the address supplied by the missing persons' officer. Neither relished the conversation they were about to have.

Twenty minutes later they arrived at a neatly kept colonial brick house in a middle-class neighborhood. They parked in the paved driveway and walked up to the front. Jacob rang the bell and the door snapped open almost instantly. The two people standing there were tall, long limbed, and fair, like their daughter. Their hair had long ago turned gray, and he found himself trying to figure out which one Amanda favored. He decided she must be a blend of the two.

"Mr. and Mrs. Sorenson, I'm Detective Jacob Warwick. This is my partner, Zack Kier."

Mr. Sorenson's gray eyes paled with worry. He held out his hand and shook Jacob's and Zack's hands. "This isn't good, is it?"

Jacob didn't want to have this conversation on the front porch. "Can we come inside?"

Mrs. Sorenson's eyes filled with unshed tears as if she knew the worst. "Please, come in," she said.

They stepped out of the cold and into the warm foyer carpeted with an Oriental runner. They followed the couple into a pristine living room that looked as if it didn't get used often.

They all sat. Mr. Sorenson was the first to speak. "What is this about?"

Mrs. Sorenson looked at her husband and squeezed his hand.

Jacob leaned forward clasping his hands in front of him until his joints ached. "Mr. and Mrs. Sorenson. We believe we found your daughter this morning. She was carrying her driver's license and her face matched the photo." He drew in a breath, dreading this part. "She was dead. We believe murdered."

Mrs. Sorenson dropped her head and started to weep. "I knew something was wrong when she didn't show up to work. I knew it. I went by her apartment on Saturday but she wasn't there."

"I'm sorry," Zack said softly.

"How did she die?" Mr. Sorenson asked. Anger mingled with sadness in his eyes.

"We can't say just yet," Jacob said.

Mrs. Sorenson's red-rimmed eyes pierced him. "Why not? She was our child."

The wall behind them was covered with pictures of their children. The pictures scanned decades and included shots of them at their graduations, during holidays, and with their sports teams. It was easy to pick Amanda out of the mix.

"The investigation is complicated. We think whoever killed your daughter may have been involved in other crimes," Jacob said.

"Two other women have been murdered in the last couple of weeks," Mr. Sorenson said. "Are you referring to those women?"

Jacob purposefully avoided the question. "Tell me about Amanda. Boyfriends, her job, friends."

Mrs. Sorenson wiped a tear from her face. "Amanda had a boyfriend last year but she broke up with him. He was a good guy and we didn't blame him for the breakup. She never stayed with anyone too long. She liked her independence. She was an artist. A painter. She was quite good and was making a name for herself."

"What about friends?" Jacob asked.

"She had some girlfriends, but again no one close."

"She kept to herself," Jacob said. He'd heard that statement when the other victims had been described.

"Basically," her mother said. "She loved her art and her work. That's what she put her energy into."

"Has she always been a loner?" Zack asked.

Her mother closed her eyes and dabbed the corners. She pulled in a breath and looked at Jacob. "Amanda was always moody. She would spend hours alone in her room listening to music and working on her art. I always assumed that that was who she was. So I left her alone so she could paint. That generally calmed her."

Three women. Each lived alone. Each couldn't sustain a relationship.

"What kind of things did she paint?" Jacob asked.

"Flowers. Clouds. A white house with a wide front porch and a picket fence. Little girls playing."

"Those images don't fit your description of a moody woman," Jacob observed.

"Her pictures always had a sadness about them." Mrs. Sorenson swallowed. "I assumed those images had to do with her life before she came to live with us."

Jacob raised his gaze. "Before?"

"Before we adopted her," Mr. Sorenson said. "We adopted Amanda when she was ten."

Jacob eased forward in his seat. "Do you know anything about her birth family?"

Mrs. Sorenson shook her head. "No. It was a closed adoption. At one point we tried to find out. She was having trouble sleeping and we thought if we understood her past better we could help her. But the agency director told us the records were sealed. She wouldn't tell us anything."

"Isn't it common to know something about an adopted child's past?" Zack asked.

Mrs. Sorenson smiled. "I suppose. Amanda was the only child we ever adopted. Our other five children are ours." Her cheeks colored. "I mean they are our birth children."

"Has her name always been Amanda?"

"That was her name when she came to us. And she never told us differently." Mrs. Sorenson frowned. "But I suspect it was some kind of code name used by the placing agency."

"Code name?"

"They used to do that. Create new names for the birth mother and the adopted child. Sometimes they made new birthdays. It was a way to protect identities."

Jacob drummed his fingers on his leg. "Did she ever talk about her birth family?"

Mrs. Sorenson shook her head. "Never. I tried to get her to open up about it but she never would. I've been told that's not so uncommon for a child who's been placed at a later age. I think the transition from Amanda's old home to ours was abrupt and traumatic."

"Abrupt?"

"We weren't given details." She frowned. "At the time I didn't question the social worker. I thought if we could love her enough we could overcome whatever she'd been through. But it was never that easy."

Mr. Sorenson frowned. "She was always testing us. Seeing how far she could go."

Mrs. Sorenson smiled, her eyes watery and red. "I think she needed to prove to herself that no matter what we wouldn't give up on her."

"She was placed in your home by the state?" Jacob asked.

"A private agency. Virginia Adoption Services."

Jacob nodded. "Where did she go to school?"

"She attended Virginia Commonwealth University. She earned a degree in painting. Later she earned a master's in art history. She was a talented painter."

"Did she sell her work?"

Mrs. Sorenson offered a faltering smile. "She'd just sold a couple of pieces a few months ago. She was so excited. Until then she'd worked as a clerk in a rental car company to pay the bills. We often had to help her with rent." Tears welled in her eyes and she started to cry again.

Mr. Sorenson wrapped his arm around his wife's shoulder. "Can these questions wait? My wife is too torn up about this."

Mrs. Sorenson raised her head. "I can keep talking. I must keep talking. I owe that to Amanda. I feel like I failed her in so many ways."

"Why do you say that?" Jacob asked.

"I wanted to bond with her so badly. I tried everything, but nothing worked. I hate to say it, but there were times when I resented her. I gave her everything and it was never enough."

"Have you ever heard the name Rachel?" Jacob asked.

"No," Mr. Sorenson said.

"What about Judith or Ruth?"

His wife looked up. "I heard her say Judith in her dreams when she first came to us. When I asked her who she was, she wouldn't tell."

Jacob looked at Zack. This was the first tangible connection between the victims. "If you think of anything that might link Amanda to the name Judith, Ruth, or Rachel would you let us know?"

"Of course," Mr. Sorenson said. "We'll give you anything you need."

The couple rose and escorted the detectives out of their house. Neither of the detectives spoke until Jacob had fired up the engine and pulled into traffic.

"What the hell does the killer see in these women that we don't?" Zack asked.

Jacob drummed his fingers on the steering wheel. "We know Vicky was in foster care. Amanda was adopted. Maybe Jackie was adopted as well."

"No one said Jackie was."

"No one said she wasn't. And it's a question we never thought to ask."

"You really think this is the connection?"

"I don't know. But it's all we've got right now."


It was past lunchtime when Cole exited his house through the back door and crossed the alley to Kendall's yard. He was certain that Kendall's house was empty. The contractor had come and gone for the day. The roommate was gone. And Kendall had left hours ago.

Now was as good a time as any to have a look around her place.

Quickly, he slipped through her garage into the back-yard and hurried to her back door. He'd been watching her for the last couple of days and knew she kept a key hidden behind a loose brick by the back door. It was a stupid habit, one that could cause her a lot of trouble. But for now he was glad because it made getting in easier. He opened the back door, moved inside, and closed the door behind him. He pocketed the key. "Hey, Kendall, it's me, Cole. Are you home? I need to borrow an egg." Lame. But he didn't care.

All he cared about was that no one answered him. And no one did.

He moved down the back hallway, listening as his foot-steps echoed in the house. He stopped in the kitchen. The new cabinets had been installed. They looked nice.

He hurried up the center staircase and headed to the room at the back of the house she used as an office. He'd watched her from his house. Generally, when she came home from work it was tea and quiet time in her office.

The space was neat and orderly. The furniture style looked French, he thought, but he couldn't be sure. She'd taken time to ensure that every piece went to-gether. Light blues, pale yellows, and whites made the space look feminine but not fussy. A man could sit on the generously stuffed couch and read while she sat at her desk.

She cared about her home. In fact, from what he'd learned, she'd taken extra care to make this house very special. A showpiece for sure, but it was also very livable and welcoming.

So unlike his place, which was furnished with a couple of lawn chairs, a TV set on crates, and a sleeping bag on a blow-up floor mattress. The furnishings were as transient as he was.

Cole couldn't remember the last time he'd felt at home. For the last couple of years, he'd either been living in cheap motels or out of his car. He'd forgotten what it felt like to have family—to know a welcoming gaze, hear laughter, or enjoy the company of those he trusted.

He ignored the tightness in his chest and moved into Kendall's office.

He didn't turn on the lights, knowing the light could draw unwanted attention even during the day. He moved behind her desk, then sat down. The papers on the desktop were neatly stacked. Pencils, pens, and paper clips were all in their proper places. The in-box had a few papers but nothing dating back for more than a week. Kendall Shaw lived a very orderly, controlled life.

He opened the front desk drawer. He wasn't sure what he was searching for. But he'd know when he saw it. Then he opened the side drawers. All the drawers, like the desktop, were neat and orderly. Nothing jumped out at him.

Cole shoved out a breath. "There has to be something here."

He sat in silence. A clock ticked. A cloud passed, robbing the room of some of its light. He tapped his fingers on the desk. Pushing back from the desk, he glanced to his right. That's when he saw her handwritten notes about Carnie Winchester, an adoption search consultant.

His heart pounded faster as he leaned under and retrieved the letter and read it. Kendall was searching for her birth family.

Just then he heard the back door open and close. Footsteps sounded in the kitchen.

"Shit." He replaced the paper and rose slowly, careful not to make a sound, and moved across the room. He stood behind the door and listened.

Footsteps sounded on the stairs. Whoever was home was coming upstairs. He curled his hands into fists. He couldn't be found. Not now.

He wedged his body back against the wall. Holding his breath, he listened as the steps paused in front of the office doorway.

"Kendall?"

It was Nicole. The roommate.

She peeked her head into the office. "Kendall, are you home?"

Cole didn't want to hurt a pregnant woman. But he couldn't be found here. If she came into the room . . .

*Go away. I don't want to hurt you.*

Nicole hesitated in the doorway and then withdrew. She moved into her room and closed the door. He waited until he heard the sound of water running before he moved out of the room and quickly down the stairs. Quietly, he opened and closed the back door and then replaced the key behind the brick. He sprinted across the backyard, through the garage, and across the alley until he was safely back in his house.

He closed the door. His heart pounded in his chest. He sensed he was so close to the answers he needed. Carnie Winchester. She was searching for Kendall's family. Time to pay her a visit and see what she knew.

Jacob, Zack, and a forensics team arrived at Amanda Sorenson's town house an hour after the detectives had talked to her parents. They had obtained a search warrant even though the Sorensons had given their consent to search.

The apartment was very ordinary. Not much furniture in the living or dining rooms. Instead, there were a couple of easels with canvases on them. The paintings were just what Amanda's mother had described: little girls playing. There were five girls in one painting, three in the other. Each painting had a happy theme, and yet the images possessed darkness under the light.

They left Jacob feeling sad, disconnected.

The detectives searched the house but found nothing out of the ordinary. They spent the next six hours talking to neighbors trying to find out everything they could about Amanda Sorenson. They learned little. She kept to herself. Very artsy. Played her music too loud sometimes. Nice. No special visitors. No known boyfriend.

Jacob stood in the living room staring at the painting of the three girls. Amanda had blurred their features. Had she done it for effect? Or was there another reason why the girls didn't have clear features?

Jacob glanced at the second painting, which depicted five faceless young girls. They sat under a tree. The sun shone brightly over their heads.

Three dead. Did the killer have two victims to go?

"What is the key to this case?" Jacob muttered as he stared at the painting. He turned to Zack, who was going through a pile of bills. "I want to know who bought her paintings a few months ago. Let's turn this place upside down if we have to."

# Chapter Nineteen

Dana Miller was very pleased with herself. She'd just closed a five million–dollar real estate deal and the 6 percent commission equated to a three hundred thousand–dollar fee. "Not bad for a morning's work."

She turned from her desk and stared out the large picture window. Her office was at the top of a skyscraper in the city of Richmond and overlooked the James River. Everyone in the company envied her. They wanted her office. Her salary. Her life.

And yet she felt bored. Empty. Sad. This last year, large deals had become nothing more than a game. And lately, she didn't even care much who won or lost.

She wanted more than what she had. She needed more.

Dana turned back to her desk and from a sleek chrome drawer she pulled out a gun. It was a thirty-eight. Small, compact, easily hidden, left no cartridges behind, and very deadly if push came to shove.

She'd not gotten as far as she had in life by playing by the rules and this latest quest of hers was no different.

She'd tried to play by the rules with Nicole. But the

woman had refused the offer she'd made for the baby. In fact, Nicole had stopped taking her calls. And time was running out.

Dana opened the gun's chamber and inspected the six bullets. She had one last offer for Nicole. It was an offer that wouldn't be rejected.


Nicole's belly weighed heavily as she scooted off the OB's exam table. The paper gown gaped open in the back, leaving her skin chilled. She'd peed not fifteen minutes ago but already her bladder felt full. "This baby can't be born fast enough."

She quietly dressed in her stretch pants and oversized shirt. She glanced in the mirror and adjusted the stray strands of her hair and moistened her lips. Her face looked bloated and round. And somewhere along the line she'd lost her cheekbones.

A soft knock at the door had her turning from the mirror. "I'm dressed."

Her doctor entered. Dr. Young was in her midforties but had an athletic body honed by a strict workout regimen. She had brown hair, pulled back at the nape of her neck, and she wore no makeup. "Well, you and the baby are doing very, very well. Your blood pressure is a bit high, though."

"I guess I'm a little stressed."

The doctor nodded. They'd talked about Nicole's adoption plan. "Are you talking to the baby? Holding your stomach?"

"Not so much, why?"

"It's good for you both. You will calm and the baby will relax. You might give her to another family to raise, but if you can make her feel loved now she'll be better off down the road."

"Really?"

Dr. Young slipped her hands into the pockets of her white jacket. "Believe me, pregnancy affects the baby as much as the mother."

"I've been so stressed during this pregnancy. So are you now telling me I've scared the kid?"

The doctor smiled. "Hardly. Just take more deep breaths and try to relax. It's time to cut back on work and put your feet up."

Both sounded like wonderful luxuries. "Okay."

"Also, your cervix is shortening and preparing for the baby's birth. It won't be much longer now. A week tops."

That news triggered a surge of panic. "There are days when this baby can't come soon enough and other days when I don't want it ever to be born." Nicole smiled. "Very normal, I suppose." She needed affirmation.

"It is." Dr. Young laid her hand on Nicole's shoulder. "You're doing a good job."

She didn't feel like she was. "Thanks, Dr. Young."

Nicole shook hands with the doctor, promised to return in a week, and shrugged on her coat. Outside the cold felt good on her skin. She shoved her hands into her pockets and cut across the parking lot toward her car.

She never noticed the car parked in the corner of the lot. Or realized she was being watched.

*Ruth. Judith. And Rachel.* Soon the family would be complete. Allen wanted to bring Eve into the family now. His hands trembled at just the thought of touching the soft skin of her neck and feeling her pulse thrum wildly. His body quivered with excitement.

He drew in a deep breath, knowing now more than ever that he had to be patient. Before Eve he had to welcome Sarah.

When he'd been alone with Rachel the devil had sorely tempted him. He'd touched her in places he shouldn't have. Done things he knew were wrong. But in the end he'd managed to keep himself for Eve.

He stood in the shadows and watched Eve cross the parking lot. She moved briskly. His body tingled with an anticipation so acute he could barely restrain himself.

*Patience.*

He chanted the word over and over like a mantra. It was so hard to be patient when he was so lonely. All he wanted was his Family gathered around him.

"Soon, Eve, soon."

Kendall had managed a few hours of sleep last night and was feeling sharper. She'd spent most of yesterday working on the triple murder story and was anxious to get to work to review the tape.

She'd made a cup of coffee and was about to step in the shower when her phone rang. "Kendall Shaw."

"Kendall, this is Brett."

"I'll be at the station in an hour. I'll have tape for you to look at by noon."

"Don't rush. I've decided to change the way we're covering this story."

She gripped the phone. "What do you mean?"

"I want you at the station. I want to do live broadcasts from each murder scene. I need you behind the anchor desk talking to the reporters."

Outrage burned inside her. "This is *my* story."

"It's the station's story now. It's too big for just you. And polling suggests that viewers don't like you in the field. They like you behind the desk."

*He* liked her behind the desk. "I don't want to give this story up."

"The decision's been made. See you at two at the station. We're having a meeting with the reporters covering the story now." He hung up.

She stared at the phone and then hurled it onto her bed. "Damn him!"

"She was a quiet and moody kid from the moment she hit my doorstep," said Janice Waters. The woman wore jeans and an oversized shirt that covered her large frame. She lived in a Victorian house on the south side of the metro area. The house was filled with the scent of macaroni and cheese and the sound of kids running around upstairs.

Around Jacob, a sea of toys and dozens of shoes cluttered the foyer's floor. The walls were plastered with dozens of school pictures, representing twelve or thirteen kids. They were Janice's foster kids, as she'd proudly said when he'd arrived.

He'd finally been able to track down someone in social services who would give him the names of Vicky Draper's foster families. Jacob chose to talk to the first family who had fostered her.

"How old was Vicky Draper when she came to you?" Jacob asked.

"Well, she wasn't Draper then. I think her name was Turner."

Jacob wanted to know why Vicky had come to foster care. It was a long shot, but something told him that there might be a connection between her and Amanda, the victim who had been adopted at an older age. Vicky's foster care file had scant information in it. "Did she ever talk about her life before she came to you?"

"No. Never said a word. But I remember she had terrible dreams. Nightmares that would wake her up in the middle of the night. Lord, those blood-curdling screams used to scare the bejesus out of me."

"Did she mention any brothers or sisters?"

"No. I remember I used to find her hiding in the closet sometimes. When I asked her why she was in the closet, she said it made her feel safe. She said no one could find her there."

Jacob tightened his jaw. "What about the scars on her hand?"

"The wounds were still fresh when she came to me. Fact, I had to take her to the doctor to get the stitches removed. Doctor said it looked like a knife wound to him 'cause it was so clean and straight. I asked her social worker about Vicky's past but she wouldn't say a word." Janice's lips flattened. "I didn't like that woman at all. She thought she was better than me—that she knew what was best for everyone."

Jacob's mind zeroed in on her initial comment about the wound. "She'd been cut with a knife before she came to you?"

The woman nodded as other memories started to return. "Yes. And Vicky hated knives, as I remember. Wouldn't come near me while I was cooking dinner."

What the hell had happened to that kid? "Why'd she leave your care?"

"She started setting fires. I couldn't have that. I had the other kids to think about."

"You have any pictures of her?"

She frowned and rested her hand on her full hip. "I think I do. Follow me."

He followed her into the kitchen to a desk tucked in the corner. It was piled high with papers, kids' artwork, and a few open cookbooks. She jerked open a door and started to rummage through old pictures and papers. Three quarters of the way down she pulled out a yearbook for Robinson Middle School. The front cover had been blackened with slashes of Magic Marker. "This one was hers. I remember being so darn sad when she ruined it." She shook her head. "I don't know why I save this stuff." She flipped to the seventh grade and found Vicky's picture. "Here you go."

Jacob studied the picture of the little girl who stared boldly into the camera. Her skin was young and fresh and her hair a dark brown. Without the tats and piercing she looked even more like Jackie White. "Can I keep this?"

"Sure. I was so sorry to hear about Vicky. But I always figured she'd come to a bad end. Whatever happened to her before she came to me damaged her good."

"Thanks for your help."

"Sure."

He hesitated. "Why didn't you like Vicky's social worker?"

Janice snorted. "She had this notion that once a child came into her care, the past no longer mattered. She'd go out of her way to erase a kid's past. She'd change their names, birth dates, even data about their birth families. I didn't like her approach. These kids need to know their past. Good or bad, they got to know."

Jacob frowned. "You ever talk to the social worker about that?"

"We had words one time. She told me she knew best and to keep my mouth shut or there'd be no more foster kids for me."

Brett had skillfully avoided Kendall, robbing her of the fight she was itching to have. When she'd finally caught up to him, there'd been no changing his mind. He'd reminded her of her contract, her duties and dropped hints of a lawsuit. In the end, she'd had no choice but to accept his changes.

Now, with less than a minute to air, Kendall stared at her copy for the six o'clock broadcast. They were leading with the third killing. The studio was tense. He had stationed three reporters around town and they were going to give live reports. Kendall was set up to question the reporters directly.

"Where's Brett?" Kendall asked. She had a quick question about the timing of the third report.

Her producer, a tall blond woman with broad shoulders, shrugged. "He's stepped out. Said he'd be back soon."

Kendall stared at her producer as if the woman had lost her mind. "You're kidding? He's left the studio?"

The producer looked equally frustrated. "He bit my head off when I asked him where he was going." She held up ten fingers. "Thirty seconds to air. Can I help?"

"No, thanks. I'll figure it out." Automatically she moistened her lips and straightened her shoulders. "Did he say when he'd be back or where he was going?"

"Nope."

Her anger seethed. "Great."

The producer held up her hand. "Ten seconds!" she shouted.

As the producer clicked off the time on her fingers, Kendall thought about Brett. What the hell was he up to now?

The red light on the camera clicked on and Kendall stared directly into the camera. She pushed aside her personal feelings. Her expression and voice somber, she said, "Good evening . . ."

It was dark when Nicole left her studio. She'd spent most of the day working as fast as she could to wrap up her projects because she wanted to heed the doctor's advice. She'd finished printing the last portrait and had boxed it for delivery.

After flipping open her cell phone, she dialed Kendall's home number. She waited for the message to play and for the beep. "I'm running late tonight. Don't freak. Just wrapping up a few more details and then I promise to put my feet up and take it easy."

Nicole hung up, dropped the phone into her purse, and ducked her head against the cold as she headed to her car. As she shoved the key in the lock, she heard footsteps behind her.

She turned and found Dana standing just feet from her. "Dana, what do you want?"

Dana's thin frame huddled in her fur coat. "I want to talk to you about the baby again."

The woman didn't understand no and that sent a ping of fear down Nicole's spine. "We've been through this. I'm not letting you adopt this child."

Dana's frustration burned through her practiced smile. "But you don't want it!"

The challenge had her taking a step back. "I don't know that! And even if I don't, I won't give it to you."

"Why not?"

"I don't like you." She'd not meant to sound so harsh. But there it was. She was through trying to dance around the woman's feelings.

Dana's face hardened. She fumbled in her coat pocket and pulled out a gun. Moonlight glinted off the barrel, which was pointing straight at Nicole. "I really don't care if you like me or not."

Nicole glanced around the dark parking lot hoping to see someone. There was no one.

Dana grinned. "No one is going to help you now. I

tried to be nice. I tried to pay you. But you give me no choice now but to take the baby."

Nicole's hand slid to her stomach. A violent protective urge rushed her senses. "You can't have her."

"I'm going to take her."

"If you shoot me you'll hurt the baby."

Dana didn't look concerned. "I can shoot you in several places that will incapacitate you but not hurt the baby. I've been practicing for this, you see."

Nicole took a step back. She'd seen this crazed look before. In her late husband's eyes. "You're insane."

"I'm practical. I know what I want and I go after it. Now start walking."

"Where?"

"My car is parked in the corner of the lot."

"I'm not going."

Dana jabbed the gun at her. "If you force my hand, you'll lose. Because if I don't get what I want I'll start going after the people you care about. Namely that snooty Kendall Shaw."

"Kendall has nothing to do with this."

"She's your friend. She's leverage. Now start walking or I go after Kendall." A dark smile twisted her lips. "I wouldn't have to kill her to ruin her. A cupful of acid to the face and her life would be destroyed forever."

Nicole felt sick. Trapped. "Leave Kendall out of this."

"That's up to you. Start walking or I go after her."

Nicole took a step toward the car. There had to be a way out of this. She'd escaped Richard. She would get away from Dana.

Dana pulled keys from her pocket and clicked the remote. The lights of a BMW flashed and the trunk popped open. "Then there's your friend Lindsay. She's expecting, I hear. I'd hate for her to have a nasty accident and lose her baby."

"You're evil."

"We all have a touch of it in us." She jabbed the gun in the air. "Now drop your purse on the ground and move!"

"No."

Dana's face twisted with rage. In a split second she rushed Nicole and brought the butt of the gun down on her head. Pain stunned Nicole and she stumbled. Dana pushed her into the trunk and grabbed her purse. She slammed the lid closed.

Nicole shook her head and immediately started to pound on the trunk lid. "Let me out! Let me out!"

Nicole then began looking for the lever, which was supposed to glow in the dark. But she couldn't see it anywhere. As her head throbbed, she frantically patted the darkness expecting to feel it. Her stomach contracted painfully. The pain pulled her attention from the lever for a moment, and she had to breathe deeply until it passed.

Suddenly a gunshot rang out.

Dana screamed. Another shot followed, and someone fell against the trunk and seemed to slide to the ground.

Nicole started to pound on the trunk, crying, "Help! I'm in here! Dana has locked me in the trunk!"

"It's all right, Nicole." The voice was masculine. Very soothing.

She nearly wept with relief. "Let me out. That woman is crazy. She's trying to take my baby."

"She's not going to take your baby," the man said. "It's all right now."

"Can you find the keys? I think they're in her pocket. You can let me out. The release lever in here is gone. I think she disabled it."

She heard him move behind the car. Then she heard the clink of the keys. Thank God! He was going to save her.

Tense seconds passed as she waited for the trunk to pop open.

"Are you going to open the trunk?!" she shouted.

"Not just yet, Nicole. Not just yet."

The stranger moved away from the car, and for several long minutes there was nothing. She screamed, "Help!"

Finally, someone tapped on the trunk. "I'm back and Dana won't bother you anymore."

She waited for the lock to turn and when it didn't she begged, "Let me out, please!"

"I can't do that." The man moved to the front of the car, got in, and fired up the engine. The car backed up and started down the road.

Nicole curled into a tight ball as tears welled in her eyes. Dear God, who had her?

# Chapter Twenty

It was past midnight when Kendall got home from the television station. She was bone tired as she stood in the kitchen and flipped on the lights. Todd had hung the cabinets, attached the hardware, and installed the new appliances. The room looked stunning. And for a flicker of a moment she felt happy. However, the feeling flittered away, as it did of late.

She moved to the phone and played back the answering machine's messages. Two messages from Brett. He prattled on about work again like nothing had happened. And then the third message replayed. It was from Carnie.

"No rush to call me back," she said, sounding a bit breathless. "I got your paperwork and I want to go over a few things with you. Like I said, no rush. Just set up an appointment. Talk to you soon. Ciao."

Kendall stood in the half-lighted hallway, her heart suddenly pounding in her chest. She was really going to do this. She was going to search for her birth family. So many years of pretending and ignoring and now she was going to look. The decision left her feeling elated and oddly troubled, afraid even. What was the old adage, "Be careful what you wish for?"

The next message played. "Kendall, this is Jenny, your mom's old neighbor. I found something in my attic. I think it'll be of interest to you."

Kendall checked her watch. It was too late to call or visit Jenny. "Damn." She'd have to wait until morning.

The last message was from Nicole. She was going to be late. She sounded tired and her promise to cut back sounded heartfelt. Kendall nodded. "Good."

The front doorbell rang, yanking her from her thoughts. Thinking it must be Nicole, she moved quickly toward the door and peeked through the curtained glass panels.

Brett smiled at her. "I need to talk to you," he said.

She let the curtain drop and groaned. She opened the door. Cold air sent a chill through her. "Go away."

"We need to talk." The faint scent of whiskey wafted toward her.

"I don't think so. You screwed me over today and then didn't have the guts to face me at the office."

His smile turned brittle. "Look, I don't want to fight. I want to talk about us. About us getting back together."

Fatigue had eroded her patience. "There is no us." She moved to slam the door.

He shoved his foot in the doorjamb, keeping the door from closing. "I'm not giving up on you."

"I'm going to call the police," Kendall warned. Her voice had attitude, but she was afraid of Brett. She'd never seen him like this before and realized he wasn't stable.

He started to shove the door. Slowly it inched open.

Kendall pushed back. "Leave me alone, Brett."

"You don't understand."

"Is there a problem here?" Jacob Warwick's stern voice cut through the night behind Brett, making the slighter man snarl. Jacob's expression was fierce and his clenched fist said he was ready to fight if need be.

"What the hell are you doing here?" Brett snapped. His gaze turned accusing as it moved from Jacob to Kendall. He released the door and faced Jacob. "Kendall and I have personal things to work out."

Jacob's glance cut to Kendall and he studied her face for a second. "That true?"

"I've asked him to leave," Kendall said. Jacob was a welcome sight.

Jacob's icy stare shifted to Brett. "You heard Kendall. Leave."

"This is none of your business." Brett's words sounded like a whine.

"It is." Jacob seemed so calm, yet there was a fierceness about him that allowed no room for argument.

Brett backed up. "I'll have your job for this."

Jacob didn't flinch. "I don't think so."

Brett's eyes narrowed. "What are you doing here? It can't be police business."

Jacob didn't answer.

Kendall folded her arms over her chest. Let Brett think what he wanted about them. "Leave now."

Brett shook his head. "Didn't take you long, did it, Kendall? How long have you been sleeping with him?"

Her gaze was pure ice. "Leave."

Brett called her something under his breath and hurried down the stairs and around the corner.

Kendall let out a breath. "I'm not sure where you came from, but thanks."

Jacob kept his gaze trained on Brett. "He's more persistent than I first thought he'd be."

"I didn't expect that from him."

He watched Brett get in his car and drive off. "I'm not surprised."

"What are you doing here?"

"Can I ask you a few questions?"

"It's late."

He checked his watch. "Yes, but you normally don't get in until late."

She stepped aside and waited for him to pass by her before she closed the door. "What can I do for you?"

His masculine scent mingled with the cold and radiated off him. "This may be nothing, but I'm following up on a lead."

She arched a brow. "You're coming to me about a lead?"

He tightened his jaw. "This is strictly confidential, Kendall."

She smiled tartly. "When are you going to give me a quote?"

His expression remained serious. "Are you adopted?"

The question took her back. No one had ever asked her that. The answer was a simple yes but she couldn't bring herself to say it. "Why would you ask a question like that?"

"The third murder victim was adopted. The second had been in foster care. We haven't been able to determine if the first was or wasn't adopted. There's no denying the first two victims look like you."

"The third doesn't."

"No." He shoved his hand through his hair. "There are too many coincidences here to ignore. My gut is telling me all three women were adopted."

Kendall's throat tightened with unexpected emotion. "Yes, I was adopted."

He released the breath he was holding. The news didn't seem to please him. "What can you tell me about your past? Your birth family?"

"Nothing, other than my parents adopted me at age three. They never discussed it. I've just started trying to track down the past. But the records are sealed. I've only just hired a search consultant to see what she can find out." She tried to stay calm. "Do you think the killer is targeting adoptees?"

"I don't know." Dark circles hung under his eyes. "Like I said, I'm trying to tie the pieces together."

"And I'm one of the pieces."

"I think so, yes."

At this moment, she felt so utterly alone. Her life felt so hollow, so rootless. "Do you think those women are related to me?"

"I don't have any evidence yet. But yes, I do."

She ran long fingers through her hair. "I've been drawn to this story from the beginning." Her voice was barely a whisper.

Jacob didn't say anything. But with him so close, she didn't feel that alone. "I don't know if I'll have answers anytime soon. Carnie, the adoption consultant, said it could take years."

He laid a hand on her shoulder. Its warmth calmed her nerves. "I'd like to go to a judge and see if I can get your adoption file opened."

"Good luck. Carnie said she doesn't know of a closed adoption file that's ever been unsealed by the courts in Virginia. Apparently, death is not considered a good enough reason to open an adoption file."

She was surprised how candid she was being. But on a gut level, she trusted Jacob. "My mother's—my adoptive mother's—old neighbor left a message on my machine. She'd found something in her attic. She wouldn't say what it was."

"You'll call in the morning?"

"As early as I can."

"Good." A silence settled between them. There wasn't much more to say to each other.

He glanced at the door as if he suddenly realized that he was overstepping.

But she didn't want him to leave. Why was it when she was with him life just felt brighter, better, edgier?

Jacob looked down at her. She read the attraction in his eyes but doubted he'd try to kiss her again. She'd blown him off the last time, and if Jacob Warwick was anything, he was a man with pride. The move would have to be hers.

And Kendall wanted to kiss Jacob. She wanted to feel the touch of his skin against hers more than anything in the world. And it wasn't just about banishing the loneliness. She wanted him. Had wanted him for a long time.

She faced him and pressed her hand to his chest, felt the rapid beat of his heart. Rising on tiptoes, she kissed his lips. He didn't close his eyes or surrender, but stared at her.

"You don't want this," he said. "You're upset. Tired."

Kendall kept her body close to his. "There's a lot of crap in my life right now that I'm not sure of. But I'm sure of this."

Jacob brushed a stray strand of hair away from her face.

"I want you, Jacob." She waited, not willing to give more than she had until he made the next move.

And then he pulled her into his arms and kissed her. A soft moan rumbled in her chest as she wrapped her arms around his neck. His hard chest brushed her nipples and they quickly firmed. He took his time exploring the inside of her mouth, and she sensed the simmering heat inside him.

Then he pulled away and nibbled her ear with his teeth. "I want you, too."

She pulled him back, pressing her breasts against his chest, and kissed him harder.

There was no denying her this time. A soft growl rumbled in his chest as he crushed her against him and he kissed her back, pushing his tongue into her mouth. Greedily, she accepted him. She dug her fingers into his shoulders and clung to him.

Jacob had imagined this moment for over a year and yet none of his fantasies compared to actually touching the woman.

She broke the kiss. Her breathing was quick, ragged. "My bedroom is upstairs."

He could barely think. "You're sure about this?"

"Yes."

Jacob kissed her again, fearing she wasn't real. And then allowed her to lead him up the stairs to her room. She turned on the light on the nightstand and it cast a warm glow over the four-poster bed.

He backed her up to the edge of the mattress until the backs of her legs pressed against it. He kissed her again. This time her hands fumbled with his jacket. She pushed it over his shoulders and he quickly shrugged it off without breaking the kiss.

He slid his hands from her silk-clad shoulders to her breasts. They felt so soft, round, full in his hands. She groaned and arched into him.

Jacob unfastened the pearl buttons of her blouse and slid her blouse off. He leaned forward and kissed the soft mounds of her breasts, which peeked out over a white lace bra. Her scent enveloped him and he realized he'd never wanted any woman as much as he wanted her now.

She pulled his V-neck sweater off and slid her manicured hands over his chest. He pushed her backward and the two fell onto the bed. His weight pressed her into the mattress. He kissed her neck as he unsnapped the bra clasp between her breasts. He captured a pink nipple between his lips and suckled. She arched her back and pressed into him.

The next few moments were blurred by desire. He shrugged off his pants with her help and then pulled her panties off. He hovered above her wanting to savor this moment but knowing that the raging desire in him wouldn't allow it.

He pushed into her tight center. She gasped with desire and cupped her hands over his bare buttocks. Desire washed over him and he started to move inside her. She matched him stroke for stroke, her desire as wanton as his.

They found their release in one blissful explosion and he collapsed down on her, resting his face in the hollow of her neck. His heart thundered in his chest and mingled with hers. He didn't raise his head. But in this moment, his life felt right. The hole that always lurked in his soul had closed. He traced circles on the scar on her shoulder, realizing for the first time that he needed assurance. "Regrets?"

"No. You?"

Her voice held no hint of the emotion he'd felt in her body when they'd made love. He met her gaze. Her expression was guarded. On reflex, he reined in his feelings. He didn't want to box her in a corner because he knew how he'd react if someone did the same to him. He'd bolt. "It does complicate things."

"Only if we let it."

The added casualness in her voice triggered caution in his. "So we go back to business as usual?"

"Why not?"

Annoyance burned in him. "Like nothing happened."

"If that's what you want."

Normally he was so guarded with his thoughts and feelings. But he sensed that if he didn't reach out he'd lose something very valuable. "That's not what I want."

She stared at him, but she didn't say anything.

He tucked a curl behind her ear. "I want you. And not just now. But tomorrow. And the next day."

She let her gaze dip to his chest. She didn't speak. Then she raised her head and kissed him on the lips. In that kiss he felt a wave of emotion and longing that seared into him.

When she broke the kiss they were both breathless. "I'm not so different from you. I don't talk about feelings so well," she said.

"Old dogs can learn new tricks."

"To be honest, you scare me."

"Why?"

"I like you."

"And that's a bad thing?"

"I have a tendency to back away when I start to like someone."

He turned her on her back and cupped her chin. "That's something I'm also famous for." He traced her lips with his fingertips.

"So maybe we should cut our losses now."

He shook his head. "Let's take it one day at a time. Keep talking to each other. See where it takes us."

"Okay." She kissed him on the lips.

Relief didn't wash over him. Nor a feeling that all would be right with the world. Whatever they had was fragile and they'd have to tread carefully. Still, he decided then that she'd be worth the risk.

They made love a second time. This time they took their time exploring each other's bodies. When the second orgasm shuddered through them, they fell asleep nestled in each other's arms.

*The banging on the closet door grew louder. "Let me in. I won't hurt you, Eve."*

*The little girl huddled in the corner, clawing at the paneling, hoping she could dissolve into the wall and never be seen.*

*"Eve, I won't hurt you." The knob twisted and the door started to open.*

*"Stop!"*

Kendall sat up in bed, her body drenched in sweat. The room was dark. Her heart raced in her chest.

"What's wrong?" Jacob's voice was clear and alert as if he'd been awake.

Kendall swallowed, shook her head trying to clear the image from her mind. "A dream."

He pulled her against him. "You're ice cold."

Cocooned in his arms, she could feel the fear abating faster than it normally did. "I'm okay now."

"You said before that you'd been having dreams."

She'd only briefly mentioned the dreams in the parking lot last week. "I'm surprised you remembered."

"I don't forget details when it comes to you." For a moment he simply held her. "Tell me about it."

"It's the same every time. I'm in a closet. I'm just a child. And I hear a woman's screams. Someone is trying to get into the closet." Her throat felt dry. "At first I thought it was just a nightmare. Now, I think it really happened before my adoption."

"All the more reason to find out where you came from."

"The past scares me," she whispered. "I don't remember it but I sense something terrible happened. And I think my mother knew what it was. I think that's why she kept the adoption a secret. Mom has erased all traces of my past and I don't think I'm ever going to find my birth family."

Jacob tightened his hold. "I'm very good at finding people. I'll help, if you want."

It was the kindest thing anyone had ever offered. "You mean that?"

"Yeah. We'll figure this out together."


The trunk of the car opened and Nicole drew back trying to press her swollen body into the recesses. Her head still ached. "Leave me alone!"

A hooded, masked figure stood over her. "Shh. There's nothing to worry about, Nicole. It's all right. I'm here to help."

"Then let me go."

"I can't do that. Not yet."

"You can't have my baby!"

"Shh. You worry too much. I would never separate a child from its mother." The figure reached into the trunk and grabbed her.

She strained against the tight grip but she might as well have been trying to break iron. "Let me go!"

He practically lifted her up with one arm and set her on the ground. Her knees felt weak and her belly ached from the weight of the child. She was exhausted, dehydrated, and barely able to stand on her own. She tried to wrench free but got nowhere.

"Don't fight me. It's not good for the baby." His voice was so damn calm. "Let me get you upstairs so you can rest."

She glanced past him through the darkness to a large white house. It was old, practically falling apart.

"Did you kill Dana?"

"She wasn't very nice to you. She wanted to steal your baby." He started to pull her toward the house.

She dug her heels into the frozen dirt. "No!"

"Yes." He jerked her hard this time and she stumbled forward.

Her belly contracted. "Please, I need to be in a hospital. I'm going into labor."

"Ah, that's a wonderful thing, Nicole. I can't wait to see the baby." He half pulled, half carried her up the front steps of the house and through the front door. "I hear it's a girl. Perfect."

Panic swelled inside Nicole as she stared around the darkened foyer. The place smelled of mold and rot. At the top of the staircase was a light. "I can't have my baby here. I can't!"

"Yes, you can. This house has seen the birth of many babies."

Tears welled in her eyes and she pulled against him as they started up the stairs. "Let me go!" She started to scream.

"No one can hear you."

She screamed louder.

He didn't respond until she'd exhausted her lungful of breath. "That's not good for you or the baby. You have to stay calm." He pulled her toward a door and pushed it open with his booted foot.

The well-lit room stood in stark contrast to the rest of the house. The room was decorated for a little girl, complete with pink walls and carpet and a white poster bed filled with stuffed animals.

"We're here," he said.

Terror slid down Nicole's spine. "Don't leave me here."

Dark eyes stared at her from behind the mask. He pushed her into the room and quickly slammed the door behind her. He locked it.

Nicole ran to the door and started to pound on it.

"Don't worry, Nicole," the man said. "Don't worry. The baby will be here soon and we'll be a family."

"Who are you? Why are you doing this?"

"Soon you will see."

His footsteps faded as he walked away.

Nicole cupped her hand over her belly as tears fell down her face. She pounded on the door until her hands hurt. Exhausted, she leaned her back into the door and slid to the floor.

# Chapter Twenty-One

*Tuesday, January 22, 7:00 A.M.*

Jacob's scent still clung to Kendall's skin as she closed her front door and watched him stride toward his car. He moved with purpose. Direction. He opened his car door and paused. He glanced back at the house, his expression stern. His gaze met hers and his face softened. He nodded toward her before sliding behind the wheel of his car and driving off.

Kendall smiled. She didn't feel alone. And she believed in him.

Kendall went to Nicole's bedroom door. She'd not heard Nicole come in last night. But assumed she had. Softly, she knocked on the door. There was no answer. No wonder. Nicole had to be exhausted. She kept brutal hours lately. Kendall understood the need for work. A busy mind kept dark thoughts at bay.

Slowly she turned the handle and pushed open the door, expecting to see Nicole curled up in her bed. But the bed was empty, neatly made, as if it had not been slept in.

Kendall frowned and moved into the room. She

peeked in Nicole's bathroom to make sure she wasn't dressing. The bathroom was neat, untouched, like the bedroom. "She couldn't have worked all night."

She moved to the table by the bed, picked up the phone, and dialed Nicole's cell. It went immediately to voice mail, a sign it was off.

"Nicole, this is Kendall. Where are you? Call me. I'm going to shower now. If I don't hear from you in the next hour, I'm headed over to your studio to track you down. Call me." She hesitated. "Better yet, I'm coming down to your studio right now."

Adrianna Barrington pushed through the doors of her interior design shop just after eight.

She'd been in Paris for the last two weeks buying antiques for several of her clients and was jetlagged and cranky. The consolation was that the days, even though they had been long and sometimes exhausting, had resulted in some stunning finds. She'd purchased several lovely French provincial chairs, two antique mirrors, and a Louis XVI secretary that would be perfect for the house she was furnishing on River Road.

Her interior design shop was small and located in a strip mall across from the area's upscale mall in the city's west end. The building space had little to no charm, but its location afforded her an excellent traffic of high-end clients.

The walls were painted in a pale yellow and covered with every imaginable accessory, from mirrors to gilded shelves. On the floor were furniture samples and in the back a large table crammed full of fabric swatches. The back wall was devoted to cubbies filled with wallpaper books. A round glass table surrounded by gray uphol-stered chairs hovered in the far corner.

"Adrianna, is that you?" Margaret Barrington, her mother, called out from the back storeroom. They'd opened the shop together four years ago after Adrianna's father had died.

Adrianna had suggested the shop as a way to keep her mother busy after her dad's death. Depression had always plagued Margaret and she was delicate by nature. Margaret had reluctantly agreed to the business, and to both their surprise, it had quickly taken off. They were doing better than either had thought possible.

"Yep, it's me, Mom. I just got in from the airport."

Margaret pushed through the chintz curtains that separated the front store from the back office. In her early sixties, she wore a blue Armani suit that fit her trim frame and accentuated silver hair swept up into a chignon. She was a petite woman and Adrianna had towered over her since she was in the seventh grade.

Her mother frowned. "You must be exhausted."

Adrianna ran slim fingers through her long blond hair, which hung loosely around her shoulders. She wore designer jeans, a silk blouse, and black heels she'd just picked up in Paris. "I slept a little on the plane. But I want to keep moving until at least nine tonight. I need to get back on schedule as soon as possible. I have a meeting tomorrow afternoon with Alderson Developers to discuss the decoration of a dozen model homes."

Margaret beamed at her daughter. The two had always been close, but Adrianna was mentally and physically so much stronger than her mother. "I know you'll be brilliant."

Adrianna picked up the stack of mail from yesterday and started to flip through it. Tired, she was only halfway paying attention. She almost missed the handwritten envelope behind an electric bill.

Handwritten items in the mail were a rarity these days

and they always caught Adrianna's eye. It's why she always made a point to write personal notes to her clients on her embossed stationery.

Adrianna held on to the envelope and tossed the other mail onto her desk. "No return address. I wonder who this is from."

Margaret smiled and her attention drifted to a stack of new fabrics that had arrived yesterday. "One of your many admirers."

Adrianna laughed. "Not likely. I swore off men after Craig." She pushed her manicured finger under the envelope's thin flap and tore it open. The paper inside was yellow legal paper.

Curious, she pulled the note out and scanned the heavy handwriting. *Sarah, when I find you, we will be a family.*

Sarah. She didn't know a Sarah. The person must have used the wrong address. She rechecked the envelope and confirmed her name was above the address. "Who the devil is Sarah?"

"Hmmm?" Margaret turned. "What did you say, dear?"

"Who is Sarah? The note is for Sarah and it says, 'Sarah, when I find you, we will be a family.' That's odd."

Margaret took the note from her daughter and read it. A frown line creased the center of her forehead. Her skin paled under her expertly applied makeup. "I don't know what it means. Likely, it's just trash. Throw it away."

Adrianna stared at her mother with intense curiosity. "Are you all right? You suddenly look pale."

"I'm fine," Margaret said. And as if to prove it she smiled. "I just don't like crank letters." She balled up the letter and tossed it into a wicker wastepaper basket by the front counter.

"Do you know who Sarah might be?"

"I've no idea. Someone is playing a stupid joke on you. And I don't like it."

Adrianna shrugged. "Frankly, I've got better things to do than worry about it. Now let me show you pictures of all the goodies I've found."

Margaret nodded, her smile tight. "I can't wait."


Jacob cradled a cup of coffee in his hand as he moved into C.C.'s office. "You left a voice mail. Said you found something."

She glanced up from a file on her desk. "I just got the land search on the families who owned that tract of land near where victim number one was found."

"Anything unusual?

"As a matter of fact, yes."

Before she could explain, the cell on his hip vibrated. He glanced at the number and saw that it was Dr. Butler. "That's the M.E. Give me a second."

She nodded her eyes, sparking with curiosity. "I wonder what he wants?"

Jacob flipped open the phone. "Dr. Butler."

"Detective." A shuffle of papers crackled in the background. "I ran DNA tests on the first two victims, as you requested. And I've gotten preliminary results. It'll be at least another week on the third, and that's only because I'm pushing with all I've got."

"What do you have?"

"The first two victims have enough genetic markers to suggest they are related."

Jacob tensed. "How related?"

"Most likely siblings. Sisters."

He clenched his jaw. "Okay. Thanks, Doc. Put a rush on the third victim's DNA. I want to know if she's related to the other two."

"Will do."

"Thanks, Doc."

Jacob hung up the phone. He recapped the information to C.C. "The third victim doesn't look like the other two. I'm only guessing they're her sisters."

C.C. lifted an auburn eyebrow. She reached behind her and picked up a picture of her taken at her sister's wedding last fall. Three tall blondes and C.C. stood arms linked and smiling. C.C. was cute by anyone's standards and had a nice figure, but the sisters were, well, goddesses. "As you can see, sometimes sisters don't look so much alike."

He stared at the picture. "Yeah."

"I'm a genetic throwback. Maybe number three was the same."

"We'll know soon enough. What did you have to say?"

"Right. I did a search on the land. I got a list of all the people who owned Alderson's land for the last twenty-five years. I really didn't think I'd find much."

"And?"

Her expression turned grim. "Twenty-five years ago Elijah Turner and his wife, who both owned a tract about a mile from where the first victim was found, were murdered."

"Details?"

"No. But I've got the name of the investigating officer. He's retired now."

Jacob glanced at the name but didn't recognize it. "Get his phone number for me."

"Sure."

Kendall opened the door to Nicole's design studio with her spare key. Nicole had given her a key, joking that she was getting so forgetful that she was afraid she'd lock herself out of the studio. "Nicole, are you in here?"

She flipped on the lights and walked around the

space. Light shone in from the tall windows onto the portraits Nicole had hanging on her whitewashed walls. The place was neat and tidy. There was no sign of trouble. No sign of Nicole.

"Where the devil are you?"

Kendall left the studio and locked the door behind her. She walked down the long stairs and out into the cold. Her gaze scanned the lot to see if her car was still here. She didn't see it.

Her cell phone rang and she flipped it open. "Kendall Shaw."

"Kendall, honey, this is Jenny."

Disappointment washed over her. "Hey, Jenny."

"You all right, dear? You sound upset."

She shoved her long fingers through her hair. "I'm fine. What's up?"

"I found your mother's old cookbook."

Kendall tightened her jaw. "Jenny, I'm kind of in the middle of something right now. Can we talk about cookbooks later?"

"No, no, dear. I didn't call you about a cookbook. I called you about what I found inside it."

"I don't understand."

"Your mom gave it to me right before you all moved. I asked to borrow it and we both just forgot I had it."

Kendall held on to her patience. "Jenny."

"In the book is an old letter. By the date it must have come within weeks of your adoption."

"What does it say?"

"It's from your adoption agency. It has your real name in the letter."

"What's my name?"

"Eve. Eve Turner."

A cold gust of air blew across her face. "Let me know if you find anything else."

"I will, honey."

Kendall closed the phone. For a moment she just stood there staring at the parking lot. "Eve Turner." It was a stranger's name. It was her name.

She burrowed her hands into her jacket pockets and started to walk the lot. As much as she wanted to learn all she could about Eve, she kept walking. First she had to find Nicole.

Nicole said she tried to park as close as she could to her office because walking made her back hurt.

She checked every car in the lot and didn't see Nicole's. The more she searched the more her sense of unease grew.

Kendall dug out her cell phone to call Jacob. Maybe she was overreacting but she was willing to take the risk. She flipped open the phone and realized she didn't know Jacob's number. They'd slept together and she couldn't even call the guy.

"Great."

She thought about Nicole's doctor. Dr. Young. West End. She'd go there and see if she was there. And if she wasn't, then she'd call in the big guns.

The drive took her less than fifteen minutes. She pushed through the lobby door, hurried down a tile hallway and into Dr. Young's reception area. The room was full of a variety of pregnant women.

She went to the appointment window. "I'm looking for a friend of mine. She's a patient of Dr. Young's. She didn't come home last night and I need to find her."

The receptionist peered over half-glasses. "I can't tell you anything about a patient."

"Is Dr. Young here?"

"She's with a patient. You can't see her for at least a few hours."

Kendall tapped her foot. She turned but instead of

leaving pushed through the door that led from the reception area into the back.

"Hey, you can't do that!" the receptionist shouted.

Kendall kept moving. She spotted Dr. Young as she came out of an exam room. "Dr. Young?"

The doctor looked up. "Yes?"

"My name is Kendall Shaw. I'm a friend of Nicole Piper's. She didn't come home last night and I'm worried. Have you seen her in the last eighteen hours?"

"Doctor, this woman burst in," the receptionist said.

The doctor held up her hand to stop the receptionist. "No, I haven't seen her."

Kendall's unease doubled. "Could she be in the hospital and you not know it?"

"She would call me if the baby was coming." The woman grimaced. "Unless she was unable to call. Let me call the hospitals."

"Okay. Thanks."

Kendall waited as Dr. Young called all four hospitals in the immediate area. No Nicole Piper. No one fitting her description.

The doctor hung up the phone on the wall. "Nothing."

Kendall nodded. Something was very, very wrong. "Thanks."

"Call me when you find her."

"I will."

Kendall left the office and kept moving until she reached her car. She called Carnie Winchester at the adoption agency and learned no one there had seen Nicole either.

This was wrong. All wrong. "Damn."

Dialing again, she waited until an officer answered, "Henrico Police."

"Jacob Warwick, please."

The operator sent her to voice mail. She pressed zero

on her phone and asked for Zack Kier. When she learned he wasn't on the premises, she asked for David Ayden. She made a point to mention this was not work related. It was personal. An emergency. Even after all that, she still wasn't sure if Ayden would take her call.

A few seconds later, a deep voice said, "Ms. Shaw."

"I need a favor."

"I don't give interviews or quotes."

"It's about my roommate. Nicole Piper."

"Something wrong with the baby?" The edge in his voice turned to concern.

"I can't find Nicole. I went by her studio and she wasn't there. I called the adoption agency. Went to her doctor's office. No one has seen her. This isn't like her."

A tense moment followed. "I'll put out a bulletin now."

Relief washed over her. "Thank you."

"Has anyone been bothering her? She had concerns about Dana Miller."

Kendall couldn't hide her distaste. "I saw Dana talking to her at Lindsay's opening."

"But you haven't seen Dana around?"

"No." She checked her watch. "I don't think Nicole came home last night. I didn't realize until this morning that she was missing." Panic laced each word.

"Okay. I'll look into this."

"I'm going by my house right now and see if she's returned."

"I'll start looking for her."

She gave him her private cell number. "Please call me as soon as you find out anything. I'll do the same."

"Good."

"I half hoped you'd tell me not to worry and that I was overreacting. But I'm not overreacting, am I?"

"No, I don't think so."

Tears burned in her throat. "Look, I know we haven't been on the best of terms."

"None of that matters. Let's find Nicole."

"Thanks." She called Brett to tell him she was going to be late.


The effects of the overnight flight were catching up with Adrianna so she headed to the Java Café, located three doors down from her shop. She'd ordered a triple espresso, extra hot.

She visited for a few minutes and then pushed out of the door back into the bitter cold. She shivered, wishing she'd taken time to put on a jacket.

Three steps away from the café, a man called out to her.

"Hey, Miss Barrington."

Smiling, she turned.

The guy standing there looked average enough. Jeans. Flannel shirt. Dark hair. But there was something about him that set her nerves on edge immediately.

Maybe it was the way he clenched and unclenched his right hand. Maybe it was the fact that his left hand was in his oversized coat pocket and she couldn't see it. Or that behind him a parked truck waited unmanned and running. All the facts collided in her brain in a fleeting moment.

She took a step back. "Yes?"

His gaze on her, he stepped toward her. "I have something for you."

Electricity snapped and popped as he jerked his hand from his pocket. He was holding a Taser.

The next seconds played out in excruciating detail.

Adrianna threw her hot coffee at him. The steaming hot black liquid hit him squarely in the face. Immediately, he pressed his hands to his face and recoiled. He dropped the Taser.

"Bitch," he growled.

Adrianna didn't bother to analyze the situation. She ran. And screamed as loud as she could.


It was close to two when Jacob and Zack parked in front of Adrianna Barrington's design shop. They'd been headed to see the retired officer who'd investigated the Turner murders when they'd gotten a call: *Woman approached by would-be attacker.* The responding officers had found a Taser on the sidewalk. The victim, Adrianna Barrington, looked like Kendall Shaw's twin.

Jacob pushed through the front door of the design shop, Zack following him. Bolts of fabrics, soft carpeting, and overstuffed chairs greeted them, along with soft scents of lavender. The place was very feminine. Very upscale.

Jacob didn't understand people who put so much time and energy into choosing their décor. But the place reminded him of Kendall. She would eat up the kinds of stuff displayed in the shop.

The place was a reminder that he and Kendall were polar opposites. The chances of them making it were slim. A smart bookie wouldn't touch a bet on their relationship.

And still he knew he wanted it to work between them. He just hoped wanting was enough to overcome the odds.

Jacob and Zack moved to the front desk, where Jacob saw a bell. He tapped it with his hand. From behind a curtained door he heard, "I'll be right there."

The curtains fluttered and an older, very distinguished woman appeared. She was dressed in sapphire pants and a blouse. Her silver shoulder-length hair was held back with a silver headband. Her smile faltered when her gaze skimmed the two men. "May I help you?"

Jacob moved forward but not so close as to spook her. He pulled out his badge, as did Zack. "We're looking for Adrianna Barrington."

Her spine stiffened. "May I ask why?"

Jacob felt as if he had an audience with the queen. "We have a couple of questions for her about the attack today."

"I'm her mother. Margaret Barrington." She said the name as if it should mean something. It didn't.

"She's in the back on a long distance call."

"We'll wait."

"I can have her contact you."

At that moment, a woman pushed through the curtains separating the back of the store from the front.

The woman damn near took his breath away. She was tall, lean, and dressed in designer jeans, a silk blouse, and high-heeled black boots. A gold link-chain belt encircled her narrow waist. Stylish blond hair framed an oval face and accentuated violet eyes.

She was stunning.

And she could have been Kendall Shaw's twin.

Jacob shook off his surprise and exchanged glances with Zack to make certain he wasn't imagining the connection. Zack looked as shocked as Jacob felt.

"Adrianna Barrington?" Jacob asked.

Adrianna's smile was cautious. After her attack today she was smart to worry. "What can I do for you gentlemen?"

"They came about that attempted mugging earlier today. They're detectives with the Henrico County Police," Margaret interjected.

Adrianna studied their badges. "I'm impressed. I didn't think an attempted mugging warranted so much attention."

Jacob tucked his badge in his back pocket, as did

Zack. "We think your attack may be linked to three murder cases."

Her expression darkened. "I'm not sure how I can help."

Zack shoved his hands into his pockets. "Anyone ever tell you that you look like Kendall Shaw?"

Adrianna didn't appear flattered. "Sure. Everyone has their double."

"Gentlemen, is there a point to this?" The annoyed question came from Margaret.

"Is there a place where we can sit and talk?" Jacob asked.

"I don't see what there is to talk about," Margaret said.

Adrianna studied Jacob for a beat. He got the sense that her patience was wearing thin. She was rushed, busy, and didn't want to deal with any more unexpected turns in her day. "Sure. Have a seat at the conference table."

The four sat around the glass tabletop. The chairs were too fancy for Jacob but he was surprised to discover they were very comfortable.

He laid his file on the table and opened it. He pulled out DMV pictures of the victims. "Do you know any of these women?" He named each as he touched her picture.

Sighing, she leaned forward and studied the images. "No. I've never seen any of these women. What's this about?"

"These women were murdered. Have you heard about the case? It's been covered in the media."

She frowned. "No. I've been out of the country. I've been in France on a buying trip. I returned only this morning."

"We believe these three women were sisters—that each was adopted by a different family. And we also believe the killer might have known this." He was fishing here but wanted to gauge her reaction.

Adrianna didn't hide her impatience now. "What are you getting at? And how does this have anything to do with me?"

Margaret started to drum her fingers on the table.

Zack leaned forward. "Were you adopted, Ms. Barrington?"

Amusement brightened Adrianna's eyes. "No."

Jacob studied Margaret trying to find similarities between her and Adrianna. They both dressed well and they carried themselves like queens. But that was all surface. He was more interested in bone structure and body types—the kind of traits created by genetics. Both women were tall but they didn't share any other similarities. Margaret's face was round, Adrianna's long and all angles. Margaret's hands were short, while her daughter's were long and slim.

"Ms. Barrington, do you have any brothers or sisters?"

"She's an only child," Margaret supplied.

"Was your father married before?" Zack asked.

"No."

Jacob looked at the older woman. "Could he have fathered any other children?"

"No. I am certain of that." Margaret hesitated. "And I can assure you that I have had no other children and that I gave birth to Adrianna. I have countless pictures to prove it."

Margaret Barrington was lying. Jacob knew it.

"It's important that you be honest with us," he said quietly. "We believe the killer knows his victims are sisters and that's why he's killing them." Again, he was fishing but he needed to dig as deep as he could to find the connection. "We think he may have attempted to take Ms. Barrington today."

The older woman paled. "Why would I lie? I have nothing to hide."

Adrianna tapped manicured fingers on the table. Her patience was dwindling. "I can appreciate you have a difficult job, Detectives. But we can't help you. I'm not adopted. Daddy had no other children."

"You have facial features similar to those of two of the victims," Zack said. He wasn't willing to give up just yet, either.

Adrianna rolled her eyes. "I'm not adopted, so it doesn't matter who I look like."

"Okay. But understand that whoever is linked to this family is in mortal danger."

Adrianna nodded. "Thank you, but we can't help you. Now, if you'll excuse us."

Jacob's gaze bore into Mrs. Barrington. She swallowed but didn't quite meet his gaze. Slowly he gathered up the pictures of the dead women. "When he takes his victims, he holds them for days before he strangles them."

The older woman paled.

"You're upsetting my mother," Adrianna said.

The older woman swallowed. She knew something but wasn't saying.

"Drugs them. Their wrists and ankles are raw from struggling."

Tears pooled in the old woman's eyes.

"Detective," Adrianna said as she rose from her chair. "Enough. Leave."

At this point Jacob couldn't force it.

He and Zack started for the door. He wasn't going to let this go. He'd be back.

"Wait," Mrs. Barrington said as she got up and started toward them.

Adrianna stared at her mother.

Tears filled Margaret Barrington's eyes as she turned to her daughter. "I planned never to tell you. Ever. Because it never mattered to me."

"Tell me what?" Adrianna asked.

"And then that letter came. Mentioned the name Sarah."

Jacob held his breath.

Margaret Barrington started to weep. "Adrianna, you *are* adopted."

Allen stood outside the design shop. He saw the cops inside. Rage roiled inside him. The cops were ruining everything. They were keeping his Sarah from him.

Time was running out. The Family had to be assembled soon.

As much as he wanted Sarah, as much as he hated leaving her behind, he realized he wanted Eve and the baby more.

The baby.

Just the thought made him smile. He had to collect Eve so they could await the birth of their baby. He got in his truck and drove across town.

Outside the temperatures had dropped and the wind had picked up. The air felt heavy with the promise of more snow.

Allen wound through evening traffic and soon parked in front of Eve's house. His heart raced as he pulled out his phone and sent her a text message. Up until now he'd been in complete control. He didn't like it when things weren't right.

Loser. Stupid. Fool. The words played in his head, beating him down. He shoved out a breath. "No!"

His fists clenched, he reached into his glove box and pulled out another Taser. Soon he would get his plan back on track. He'd take Eve and the baby and then double back for Sarah.

Eve pulled up in front of her house and dashed up the

front steps. She opened the door and shouted as she flipped on lights.

He shoved the Taser into his pocket and got out of the truck. He strode up to Eve's front door.

He rang the bell. Impatience boiled. His need for her overrode all sense of logic and fear.

He rang the front doorbell again.

This time he heard footsteps. He blew out the breath he was holding. "Keep it together."

The door snapped open. Eve stood before him. She was as glorious as she always was. His perfect woman.

Recognition softened her eyes. "I can't talk now. I'm in a bit of a crisis."

"I know."

Confusion darkened her eyes. "You know?"

"It's going to be okay, Kendall." Smiling, he shoved the Taser into her belly. She convulsed and stared at him with frightened eyes before she collapsed into his arms. "We're going to be a family."

# Chapter Twenty-Two

Adrianna's laughter held no mirth. "This is some kind of sick joke, isn't it? I'm not adopted."

Tears filled her mother's eyes as she stared at her. The immediate lack of denial from her mother scared Adrianna. Chest tightening, she stared at her mother's face, now so tight with worry. This was insane.

"Adrianna."

"Mom, what is this about? You need to say that I'm not adopted."

Tears streamed down Margaret's face, ruining the makeup that had taken a half hour to apply. "I want you to understand that I love you more than anything in the world."

Adrianna swallowed, had the sense that the earth shifted under her feet. She was aware that the detectives were staring at them and absorbing every detail of the conversation. At this moment, she resented their presence. Whatever her mother had to say was private and between the two of them. "Can you gentlemen give us some privacy?"

They didn't budge.

"We can't do that," Jacob said. "For your own safety we need to hear what your mother has to say."

Dread hardened in Adrianna's stomach. She could barely speak. "Please, just give us a minute."

Margaret shook her head. "Let them stay. If what they say is true about these murders, I want them here. You might need them."

Somewhere deep inside Adrianna the whispers of old doubts grew louder. She'd never felt like she fit in with her family. At family reunions, she was the fair-haired one, not dark, like her cousins. The one who loved art and hated math.

"Why would I need police protection?" Adrianna clung to logic even as she stared at the growing panic in her mother's eyes. "I didn't know these women. I have nothing in common with them."

Margaret drew in a breath. "You might."

Her mother had always had a flare for the dramatic. She could turn a hangnail into a major event. But the directness in her gaze set off alarm bells. "What do you mean? How am I connected to these murders?" Adrianna could hear the slight hysteria in her voice. "I'm *not* adopted." The last statement came out of desperation. God, she needed her mother to say the words.

Margaret shook her head no. "You *are* adopted."

This was like a bad dream. She fully expected to wake up any moment. Or better, a celebrity would burst into the room and announce she'd been punked. Neither happened. "But I've seen the pictures of when you were pregnant with me. You told me I was a long delivery."

"I wasn't pregnant with *you*." She dragged in a shuddering sigh.

Adrianna's head was spinning. "I don't understand."

"I need to sit down," Margaret said.

Adrianna helped her mother to a chair and took the one across from her. The detectives still stared, still hovered. "Tell me."

"I love you."

"Tell me."

Tears ran down her face as she started to recount the old nightmare. "A month before you were born, I gave birth to a little girl. She was so pretty and so perfect. She was everything to me. My sweet Adrianna."

Adrianna stiffened. "*I'm* Adrianna."

Margaret sighed. "That was her name too."

Adrianna couldn't speak. Her mother hadn't given birth to her. She'd been given the name of a dead child? Her voice hardened with shock and anger. "*Tell me.*"

"I came in to check on her one morning. She would have been just four weeks old. Normally, she woke early and was kicking and trying to roll over. Only that morning she was very still. I touched her and she was cold." She raised a shaking hand to her temple as if the recollection made her head hurt. "I remember screaming and calling your father. When he came in and saw our little girl that way, he called our family doctor. The doctor lived next door and came right over. He told us we'd lost our daughter to crib death."

Adrianna's heart beat faster and sweat beaded on her forehead. She thought she'd throw up.

"I was so lost during those days. I wanted to die. Your father panicked. He was terrified I'd try to kill myself." Margaret smiled. "Your dad had all kinds of connections in the legal community. He heard about a baby who had just been seized from a bad home situation."

"Me?"

"Yes. He pulled a lot of strings. Money changed hands, but he was careful that all the paperwork was above board. Within a day, he laid you in my arms. In that moment, I felt as if I'd been given my life back. I felt whole again. I never looked back."

Adrianna's face flushed. In one moment, the life she'd known had been changed forever. Everything she'd known as truth shattered.

Margaret laid her hand on Adrianna's. "I love you."

Adrianna pulled her hand away. "Do you?" The primal urge to lash out was so strong. It wasn't logical. And she didn't care. "Or am I just a replacement?"

Jacbo cleared his throat. "Mrs. Barrington, do you know anything about Adrianna's birth family?"

Her shoulders had crumpled, but her gaze remained on Adrianna. "I never asked questions. But my husband kept records." She knitted her fingers together. "I have them at my house, locked in the safe."

Zack, silent until now, spoke up. "I know this is a tough time, but those papers could help us figure out who's behind the killings. Perhaps even link back to an unsolved double homicide twenty-five years ago."

Adrianna's life was crumbling. She couldn't think clearly.

Margaret lifted her chin. "I'll contact you when my *daughter* is ready to speak to you. She has the right to see these papers before anyone else."

The word *daughter* held an extra emphasis. And Adrianna found she resented it. "I'll give you the papers as soon as I find them."

Jacob nodded. "I'm going to order a patrolman watch over you, Ms. Barrington. Right now I believe you're not safe. I'd like for you to take a DNA test."

She glanced up at him. "Why?"

"If your DNA is a match to the murder victims, then you need to be very careful. You could be next on the killer's list."

\* \* \*

The cold outside the shop was a welcome relief for Jacob. He had come on a hunch and unearthed a mess. He felt for Adrianna Barrington. She had just taken a right hook to the chin and had had her feet knocked out from under her.

He glanced at Zack. "That was something."

Zack nodded. "Yeah."

A marked patrol car pulled up in front of the design shop. Jacob nodded to the officer and held up his hand as a signal to wait. He flipped open his phone and called Vega. He requested a forensics tech to do a DNA swab on Adrianna. And soon as he called Kendall he was going to ask the same of her.

"I've got news for you as well," Vega said. His voice sounded tense. "Dana Miller's body was found near Carytown."

Jacob hesitated. "Strangled?"

"Neck broken."

"She doesn't fit the profile of our last three victims."

"Her body was found in the trunk of Nicole Piper's car. Nicole's purse was also in the trunk."

"Kendall's roommate."

"Yeah, I know. Ayden is on the warpath. Kendall called about an hour ago and reported her missing." Worry coated each word. "Nicole's not answering her cell phone and now neither is Kendall."

The muscles on the back of Jacob's neck tensed. "Is Kendall at work?"

"No. Supposedly, she ran home to check to see if Nicole had returned. No one has heard from her and she's not answering her cell."

"Shit." He glanced back at the shop.

"And remember that guy you asked Mundey to check out? The guy who lives behind Kendall? Cole Markham?"

"Yeah."

"Mundey just called and said Markham's story doesn't check out. He doesn't sell insurance. No one's heard of him. And he's not renting the place behind Kendall's. He's squatting."

"Get a warrant and meet us at the house."


Allen lifted an unconscious Kendall from the cab of his truck and carried her toward the old home. In the setting sun's soft glow, the house's imperfections weren't so visible. If he squinted, the house almost looked like it had twenty-five years ago, when it had been so full of life and laughter.

He'd hated the house then because it had been a stark reminder of what he didn't have. Its lush gardens, flower boxes, and welcome mat seemed to taunt and remind him that he didn't belong. In those days he'd felt so adrift. The outsider.

God, but he'd wanted to belong then and to feel like he was loved and wanted.

Only years later during his exile did he come to miss this place. Here he'd at least had a connection to the people who lived in this house. Here he'd at least had his sisters.

He'd tried to re-create that connection with other women so many times but each attempt had failed.

Allen glanced down at Kendall's face. So beautiful. He leaned forward burying his face in her hair. It smelled soft with a touch of spice. God, but she was so perfect.

A gentle nudge to her cheek only coaxed a soft moan from her. "Honey, we're home."

She didn't speak. Not that he expected her to. After he stunned her with the Taser, he'd injected her with a knockout drug. She'd sleep for another hour or two.

He carried her up the stairs and through the front door. Inside, the house's warmth wrapped around him. Smiling, he climbed the stairs with Kendall, easily managing her weight. She'd gained a couple of pounds since last summer. Then, her features had been too sharp and angular. But the last year had mellowed her. He liked to think that God had been preparing her for his arrival.

On the second floor he heard Nicole's moans. They were deep, labored. Good. It was all coming together. Soon the Family would be complete.

He laid Kendall by the door, propping her back against the wall. He reached into his pocket, pulled out his mask, and put it on. He wasn't ready to reveal himself. Not yet. The moment wasn't perfect. He unlocked the door, pulled Kendall's limp body up and pushed the door open. Nicole lay on the bed, curled on her left side. She'd drawn her legs up close into a fetal position. Sweat covered her body.

She raised her head and pushed herself into a sitting position. It took her a moment to focus and to absorb the scene. "Kendall?"

"I brought her to you. She's going to deliver our baby."

Sweat had plastered her hair against her head. "*Our* baby?"

He smiled. She'd understand soon. "Yes. Ours."

He laid Kendall on the floor. "Did you find the water and crackers in the little refrigerator? There are ice chips too. That's supposed to be good for women in labor."

Nicole ignored him. "Is Kendall all right?"

"She's fine." He laid her on the floor in front of the bed, all the while keeping his gaze on Nicole. He didn't fully trust that she really was in labor.

Both women would fight the journey home, just as the others did. So he had to be careful. "I'll be back soon. There's still one more sister I need to bring to the fold."

Nicole's stomach contracted painfully as she tried to stand. "Don't leave us here."

He backed away from her. "I'll be back."

Nicole climbed off the bed and walked doubled over to Kendall. She dropped to her knees and pressed her fingertips to her throat searching for a pulse. "She's barely breathing."

"I might have given her a bit too much, but she'll be fine."

Disapproval burned in Nicole's blue eyes. He took a step back, remembering that his mother had always looked at him that way. No matter what he'd done, she'd hated him for it. She'd resented his presence every minute of every day.

Anger surged in him. "Stop it."

She cupped her hand to her belly. "Stop what?"

"Looking at me like that. I'm doing what is right."

Nicole held her gaze, seemingly taking pleasure in his discomfort. "You're a monster. And what you're doing is evil."

For an instant, his heart froze. He remembered when others had called him a monster and a freak. He remembered scorn. He clenched and unclenched his fingers. "If not for the baby, I would kill you right now."

She didn't flinch. Instead, she boldly stared at him. "You come near me and I'll fight you until one of us dies."

His heart raced. "The kitten has grown claws."

With trembling hands, he backed out of the room and slammed the door. He had to get the last sister. He needed Sarah to complete the Family.


It took almost an hour for Jacob to get a search warrant for the house where Cole Markham was staying. When he and Zack arrived at the house it was six in the evening. They'd brought Vega and Ayden and two detectives from the city as backup.

Before Jacob rang the front bell, Zack drew his gun and ducked down the alley behind the house. He returned and reported Cole's car was in the driveway. Jacob rang the bell. Seconds passed and they heard nothing. Jacob rang the bell again. Finally, footsteps sounded in the house. The door opened.

The man standing before them was tall, lean and possessed an intensity in his eyes that caught Jacob by surprise. This guy was no insurance agent.

"Cole Markham?" Jacob asked.

Markham's eyes narrowed. "Yeah. Can I help you?"

Jacob pulled out his badge. "We're with the police. We have a warrant to search this house."

Markham stiffened. "On what grounds?"

"We have reason to believe you might have knowledge about a recent murder."

Markham didn't blink. He wasn't intimidated or surprised. "That's ridiculous."

"We don't think so." In fact, he was more certain than ever that this guy was into something up to his neck.

Blue eyes narrowed. "Let me see your warrant."

Jacob handed it to him, carefully watching him as he surveyed the document. "It's all very legitimate."

Markham shoved out a breath. "I want my attorney to look at this first."

Lawyering up so quickly. "Feel free to call him. In the meantime we're going to be searching the house." Jacob raised his hand signaling Ayden, Vega, Zack, and the city detectives to advance toward the front steps. "We're coming in now."

"This is *my* house!" Markham shouted. "I want you the hell out of here!"

"Save it," Jacob said. He pushed past Markham. Zack moved in right behind him and blocked Markham so he couldn't stop Jacob.

Jacob's gaze roamed the room. It was furnished with only a lawn chair and a TV set up on crates. Tinfoil dangled from the set's rabbit ears. His footsteps echoed as he moved through the main room and looked in the vacant sitting and dining rooms. The kitchen had a refrigerator, but it was empty save for a couple of beers.

"This is bullshit!" Markham's voice echoed through the house.

Jacob had hit a nerve with the guy. Good. He started to climb the stairs to the second floor. He glanced back and saw that Markham looked visibly upset now.

"I'm going to sue your ass for everything you're worth!" Markham shouted.

Jacob winked at him. "Go for it, sport."

He moved down the center hallway. To the master bedroom. He pushed the door open and stopped dead in his tracks.

The room was papered with pictures of ten women. All dark haired. All young. He didn't recognize the faces of all the women, but he did recognize newspaper pictures of Jackie and Vicky. There were also several pictures of Kendall.

Anger roiled inside Jacob as he stared at the pictures. "Zack! Get up here!"


Kendall woke in phases to the sound of Nicole's frantic voice. She struggled to clear her mind and to shake off the fog that seemed to surround her. Her limbs felt so heavy and her side ached. She wanted to roll over and let the sleep take her.

"Kendall!" Nicole's voice was so sharp and angry. What was her problem? Nicole was such an easygoing person.

She felt the sharp sting of a slap on her face. The pain made her angry. "Stop."

"Wake up!" Nicole shook her shoulders.

Kendall's eyes fluttered open. The image above her was a blur. She blinked a second time and shook her head. "Nicole? What's going on?"

"Wake up! You've been drugged." Nicole pulled Kendall into a sitting position.

Her head spun. She felt nauseous. As her vision cleared a fraction she looked around the room. Pink. It was filled with the color pink. "Where the hell are we?"

Nicole shoved out a sigh. "I don't know. He brought me here in the middle of last night."

Kendall shoved long fingers through her hair. She couldn't concentrate. Couldn't remember how she got here. "Who is he?"

"I don't know. His face was covered and he keeps talking about us joining some family."

God, think. Her brain felt as if it were wrapped in cotton. "Family?"

Nicole rose gingerly, cupping her hand to her belly. She picked up a photo album from the nightstand and handed it to Kendall. "He killed those three women. And others, I think."

She glanced down at the pictures secured in the album's clear plastic pockets. They were of the women who'd been killed. Only the pictures had been taken when they were alive. Snapshots taken while they walked down the street, talked to their grocery store clerk, came out of a shoe store.

Someone had been following them and taking pictures. "My God."

Nicole flipped through several pages. "Look at the last page."

Kendall saw a picture of herself and Nicole. They were having lunch. She remembered that lunch. It had been taken just before Christmas. "He's been following us."

"He considers us family."

Kendall clawed through the fog in her brain until she remembered the face of the man who'd taken her. "I know who he is."

Zack, with four uniformed officers behind him, brought Markham upstairs to the room dedicated to the dead women and Kendall. Markham wasn't cuffed but was surrounded by tense cops waiting for an excuse.

Jacob turned from the wall of photos and stared at him. "Mind explaining this?"

Markham folded his arms. "It's not a crime to collect pictures."

Jacob flexed the fingers of his right hand. "No. But it's mighty suspicious when those women show up dead. Where's Kendall?"

Markham frowned. "I don't know. Is she missing?"

Jacob's eyes narrowed. Rage pumped in his veins. "Like you don't know."

Markham met his gaze. "I *don't* know. I've been gone most of the day."

"That's crap. You know where she is. It's clear you've been watching her for days, weeks even."

"Yeah, I've been watching her for about a week. But I don't know where she is. Like I said, I've been out most of the day."

"Where the hell were you?"

Markham set his jaw as if mentally digging in his heels. Clearly, he didn't like cops. "Across the river."

"Killing another woman?"

Markham shook his head. "So like the cops to take the easy way out."

"Believe me, pal," Jacob said, "none of this is going to

be easy." He shifted tactics. "Who are these women on the wall?"

"I want my lawyer."

Jacob moved so that his face was within inches of Markham's. "I've got two missing women. I swear to God if anything happens to them because you didn't talk . . ." He let the sentence trail.

Markham's brow knitted and he let out a sigh. "They're women who've been murdered. Most were strangled. A couple were beaten to death. It's easy enough for you to check. I've got all their names."

Jacob cursed. "Checking takes time, but you've already figured that part out. And I think you know Kendall doesn't have much time."

"If he has her, she has time," Markham said. There was no joy in his statement.

"If he's got Nicole," Ayden ground out, "she doesn't have time. She's about to give birth."

"Who the hell is *he*?" Jacob demanded.

"I don't know his real name," Markham answered.

Jacob shook his head. "Where would he be holding them?"

"That's what I was trying to figure out today." Markham fisted his hands. "I don't think he'll hurt either of them right away."

"How the hell can you be so sure?!" Jacob shouted.

"Because he likes to hold his victims," Markham said. "He held some for months."

"His last three victims weren't held for months," Jacob countered. "He killed them within forty-eight hours."

Ayden checked his watch. "Nicole has been missing for almost twenty-four hours. And I spoke to her doctor. The baby could come any day now."

Markham shook his head. "I don't know why he'd want Nicole. She doesn't fit the profile."

"Well, she's missing," Ayden said.

Jacob folded his arms over his chest. He was afraid he'd pummel the smug bastard if he wasn't careful. "Start talking, Markham. Fast."

Markham's jaw tightened and released. His distaste and defiance were clear. "I'm from Denver. I owned a computer software business that was doing real well until eighteen months ago when my girlfriend, Diane, vanished. The police thought I had something to do with the disappearance. They hounded me for months. They took all my computer equipment. When they found out I had a record, they called clients and told them I was under investigation. Within weeks, my life was destroyed. Then Diane's sister, Courtney, vanished. The cops really started to squeeze me then. My income stopped and I lost my house."

Jacob shook his head. "Save the sad story."

Markham glared at him. "January of last year, Diane and Courtney's bodies were found. Diane had been strangled just days before. Her sister had been beaten to death the same day." He seemed to struggle with the memories. "I had an alibi for the time of their deaths."

"Really?" Jacob said.

"Yeah. I had been arrested—broken taillight. The cops were always looking for an excuse to hold me. Anyway, I was in jail when Diane and her sister were murdered. All that time the cops had been hounding me and some sicko had them. They were alive and could have been saved."

Jacob stared at him. He was either one hell of a liar or one talented actor. "Keep talking."

"When the cops realized I hadn't killed the women, they quickly lost interest in me and the case. Since early October the case has languished. I needed to find out who had killed Diane and her sister." Contempt dripped from his words.

"So how the hell do you land on the East Coast two thousand miles away from home squatting in a vacant house?" Jacob itched to grab this guy by the collar and rattle the truth out of him.

"Like I said, I owned a computer company. I can hack into any system and I don't need a warrant to collect data. I checked ViCap. There was an old killing in Alaska."

Jacob narrowed his eyes. "Keep talking."

"I started watching ViCap. Nothing for months. And then you filed a report on the thirteenth. It was the first lead I'd had in months. So I drove to Richmond from Denver."

"That's bullshit."

Markham sighed. "Have you talked to the trooper in Alaska?"

The guy's knowledge of the Alaska killings added credibility to his story.

"When I saw Kendall on the news shortly after I arrived, I noticed the similarity to Diane immediately," Markham said. "I decided to keep an eye on her."

"Why not come to us?" Ayden challenged.

Markham glared at Ayden. "I don't trust cops. The cops out West made my life hell. And let's face it—I show up after two women are killed. It would be easy to assume that after what happened in Denver I was behind these killings."

"If you know so much, then who the hell is behind this?" Jacob asked.

"I spoke with all of Diane's friends and family many times. It wasn't until the fourth interview with her neighbor that the woman remembered a man. This guy had done a little carpentry work for Diane a few days before she vanished. The neighbor only saw him the one time so she'd forgotten all about him."

Jacob thought about Kendall's newly renovated kitchen.

"By the time I figured out who Kendall's carpenter was

and where he lived, the third victim had been found. The carpenter didn't show up for work yesterday. I've been watching his house but he hasn't been home either."

"What's the guy's name?"

Markham shoved out a breath. "Todd Franklin."

"You got an address?"

Markham gave him the address of a motel on the south side of town. "He hasn't been at his motel room since yesterday." He folded his arms over his chest.

Jacob stared at Markham and flipped open his phone. He quickly verified Franklin's address. "Ayden, hold this guy while Zack and I check out his story."

"Be glad to."

An hour later, Jacob and Zack arrived at the address Markham had given them. Todd was living in a seedy motel on Route 60. A search warrant in hand, they got a key from the manager and with guns drawn opened the door.

It was dimly lit and smelled of mold. The bed was made neatly and everything on the cheap bureau was laid out in precise lines. "This guy has a thing for organization and detail."

There was no evidence that linked the guy to any of the killings. "The killer we're looking for is very organized and neat."

"Like this guy."

"Yeah."

Jacob moved around the room trying to disturb as little as possible. "So where did he take them?"

"Let's talk to the detective who investigated the Turner murders."

"Yeah."

# Chapter Twenty-Three

*Tuesday, January 22, 8:00 P.M.*

A contraction hit Nicole and she winced as she leaned forward on the bed to ride it out. Kendall laid her hand on Nicole's shoulder. Kendall's own worry doubled. She knew nothing about babies, let alone bringing one into the world. "I think you're supposed to breathe deeply."

Nicole glanced up at her. "Your guess is as good as mine. I skipped the birthing classes."

Kendall shoved her hair out of her eyes, annoyed she didn't have a rubber band to tie it back. "Didn't your doctor tell you what to do?

"She did. But I didn't pay attention."

Her panic rose. "For God's sake, why not?"

Wincing again, Nicole blew out a breath as the contraction passed. "If you haven't noticed, I've been in denial about the baby."

"I know the adoption has been an issue but I thought you were handling all the medical stuff okay."

"I made checkups, but frankly, once I got the thumbs-up from the doc each month, I tuned the rest out. I have no idea what I'm doing."

Kendall glanced at the locked door. Her head had cleared and she was coherent enough to think and plan. "Why would he come after us? It makes no sense."

The dream Kendall had had over and over again flashed in her mind. The child in the closet. The screams. The soft, soothing voice beckoning her to come out. It was all connected to this place. "I've got to get you out of here."

"How? He's locked every door."

"Todd has got to come back sometime. When he does, he'll be expecting to find me unconscious and you in labor. We're not as helpless as we might seem." As Kendall rose from the bed to look around the room, a wave of nausea passed over her. She stomped it down, straightened, and concentrated on the room. It was so familiar.

Tears filled Nicole's eyes. "God, I'm scared."

Kendall managed a brave tone. "It's going to be fine."

Where had she seen this room before? The place was garishly pink. The smell of the house triggered deep emotions long since buried. This room had never been in her dreams, yet there was a familiarity.

She moved around staring at the posters on the wall. All from the eighties, all considered vintage now. She ran her finger along the edge of a white desk as her gaze drifted to a closet door.

Kendall's heart pounded in her chest.

"What is it?" Nicole said.

"I've been here before." Kendall moved toward the closet. With a trembling hand she twisted the knob.

Hinges squeaked as she opened the door and peered into the blackness. *Stay in here. Stay quiet. Protect your sister.*

Kendall went to the main door of the room and rattled the handle. Locked. She crossed to the window. Nailed shut. And a glance out the icy pane revealed they were in a room three stories up. A jump to the ground would at best break her leg and at worse kill her.

She took a wooden chair from behind a small desk and returned to the main door. She started to beat the doorknob with the chair. Each impact stung her hands.

Nicole rolled to her side and got off the bed. She moved to the window. "If he comes back he's going to hear."

She kept hitting the door. Some of the wood around the lock chipped but the lock held strong. The exertion made her heart race and combined with the drugs in her system left her light-headed. She stopped and brushed the sweat from her head. "This bastard has built a fort."

Nicole cupped her hand under her belly and grimaced as her gaze skimmed the room. "What is it with this room? It's like he's expecting little girls."

A memory danced at the edge of Kendall's consciousness, just out of her reach. "I think I'm one of those little girls."

Nicole glanced toward the window as headlights shone in the driveway below. "Headlights."

Kendall rushed to the window and glanced out. "It's a truck."

"Do you think it's help?"

Her fingertips touched the icy windowpane. "We're in the middle of nowhere. The chances of someone finding us are slim. I don't think this is good." She glanced at the door and the battered chair. "Get back in bed and lie on your side. And make it sound like the baby is coming."

"That won't be hard." Nicole lay back down. A sigh escaped her lips as she rolled on her left side and curled up in a ball.

Kendall picked up the chair and moved behind the door. "When he comes in, I'm going to hit him with everything I have."

Nicole nodded. "Put all your weight into it."

Kendall nodded. Her heart hammered.

Downstairs, the front door opened and slammed shut. Kendall winced at the sound. She tightened her grip on the chair. She'd only have the element of surprise once. The steady thud of footsteps sounded on the stairs. They grew louder. Closer.

Kendall's palms grew slick with sweat. "Be ready to run," she whispered.

"Got it."

"Showtime."

Nicole closed her eyes and started to moan loudly.

The dead bolt on the door turned, followed by the knob. Kendall raised the chair. Her bangs fell in her eyes and made her nose twitch but she ignored it.

Hinges creaked. Nicole moaned as the door opened. A dark, masked head appeared. Todd was holding a fast-food bag. Kendall didn't give herself time to think. She brought the chair crashing down. Wood contacted with the side of his head and Todd dropped to his knees and forward onto the floor.

"Hit him again!" Nicole shouted. Wincing, she scrambled off the bed as Kendall stood guard over Todd, the chair still held high over her head.

Adrenaline pumped through her veins. Kendall hit him between the shoulder blades.

"Get out, Nicole," Kendall said. "I'm right behind you."

Tears ran down Nicole's face but she kept moving forward. Carefully she stepped around Todd as if she expected his hand to shoot up and grab her ankle.

Only when Nicole had started down the stairs did Kendall step over Todd, who still gripped his keys in his hands. Keys. She thought about the truck. Her heart racing, she reached down and tugged the keys free from his grip. He groaned and tried to lift his head but couldn't manage it.

Kendall jerked back and dropped the chair. Keys clutched in her hands, she sprinted across the landing toward the stairs. She caught up to Nicole halfway down the stairs. Wrapping her arm around Nicole's waist, she hurried her the rest of the way.

Nicole's breathing sounded ragged when they reached the front door.

Kendall turned the knob and discovered it was locked. "Oh, God."

"Damn him!" Nicole gripped her belly and doubled over.

Hands trembling, Kendall searched all the keys on the chain trying to find one that looked like a door key. She picked one that looked right and shoved it in the lock. It didn't work. She tried another and then another.

An angry wail emanated from the room upstairs. "Eve!"

Kendall dropped the keys. Panic exploded as she reached down and picked them up. She'd lost track of which keys she'd tried. Upstairs, Todd sounded as if he'd stumbled to his feet.

Nicole gripped her belly again. She bit her lip and sucked in a deep breath.

Kendall pushed another key in the lock just as Todd appeared at the top of the stairs. He staggered and gripped the banister. "Eve! No! You can't leave!"

This time the dead bolt turned. She opened the front door as he started down the stairs. Wrapping her arm around Nicole, she helped her outside. Cold air hit them hard in the face but Kendall barely cared. Her only goal was to get Nicole to the truck.

Nicole stumbled. "My water has broke." And in a rush her water splashed over Kendall's and Nicole's shoes.

"Keep moving," Kendall ordered. "Your baby isn't going to be born in this house."

Nicole gritted her teeth, gripped Kendall's hand and the two hurried down the house's front steps toward the truck. Kendall opened the passenger door and helped Nicole inside.

She'd just started around the front of the cab when a shot rang out. An unmasked Todd appeared on the top step. He shouted, "Eve!"

Kendall ran to the driver's side door and slid behind the wheel. She shoved the key in the lock. "Please start."

Todd fired. The back wheel deflated.

"You're not leaving me, Eve!" His voice sounded ragged with anger.

Kendall clenched the keys in her hand. "I'm not Eve! I'm Kendall!" She'd drive the truck on its rims if that's what it took. She cranked the engine.

Running, he fired again and hit the front tire as the engine ignited. "You won't make it far! I'll find you!"

Kendall put the truck in drive. "Just try!"

He pointed the gun at Kendall's window and fired. Glass shattered as the bullet whizzed by their heads. Nicole ducked and screamed.

The explosion of noise stunned Kendall and confused her. She slammed on the breaks. She jerked forward and hit the steering wheel with her head. Stunned, she hesitated just long enough for Todd to yank open the driver's door and point the gun into the cab. "I don't want to kill Nicole but I will."

Kendall's head pounded as she glanced at Nicole's ashen face. "The baby is coming. She needs a hospital. Let her go. I'll stay."

"No," Nicole said. "I'm not leaving you."

"You have no choice," Kendall said. She didn't want to imagine what his sick and twisted mind was planning. "Let Nicole go and I'll stay."

"I can't do that." His voice was deadly calm.

Kendall tensed. "Let her go."

"I need you and the baby to complete the Family, Eve."

Cold and fear made her teeth start to chatter. "What family?"

"Our family, Eve."

"My name is Kendall Shaw."

"Your name is Eve Turner."

She'd only just learned of it today. "How do you know that name?"

"I know all about you. Where you came from and who your real parents are." He smiled. "And soon you'll join the Family, just like the others."

Kendall remembered the monogrammed *E* on the silver mirror he had given her. "You didn't find that mirror in my kitchen."

"No. I gave it to you when you turned three. You loved it. You loved *me.*"

Maybe she had at one time. But not now.

Nicole opened her door. Pain constricted her face. "Kendall, the baby is coming."

Kendall searched Todd's eyes. The million questions that had plagued her for a lifetime didn't matter now. All that mattered was Nicole and the baby. "Please let her go."

"No." He waved the gun. "Now help her up the stairs. Our baby is about to be born."


It was nearly nine when Jacob and Zack drove to the house of the retired detective who had investigated the Turner murders. It was a small brick rancher. A low-wattage bulb shone down on a small front porch. Snow covered the front lawn and the trees dipped low under the weight of the snow.

The detectives got out and moved to the front door. Jacob rang the bell. Seconds later the door jerked open.

Standing in the doorway was a short burly man with thick graying hair. He wore a red sweater that stretched tightly over his round belly. "Warwick and Kier?"

Jacob nodded. "Detective Houseman?"

He nodded and pushed open the screened door. "Come in."

They wiped their feet on the mat outside and moved into the warmth of the house. The living room was furnished with formal-looking furniture covered in clear protective plastic. Sitting on top of the polished coffee table was a dusty file box. It was open, as was one of its files.

Houseman closed the front door. "Have a seat. After you called I pulled my files. Didn't take me a minute to refresh my memory on that case."

Jacob felt antsy and didn't want to sit but he and Kier dutifully took seats across from the couch. Houseman picked up reading glasses from the table and put them on. "I won't waste your time with small talk."

"Thanks," Jacob said.

"I remember what it's like to be under the gun." He dropped his gaze to the file. "Elijah and Delia Turner married in the late seventies. It was her first marriage, his second. He was a religion professor at the college and she stayed home with the kids. They had five daughters in a decade. There was also a son."

"A son?" Jacob prompted.

"Yes. From Turner's first marriage. Turner's first wife had gotten pregnant while they were in high school and he wanted to do right by her. But the marriage never worked. His first wife had never been very balanced and after four years of marriage he moved out. He paid his child support but he didn't visit the boy much." He sipped his coffee. "The boy was about six when Turner married the second wife. From what neighbors say, wife number two encouraged her husband to include the boy in their lives, so he did. The boy was quiet, but he seemed to enjoy his visits with the new family. Allen seemed to adore his sisters. Especially the second to the youngest, Eve."

Jacob sat forward in his chair. "What were the girls' names?"

"Ruth, Judith, Rachel, Eve, and Sarah."

Jacob shoved out a breath. The charms were engraved with the girls' birth names. "What happened?"

"From what we could piece together, Delia caught Allen with the two oldest sisters in the back shed. The girls were partially clothed. Delia went nuts. She told Allen he could never visit them again."

"Her husband backed her up?" Zack asked.

"According to Delia's next-door neighbor, he did. He'd never wanted the boy around anyway. The kid reminded him of all the mistakes he'd made. He took the boy back to his mother and informed both of them that Allen was never welcome again."

"How old was Allen at the time?"

"Sixteen." Houseman shuffled through his papers. "Here's a picture taken shortly before Elijah and Delia were murdered."

The family portrait was of Mother, Dad, oldest son, and five daughters.

Jacob drew in a breath. "Look at the girls. The oldest must be Jackie White, then Vicky, and then Amanda. That infant has to be Adrianna and the toddler beside her is Kendall."

"And our killer is the son," Zack said.

Houseman sighed. "I read about the recent murders but the names were different and so much time has passed. I didn't connect the dots."

"There's no way you could have," Jacob said. "The names on the charms had never been released to the public."

Houseman frowned. "No one realized how upset Allen Turner was. A week later he stole a car and came back to the Turners' house. Using a kitchen knife, he first stabbed Elijah in the garden. It looks like Delia saw what was happening and hid the two youngest children in a closet. She didn't have time to find the other three. He killed her in the kitchen as she was calling the police. He cut up the second daughter's hands as she fought him off."

"Vicky," Jacob said. "That explains the old defensive wounds the coroner found." Kendall's dream hadn't been a dream at all. It had been a repressed memory.

"He'd have killed the older girls if a neighbor hadn't intervened. The neighbor showed up with a baseball bat and knocked the knife out of the kid's hand. He thought he broke the kid's hand. But Allen was able to get away. He and his mother vanished."

"They were never found."

Houseman shook his head. "We couldn't find them."

Jacob nodded. "We think now they went to Alaska."

Houseman had been briefed on the recent homicides. "Now he's back to kill the sisters."

"That's what we think."

"And the two younger sisters?"

"We found the youngest. I've been trying to reach the older sister for a couple of hours but she's not answering her cell."

"Who is it?"

Jacob clenched his right hand. "Kendall Shaw. She's missing and so is her very pregnant roommate."

Houseman raised an eyebrow and glanced back at his files. "Mrs. Turner was pregnant with her sixth child when she was killed."

"Damn," Zack said. "We know the Turners owned land east of the city."

"They hunted there but didn't live there. They lived in a farmhouse in Hanover County." Houseman flipped through his notes and read out the address. It was still raw, rural land—a perfect place to hide women.

Jacob and Zack rose at the same time. "Thanks."

Sweat dampened Nicole's brow as she lay panting in the center of the bed. Her contractions were less than a minute apart.

Kendall had tied back her hair with a shoelace and now held Nicole's hand as another contraction gripped her body. The baby would be here any second. When the contraction passed and Nicole collapsed against the pillows, Kendall moved to the end of the bed and pushed up the sheets. She helped Nicole out of her pants, careful to keep her covered from Todd's watchful eye.

He stood by the door. A gleeful smile turned up the edges of his lips.

Kendall tried to look calm for Nicole's sake. "We're right on schedule."

Nicole gritted her teeth. "I want to push."

"Okay. Okay." Was that a good thing or not? She glanced down and thought she saw the tip of the baby's head. "I think I see her."

"Can I push?"

Kendall had no idea. "Yes."

Nicole moistened her lips. "How would you know?"

"I just do." She didn't look over her shoulder at Todd. "I'm going to need hot water so I can wash my hands and clean the baby off."

Todd shook his head. "Make do with what you have."

"I'm worried about infection."

"I'm not. As long as the baby is fine that's all I care about."

"Kendalllll!" Nicole arched her back and started to pant.

Kendall looked down. The baby's head had started to crown. She had no idea what was going to happen once the child was born, but now all she could worry about was the birth. "She's coming, Nic. Push. Push hard!"

Nicole bore down and screamed through clenched teeth. Todd moved closer, peering with great interest. The head emerged.

"Push!" Kendall said.

One final scream and the baby's shoulders passed. Kendall caught the wet, blood-soaked baby as she moved out in one final whoosh. Immediately, she turned the baby on her side, cleaned the mucus out of her mouth, and rubbed her between the shoulders. The baby started to wail.

Nicole started to weep. "Is she all right?"

"She's fine," Todd said. There was pride in his voice.

Kendall took the other lace she'd removed from her shoe and tied off the umbilical cord. Seconds later the placenta emerged. "I need to cut the cord."

Todd flipped open a pocketknife. "I'll do it."

Kendall covered the baby with her hands while Nicole pushed up on her elbows to watch Todd. The worry in her eyes was not for herself but the baby.

However, Todd's hands were as steady as a surgeon's. He cut the cord.

Kendall wrapped the baby in a blanket from the bed and laid her in Nicole's arms. Nicole glanced down at the child. Tears spilled down her cheeks as she gazed upon the baby.

Kendall covered Nicole and wiped the blood from her hands on the sheet. She met Todd's gaze. "Leave them and I will go with you. Please. Just leave them be."

He stared at her for a long moment. "You would go with me?"

She used the word she'd heard him utter so many times. "We can be a family."

He reached out and touched her face. "Family."

She stiffened at his touch but she managed a smile. "Yes. It will be better if it's just the two of us."

For a moment he hesitated. Nicole cradled the baby close.

Todd shook his head, moving to the head of the bed beside Nicole. He reached down and pulled the baby from her arms. "It has to be the three of us to complete the Family."

"No!" Nicole yelled.

He moved toward Kendall. "Take our baby, Kendall."

Kendall took the child, not daring a glance at Nicole's stricken face. The bundled infant squirmed in her arms as if sensing she'd been wrenched away from her mother.

Todd leveled his gun at Nicole's head. "It's just the three of us now."

Kendall clutched the baby tight against her. "Don't kill her, Todd. You and I and the baby will leave but don't kill Nicole. Don't make me hate you."

The memory of her mother's screams echoed in her head. "You killed my mother. If you kill Nicole I will never forgive you."

He frowned. "We are family. You can't hate me."

"Families hate all the time. If you want me to love you, leave Nicole alone. She can't hurt us now."

Tears streamed down Nicole's face.

Todd stared at Kendall. The raw pain in his eyes was almost heartbreaking. "I didn't want to kill her. I just came back to talk to her. But she got so angry. She found me with Ruth and Judith. She didn't understand how much I loved them."

Tears choked Kendall's throat. "And you stabbed her."

Todd lifted the gun, holding it to his temple. "I didn't want to."

"Don't kill Nicole. If you love me you'll leave her be."

A tense silence followed and then he nodded. "Okay. For you, I'll let her live."

He moved toward Kendall, the gun in his left hand. He wrapped his right arm around her and guided her and the baby out of the room and down the stairs.

Behind them, Nicole's weeping filled the house. "My baby!" Her moans mingled with the child's cries.

The front door opened. Cold air hit Kendall's face and she held the baby closer. He put her in the cab of the truck and hurried around the front of the vehicle, all the while keeping his gaze on her. He got behind the wheel and fired up the engine. He took a moment to adjust the heater so that she and the baby would be comfortable. But the windows, shattered from his bullets, allowed the cold air into the cab. The baby cried louder.

"Why is she crying?" He sounded angry, annoyed.

"I don't know."

"Tell her to shut up or I'm tossing her out the window."

Kendall held the baby close and started to rock her gently back and forth.

Todd put the truck in drive just as flashing blue lights appeared at the top of the driveway. Kendall clutched the baby. At least ten police cars blocked the entrance.

She nearly wept with relief.

Todd cursed and thrust the truck into reverse. He started driving toward them, then quickly veered onto a dirt road that intersected the driveway.

The side road was bumpy and rough and the flat tires made the truck unwieldy. Kendall bounced in the seat. With the baby in her arms, it was nearly impossible to keep her balance. She fell forward and hit the dash hard with her shoulder before she righted herself.

Todd didn't even toss her a side glance. He kept driving down the narrowing road. Snow started to fall and soon the windshield wipers couldn't keep pace.

Without any notice, the truck's tires hit a slick spot and the vehicle skidded sideways until it hit the side of a tree.


Ayden parked his car at the top of the driveway. Gun drawn, he pushed through the house's front door. His gaze swept the dimly lighted interior.

From upstairs, he heard Nicole's cries. He didn't rush up as instinct demanded. Instead, he and the uniformed cops flanking him methodically swept the house's interior. Until he knew differently he wouldn't assume Todd was working alone.

Once the house was cleared, he followed Nicole's cries to the third floor. He moved down the hallway toward the lighted room at the end. Her cries tore at his heart.

"My baby," Nicole cried.

Ayden burst into the room. Nicole lay back against the pillow, her body wrapped in blood-stained sheets.

"He's taken the baby," she said.

"Is there anyone else working with him?"

"No."

Immediately, Ayden holstered his gun and went to Nicole. He got on his phone. "This is Sergeant David Ayden. I need a rescue squad." He gave the address before closing the phone. "Nicole."

She stared up at him with bloodshot eyes. Sweat had matted her hair to her head. "He took my baby. And he took Kendall."

"Where are they going?"

"He didn't say."

Blood was normal at birth. But Nicole was losing too

much. And her face was deadly pale. He raised the sheet and realized Nicole was hemorrhaging.

Jacob cursed when he saw the truck careen off the road. The driver's side took the brunt of the impact but he feared for Kendall.

"Jesus," he said.

Zack pulled out his gun.

Jacob slammed on his brakes and put the car in park. He drew his gun and jumped out of the driver's seat. He was less than twenty feet from the truck.

"Get out with your hands where I can see them!" Jacob shouted.

Todd appeared to be slumped over the steering wheel but straightened at the sound of Jacob's voice. He grabbed a handful of Kendall's hair and pulled her toward him and pressed the gun to her head. A baby's cry broke the tense silence.

Todd pulled Kendall out of the driver's side of the cab and held her in front of him as a shield. She clutched the baby, trying to turn sideways so she could protect the child. Todd forced her to face Jacob. "Leave us alone or I'll kill them both now."

Zack and Jacob kept their weapons trained on Todd. "Okay," Jacob said, but the detectives didn't move.

Todd snarled at Jacob. "Put your guns down!" He cocked the hammer of his gun and pressed it to Kendall's temple.

Terrified, Kendall kept her head bowed low over the baby.

"Okay. Okay." Zack didn't budge. He kept his gun pointed at Todd.

Jacob also kept his gun pointed at Todd.

Agitated, Todd jerked back Kendall's head. For just a

brief instant Jacob's gaze locked with hers. There was fire in her eyes.

"Put your gun down, Detective, or I'll kill her!"

The baby's cries cut though the night. The air was bitter cold and the snowflakes were heavily falling.

In that moment, Kendall racked her heeled boot down his shin.

Todd winced and for just a split second was distracted. That was all Jacob needed. He fired. The bullet hit Todd in the head.

Blood splattered on Kendall's face. For a moment, Todd stood frozen, his eyes wide, the hole in his forehead oozing blood. Then he teetered back and fell into the snow. Kendall, the baby still in her arms, collapsed to her knees.

Jacob moved quickly toward Todd, his gun pointed at him. Zack followed. Their gazes were not on Kendall but Todd. Both were ready to fire again if need be.

Only when Jacob was certain that the man was dead did he spare a glance at Kendall. He holstered his weapon.

Dropping to his knees, he pulled Kendall into his arms. The baby squirmed and wailed between them.

"Is he dead?" Kendall said.

"Yes."

The baby's cries quieted.

Jacob stroked Kendall's hair, now coated with snow and blood. "I was afraid I wouldn't find you."

"Me too." She savored his warmth. Only now did she realize just how cold she was. She started to tremble.

He shrugged off his jacket and wrapped it around her shoulders. His scent clung to the worn leather and calmed her nerves.

"How is Nicole?"

"Ayden is with her." She glanced down at the baby, who had calmed. "I want to see her."

"Sure."

When they returned to the house the ambulance had arrived. The flashing blue lights of the cop cars and the red lights of the rescue squad lighted up the night.

Nicole had been loaded onto a gurney and was being wheeled to the ambulance. A grim-faced Ayden was at her side. Kendall hurried over and glanced down at Nicole's pale face.

"Nicole."

Her eyes opened slowly. "The baby?"

Kendall lowered the child so Nicole could see her daughter. "She's here. She's fine."

Nicole started to cry. "Thank you."

The rescue squad worker glanced at Kendall. "We need to get her to the hospital right away."

Kendall moved back so they could load Nicole into the ambulance bay. She handed the baby to the attendant. "What's wrong with her?"

"She's hemorrhaging." He got into the back of the cab and Ayden shut the doors. The rescue squad raced off into the night.

Jacob wrapped his arm around Kendall's shoulders and she turned her face into his chest and started to weep.

# Epilogue

*Saturday, April 12, noon*

The April morning was warm and the sky a vivid azure. The small stone church was filled with people as Nicole stood by the christening font holding her three-month-old daughter, whom she'd named Elizabeth. Jacob, wearing a dark suit, sat in the front row. On his left sat Zack and Lindsay. She was in her second trimester and her stomach delicately rounded. To Zack's left sat David Ayden and his two boys. The boys looked uncomfortable in their new suits and squirmed when their father wasn't looking.

Kendall stood at the front of the church next to Nicole. Kendall wore a silk blue wrap dress and had pulled her hair into some kind of twist. Her high heels accentuated long legs that always took Jacob's breath away when he watched her walk.

"And who offers this child for baptism?" the priest asked.

"I do," Nicole said proudly. She looked radiant. Her cream-colored dress accentuated her slim figure. Dark hair skimmed her shoulders.

Nicole handed the baby to the priest and watched as

he settled the baby into the crook of his arm. He moved to the stone font and scooped a handful of water and gently trickled it over Elizabeth's small head.

"Elizabeth Kendall Piper, I baptize you in the name of the father and the son and the holy ghost." The priest turned to Kendall. "Who stands up for this child?"

Kendall smiled proudly. "I do."

After the baptism was complete, Kendall took her place back on the pew beside Jacob. She smiled up at him. He took her hand in his and squeezed gently. He loved her scent. Loved touching her. And already, he ached to be alone with her.

The last few months had been filled with so much change. The first days after Elizabeth's birth, Nicole had been in serious condition. She'd lost a lot of blood during the delivery and it had taken an emergency hysterectomy to save her life. When she'd finally been able to sit up and nurse her baby girl, all her fears about loving the child had vanished. She'd banished all thoughts of relinquishing the baby.

Two weeks after the baby's harrowing birth, Kendall had driven mother and daughter home from the hospital. The first weeks after Elizabeth came home had been rocky. Neither Kendall nor Nicole had gotten much sleep, but by late February the three had settled into a routine. By mid-March, Nicole, with Elizabeth in a front pack baby carrier, had returned to her studio.

Kendall had requested a leave of absence from the station to care for Nicole and recover from her own trauma. Brett had insisted she stay on the job. She'd quit. She'd put her house up for sale and was looking for another job.

\* \* \*

The service ended and the congregation stood. Jacob pressed his hand into the small of Kendall's back and guided her out of the church. Bright sunshine shone down on them.

David stood by Nicole as his boys made goofy faces at Elizabeth. The baby seemed to thoroughly enjoy the attention.

Kendall leaned close to Jacob. "Do you think Ayden is ever going to ask Nicole out on a real date?"

Jacob grinned. "He wants to, but he's waiting for the right time. She was so sick and weak at first and then she was so worried about getting back to work."

She turned her gaze to Jacob. "Tell him that life has settled down and he should get a move on."

Jacob shook his head. "I'm not getting in on that."

"On what?" The question came from Lindsay. Zack's arm casually draped over her arm.

"Ayden and Nicole."

Zack rolled his eyes. "I'm not a part of this."

Lindsay laughed. "If you don't prod the man along I will."

Zack chuckled. "He'll get around to asking her out."

Kendall stared at Ayden. The man had been a rock during the weeks following Todd's death.


Ayden and Jacob had worked with Detective Houseman and Cole Markham to piece together Todd's troubled and dangerous past. What they'd learned was that Todd had never gotten over his parents' divorce. He'd resented and envied the life his father had built with his new wife. During his brief visits to the Turner house, Todd had developed an unhealthy obsession with his half sisters. Police now believe he'd assaulted the oldest two. When his stepmother caught him with Ruth and Judith, she'd gone into a rage. Todd had left but had returned two days later, on Saturday morning. That's when he'd stabbed the Turners, injured Vicky, and tried to get to Kendall and Adrianna, who were locked in the closet, where Mrs. Turner had hidden them. If not for the neighbor's intervention, Todd likely would have killed the whole family that day.

Alaska troopers believed that Todd had fled to Alaska, where he lived for twenty-five years. That's where Todd had started killing prostitutes. He'd chosen sisters to murder because he was continuing with his obsession with his own sisters. In Denver, he'd killed Diane and her sister, Courtney, before heading east.

It was Adrianna's father's files that had supplied the last few pieces of the puzzle. Social workers discovered Delia Turner had had a brother who had been awarded the girls. He'd wrongly believed that the girls should be separated and their names changed to protect them. The five little girls had needed each other, but the uncle and social worker had decided differently.

In Virginia, Todd had tracked down the uncle and through him the adoption agency that had placed the sisters. He had broken into the agency and stolen the girls' records. He'd set fire to the agency to cover up the theft.

The day Jackie had been murdered marked the twenty-fifth anniversary of the Turners' killings.

Kendall had had lunch with Adrianna a couple of times. Adrianna was still reeling from what she'd learned. They were both taking their reunion slowly, understanding that family bonds could only be built over time.

And as she'd gotten to know Adrianna she'd started to remember her older sisters. The memories were just flashes: laughing by a swing set, eating ice cream cones in the cool grass, and holding hands as they danced in circles. The memories weren't much, but they gave her a sense of peace and of feeling connected.

\* \* \*

Jacob looped his fingers with Kendall's. He leaned over so that his lips brushed her ear. He spoke in a low voice that only she could hear. "I love you."

The words came hard for him. He'd spent his life closed and afraid to love but he'd found the courage to love Kendall.

Kendall smiled warmly and met his gaze. "I love you too."

He traced his calloused thumb over the palm of her hand. "Marry me."

That surprised her. They'd not spoken of marriage at all. She lifted an eyebrow. "Did I hear you correctly?"

"Marry me."

She could be just as cautious as he was. "Are you sure about this? You're not just overwhelmed by the emotion of the day? Because it's understandable that you would be thinking about the future. . . ."

Jacob kissed her, stopping her midsentence. "I love you. I want us to get married."

Kendall stared into his eyes. Her gaze reflected so much love, hope, and vulnerability that it made his knees weak. "Yes. I'll marry you."